A SOWER WENT FORTH

Nothing was any use any more. Everything was wrecked.

When they left her, falling back to find the rum pot and refresh themselves, she lay for a while half-fainting. Then she dragged herself up and crawled away, on her hands and knees at first, and then in a staggering run . . .

She felt degraded, dirty. She shivered as she thought of the words she had sometimes heard or puzzled over in the Bible – words that were names for bad women. Such women were outside the bounds of society. Decent folk turned away from them.

And now she was one.

A SOWER WENT FORTH

Tessa Barclay

A STAR BOOK

published by
the Paperback Division of
W. H. ALLEN & Co. PLC

A Star Book

Published in 1980
by the Paperback Division of
W. H. Allen & Co. PLC
44 Hill Street, London W1X 8LB

Reprinted 1985 (Twice)

Printed and bound in Great Britain by
Anchor Brendon Ltd, Tiptree, Essex

ISBN 0 352 30425 1

1

SHE WAS AWARE OF him from the outset. While Mr Henderson was giving her her final instructions – warnings, rather – Morag's eyes were fixed on the tall young man with the auburn hair.

'Don't take up with ill characters on the ship,' the warden was saying. 'Be demure. Remember, "He that keeps a still tongue and a downcast eye can scarce be tempted", as the Reverend James McHugh so aptly put it.'

'Yes, Mr Henderson.'

'Say your prayers night and morning. Read your prescribed passage of the Bible each day.'

'Yes, Mr Henderson.'

'Mr and Mrs Aggerley will have you fetched to them when you land in New York. You are to wear your Sunday bonnet – you have it with you? The one with the pheasant feather?'

'Yes, Mr Henderson.'

'And carry your Bible. Those two points of identification will make everything simple.'

'Yes, Mr Henderson.'

'Remember, too, that seasickness is all in the mind. You will not suffer from it if you set yourself against it from the outset. But you are not one of those who likes to fancy herself ill.'

'Yes, Mr Henderson.'

'What?' he challenged, his bushy grey eyebrows coming

together under the brim of his tall black hat.

Morag McGarth realised she'd been answering at random, assenting in the pauses she sensed rather than heard. She pulled herself together so as to behave with propriety towards her companion. Not that it mattered, in one sense. After today she would never see the warden of St Hilliar's again.

A benefactor of the orphanage, now living in New York, had written asking for a good, reliable maid to be despatched to them from among the girls of the institution. Who more suitable than Morag McGarth? Trained in housework, a skilled needle-woman, biddable, neat, well-mannered – and moreover, she was living in the orphanage beyond the age at which girls were normally sent out to earn their keep. It was time she was sent away, to leave a space for another foundling.

Now here she was, pressed in upon by the throng of would-be passengers for the *Esperance* on Leith Docks, her trunk containing the essentials for a steerage passage of the Atlantic: tin cup and saucepan, tin plate, spoon, fork and knife, salt, oatmeal, and two new-baked loaves. 'That'll last you until the end of the first week, with luck,' the cook at St Hilliar's had said with satisfaction. 'And if you have the seasickness, they'll last you longer.'

Mr Henderson was staring about him in the gloaming. This unexplained delay was extremely inconvenient. He really must get back to St Hilliar's. He debated seeking out someone in authority to make an inquiry, but the crowd was so great it would be disagreeable to push one's way through.

He needed to find a respectable married woman to whom he could entrust the girl, to see that she got safely aboard and into a berth. He himself had never seen the inside of a ship, but he understood that berths on an emigrant ship had to be shared; decency required that he should place Morag with a mature woman of good repute – and preferably a married woman with a husband to fend for her – for one heard the most scandalous rumours about conduct aboard ship . . .

Certainly not that young woman, flirting at this moment with the tall rangy young man. Mr Henderson had noticed him arrive about half an hour ago, rather late in the day if he had his passage booked. But perhaps he had not; perhaps he was one of those fly-by-night youngsters who made the decision to emigrate suddenly, when things went wrong. He seemed to have no kit with him, no valise or bundle, like most of the others.

Mr Henderson's eye lighted on just the woman he needed. A buxom soul, wrapped in a plaid shawl against the keen wind, and using her bulk to shelter a man at her side – smaller than she, and stooped in the shoulder, but tidily dressed.

'Excuse me, madam?' said Mr Henderson, edging nearer and touching the brim of his stiff hat.

'Aye, maister?' said the woman.

'You're boarding the boat?'

'If it ever happens that we're allowed on her,' she agreed, with an impatient toss of her head.

'I'm Walter Henderson, warden of the St Hilliar Orphanage for Foundling Girls. Madam, I wonder if you'd be so good as to keep an eye on my charge here – Morag, stand forward.'

Shivering, Morag obeyed. Lizzie Armitage examined her. She saw a slight figure in grey, with a handknit grey shawl wrapped close to a tiny waist. From under the brim of a plain bonnet two great dark brown eyes gazed at her, and two curling strands of dark hair – a rich, chestnut brown – were caught by the breeze.

'Well now, sir, ye ken I've my own family to think of,' Lizzie said, unwilling to be burdened.

'Pardon me, madam, but I don't see any bairns . . . ?'

'It's my husband I speak of. He's not the picture of health – are you now, Charlie, eh? Suffers with his chest,' Lizzie added in an aside to the warden. 'The sea voyage'll do him the world of good, I'm told.'

'No doubt,' Mr Henderson agreed. 'I don't ask you to take any further responsibility for Morag, my good woman – just to see her safely settled when you go aboard. Alongside yourself, for example.'

'Ah, well now . . .'

Mr Henderson produced his purse. A sixpence changed hands. 'You leave it with me, maister,' Lizzie said. 'I'll see the lass finds a place to make herself comfortable.'

'I'm obliged,' said the warden. He turned to Morag. 'Now, child, it's time to part. I must away home. This lady will take care of you until you're settled aboard.'

'Yes, Mr Henderson.'

'Fare you well, then, Morag. Work hard and be a credit to myself and Mrs Henderson.'

'Yes, sir. Goodbye . . .'

Mr Henderson was about to go, but found to his astonishment that he was being detained: the girl was clutching his hand!

'Now, Morag! What is the meaning of this?'

'Sir . . . I wondered, sir . . . If you would be so kind as to kiss me goodbye?'

'Kiss you?' He stared at her, his bushy eyebrows leaping in astonishment. 'There is no need for such displays of sentiment. I wish you well, Morag. That is all you need to know.'

'Yes, Mr Henderson.' She let go of his hand and stood back, looking down.

He shouldered his way through the press of people and was gone. Morag saw the spot where he had stood fill up with others; it was as if her past life had vanished with his going.

'Ah, lass, cheer up,' cried Lizzie Armitage, digging her in the ribs with a plump elbow. 'You're none the worse for seeing the back of *him*! A cold one, that.'

Morag made no reply. She felt her throat closing up with unshed tears. She was leaving Scotland. She wanted to be gone – but she wished her friend Fiona Johnson could have come to the docks, to see her off, to cry with her and hug her in farewell.

'Ye've a post arranged in America?' Lizzie went on. 'You're lucky. Charlie and me, we'll have to be bonded. But he'll get a sponsor, I'm not doubting that. He's the best shoemaker in Berwick – are you no, Charlie?'

Charlie Armitage nodded and laughed, then coughed. His wife put a meaty arm around his hunched shoulders. 'Ah, my laddie,' she said with unexpected fondness, 'the New World will give you a new pair of lungs, eh? It's the great man you'll be in America, with all the fine ladies queueing up to buy your shoes.'

'I hear they're very rich,' Charlie said when he'd recovered from his coughing fit. 'I saw in a newspaper where they'd given a fancy dress ball in a mansion on Fifth Avenue, and it said – man, can you credit it? – that the leddies' dresses cost not less than fifteen thousand pounds a go.'

Lizzie questioned her about her prospects in America and her past life. But, bossy and garrulous, she was soon talking about herself and her Charlie. The account was interrupted by a bustle of movement at the seaward side of the jetty. The crowd surged in that direction. A man in sailor's uniform was addressing them through a speaking horn.

But the lively breeze whipped the words away. 'What's he saying?' urged Lizzie. 'Eh? What's he on about?'

'He's telling us we can't go aboard until morning,' a young man now at her elbow reported. He was that same young man of whom Mr Henderson had instinctively disapproved. Taller than most of those around him, he had been able to catch something of the loud mutter now growing in the front ranks.

'Not till the morning? But what's to become of us in the meantime?' Lizzie demanded with an anxious glance at her husband.

'That's what they're all asking him,' her informant said. He craned his neck to hear, his auburn hair glinting in the lamplight. 'I don't exactly gather . . . What was that last part?' he asked the man ahead of him as the spokesman jumped down from his perch and vanished.

'He says we must find our own overnight lodging,' was the angry reply. 'He says it's not the responsibility of the shipping line –'

'That's all wrong! "Boarding the 14th March",' Lizzie declared, delving into her pocket and finding the embarkation permit.

'We'll just march on board –'

'Lad, you cannot,' said the man in front. 'They've put guards at the gangway –'

'Oh, a few men – we could easily push them aside –'

'Speak for yourself, lad. They've got cudgels. I don't want to get knocked senseless and end in the water. No, I'm for finding myself a snug spot to sleep.' With that, the speaker hurried off.

All around them others were doing the same, seeking shelter among the crates and boxes, the bales and parcels on the quay, or in the doorways of the warehouses. Few had the money for a night's lodgings. If they had, they wouldn't be travelling steerage to the United States.

Lizzie Armitage's first thought was for her weakly husband. She took him by the arm and hustled him away. In a moment she was lost among the scurrying figures in the gloom of the wharf. Encumbered by the small tin trunk provided by the orphanage, Morag couldn't move so fast. She dared not leave her belongings. Having seen the poverty of the other passengers she was frightened the box wouldn't be there when she got back.

The chill wind caught at her shawl. She wrapped it more closely about her, shivering.

'Well, lass, what are you going to do?' the redhaired young man enquired.

'I . . . don't know.' She glanced about helplessly. 'Stay here, I suppose.'

'Haven't you money for a room?'

She shook her head. 'I haven't any money at all.'

'None?'

'Mr Henderson said I wouldn't need it. I've had my passage paid, and I'm being met at the dockside in New York . . .'

'You're in a sad plight,' he said with a little laugh. 'I was going to offer to mind your trunk for you while you went somewhere more sheltered to spend the night! But if you cannot pay me . . .'

'No, sir, not a penny.'

'Ah well.' He squatted on the little tin trunk. 'Never mind, I'll stay with it just the same. Go you, and creep in some nook out of the wind. It'll knife you to the heart if you do not.'

'Oh, that's . . . that's kind of you, sir. But I feel I ought not –'

'Ought not to leave the box? You think I'll make off with it,' He laughed in genuine amusement. 'And what would I do with your spare petticoat and your flannel wrap?'

She blushed at his naming intimate garments, but in the dark her embarrassment was unseen. She disclaimed any suspicion. 'It's just that . . . I was told to keep it with me . . .'

'I'll carry it for you to any spot you choose,' he offered, putting his hand through the rope carrier at one end. 'But you're better off not to be encumbered with it for the moment.'

'But I don't even know where to go, sir.'

'Aye, all the warmest places were taken while you stood here hesitating,' he agreed. He stared over her head at the warehouses and stores, bulky outlines against the racing clouds of the March night. 'See there, lass – yonder, where the lamp is swinging on the bracket? It's the office of some harbour official, I suppose. D'you see the stack of boxes to one side? That would make a cosy little cave for you.'

'But if the official saw me . . .' She was alarmed at the idea of taking up even a few feet of ground near someone of authority.

'What could he do? Wake you and order you off? That's no great thing, is it?'

'That's true,' she murmured, heartened by his confidence. 'Perhaps I . . .'

'Go on,' he urged, 'before someone else spies the spot.'

'I will then,' she agreed, with a sudden surge of audacity. She was about to go but paused. 'To whom am I beholden for help, sir?'

'My name is Robert Craigallan of Glen Bairach,' he said.

There was a sort of natural dignity in the announcement that almost made her drop him a curtsey. 'I'm Morag McGarth, sir.'

'Well then, little mouse of a Morag McGarth, scurry away to your nest for the night.'

She approached the stack of boxes under the hanging lamp with a heart beating fast, expecting some loud voice to order her away. But the night watch of the harbourmaster's office was snugly installed for the next six hours and wouldn't come out unless summoned. Between the boxes and an angle of the building there was a sheltered cranny. She crept in, sat down, wrapped her shawl close round her shoulders, and closed her eyes to sleep.

The thought that came to her before she drifted off was:

'Robert Craigallan of Glen Bairach, indeed! What a dignified name for an out-at-elbows lad emigrating to America . . .'

The night grew colder as it wore on. A flurry of sleet blew in among the sleepers in the less sheltered places. They woke and muttered, and some got up to look for a better bolthole.

This was how it came about that Morag woke with a heavy hand pawing at her. She gave an exclamation of alarm, not quite aware of what was happening.

'Hah!' said a voice. 'Not just a sheltered bed, but a bedmate, eh?'

The hand tightened on the fold of shawl it had grasped, and pulled at her. She was dragged out of the alcove, into the light of the hanging lamp. 'By the holy, and pretty too –'

'Let me go!' she cried, thrusting with her palms against the brawny chest of her captor. 'Let go of me –'

'Not a bit of it, sweetheart! I'm in luck –'

Morag found herself being pulled against a rough coat, while with his free hand the man explored the front of her bodice for its opening. She kicked and struggled, half-stifled by the coarse cloth against which her mouth was being ground. Her assailant laughed at her struggles. She felt the buttons of her dress being rent from the cloth. Strong calloused fingers clawed at her flesh.

With a last rush of strength she threw herself backward from him and screamed. He grunted in surprise and threw himself upon her, bearing her backwards so that she fell in among the boxes, bruising her shoulders against the wood. He was heavy upon her, holding her down with his forearm while he dragged her skirts up.

A thudding of footsteps, a crashing impact on top of her and then – the blessed relief of the man being hauled away. She scrambled back into the furthest angle of the alcove, away from the grunting, flailing figures. She heard the sound of blows, angry curses, gasps of pain. She couldn't make out what was happening for though the two men were under the lamp, she caught only glimpses of them from her shelter among the boxes.

But the glint of reddish-brown hair had told her that her rescuer was Robert Craigallan.

Suddenly the door of the office opened. 'What's all the racket?' demanded an irritated voice.

A scramble of footsteps and a running figure told Morag that one of the combatants had made off. The other moved forward towards the door, panting a little.

'No trouble, sir,' said Robert. 'Sorry if we disturbed you.'

'A fight, was it?'

'Just a bit of fun, sir. It's over now.'

'Ah . . . well, make less noise, will you? It's the middle of the night.'

The harbour official went in again and closed the door. Morag crept out of her hiding-place. 'Oh, Mr Craigallan! Are you hurt?'

He was dabbing at the corner of his mouth with a corner of his shirt tail. 'It's nothing. He split my lip, I think. Are you all right?'

'Yes, sir, but it's only thanks to you. He . . . he . . .'

'Yes,' Robert said grimly. 'I see what he did.'

She became shockingly aware that her bodice was gaping open where the buttons had been ripped off, exposing an expanse of creamy skin from her throat to the cleft of her bosom. She clutched her shawl against her, colouring to the roots of her hair. She was so overwhelmed that she swayed with emotion.

'Nay, now, it's no great matter,' he said, putting an arm about her to steady her. ''Great ladies in Edinburgh show a deal more than that when they go to a ball.'

'Oh, Mr Craigallan,' she muttered, turning her head away.

'You'd best get back to sleep,' he advised, ushering her towards her bedroom.

She resisted. 'No, he . . . might come back . . .'

'I doubt it –'

'But I couldn't sleep now, not there. I'll come and join you by the baggage –'

'Ah, that's foolish. The wind will slice you in pieces –'

'I can't lie there waiting and wondering if that man will come!'

There was a pause. 'It would make more sense,' Robert said, 'if I were to join you there instead of the other way about –'

'Oh sir!'

He laughed, then gave an exclamation of annoyance as the

laugh split open the cut on his lip again. 'Dammit,' he said, patting at it as it began to bleed.

'Here, let me.' She produced a worn little handkerchief from the pocket of her skirt and dabbed the cut.

Rob Craigallan looked down at the chestnut hair half-covered by the knitted shawl, and at the curve of the paleskinned cheek where the soft hair rested. She was a pretty little thing, too shy and timid for her own good yet with a strange sturdiness about her.

As if she felt his gaze upon her, she looked up. She had brown eyes, like a deer, velvety-dark and innocent. She met his glance and gave a little smile. 'I trusted you with my worldly possessions,' she said, with a demure mockery. 'Can I trust you further yet?'

'Perhaps not,' he teased. 'But it would be warmer if there were two of us in your nest, little mouse.'

'Warmth would be welcome, sir. But . . .' She scarcely knew what she was afraid of. She was sure Robert Craigallan wouldn't paw at her as the other man had done. Yet men were to be feared: Mrs Henderson always said so.

'Devil take it, I'm prepared to promise to be good if we can get out of this damned wind!'

'You promise, Mr Craigallan?'

'I promise.'

To her surprise he took a step away from her. 'Where are you going?' she exclaimed.

'To fetch your trunk, of course. It will not be there, I'm thinking, if we leave it out on the quay for the morning.'

He stalked away, and was back a moment later carrying the tin box quite easily under one arm. It astonished her when she thought about how much effort it took her to move it. She realised with some satisfaction that her assailant had probably received something worse in exchange for the cut lip he had given Robert Craigallan.

As they edged into the narrow alcove, something crunched under his foot. 'Ah, the buttons of my dress!' she cried in dismay. 'Pray, sir, let's pick them up, for I've no others to replace them with.'

'And you'd not be wanting to arrive in New York looking like an abandoned woman.'

'You can laugh, sir, but this is my best dress. And I greatly fear he tore it at the collar.'

'I wish I'd broken his neck!'

They gathered up the six buttons, one, alas, broken in half. Morag folded them in her handkerchief and put them safely in her pocket. Then, with her knitted shawl tied round her upper body to make sure she was thoroughly decent, she snuggled down to sleep again. She tensed a little as Robert lay down beside her, putting an arm about her. She edged away.

'Come now,' he said, 'it's very cold and this way we keep each other warm. Come, Morag, don't be foolish. Didn't I promise to be good?'

'Well, I . . . I . . . suppose you're right.'

They settled down together, she turned in towards the warmth of the alcove and he with his arms around her and his back to the night wind. She was slight and soft in his embrace. He half-regretted he had promised to behave himself, and more than half-regretted that he felt obliged to honour his promise.

'Are you comfortable, Mr Craigallan?'

'Nay, now, d'you think you could stop calling me Mr Craigallan? It sounds odd from a bed companion!'

She gave a little sound of embarrassed amusement. 'How should I call you then? Robert? Bob?'

'My friends call me Rob.'

'Well then, Rob . . . Are you comfortable?'

'Better than I was out on the jetty, for sure. At least I won't be discovered stiff and frozen when morning comes and they allow us aboard.'

'I wonder why they delayed the embarkation?'

'Some problem over a certificate of hygiene, I heard the officers say. There are regulations, it seems, about the amount of space allowed to each passenger, and there'd been an inpsection this afternoon on board the *Esperance*.'

'The *Esperance*. That means hope, doesn't it?'

'Aye, well chosen, for those like us setting off to a new life.'

'What are you going to do when you get to America, Rob? Have you a job awaiting you?'

'I . . . well, I . . . No, to be truthful, I have not. But the man from whom I bought his berth last night sold me his papers too – so his job is available to me when I land.'

She half turned towards him in the darkness. 'You only bought your passage last night?'

'Aye, I reached the docks late in the afternoon and questioned one or two of the men waiting to embark. I was pretty sure there'd be someone in two minds about leaving his native land, at the last moment.'

'But Rob! Didn't you have to plan a long way ahead? Did you only make up your mind yesterday?'

'I had my mind made up for me.'

'What do you mean?'

'The constable was after me.'

'After you?' She sat up, with a gasp of dismay. 'You mean you . . . you're a criminal?'

'Oh yes.' There was bitter irony in the agreement. 'A dire evildoer.'

'What did you do?'

'Shot a deer.'

'Shot a –?' At the word 'shot' she felt a frisson of fear, but as his full meaning sank in, she gave a little laugh of relief. 'A deer? Is that a crime?'

'Aye, indeed! If the deer are being preserved so that the laird's friends can come north to shoot them, no one else must touch them. Not even if they come nibbling the green shoots of the crops.'

'Is that what happened? You shot a deer in your garden?'

'It was in my field – eating my young oats!' he said indignantly. 'I chased it off twice, then in the end I took a shotgun to it.'

'But that doesn't seem so criminal to me –'

'Nor to me, but you should understand that the laird has no cause to love me.' He sighed in angry recollection. 'The laird might even be thinking it's cheap at the price, to lose a deer if it provided me with funds for a ticket to the United States.'

'How? I don't understand? How does shooting a deer provide you with funds?'

'Well, for the love of heaven, girl! You didn't think I'd leave a great hunk of venison lying useless among the oats? I carted it to Edinburgh and sold it to a butcher, and that's how I think the constable got on to me ... Well, what does it matter? It was time to get away. There was never going to be any future for me in Glen Bairach.'

'Everything will be different in America,' Morag whispered. 'It'll be different there, Rob – different, and better.'

'I hope so,' he said, with a stifled sigh. 'Goodnight, Morag.'

'Goodnight, Rob.'

She fell asleep quickly, but he lay for a long time thinking about Glen Bairach. Say what he might, he was loath to leave the valley where he was born. His father was the laird's son – on the wrong side of the blanket, true enough, but everyone in the valley knew well that he was of aristocratic blood. His grandmother had been married off to Archie Craigallan to provide a name for the expected child, and a little piece of land had been provided for him to farm. In time the son succeeded to the farm then married and settled down to raise a family.

Rob was the only surviving child, making a hard living for himself and his widowed mother on the croft. But the laird – the legitimate line of descent – had always resented his presence there. Lord Bairach wanted to turn the entire hillside and valley over to the deer. There was more money to be made by using the land that way.

Rob had to agree. Crops had a hard time on the shallow soil. But that little patch of land was all Rob had. One way or another it had to yield a living for himself and his mother. Lord Bairach offered to buy the croft, but the price wouldn't have been enough to set Rob up in any other livelihood.

So Rob had struggled on with the farm. He had been the bread-winner for four years, since he was thirteen. He was always aware that Lord Bairach was waiting for the chance to get rid of him, but it only made him more stubborn, and more arrogant.

He half regretted now the impulse of anger and frustration that made him take the gun to the deer. But perhaps it had been inevitable. If it hadn't been that, it would have been something else. Once it was done, the laird's men were at his heels. Lord Bairach was a magistrate. He had only to put his name to a warrant, and Rob Craigallan was a wanted man.

Goodbye to it all, and the devil with it! As Morag said, there was a new life waiting for him in America. No one would know the dark side of Rob Craigallan's story there. He would make a new start, he'd make the name of Craigallan count for something at last, there in the New World . . .

He fell asleep eventually, his arms round the sleeping girl, the warmth from her fragile body comforting him through this bitter night. Already she had become strangely important to him – a fact which he might later regret, for he had meant to be singleminded and unhampered when he began his new life.

The sounds of activity roused him before light next morning. Some of the men, unable to sleep any longer in the cold, had moved off in search of broken crates and billets of wood, with which they'd started a fire. Saucepans and kettles had been produced, water was drawn from a well in the main square of Leith Harbour, a sprinkling of tea was provided and a hot drink was handed round. Rob went in search of something to eat, and came back with a penny loaf from the baker. Morag had unstrapped her tin trunk and brought out an enamel mug, in which he fetched a ha'penny worth of hot tea.

They had just finished this breakfast when a rush to the water-side told them that embarkation was now being permitted. Hastily they gathered up her belongings. Rob carried the little trunk on his shoulder. Clutching at his jacket, she hurried along at his side.

They had to cling together hard to avoid being separated in the shoving and pushing of the embarkation. When they at last had edged their way up the gangplank and were on the deck of *Esperance*, the purser's assistant waved them towards the hatchway which led to the steerage.

Rob went down first, in the wake of Lizzie Armitage and her husband Charlie. Morag came behind him, buffeted and pushed by the next in line behind her.

'Dear God!' Rob gasped, drawing up short.

'What? What is it?' she asked, coming to a stop immediately behind him. He leaned a little to one side so that she could see.

'Oh, no . . .' She bent her head and looked away in horror.

The hold of the *Esperance* was a seething mass of people, pressing forward into the stern through narrow alleys between rows of bunks. The bunks were strange erections, two tiers high, and built so as to accommodate four people with a bed and, in the centre, a small amount of floor space. They were like hutches. In these, the steerage passengers were expected to sleep and live for the six weeks of the voyage to New York.

At each end of the long hold there was an alcove with a cooking stove. Here the passengers would cook their food and heat water for ablutions. There was no bathroom, although there were sanitary facilities in the passage outside. A small open area of decking had been left for 'social gatherings' – prayer meetings, concerts, lessons for the children if anyone could be found to teach them.

The only light came from candles swinging on gimbels. Later in the voyage, when the frequent high winds blew them out, the emigrant's would know the misery of creeping about in darkness for hours on end.

'I . . . I can't!' Morag moaned as the full squalor of the arrangements sank in upon her. She turned to go back, but the press of people coming down the companionway was so strong that she couldn't retreat, no matter how much she wanted to.

'It'll be all right,' Rob said, putting an arm round her. He shouldered his way past a group who were hesitating which bunk to claim, and put Morag's trunk down in one of the lower tier bunks. Then he grabbed the arm of Lizzie Armitage as she came by. 'Here – you! You were supposed to look after Morag, weren't you?'

'Me?' she retorted, far too concerned about herself and Charlie to spare a thought for anyone else.

'I saw money change hands. And since then you've not done a

damn thing. Here, put your gear in this bunk –'

'I don't know that I want to –'

'You've got to choose somewhere, so it might as well be here. Four to a berth – you can see that's the arrangement. You and your husband, Morag and me – that makes a foursome –'

'But I want to be –'

'This isn't a bad spot. We're near the door –'

'It'll be draughty –'

'But handy to get on deck when we're allowed, and near one of the cooking stoves. Come on, put your bundle down. You owe it to Morag to share with her – she needs somebody to help fight her battles.'

'You seem to have taken that on yourself, young man –'

'Don't be daft! She needs a woman to look after her. She'll go under in a place like this if you don't help her.'

'I'll be all right,' Morag said, trying to keep her mouth from trembling.

'Lizzie my dear,' Charlie Armitage said, sinking onto the bunk nearest him, 'let's settle here. I'm not for struggling further up the boat. It's as bad wherever you settle.'

'We-ell . . . All right,' Lizzie said, having realised that there was little to be said for any particular berth. And after all, since one had to share, why not with this pretty biddable girl and her forceful young friend? Her Charlie wasn't fit to fight for anything; here was a strong young pair of arms to defend them.

They put their belongings in the berths and sat down, watching the rest of the passengers struggle to find a place. Soon a tremor in the deck beneath their feet told them *Esperance* was beginning to move. Near the hatch, Morag and Rob were first up on deck to see the ship inching away from the wharf, while the crewmen ran along the decks coiling ropes or sprang like monkeys up among the shrouds to unfurl sail.

The March morning was grey, and the light was still poor. The tide was setting out in a fast eddy of grey-black water that drifted the ship into the seaway and towards the harbour mouth. There were few on the jetty to wave farewell to *Esperance* as she made her slow way out to the North Sea.

Those on deck stood watching the port of Leith slowly diminish in size as the distance increased. The warehouses, the clock tower, the roofs of the tall stone dwelling-houses – gradually they faded into a huddle of indistinguishable brownish-grey. Then the coastline could be seen, with the town like a dark smudge upon its green, and the mouth of the River Forth making an opening in it.

That too vanished in the mist. There was nothing now except the waves and a lonely gull crying as it swept on white wings in their wake.

Morag McGarth watched it, envying its freedom, cringing from the thought of having to go below to the huddle of humanity in the steerage. But then she told herself she was lucky. She had a friend, a knight errant. She glanced up at Rob.

He had forgotten her existence. His eyes were on the sails of *Esperance*, filling now with the bluster of the North Sea breeze and taking them in a rush of smooth movement towards that new life he longed for.

2

WITHIN TWO DAYS NINE-TENTHS of the passengers on *Esperance* were laid low by seasickness. Even the cabin passengers kept to their rooms, failing to turn up in the dining salon, and praying for death.

The steerage crowd thought they already had died, and gone to hell. The misery and indignity of seasickness was made a thousand times worse by the lack of space in which to be sick, the lack of water to cleanse away the vomit and the bile, and the lack of care from any stewards or nurses.

The children recovered soonest; many of them, in fact, were never overtaken by this mysterious ailment which caused the head to swim, the stomach to heave even though it was empty. Then a few hardy spirits got up and began to move about. Rob Craigallan was one of these; on the second day he was on his feet, accustomed to the swaying deck and the plunging movement of the ship.

It took Morag much longer. Even when her stomach had quieted down, the revulsion she felt at what was happening around her made her faint and ill. The spartan cleanliness of the orphanage had not prepared her for the foetid atmosphere of the steerage compartment. Lack of privacy wasn't new to her – she had been accustomed to sleeping in a dormitory with nineteen other girls. But there had always been decency and order, there had always been water to wash in, even if icy cold, and there had always been regard for modesty – perhaps too much so.

Now she was at the closest possible quarters with both men and women too sick to care what they did. Shock and dismay beset her every time she raised her head from her hard pillow.

She was roused at last by the need to help Charlie Armitage. He wasn't just seasick; the conditions in the hold brought on a terrible attack of chest pain and coughing. His wife Lizzie, generally a tower of strength, was beyond helping him; she lay on her bunk sweating and groaning, wracked with the need to vomit and unable to do so, and aware that her darling Charlie was choking from his cough.

Morag dragged herself off her bunk and onto her feet. Swaying, she clung to the uprights and then leaned over Charlie. 'Come, sit up,' she urged. 'It's worse for you if you lie down.'

'I canna, I canna,' he moaned.

'You must. Come, I'll help you.' She let go of the wooden post, almost fell, but by a great effort kept her head clear. She put both arms round Charlie and heaved him off the straw-filled mattress. He tried to help, pushed with his elbows against the bunk, and finally lay half-propped against the wooden support. He coughed weakly. His striped cotton shirt was damp with sweat.

Morag staggered to the water-pot at the end of the hold. There was no dipper with which to fetch a drink so she had to make her way back for her enamel mug. At last she put it to Charlie's lips. He sipped a little, choked on it and coughed again, but by and by swallowed down enough to soothe him.

Around her others begged for a drink. Morag struggled to and fro, fetching water. When the moaning cries died down, she forced herself to heat water and wash herself. Weak and still half-dazed, she crept on deck.

The weather was not in fact very bad. *Esperance* was spinning along in front of a south-westerly breeze on a starboard tack, rising and falling on the swell of the waves, but not pitching dramatically today.

One or two of the cabin passengers, well-wrapped against the wind in coats and pelisses of thick velour or merino, were lying in long chairs on the first class deck. This was railed off from the steerage passengers. As Morag emerged, a crewman passing by nodded at the deck immediately roofing the steerage compartment.

'That's your area, Missie,' he said.

She climbed the few steps and found Rob leaning with a few others against the rail. 'Well,' he said in greeting, 'there's a white little face!'

'It's cold up here,' she said, shivering.

'You feel it because you're still not fit. It's not very cold, really.'

'What day is it?'

'Wednesday.'

'Wednesday? But that was the day we boarded –'

'A week ago.'

'You mean I've been sick for a week?'

'Amazing, isn't it? Time doesn't have any meaning when you're sick.'

'I'd no idea it would be like this,' she whispered, gripping the rail for support, and drinking in the clean air.

'The worst is over now. You're on your feet again. I found that once I was up and moving about, I felt fine.'

'But you didn't –'

'What?'

She was going to say that he hadn't done anything to alleviate the distress of the others still suffering. But she let the words die, for it was no part of her character to criticise others. Besides, what could he have done? What had she been able to do? Merely bring cups of water to a few sufferers.

Esperance's voyage was uneventful in the annals of merchant shipping – there were no great storms, no shipwreck, no visitation of plague or sickness. But none of the steerage passengers would ever recall it without a shudder for the misery, the dirt, the darkness and the stench of that crowded hold.

It was bad enough for the men. But the women had the added danger of finding themselves the object of the crude desires of the crew and men in the steerage hold. Any woman was fair game, and any young and pretty woman was in danger if she strayed near a quiet spot. Luckily there were few on *Esperance*. Morag was grateful that she had Rob's support. His tall muscular frame was a fine shield against unwelcome attentions.

The men were of the greatest use in queuing for the food allowance. Included in the fare was a supply of staples: ship's biscuit, oatmeal, salt pork, water. But the commissary calculated the supplies on the basis that a great number of the passengers would be seasick for several days, so never had sufficient aboard to satisfy the needs of all the steerage travellers. A daily allowance was issued; it grew smaller as the voyage progressed, and the quality deteriorated dramatically. The water supply grew more and more rank.

Those at the head of the queue got the best of what was available. At the beginning, Rob had few scruples about using his elbows: by the end of the passage he was ruthless. Thus the three people who relied on him for their food did relatively well – but that meant little when the oatmeal was scant, the biscuit was weevil-ridden, the pork was tainted and the water foul. Only those with a little money could get anything fit to eat. The few shillings Lizzie Armitage carried were soon exhausted, and Morag had nothing to begin with. Rob's funds consisted of a little under a pound, the remains of what he had got for the venison; reluctantly he let it dwindle until half was gone. Then he had a brilliant idea.

He had watched Morag carefully mending the tear on her best dress so that it was almost invisible, and then sewing on the buttons. It occurred to him that the crewmen ought to be glad to have the services of a needlewoman. Their clothes were subject to rough usage as they hauled and pulled, climbed and scrambled.

He'd made it his business to get friendly with some of the sailors. He didn't attempt to get money from them for the mending he brought to Morag. Instead, he got them to steal food from the galley.

What they brought was not much, for the stores were carefully supervised. But it was better in quality than was doled out to the steerage, for the crew stole from the galley of the cabin passengers.

Lizzie Armitage was too thankful to query this blessing. As for

Morag, it didn't occur to her that there was anything underhand about what was going on. She took it for granted that she was being paid out of the allowance of the sailor whose clothes she was mending; she would have been stricken if she knew she was handling stolen goods when she and Lizzie took their turn at the cooking.

So the weary, stifling days passed. On 4th May, *Esperance* moved with graceful ease into the East River of New York. Ropes were thrown to loungers on the South Street Wharf, and the journey was over.

The passengers had been crowding the decks since the lookout first called the sighting of the mouth of the river. They saw a green landscape, well wooded, with meadows and pastures coming down to the waterside. Then a huddle of buildings, jetties pointing out into the dirty water of the firth where it narrowed.

'Manhattan Island,' announced one of the sailors.

The jetties grew nearer, and could be distinguished as long walkways of timber and iron. Ships were tied up there, tugs and ferryboats hustled between them and between the shores of Manhattan and the as-yet open coast of Brooklyn. New-fangled steamboats chugged about, smoke feathering out from their stacks.

It was time to go below and put on best clothes for the momentous event of stepping ashore in the New World. The cabin passengers, of course, were allowed ashore first. Morag watched the ladies lift their soft, voluminous skirts clear of the gangplank to reveal lace edging on petticoats and little velvet-sided boots with Louis heels. They raised elegantly gloved hands to wave to those who had come to meet them. Their little flat bonnets of straw or felt, trimmed with artistic ribbons, feathers, or flowers, were set above curls and bows and plaits pinned with tortoise-shell and gilt combs.

She viewed them with awe but without envy. These were the gentry, the wealthy, and it was only right that the ladies should be pretty and well-dressed. If she compared their clothes with her own, it was only to resolve that she would save up her wages so that next year she might buy a piece of rose-coloured silk to trim up her plain bonnet and make it more modish.

She took her turn heating water to wash and make herself fresh and clean. She put on her good dress, although the serge was rather too heavy for the fine May weather which bathed the grimy jetty in warmth and light. She smoothed the pheasant feather on her bonnet; this was to be the recognition signal, this and her Bible. Wishing she had pretty hairpins or a bow for her thick hair, she tied the bonnet on to hide most of it, as had always been the rule at the orphanage.

When she pushed her way on deck again, it was to meet the ironic eye of Rob Craigallan.

'Well, and aren't you the picture of respectability,' he remarked. 'No one's going to turn *you* away, that's certain.'

'Is there much trouble?' she asked, for the conversation in the last few days in steerage had been about the difficulties of being allowed ashore.

Since 1850 the United States had had a huge influx of immigrants. Although as a whole they had brought immense benefits to their adopted country, some had brought problems too. The greatest of these was sickness; typhus and cholera were imported along with the steerage passengers. Moreover, some of those coming from bad conditions at home had no skills, no funds, nothing but their need to start anew. These had become enough of a charge on the taxes to make the cities wary. Now it was necessary to prove that you had enough money to maintain yourself, or had a family willing to support you until you could support yourself, or had a job lined up.

Officials were sitting at trestle tables in a long shed behind the wharf at South Street, looking over the steerage passengers as they filed through. Already several had been taken to one side to await further questioning. Some would be 'bonded'; prospective employers coming down to the docks would question them and hire them, guaranteeing their wages for a year in exchange for a signed promise to remain in that master's employ and not take off in search of land or gold or some other fantasy.

If sickness was suspected, a medical officer was on hand to make an examination. Charlie Armitage, who under his wife's bustling guidance had been one of the first on the dockside, was taken to an inner room to be questioned further. Morag never saw

Charlie or Lizzie again; the medical examiner diagnosed advanced lung sickness in Charlie and despite his skill as a master-shoemaker, he was shipped home again at the expense of the City of New York to prevent him spreading infection in the mysterious fashion which made the consumptive so frightening.

It was lucky Morag didn't know about it. It would have broken her heart, for she had grown very fond of Charlie and Lizzie during the voyage. Many a time she had wakened in the night to talk quietly with Charlie after he had been roused from his sleep by a coughing fit. Perhaps as a result of spending so much time in his company, Morag too had developed a little cough. But the fresh air and good living of the New World would soon clear that up.

She took her place in the line making its slow way down the gang-plank. Rob Craigallan was behind her. Rob only had the tweed trousers and jacket he stood up in. But he had borrowed Charlie's razor to have a good shave, and his glowing dark red hair had been cut by one of the immigrants who was a barber. Early in the voyage he had bartered his services as a strong-arm in the food queue for a spare shirt from one of the other men. He looked neat and fit and strong. To Morag's eyes, he had no faults.

He was carrying her tin trunk for her. It was lighter now, for the linen bag of oatmeal was empty, the salt had gone into the cooking pot, and the loaves were long since eaten. But the fact that Rob was in charge of it gave the appearance of being together, so that when Morag stepped up to the table to hand over her papers, the official glanced past her at Rob.

'Your husband?' he asked.

'Oh!' She blushed. 'No, sir. Just a friend.' And then, for the first time, it dawned upon her that in a moment they were about to part. She went pale. Her change of colour was noticeable, so that the man across the table frowned at her.

'You all right?' he said. 'Had any sickness on the journey?'

'No..no, sir,' she faltered. 'I'm f..fine, sir.'

'Morag McGarth, to be employed by Mr Jonathan Aggerley of Fourth Avenue . . . Mm.m . . . Have you money to get to your employer's house?'

'I'm being met, sir.'

'I see. Very well.' He nodded and waved her on. She took two or three paces and then turned, waiting for Rob.

Rob stepped up to the table and handed over the papers he had bought from the man on Leith Docks: David Grant of Prestonpans.

'Now then . . . David Grant?' said the official, studying Rob.

Rob nodded. Morag gasped in surprise, for until that moment it hadn't occurred to her that Rob was really making his way into the United States by deceit. She had listened to his story and accepted it; he was unjustly accused, and to evade his pursuers he had bought the ticket of another man. But she suddenly understood that, looked at from the official viewpoint, Rob was a man with the police after him, travelling under a false name.

'You've got a job waiting for you at Dalgow's Grain and Feed Supplies, St George?'

'That's right.'

'Have you money to get to your place of employment?'

'Yes, sir.' Robert produced an English florin.

The other man gave a snort of laughter. 'You won't get far with that, boy! Haven't you got money to change for dollars?'

Rob coloured. 'How much would I need, then?'

'At least two of those, my bucko, to get one American dollar. And the ferry to the Island will cost two bits.'

'That's . . . how much?'

'Twenty-five cents,' said the official, 'leaving you seventy-five out of a dollar, if you have enough to exchange.'

Rob delved in his pockets to produce the last few coins he possessed. But he produced them negligently, as if they were of no importance. 'How about these?' he asked.

The immigration officer glanced at them and shrugged. 'You'll make it, I reckon. Okay, then, you can go through.'

Rob stalked past him, his head held high. Inwardly he was seething, furious that he had had to undergo this cross-examination which brought his poverty out into the open. No matter that every other person in the shed was in the same case as himself – it was an affront to his self-respect to be dealt with in that fashion.

He almost walked straight past Morag, he was so angry.

'Rob!' she exclaimed, grasping his jacket.

He stopped.

'Rob . . . I've got to go and look for Mr Aggerley now. Will you come with me?'

'What?' He was about to shake her off, but her brown eyes were fixed on his face in appeal. She looked scared and small. He had an impulse of pity. They had spent six weeks in close proximity and he was somehow accustomed to her. 'Oh, all right,' he said ungraciously, but not entirely displeased to be with her a few moments longer.

They walked the length of the yard behind the shed, looking for Mr Aggerley. Morag was sure he'd be a tall portly gentleman in black clothes, something like Mr Henderson but more affluent. But no one of that kind was to be seen, and the men who lounged about weren't exactly of the type she expected.

'Perhaps it's too early yet?' she suggested to Rob.

'Early? It's getting on for five o'clock in the evening!' He was impatient and displeased. He didn't want to be delayed by her problems, but something prevented him from saying outright that he felt she was a nuisance. 'I'll take a look out on the street,' he said, and went towards the roadway.

Morag remained hesitating, with her tin trunk at her feet. She turned this way and that, holding her Bible conspicuously, but no one seemed to be paying any attention. Then someone tapped her on the shoulder. She turned. A quietly dressed woman, not young, not old, was regarding her with raised eyebrows. 'Morag Mcgraw?'

'McGarth,' Morag said in automatic correction. Then, fearing it had sounded impolite, dropped a curtsey. 'Mrs Aggerley?'

The young woman gave a snort of laughter. 'My, you're really green if you think Mrs Aggerley would come to meet someone off the boats!'

'Oh . . . no . . . of course. I'm sorry.'

'I'm Bertha Boxwell, the upper housemaid. This is the third time I've been here looking for you. What kept you?'

'It's . . . the men at the desks . . . they take a time . . . I'm sorry.'

'This your baggage?'

'Yes, Miss Boxwell.'

Bertha Boxwell was mollified by the girl's polite and respectful demeanour. Almost no one addressed her as Miss Boxwell – it made her feel less resentful of the time she'd wasted making the trip from Fourth Avenue.

'Well, come on then, the missus is expecting you. Pick up your box and let's get going.'

Morag did as she was bid. The box wasn't beyond her ability to lift, but it was by no means weightless, containing as it did her heavy-duty boots, her night attire and working dress and apron, and her few books. The box itself was made of tin and had sharp corners. Bertha made no concession to her problems, however, leading the way briskly from the wharf.

Outside on the sidewalk they found Rob, still gazing about in search of a gentleman who might be Mr Aggerley. He looked at Morag for an explanation. She said, rather breathlessly, 'This is Mrs Aggerley's housemaid –'

'Upper housemaid. And who might you be, young feller?'

'We travelled on the ship together,' Morag explained. 'He . . . er . . .'

'Huh,' Bertha said. 'You may as well know now . . . Mrs Aggerley doesn't allow followers.'

'Followers?'

'Beaux, gentlemen friends . . . Not allowed at the house, get me?'

'That's all right,' Rob said with chill acceptance. 'I'm bound for Richmond Borough anyhow. This looks like goodbye, Morag.'

She gazed at him, wordless. Wouldn't he say that he'd come and see her at some arranged meeting place? Wouldn't he ask if he could write to her?

'Goodbye, Rob. Good luck.'

'The same to you.' He touched his cap and was gone.

'He might have offered to carry your box to the streetcar,' grumbled Bertha. 'A fine friend he seemed to be!'

Morag said nothing. She didn't want to explain how much Rob had meant to her on the voyage, how much she had relied on his strength and his indomitable will to survive. A wave of loneliness engulfed her. Everything was gone now. Her homeland was far behind her, the Armitages had vanished from her ken, and now Rob had simply walked away.

All around her was the noisy hustle of New York. She trudged after Bertha to the corner of South and Fulton, where the older woman hailed a horse omnibus. It was packed with home-going workers, who growled at having to make space for the tin trunk. Wedged in between two men in coveralls, Morag and Bertha clutched the leather straps hanging from overhead and swayed with the motion of the vehicle.

It went via Fulton and Broadway to Fourth, avoiding the Bowery where tough gang-boys were apt to swing aboard and take wallets at knife-point. Morag looked out between the shoulders of the other passengers at Broadway, over-awed by what she saw. She had thought Dunbar a busy place when from time to time the girls from the orphanage were marched into the town to hear some famous preacher on a Sunday. But the crowds on Broadway were overwhelming. Alongside the omnibus, other vehicles competed for road space – public transport, hire carriages, vans, smart landaus and barouches. The drivers of the private carriages wore elegant livery, while the master or mistress leaned back on leather seats. The ladies were in the height of fashion; the men, though more sombre, showed their wealth by the smoothness of cloth and cut and sometimes by the costly stickpin or watch chain.

Morag had never seen an omnibus before, let alone travelled on one. She couldn't envisage a town so large that it needed public transportation to move its citizens about. But she understood that Broadway was only one street of many, for she saw the intersections at which the vehicles competed to force a way ahead, and at each of them during the necessary delay she looked along the street at right angles to see yet more people, yet more buildings.

The shops were unbelievable. They had huge windows – she couldn't imagine how the glass was kept in place. Beyond the glass, goods were on display: bolts of cloth cascading in glowing colours, boots and shoes in the finest leather, household goods, furniture, paintings, food . . .

It was overpowering. And the noise was deafening, what with the trampling of hooves, the trundle of wheels, the shouts and oaths of the carmen, the crying of the street traders, the chatter of conversation, the braying of mules straining at harness, the barking of dogs . . .

The lurching of the omnibus and the smell of tobacco from the male passengers was making Morag feel nauseous. She'd heard that when you stepped ashore you had the reverse of seasickness for a few hours, and perhaps that was what she felt now. She tried not to think about it. At her elbow Bertha was saying: 'There, that spire, that's St Mark's. We're nearly there. Pick up your box.'

They stepped down in a street not so well paved as Broadway, although to Morag it seemed imposing. She knew so little about New York that she was unaware Fourth Avenue wasn't considered of the first importance socially, because it had the New Haven and Harlem Railroad running alongside. To her, this broad street was very fine indeed; to think that she was to work for people who lived here!

Bertha led her to a house that faced immediately on the street, but took her down into the basement area instead of up the six steps leading to the front door. They went in at a glass-paned door under the steps, into a stone-floored hall. From a door further down, a white-aproned woman appeared.

'That you, Bertha? Got her at last, have you? She's been asking after you.'

'Yeah, well, there was some kind of delay with the immigration officials, I hear. Let's have a cup of coffee, for the Lord's sake. Morag, this is Mrs O'Malley, the cook.'

'How do you do?' Morag said, curtseying.

'Pretty well, I thank ye. Can't say the same for you. You're as white as a sheet.'

'No, I'm . . . I'm all right, thank you.'

'You'd better be. The missus wants to see you right away. She's anxious to dress and go out to dinner and you're keeping her back.'

'I'm sorry. I didn't . . . I couldn't help it . . .'

'Yeah, yeah, all right. Tidy yourself up, and be ready to go with Bertha when she's drunk her coffee.' As an afterthought Mrs O'Malley said, 'Want some?'

'No, thanks,' Morag said, her stomach heaving at the idea. 'But if I could wash up . . .?'

Bertha showed her a sink with cold water coming from a faucet. Morag was taken aback, for in the kitchen at St Hilliar's they had had to pump the water up from the well. She bathed her face in cold water, brushed her hair back, and was ready when Bertha had finished her coffee.

The way up to Mrs Aggerley's parlour was intimidating. They went up a flight of stairs carpeted with coarse cloth, then through a door into a hallway paved in chequered black and white. A gasolier of enormous proportions shed light into this gloomy cavern, from which doors seemed to open off in bewildering profusion – though when she became accustomed to the house later Morag discovered there were only five downstairs rooms.

Mrs Aggerley's parlour was on a mezzanine landing. It was a small room, heavily curtained with chenille drapes and carpeted with imitation turkey rugs. Little tables stood about, laden with photographs in silver and mother-of-pearl frames. In this room too there was gas lighting; to her amazement Morag discovered afterwards that there was gaslight in every room, even the maids' attics under the eaves.

The lady of the house was a tall, rather thin figure in dark shot silk, with much lace at her neck and wrists and a cap of ruched muslin trimmed with looped ribbons. Her hair was greying, but had been carefully curled and primped to frame her face becomingly. She turned pale grey eyes upon Morag as she came in behind Bertha Boxwell.

'Here's the new girl, ma'am.'

'So! You've taken your time getting here! We expected you this morning.'

'Yes, madam, I'm sorry,' said Morag, and explained once more that there had been a long file of people going through the exit sheds.

'I see. Well, now you're here, I hope you'll try to be punctual in future. You're sixteen years old?'

'Yes, madam.'

'Mrs Henderson says you're handy with the needle?'

'Yes, madam.'

'I'll be able to use you on clothes for my grandchildren. After you've done your kitchen chores, of course.'

'Yes, madam. Thank you.'

'You have the letter explaining your conditions of employment?'

'Yes, I've got it here, madam.' Morag produced it from the pocket of her skirt.

'You can read, can you?'

'Oh yes, of course, Mrs Aggerley.'

'There's no of course about it. The last girl I had couldn't read or write. Well, you must write back to Mr Henderson telling him you have arrived safely and feel quite happy in your new home – let me see the letter before you seal it up.'

'Yes, madam.'

'Your wages are ten dollars a month and all found, except that your first uniform and caps must be your own supply – because of course I didn't know what size to buy. You have caps and aprons?'

'One set, madam.'

'Oh, only one? We-ell . . . I'll give you some cotton goods, you must make a second set for yourself. I insist on clean caps and aprons after midday each day – although in your case it doesn't matter so much because you won't be answering the door or dealing with callers.'

'No, madam,' Morag said thankfully. The idea of having to deal with strangers unnerved her. 'What are my duties, please, Mrs Aggerley?'

Her employer looked displeased. 'Boxwell will explain all that to you. But there is one point I want to make: my daughter and her three children are staying with us for the present. It will be your duty to help care for the children and see to their laundry, and so forth. Is that understood?'

'Yes, thank you, madam.'

'Very well. That will be all.'

Morag curtseyed at her dismissal and followed Bertha out. The housemaid sniffed as she led the way back below stairs. 'Staying with us for the present,' she scoffed. 'She's here for the foreseeable future, and well the missus knows it. Vanished, he has.'

'Who?'

'The husband – Mrs Aggerley's son-in-law. Couldn't settle after the War, you see. Now Miss Cecilia's back with three kids hanging on her apron strings, and *he's* made off with her money – gone out to the Colorado to make a new life, I hear.' Bertha sighed. 'This is a hard house to run. There's too many people in it all pulling in different directions. There's the mister, out all hours of the day and night supervising the construction jobs. Making money hand over fist, he is – but he don't like to lay it out on anything to make life easier for the likes of us. Then there's the missus, longing to be a success in society. If I've heard them arguing once over keeping their own carriage, I've heard them a hundred times. Then there's Mister Claude – that's their younger son. Ought to have left home by now but not him – likes to be comfy, to have his four meals a day and no expense to himself. Then there's Miss Cecilia, Mrs Portigo as she is now, and the three little 'uns. Four, three and thirteen months – and she's got no control over them, so you'll have your work cut out. Messy eaters too. Nothing but bibs and pinnies to wash every meal! Then there's the mister's Pa – sits about talking about how he laid the foundations of the family firm and how the mister owes it all to him and how he's treated like a dog . . . Not a bad life for a dog, if you ask me! But it makes him crotchety.'

'That's five adults and three children,' Morag said, a little alarmed.

'Yeah, and only four of us to keep the place going for them. Four, that is, if you discount Mr O'Malley, which you better do, 'cos he's generally half-seas-over. Still, he does the rough work, keeps the furnace going, sees to the garden.'

'Mrs O'Malley does the cooking, and you attend to the house?'

'Yeah, with Peggy to clean and lay the fires and wax the floors.

Your job'll be to see to the kitchen chores and help with the kids upstairs. That's where you'll sleep, up in the nursery with the kids. I wish you joy of it,' Bertha said in cynical amusement. 'Awake all hours of the night, they are. I can hear them the other side of the house, screaming their heads off when I'm trying to get my rest. I quite see why Arthur Portigo pulled up stumps and left, if he had to put up with that night after night! Worse than the Battle of Bull Run!'

This was disheartening to listen to, but luckily Mrs Portigo was out visiting friends with her children at the moment, so there was a respite before Morag had to deal with them. Bertha took her to the night nursery to show her where she was to sleep, pointing out a cupboard where she could put her belongings. She looked expectantly at Morag, waiting for her protest; but Morag was so accustomed to sleeping cooped up with other people that it didn't occur to her these quarters left anything to be desired. She carried her tin trunk upstairs to the night nursery, unpacked, put on her cap and apron, and was ready to plunge into her new role as kitchen maid and nursery maid to the Aggerley family.

The children were brought home at nine o'clock, overtired, over-excited, nauseous from having been given too many goodies. Little Jonathan, named after his grandpapa and known as Jonnie, little Cecilia known as Cissie, and the baby, Claudie ... Mrs Portigo handed them over to the new nursery maid thankfully, hardly even pausing to look at the girl to see if she was capable or suitable.

Morag put them to bed but had to stay with them for over an hour before they fell asleep. Then she she was expected downstairs to wash up after the servants' evening meal and to clean the pans left after the day's cooking. After that she had the cook-stove to tend; there was gas lighting but the heating and cooking were done by coal, so the stove had to be raked out and re-fuelled and damped down. Then there was the kitchen floor to wash, and the tables to scrub, so that all would be in order when Mrs O'Malley came down to start on the breakfast of buckwheat cakes, ham and eggs, lamb chops, kidneys, and fresh-milled coffee.

She went to bed about twenty minutes to one, but had to be up again at five when the baby, Claudie, woke demanding a drink. Bertha warned her she had to keep the children from annoying the household until Mrs Portigo was ready to play with them about eight o'clock. That first morning, Morag spent her time running up and down the forty-three steps from the kitchen to the night nursery, but learned from that experience to get the children washed and dressed and into the day nursery as soon as they woke – it was only twenty-one steps to the day nursery. In fact, once she had made friends with the other servants, it was possible to bring the children into the kitchen, where they could amuse themselves with pieces of dough or apple peelings, until their mother wanted them dressed to go out.

The work seemed to be unending. As Bertha Boxwell had said, it was a hard house to run. Mrs Aggerley had social pretensions which led her to give parties at which endless little refreshments had to be served, or else Mr Aggerley had business friends in to dinner. In either case the servants had to stay up until the last guest had gone and the master and mistress had retired, so as to clean up the mess. The kitchen, which was Morag's charge, was always the last place to be put to rights, because someone was sure to call for a cup of hot chocolate and cinnamon toast just when everything had been washed and put away.

Morag joined the household on a Thursday. Her first period of rest was the Sunday, when she was expected to go to church with the family. She slept all through the sermon. In the afternoon the Aggerleys went visiting so a relative calm descended on the house, but Morag had her new caps and aprons to make and a letter to write to St Hilliar's. Mrs Aggerley cast an eye over the letter that evening and said, in some surprise, 'You express yourself quite nicely, child. I won't make any corrections – although I would have thought you would have included some expression of gratitude for your good fortune in being placed in our household.'

'Oh, of course, Mrs Aggerley,' Morag agreed, colouring. 'I'll put that in above my signature –'

'No, no, you can mention it in your next letter. You had better write again in about three months time.'

Three months. At mention of the time span, Morag saw it stretching before her – a long tunnel, going on for ever, with no light at the end of it, and lined on each side with children's garments that needed washing and mending, kettles and pans to scour, tables to scrub, grates to polish, steps to hearthstone . . .

No one was exactly unkind to her. The other servants worked hard too, but it was only logical that they should put on to her the tasks they themselves thought beneath them. Peggy, the under-housemaid, ordered her about with just as lofty an air as Mrs O'Malley. It didn't occur to Morag to protest. She had nothing with which to compare her lot. Life at the orphanage had been just as hard as this, only in a different way.

But at least at St Hilliar's she had had friends. She'd had Fiona Johnson to share secrets with, to laugh and talk with. At St Hilliar's she had known everybody, she had known what lay beyond the garden walls, and she had been accustomed to the scale of existence there.

Here in the Aggerley house on Fourth Avenue, everything seemed to go by too fast, too big for comprehension. The railroad thundered by not far from the house, the traffic trundled past the door. The doorbell rang all day and all evening. People came and went, strangers, far better dressed than anyone she'd ever seen before, who swept past her as if she were invisible.

She told herself she'd get used to it. But a growing sense of loneliness and alienation seemed to envelop her, making her more silent with everyone except the children. The children, indeed, were the saving grace. They were wayward and spoiled, but they could be loved and could give love in return. She even began to think, by the end of the third week, that she was having some effect on their behaviour.

To her astonishment, she was told on the Sunday of the third week that after breakfast, she could have the rest of the day off. 'Don't look so staggered,' Mrs O'Malley said with a frown. 'One day off a month, that's the rule.'

'But . . . but what should I do with it, Mrs O'Malley?'

'Go out and enjoy yourself, of course.'

'But how? Where should I go?'

'You should get some fresh air, my girl,' Mrs O'Malley's husband put in. 'Not a scrap of colour in those little thin cheeks! You go and stroll among the flowers in Jones's Wood –'

'There's no fun in that,' Peggy objected, 'not unless you've got a feller. No, what you ought to do is go and have an ice-cream at Wintergreen's –'

'She's better off staying indoors and putting her feet up,' Bertha said.

'How can she do that without being interrupted by the kids? No, you go out, girlie – get out of the house and see something of the world. Cooped up here, like a little dormouse!'

Morag was inclined to agree with him. Her head ached and her shoulders had a strange tightness between them, due – no doubt – to running about after the children or carrying buckets of coal for the stove. Though she seemed to have little energy for the walk, she longed to get out into the fresh air. Buoyed up by the excitement of having a day to herself, she ran upstairs to put on her good dress. It was much too heavy for this warm day, a late May day with the sun glowing in a pale blue sky, but it was the only walking-out dress she had.

When she came down again, Mr O'Malley took his pipe out of his mouth to give her directions to Jones's Wood – on along Fourth Avenue to Fifty-seventh Street then north for a block or so: 'You can't miss it, there's some fine trees and a little stream...'

She set off full of determination, but almost at once the racket in the street unnerved her. She paused, half inclined to turn back.

But, like an angel sent from heaven, she saw a familiar figure walking towards her – tall, upright, fine red hair gleaming in the sun.

'Hello, Morag!' Rob said. 'I was just coming to wait outside the house and see if you came out to go to church!'

'Hello, Rob,' she replied, smiling at him with eyes that had a glint of tears. 'This is a surprise . . .'

'Yes, well. . . .I just thought, as the shop's closed on Sunday ... I thought . . . it wouldn't be bad to see you again.'

All at once her tiredness slipped from her. The headache was gone. Happiness raced through her. She wasn't alone, after all.

3

THE BEGINNING OF ROB'S life in the New World had been little better than Morag's.

After he left her at South Street, he went in search of the ferry to Richmond, and at first wasn't helped in his quest by the fact that all the watermen still referred to the place by its Dutch name, Staten Island. The ferry was now owned and run by the Vanderbilt family which, being of Dutch origin, preferred the Dutch name.

The ferry took him across the grey waters of The Narrows to St George, a little town huddled on a flat shore looking across to the Battery. By now the day was ending; Rob had been up and about since four in the morning and wanted nothing more than to present himself to his new employer and fall into bed. But when he inquired on St George Quay for Dalgow's Grain and Feed Supplies, he was told it was out on the Arthur Kill Road.

'Far out?'

''bout two mile.'

'Can I get a lift?'

'Ain't nobody goin' there this time of night, boy. If you're goin' you'll have to find your own way – or wait till morning. You mebbe get a lift out there round breakfast time. Ferry comes in then, there'll be mail to take out.'

Rob hesitated. If his informant had offered a place to bed down for the night, he would have waited until morning to present himself at Dalgow's. But the inhabitants of Staten Island were reticent and distrustful. They'd had plenty of trouble in days gone by with drunken longshoremen, mutinous gangs of runaway sailors, and other interlopers. No offer of help was made. Rob nodded his thanks for the information and set off along the unmade road pointed out to him.

The light died on him as he trudged along the sandy track. The houses of St George were soon left behind, although now and again he saw a farm-house roof against the blue-black sky. After about half an hour he came to a group of rather fine buildings at a crossroads; this was the outer suburb of St George, where the businessmen had their homes, on Grymes Hill. Lights shone in windows and on gateposts. He saw a nameboard over a store: Dalgows Grain and Feed, Finest Supplies for Gentlemen Farmers.

The store was still open although there were no customers. A fleshy man in shirt sleeves and a coarse sailcloth apron was counting sacks of oats as he came in. 'Help you?'

'I'm looking for Mr Dalgow. I just got off the ship from Leith this morning.'

'Oh? You'll be David Grant, then. I'm Joe Dalgow.'

'How do you do, Mr Dalgow.'

'Just got in, eh? I been expecting you the last day or two.'

'I came straight from the pier, sir.'

'Hm. That's okay. Help me move these sacks, will you? I'm stocktaking.'

'Yes, Mr Dalgow.'

The next half hour was spent heaving sacks of meal and tubs of tack. He had a feeling it was a kind of test, to see if he was strong and hearty. About eight-thirty the storekeeper said, 'Well, I guess it's suppertime. You hungry?'

'Yes, Mr Dalgow, I must admit I am.'

'You can eat with us this evening. Generally you'd eat with the boys in back, but I reckon they wouldn't have enough cooked up for an extra belly. You look as if you eat hearty.'

'I believe I do, Mr Dalgow.'

Dalgow looked at him under tufted grey eyebrows. 'You're younger than I expected. Somehow got the idea Grant was in his thirties. Well, that's great with me. The younger you are, the more muscle you're likely to develop. It's no rest cure, humping sacks of feed around. Come on then.'

Mrs Dalgow had the food on the table when they went into the living accommodation built on to the side of the grain store. She looked surprised when her husband brought in a guest, but shrugged and put an extra tin plate on the table. The food was plentiful and basically good, even if not well-treated. Rob ate ravenously, for it was his first meal since dawn.

'Land sakes,' Mrs Dalgow remarked to her husband, 'if he's goin' on like that, you'll have to double supplies to the men's cookhouse.'

'He can eat as much as he likes,' Dalgow said. 'It comes out of his wages, don't it?'

Rob was too weary to ask any questions. He was falling asleep over his dessert, a rich pudding of molasses and dried apples in dough.

'Come on, boy, wake up. Don't fall asleep here . . . I'll show you where you bed down.'

Rob stumbled up and followed the storekeeper. He was taken to a store-room smelling sweetly of hay and chaff. 'Here you are,' Dalgow said. 'Anywhere here, except the corners. The other men sleep in the corners.'

'But . . . but . . .' Rob was trying to clear his head. 'Don't I get a bed?'

'A bed? What d'you want a bed for? Ain't the barn good enough for you?'

'It's all right. I just . . . took it for granted . . .'

'You sleep here. If you want anything fancy, you can get a room at Clancy's Boarding House, but that'll cost you. Want a blanket?'

'Yes, I think . . .'

'You won't need one come the warm weather. They're hanging over the partition – help yourself. Start work six in the morning.'

It was too difficult to keep a conversation going. He nodded,

Dalgow hung his lantern on a nail with a warning that he should turn it out before he went to sleep, and went away.

Rob found a pump outside where he washed away some of the grime and sweat of the long day. Then, folding his jacket, he used it as a pillow. Within minutes he was fast asleep in the warm hay.

Some time later he felt someone prodding him in the ribs. He roused and turned over.

'Davey! Davey boy! Dalgow told me you –' The voice broke off.

'Huh?' Rob said, blinking in the lantern light.

'You're not Davey,' said the man holding the lantern.

'Yes I am,' Rob protested, half-asleep.

'You are?' A pause. 'Well, it's late. We'll talk about it in the morning.'

'Yes,' Rob said, already sinking back into the hay.

When he woke he heard sounds of activity. He got up, stretching. The door of the barn was open. In the yard, men were sitting round a fire, cooking bacon and brewing coffee. Appetising smells drifted in. Rob came out to see if he could claim some breakfast.

'Hello there!' said the man with the skillet. 'You were asleep when we got back from the saloon last night.'

'Yes, I was dead tired.'

'David Grant, that's your name, isn't it?'

'That's right.'

'Want some bacon?'

'Is there enough?'

'Yeah, the old lady give us extra last night when we came in. She gives us the makings, we cook for ourselves. Take turns, y'know. Can you cook?'

Rob shook his head.

'You'll learn. But we don't ask for anything fancy. Sundays, we generally go for a meal at Clancy's to get some proper food, but the rest of the time we just fix up whatever's easy. Here.'

He was handed a plate of fat bacon fried very crisp, and a hunk of bread. There seemed to be no forks or knives. He picked up the

[44]

strips of bacon and crunched them hungrily, dipping up the fat from the plate with the bread.

The coffee was bitter and strong. He had never tasted anything like it before, but he knew better than to make any remark about it. The men introduced themselves. There were four of them: Siddall the foreman, Prior who specialised in seed grain, MacLain who looked after the feedstuffs and the boy Nahum, learning the business. They worked from six in the morning until customers ceased to need their services, usually about six in the evening during winter but longer in the growing season.

They slept in the barn and kept their few belongings in the tool store. Cooking equipment was on loan from Mrs Dalgow. Supplies were doled out at cost price, deducted from their wages. Rob's wages were five dollars a week; he guessed that the others, except for Nahum, were getting a little more, because they were expert in their trade.

As they were finishing the food they heard the sound of the door being unlocked in the main store. Herb Siddall gave a short laugh, glancing at his watch. 'Never late,' he said. 'Six o'clock, boys. Time to start work.'

They rose without reluctance, stacking their plates to one side to be washed when they had a moment during the day. As they were moving towards the store, Siddall jerked his head at Rob.

'Word with you,' he said.

Rob hung back as the others hurried away.

'Now,' Siddall said, 'what're you up to? You're not Davey Grant.'

'I am.'

'No you are not. I met Davey when I was over in Scotland two years gone. He and I shared many a glass of whisky.'

Rob gave a shrug. 'All right. I bought his papers from Grant on the docks at Leith. He'd got cold feet about leaving home, and I wanted to get to America. That's all.'

'Is it, now? You were in a damned hurry, weren't you? Going down to the docks with no ticket to sail, and buying one off another guy?'

'What difference does it make? You want a man to handle the

sacks, I want a job – it's a good arrangement.'

'No it ain't. I writ to Davey offering him that job. I felt it was fit for him to have. I don't know that I want any Johnny-come-lately taking a job when it's mine to give. Dalgow leaves the hiring and firing to me, get me?'

Rob eyed him. He was a lean, grey-faced man, with the air of deserving something better out of life than to deal in corn and hay in this tiny township. He was the kind who wanted to feel his importance. If he had the right to say who was to be hired, Rob mustn't antagonise him.

'I didn't know you and David Grant were acquainted,' he said. 'I just thought he'd got a job lined up through some agency or charity –'

'There's no charity involved in this, sonny! I get my cut off everything in this business, and don't you forget it. So what we have to decide now is, if you want to stay here as David Grant and keep this job, what's it worth to you?'

Rob sighed inwardly. He might have guessed there was something like this involved. 'How much was Grant going to pay you?'

'Ten per cent of his wages. But for you it's different. You're here under false pretences in the first place. And you don't know anything about the hay and feed business. It ought to cost you something to learn your trade.'

'I can see that, Mr Siddall,' Rob agreed.

'Good. You're showing sense. Let's say, twenty per cent, eh? Every Saturday when Dalgow pays you, I get one dollar from your five.'

'Twenty per cent? But it's downright robbery –'

'What'd you prefer? That I go to Dalgow and tell him you're not Davey Grant? And if you don't have a job, you know – the authorities can get mighty hard-faced at the moment. They've had trouble enough from starving immigrants. You might find yourself on a ship going back where you came from – which you seemed mighty keen to leave in the first place.'

'I don't want to go back,' Rob said.

'I didn't think you did. Twenty per cent then?'

'All right.'

Rob learned later that all the men let Siddall have a little something each week out of their wages. It was known as 'kick-back', and it had become general over the past twenty years, for a huge influx of immigrants had brought too many men for too few jobs. To stay in work, you agreed to let the foreman take a percentage off the top. It was taken for granted around New York. On the wharves, in the factories – everyone had to submit to kick-back, which in its turn gave tremendous power to overseers, foremen, supervisors. Men who would do anything to stay in work could be depended on to vote how they were told, to turn out on the streets and demonstrate in support of a politician, to make no complaint about corruption.

Here on Staten Island, the system had little political importance. But men like Siddall could make money out of it and boost up their importance, so it had its grip here too. Rob had to accept it, as he accepted the hard physical labour. At the end of the first day he felt as if his back was broken, as if every bone in his body had been shaken loose from its joint, as if every muscle had been wrenched out of its sheath and every tendon broken. All the men worked hard, but he and Nahum were bottom rung of the pecking order. If anything had to be loaded, they had to load it; if tools needed to be fetched, they fetched them.

They broke at noon for a meal – cold meat and bread washed down by cider. About five there was a short breathing space during which they had hot strong coffee. About eight, Dalgow decided there would be no more customers and put up his shutters. Sighing and stretching, the staff wandered away to eat their evening meal, which turned out to be surprisingly good – a pot of stew brought out from Mrs Dalgow's kitchen, potatoes and greens, and a pie of dried apricots, apples, or pears.

The food brought on in Rob an intense sleepiness. The other men, accustomed to the routine, went out to amuse themselves at the saloon but Rob fell into his sleeping place in the straw and was lost to the world.

It took him four days to acclimatise. Then he raised his eyes a little to look around him. He saw a neat little community, composed of half a dozen fine houses dating back to the sixteen-hundreds, some lesser dwellings of brick, and some splitboard cottages where the seagoing community lived. The island was the home of watermen and tugboat men, with a few farmers and businessmen as an aristocracy.

Dalgow was the only corn chandler and feed supplier on the island. In an area of about a hundred square miles, he was the only source of grain for wheat, seed for vegetables, feed for horses and cattle. Moreover, he acted as middleman for supplies going east by sea to New Jersey, having contacts in Tammany Hall which gave him exclusive rights to move supplies to Elizabeth or Newark. This was why the firm was so busy and why there was a constant stream of vans coming to load and unload.

Two miles away in St George, there was an active and rather elegant society, the remains of the old Dutch settlers forming its basis. Dalgow was the main supplier to all the gentlemen who owned stables and kept their carriage. Rob watched with interest as liveried coachmen called in with orders, and by the Sunday of his second week had enough curiosity to go into the little port to see what went on there.

There were snug little bars by the harbour, with pretty girls to entertain those with money to spend on them. Rob got back to Dalgow's long after midnight, having spent every cent of his week's wages. He was still naïve enough to imagine that the girl who smiled on him on Sunday would do the same on Monday evening when he walked in to see her after the day's work. But he had no money on Monday, and she turned her back on him. It was his first lesson that some girls are different from others. Until then, in the home village he had left and on his short wandering through Scotland until he got aboard *Esperance* at Leith, he'd always found girls eager to please him; he'd only to smile and say a few pretty things, and they melted. But the lady in the bar at St George didn't melt.

The working week kept him busy enough to have little energy for the walk into St George. Instead he went with the others to the local saloon, but there were no girls there. Grymes Hill Crossroads was a respectable little community; it was thought improper for women to go into a bar there. If you wanted feminine company you had to make other arrangements, which meant finding time to get friendly with a girl or putting out money for an hour with Tibby Newgate. Rob had no money and not enough time.

That was how it came about that on the Sunday at the end of May he thought of Morag McGarth. For twenty-five cents he could cross on the ferry to Manhattan and visit her. She might not be as exciting as the girl in the bar at St George, but she would expect a lot less spent on her. Moreover, he had things in common with Morag. They had shared a lot of troubles on the voyage over. And despite himself he felt a faint curiosity to know how she'd got on in her new home.

He'd been warned that 'followers' weren't permitted. But he knew that every respectable family must allow its servants to go to church on Sundays – so all he had to do was wait about outside the Aggerley house and he would probably see Morag. If not ... well, there was always New York waiting to be explored. New York was a lot bigger than St George and presumably would have many more pleasures to offer – and this time he'd be more careful about spending his money on ungrateful girls in saloon bars.

Luck was with him. He'd only been loitering a short time near the Aggerley home, which a passer-by had pointed out to him, when Morag herself made her appearance. He was surprised at the pleasure he felt in seeing her. She was wearing the dress in which he'd seen her last, but this time she had no shawl. Her slight figure looked fragile and fine-boned, her waist the proverbial handspan. Under the plain bonnet, her hair was pulled back in a simple knot at the back, but little tendrils had escaped to make wisps of curls on her cheeks. Her face was pale, almost as white as the muslin collar of her dress.

He held out his hand to her. She put hers in his. They walked on in the direction she'd been heading.

'Where are we going?' he asked. 'Church?'

'It's my day off,' she said. 'I *ought* to go to church, but . . .'

'But it seems a waste to go to church on your day off.'

'That's what I was thinking,' she said, with a guilty little laugh.

It was the first time she had been at liberty on a Sunday in her entire life. At the orphanage, Sunday had always been laid out as a series of fore-ordained events – to be looked forward to, of course, because it was the duty of every good child to worship the Lord and listen to improving sermons, and also because there was no housework to be done on a Sunday. Now she found herself out of doors by herself, with the whole day before her and no one to tell her what to do, nor to disapprove if she pleased herself.

'Mr O'Malley suggested I should take a walk to Jones's Wood,' she said.

'Jones's Wood? What's that?'

'I don't know. I haven't been there yet. In fact, this is the first time I've been further than the house-garden since I got here.'

'Keep you busy, do they?'

She shook her head. 'It's only to be expected, with three young children to look after.'

She explained to him about the Aggerley household. As he listened, Rob began to appreciate that he was better off. At least he had his evenings free. His living quarters were perhaps more primitive than Morag's, but he didn't have to share them with three squawling kids. His hours might be filled with hard physical labour, but they ended before Morag's did, and his nights were undisturbed.

'You don't look well,' he remarked as they walked slowly up Fourth Avenue looking at the city coming out to enjoy the Sabbath. 'I think they're working you too hard.'

'Can't be helped,' she said, in complete acceptance of her lot. 'How about you? You look as if you're enjoying life.'

'Oh, it's all right.' He made no complaint to her, although until that moment he'd felt he was being hard used. 'Come on, let's find this place where it's supposed to be so pretty.'

'Oh, don't let's hurry. I like to look at the ladies – they're so smart! I've never seen clothes like the gowns and pelisses going by! Oh, Rob, isn't New York a grand place?'

She was so easy to please! He put her arm through his and pressed it to his side, and she smiled up at him, delighted by his sign of affection and grateful to him for just being here. To have someone of her own, someone to turn to and talk with . . . It lit up her entire life.

They strolled along the avenue, watching the families heading for church. Rob had no interest in fashion but he listened to her approving commentary, agreed when he thought she wanted agreement, and teased her when he thought the clothes were outré. The idea of looping back the skirt to display ruched and frilled underskirts struck him as very odd – 'Why don't they wear the underskirt on top?' he asked.

They stopped at a stall at the top of the avenue and drank some lemonade. It had a strange metallic taste compared with what they'd been used to at home, but when Morag mentioned it to the stall-holder she was told, with a haughty stare, 'This is the New Improved Lemonade Mixture, made from best purified ingredients including citric essence, scientific yellow colouring, and chemical sugars.'

'In other words, it's not real lemons,' Rob said.

'What d'you expect for two cents a glass – brandywine?'

Rob laughed. 'No, I suppose not. Do you want a cookie too, Morag?'

'Will that be made from new improved flour produced from essence and colourings?'

'Seems likely.'

'Then let's not bother.'

They wandered on until they found Jones's Wood. One or two families were already there, spreading chequered napkins on the grass in the shade, pouring real lemonade into glasses and putting pieces of pie on plates. Children were rushing about playing ball and bowling hoops, the girls leaping so that bow-tied pigtails escaped from under wide-brimmed straw hats, the boys unfastening prissy lace collars and losing braided buttons off their jackets.

'They look so *rich*,' Morag whispered to Rob.

He looked thoughtful. 'One thing's certain about this New World. There's money here.'

'You should see Mr. Aggerley's house,' she said. 'There are carpets on every floor! And the drapes – ! I'm sure there's the width of the windows twice over in every set of drapes. And some of the downstairs rooms have chenille velvet edgings to the mantelpieces and the pelmets and everything.'

'I wish there was some way of getting a share of all that. Seems all wrong to me, you working like a slave for next to nothing and me sleeping in the hay-barn, when there's so much comfort and luxury around.'

'It won't always be so, Rob,' she said on a note of rising hope. 'If we work hard, we can improve our lives. Mrs Aggerley says I've a good eye for needlework, so by and by perhaps I'll be allowed to make a little extra that way, and what I'm hoping is that in a year or so I'll be able to move on to a job in a dressmaker's —'

'Always at someone else's beck and call, though,' he put in with exasperation. 'Is that all you want out of life?'

'Oh no – one day I'd love to have a dress shop of my own. But that's a dream, I suppose,' she sighed. 'It would take an awful lot of money to set up on my own.'

'Doesn't seem much of a dream to me. Bowing and scraping to other people, always having to say yes-sir and no-sir —'

'It would be yes-madam and no-madam,' she teased. 'Men don't come into dress shops much.'

'That's why it doesn't appeal to me, I suppose. If it's what you want, I wish you luck with it. But I'm a different sort of person. I'm Craigallan of Glen Bairach – I've got chieftains' blood in my veins, Morag. One day I want to have land, as my forebears did.'

They walked about in the parkland until hunger forced them to look for an eating-house. There they had cold ham and cucumber salad with English tea for fifteen cents apiece. Then Morag begged to be taken down Broadway, the thoroughfare she most often heard mentioned by the Aggerley household.

They began the walk far out by Wood Lawns at 77th Street, where everything still seemed unformed and touched with country air. But as they approached the Fifties there were houses or building lots for houses, while behind them rose the great walls of the building that was to be the Museum of Art, on Fifth Avenue.

The middle of the roadway had been paved. Carriages bowled along upon it, heading for Central Park, to show off the equipage, the horses, and the finery of the occupants. Everywhere silks gleamed, jewels flashed, the sleek coats of the horses shone in the sunshine.

By the time they reached Madison Square Park, Morag was too weary to go any further. They sat on a park bench to talk, but her energy was spent; even for Rob, she couldn't keep up a conversation.

'Come on,' he said, 'it's time you were home.'

'No, no – I'll be all right when I've had a rest –'

'I've made you walk too far. I should have realised you needed rest. Come on, Morag – I'll take you home in a cab.'

'A cab?' She was horrified. 'That's ridiculous – think of the expense!'

'Never mind. It'll be worth it, to save you any more exertion –'

'No Rob, really, it's sheer extravagance –'

'Don't be daft.' He hailed a cab and helped her in. She was still protesting weakly when the driver slapped the reins and they were on their way.

All through the short journey she sat forward staring out of the window at the passing scene. She'd never ridden in a carriage before. She was overwhelmed by the sense of luxury and importance, by Rob's thoughfulness in giving her this treat.

She didn't sense that he'd grown bored by her exhaustion. He liked her, but when she was too tired to talk it was no fun. Better to take her home and set out by himself for some amusement. It was still only early evening – plenty of time to find a saloon and a relaxing atmosphere before he had to head for the Staten Island Ferry.

When they drew up at the door of the Aggerley house, he helped her out and paid the driver. She stood on the sidewalk, looking somehow small and lost. For a moment he hesitated, wondering if there was something he ought to do for her. But in a way their day out was over, brought to an end by her lack of energy. It wasn't her fault, but it had put a damper on their activity.

She held out her hand. 'Thank you, Rob. It's been absolutely lovely. I've never had such a wonderful time.'

'Glad you liked it. You go in now and take it easy.'

'Yes, I will. Shall I...shall I see you again soon?'

'Of course,' he assured her. 'I'll come again next week.'

'I don't have another day off until another month.'

'But you go to church on Sundays, don't you? They can't object if I come along and walk with you to church and back?'

'Well... no... I suppose not.'

'I'll be there, then.' Why was he saying this? What sort of a day off was that, to come to Manhattan and hang about waiting to walk with a girl to church? But she had this air of being lonesome and forlorn...

'You're so kind to me, Rob! It's wonderful to have a friend who thinks so much of me.'

'It's natural, isn't it,' he said with a grin. 'We're fellow-sufferers – strangers in a strange land. It's only right you and I should stick together.'

' So I'll see you next week?'

'Next week for sure.'

They stood hesitating. Morag was wondering whether she should offer her cheek to be kissed, and Rob was wondering if she would read too much into it if he kissed her. In the end he pressed her hand with open affection and hurried away.

She went down the stairs to the basement area door, her heart on wings. To think that he had given up almost a whole day to her when he had so little free time! And he was coming again next week. It was almost too much happiness. She went upstairs to the night nursery, undressed quickly, and lay down on her cot to the left of the door. She was physically very tired, although her mind was alive with memories of the day spent with Rob. She fell asleep at last, to dream about this wonderful day until she was roused by Mrs Portigo coming home from an evening party with the children. But it was only a small interruption to her dreams, for the children were as tired as she was and settled down at once.

Morag went back to her wonderland world. She walked again along the busy avenue with Rob at her side, drinking in the splendour of New York life and sharing her delight with him. Always, as a refrain to the dream, was the thought, 'I'll see him next week, I'll see him next week...'

But next Sunday came, and he wasn't there. She had spent fifty cents of her first month's wages on a little length of ribbon to edge the collar of her best dress, and freshened the sateen of her bonnet with a little gum-arabic starch. She had even begged a little glycerine and lemon from Cook to smooth and whiten her hands, which were roughened by the continual laundering of the children's clothes. She felt she looked her best that Sunday as she came up the area steps to fall in behind Bertha and Peggy as they followed Mr and Mrs Aggerley and their family to Grace Church.

As she walked, Morag let her glance wander ahead, looking for Rob. But although several men were to be seen loitering further along the sidewalk, Rob wasn't among them. She glanced behind her. He wasn't there either. All the way to church she was on the alert, but he didn't come.

In church her attention was never on the service. She kept glancing over her shoulder to see if he would come in. On the way home she was sure she would see him: he must have been delayed, and he'd be waiting by the house door.

Indoors, almost disbelieving in her own disappointment, she took the children upstairs to the day nursery. She stole to the window to look out from time to time. She was certain he would come.

But that tall, spare figure never appeared. The June dusk fell, the day was over. She went to bed, but this time she lay awake struggling with her dejection. It was only when she consoled herself that he had been prevented and would write, that she drifted off to sleep.

The week went by. No message came. She watched the mail eagerly every day, but though there were one or two letters for the belowstairs occupants, there was never one for Morag. Monday, Tuesday, Wednesday, she watched and hoped. When Thursday came she thought: Well, of course – it's so near Sunday now that he won't write. He'll come on Sunday.

[55]

But he didn't. Not that Sunday, nor the next. And sent no word.

By now she was sure that something terrible had happened. Rob had promised to come. He would come if he could. So something must be wrong.

She begged a piece of notepaper and an envelope from Bertha and wrote to him. A very brief, undemanding letter.

'Dear Rob, I feel sure something must have happened to prevent you coming as you said you would. Please let me know you're all right or, if sick, get someone to send word. Your affectionate friend, Morag McGarth.'

She sent it on the Monday. She knew it would reach him the following day, so she could expect a reply by Wednesday. But Wednesday passed, and Thursday, and Friday, and Saturday.

Then it was Sunday, and her day off. She still hadn't had any message. With a heart as heavy as a stone, she set about getting the children ready to accompany their mother on a visit to relatives at Manhattan Beach.

Almost at once, things began to go wrong.

4

CECILIA PORTIGO FELT SHE had nothing left in her life but her children. They were her claim on her husband, her proof that she'd been a good and loving wife. It was a pity she had no talent for handling them – she couldn't see them as human beings with lives of their own, but only as extensions of herself, to be put on and taken off like ornaments.

In the two months since Morag had been with the Aggerleys, Cecilia Portigo had been growing more and more jealous of her. She seemed to have some magic influence with the children. When they were with Morag, they were less noisy and demanding. When Morag chided them, they heeded. When she played with them, they were interested and quiet.

Mrs Portigo was sure Morag must be bribing them somehow, or spoiling them. What could be her secret?

Mrs Portigo came into the day nursery to see that the children were properly attired for their day at the beach. Jonnie was in his sailor suit and panama hat, the baby Claudie was in a short frock of flannel and white button leggings.

Little Cissie ran towards her mother, holding out her pinafore for inspection. 'Look, Mommy, isn't it pretty? Morag done it.'

'Morag *did* it, dear,' corrected her mother.

'Yes, I just tole you that,' agreed Cissie. She twirled. 'Do you like it? It's real pretty, isn't it?'

If Cissie hadn't been so eager to show it off, Mrs Portigo might not even have noticed the work done on the little girl's pinafore. But now, stooping, she saw that tiny rosettes of blue ribbon had been strewn across the edge of the starched cotton bib. To amuse and please the child, who hated to be encased in the stiff starched garments that felt like armour to her pudgy body, Morag had used up the remnants of the ribbon with which she'd trimmed her plain bonnet. By gathering one edge she had with tiny stitches shaped little flowers. They had made Cissie actually keen to put on her pinafore.

Cecilia felt an unreasoning wave of annoyance. 'What do you think you're up to, decking the child out to look like a little doll!' she cried. 'Take that off at once, Cissie. It's absurdly unsuitable.'

'But, Mrs Portigo –'

'And you hold your tongue,' Mrs Portigo exclaimed, whirling on Morag. 'Who asked you to garnish a perfectly good Swiss toile garment with gew-gaws like that?'

'I only did it to give pleasure to Cissie –'

'You take too much upon yourself!' cried Mrs Portigo. 'Scarcely a minute in the family and you're deciding how my children should be dressed –'

Cissie sat down fatly on the rug and began to wail with anguish. 'Don't be cross with Morag!' she wept. 'Don't you be naughty to her!'

Her brother, elder by one year, flew to her side. He knelt beside her and put his arms around her. Over his shoulder he said to his mother, 'You're horrid! You've made Cissie cry!'

Little Claudie, sitting as good as gold in his high chair, looked from one to the other and the corners of his mouth began to turn down. 'Ma-ma-ma,' he hiccuped.

Mrs Portigo snatched him up and held him to her bosom. 'Ah, my own little boy,' she crooned, 'you love your Mommy, don't you?'

Claudie, half-stifled against an expanse of maroon taffeta ruffles, writhed and struggled to be free. In panic he began to shout for help. "Wa-a!" he roared. 'Wa-a –'

'Mrs Portigo,' begged Morag, trying to take the baby from her, 'he can't breathe –'

'Take your hands off,' cried Mrs Portigo. 'Get out of my sight, you impertinent girl!'

'But madam –'

'Get out! I order you!'

There was nothing for it but to go. Morag curtseyed and hurried out, hearing the two toddlers clattering after her and hitting the door with their fists when they reached it too late to stop her.

She ran up to the day nursery and fetched her bonnet. It was, after all, her Sunday off. She'd intended to stay at home, to do some needlework for Mrs O'Malley. But now she was desperate to get out of the house.

She set off with no conscious plan in mind. All she knew was that for some hours at least she must stay out of the Aggerleys' house, until the annoyance over the children's outcry had subsided, until Mrs Portigo had had time to complain to her mother and to be soothed with the reply that the nurserymaid was of no importance.

Her footsteps had taken her northward, in the general direction of Madison Square. She was walking quickly, head bent. It made her start when someone touched her on the shoulder.

'Where are you going in such a hurry, Morag?'

She gasped and turned. 'Rob!'

'Hello,' he said. 'Why so surprised? Didn't you expect me?'

'Rob! I . . . I . . . You didn't reply to my letter.'

'*This* is the reply,' he said, linking her arm with his. 'Surely you must have known I'd come?'

'No, I . . . You didn't, before.'

'Well, that was just one of those things. Mr Dalgow had some big loads of fodder to put into store. There was just too much work to be able to come visiting on Sundays.'

'Oh, I'm sorry, Rob! You must be tired.'

'Well, yes, I am – but I'm better for seeing you.'

Her letter had pricked his conscience. Against his will, he had felt a pang at his own neglect. He looked back to the day he'd spent with her, and somehow it seemed very pleasant. True, he'd felt he got more excitement out of the evening in the bar on Broadway, and hadn't felt much urge to seek her out the following weekend. But when her letter came, he found himself thinking about how undemanding she was, how tranquil and easy to talk to. Other girls he picked up always seemed to be playing a part – acting coy, expecting compliments. And when he spent his time with the men, he drank too much, woke up feeling thickheaded and dull.

'What would you like to do?' he asked.

'I don't mind. What would *you* like to do?'

'Let's go for a ride on a horse-car.'

'All right.'

They walked to Sixth and boarded the car for 59th Street. As yet there weren't too many passengers, so they found seats together on a bench. Rob let Morag sit by the window, remembering how she loved to look at passers-by to admire their clothes. But today she didn't seem so interested. He thought she was a bit down in her spirits. When he chatted to her, she replied with interest, but he caught glimpses of sadness at the back of her eyes.

Central Park didn't seem to be central to anything, so far as Rob could make out when they alighted. Hopefully named by the city fathers, it was still a long way north of New York's main thoroughfares. Wild and unformed, it was nevertheless popular with the New Yorkers who liked to show off their fine horses and carriages. As yet it was too early in the day for the high society parade; that didn't reach its peak until about four in the afternoon. But already lesser notables were sitting back to be admired in a glossy landau, or whizzing past in a phaeton.

They strolled along the walk that bordered the east carriage drive. The sun was now high in a blue sky. The pedestrians were mostly young married people with young children, or engaged couples under the watchful eye of a mother or an aunt. Everyone was in their best clothes – the women in fine taffeta or silk or lawn, the colours rather dark, trimmed up with bright ribbons or well laundered lace, the men in walking suits of light coloured pants and short dark jackets set off by high collars glossily starched.

[60]

But there were plenty of walkers who hadn't yet reached that rank in society where they could afford fine clothes. Rob and Morag weren't out of place in their dark, worn garments. They were part of that hopeful group who looked at those around them and vowed that one day they, too, would wear silk and fine linen, and own a fine carriage.

In the early afternoon, when the crowd began to thicken for the carriage parade, they made their way eastward through some rough ground to the farm at Fourth Avenue and 57th Street, where Rob bought milk and home-made muffins for a picnic lunch. They sat on the grass by the farm gate to eat. After they'd returned the milk pitcher they wandered on again, down a lane at the side of the pasture and into a little wood from the outskirts of which they could see the East River sparkling in the sun about a quarter of a mile away. Here they sat down in the shade, but what with the warmth of the day and the weariness of many disturbed nights and long hours of work, Morag fell asleep.

She lay with one arm thrown across her eyes to keep out the light, her chestnut brown hair tangled in the long grass already turning dry and yellow in the early summer sun. Rob sat with his arms clasped round his knees, studying her. It struck him she was thinner than when he last saw her, and the wrists escaping from the narrow sleeve of her dark dress looked almost brittle under their thin covering of skin. Her hands, small and fragile, were reddened by frequent immersion in hot water.

He felt an impulse of pity for her. He could guess that her employers expected – naturally – to get their money's worth out of her. But where a more guileful girl might have protested or evaded the work, Morag was too openhearted to refuse any task. From what he'd heard her say, the children were demanding and unchecked, but she had given her heart to them – which didn't help in the struggle to keep some time to herself.

She stirred and moved her arm. Her great dark eyes looked straight up into his. He smiled. 'Had a good sleep?'

'Oh! Rob, I'm so sorry! I didn't mean –'

'It's all right. I've been watching the boats out on the river. But I reckon it's time to be heading home now.'

She had sat up and was brushing her hair into order with her hands, but at his words she turned sharply. 'Must we?' she whispered.

'We-ell . . .' Rob could use the evening hours more to his own advantage than sitting on a knoll looking at the view. 'We ought to be getting back,' he said.

To his astonishment her eyes filled with tears. 'Oh, I don't want to!' she cried.

'But – Good Lord, what's the matter?'

'It's so awful there, Rob! Nobody really to belong to, and when I try to make friends with the children, their Mama gets jealous and angry –'

'Oh, come on now, you mustn't let it bother you –'

'You don't understand,' she said in desperation. 'You're the only real friend I've got.' She threw herself against him, her hands on his shoulder to pull him towards her. Her cheek was against his chest. 'You're so kind to me, Rob. You're the only person who seems to know I *exist*.'

'Poor little lass,' he said. He put his arms round her and stroked her hair. 'You take it so much to heart –'

'I'm sorry,' she wept, keeping her face turned away. 'I'm being silly, I know I am. You must think I'm a fool –'

'I think you're a dear wee thing,' he said, holding her closer.

She felt like a bird nestling against him – small and light and delicate. He could feel the narrow bones of her shoulders and arms, smell a faint fragrance from her hair, sense the quick distressed beating of her heart.

With one hand he turned her face up to his. Her eyes were swimming in tears, enhancing their helpless appeal; tears trembled on her lashes as if they asked to be kissed away. With his lips he brushed them lightly, and felt the lids close under his touch. It was strangely moving. He kissed her mouth, pressing so close that he tasted the salt of fallen tears.

To his surprise, she responded eagerly. To her, his kisses were warmth and love and belonging. They brought a little surge of new emotion, something to do with the need to be with Rob, with Rob rather than anyone else in the world.

[62]

When he began to explore her neck and throat with his lips, she tilted her head back to let the glow from that caress spread through her body. A moment later she was kissing him again, her lips as urgent and eager as his. Her whole being was beginning to waken to wonder and delight as his hands sought out her secret parts.

For the first time in her life she felt loved; her being was drawn out of her towards another who merged with her in this magical encounter of body and soul. She had no thought of drawing back. She had never known such joy, and couldn't turn away from it.

Even when his grasp became harsh and demanding, she didn't protest. She didn't understand that this was physical desire. All she knew was that Rob desired something from her that she wanted to give, and if there was a moment of pain, of anguish, it was swept away almost at once by a growing rapture. She heard voices, muffled and gasping – could that be herself and Rob, speaking to each other in passion? She hardly knew, hardly cared, as the gates of paradise burst open for her.

She came back to her everyday self to find Rob's arms around her, Rob's voice crooning endearments against her cheek. She lay languid and drowsy, unable to sort out her reactions to what had happened.

She was totally innocent. When the minister in the kirk at home thundered about 'the sins of the flesh', she had no idea what he meant: she pictured them as being surrender to the wish to stay in bed in the morning, the guilty enjoyment of soft fabrics against the skin. She had no experience . . . no knowledge of men. The episode on the docks at Leith when the big ruffian attacked her, she had always supposed was mere brutishness and greed, the wish to oust her from her little shelter and escape from the cold. That anything like a sexual attack had been intended, she didn't understand.

What had happened with Rob just now was utterly new, utterly unknown. How could this splendour and joy be sinful? She knew Rob to be good and noble, her knight-errant of the steerage quarters.

'Ah, my love, my love,' Rob whispered. 'Who would have suspected you had so much passion in that little body?'

'I'm so happy, Rob.'

He kissed her with gentleness.

What had happened was entirely unforeseen, almost unwished-for. Morag had taken him by surprise. It had never occurred to him that she could make love. So far in his life, 'love' was a word he associated with saucy girls, knowing little lasses who teased and cajoled and expected to be paid in some way.

The generous and open response of Morag was a revelation to him. He hardly knew what to say, what to do. His upbringing urged him to tell her that all would be well, that he would marry her and repair the damage he had just done. But she didn't even seem to suspect that he owed her any such reparation. To talk in that way to her would be wrong; it would mar their love.

She blushed and laughed when he helped her put her clothing to rights and pulled her to her feet. There was colour in her cheeks. She glowed with happiness. As they made their way back to the rattling roar of the main thoroughfare she clung to him, gently confident that she belonged to him now and could let it be seen.

They walked back without speaking much to each other. Morag was still too bewildered to have many words, and Rob was busy with his thoughts – his sense of guilt, his happy feeling of triumph and affection, his worry about where it might all lead.

He was almost eager to part from her so that he could think about everything. He loved her, but wasn't sure that he wanted to. For her part, Morag accepted his decision and tilted her face for his farewell kiss.

'I'll see you next Sunday,' he promised.

'It isn't a day off –'

'That doesn't matter. I'll come at church time.'

'All right, Rob.' She gave him a little teasing smile. 'You really will come this time?'

He felt himself flushing at her words. She expected so little. She had no notion of what she had just given him, no idea that at this moment he felt as if he had been made a millionaire. 'I'll come,' he said, and meant it.

After a last hug she walked the remaining block to the Aggerley house and went down the steps to the servants' entrance. She was still flowing with happiness, still drunk with the after-effects of physical love.

Mrs O'Malley was preparing supper for her employers. She looked over her shoulder as Morag came in, about to demand her help in preparing the vegetables, but Morag slipped past quickly, remembering it was still her day off and eager to be alone with her thoughts.

She went upstairs to the empty day nursery. Mrs Portigo was still out on the visit with the children. Morag threw her bonnet on the nursery table and sat down on a stool by the window, staring out at the early evening sky. She knew she ought to go and brush her tangled hair, get out of her rumpled gown, but not yet. Just for a moment, she wanted to treasure her memory of Rob's nearness.

She had left the door open. The son of the house, Claude Aggerley, glanced in as he passed on his way upstairs to change for a social gathering later in the evening. He saw a little figure sitting on the low stool, her head tilted back, her dreaming eyes fixed on the drifting clouds. The thick rich hair was in disarray. The usually demure skirts had caught up on the little black boot, exposing a length of slender leg in a black cotton stocking. Her arms were clasped about herself so that her breasts were pushed against the dark fabric of her bodice. The prim white muslin collar had been partly torn from the neckline, so that the white throat was rising from the whiter bosom.

Claude had often glanced at the new kitchenmaid and thought she was a neat little piece. But it had been an idle notion, until now. In her plain white cap and big coarse apron, there had been little to invite further examination. There was something different about her this evening. Now she was suddenly enticing.

He stepped into the day nursery. At the sound, Morag turned. Seeing it was the master's son, she rose. 'Is there something you want, Mr Claude?' she asked, expecting to be sent to fetch it.

'Oh yes, my dear, you could say that,' he replied. He came close, putting his hands on her shoulders. 'All on your lonesome, are you?'

She didn't really understand what his tone meant, but she found that she couldn't bear him to touch her. No one must touch her except Rob. She shrugged off his hands and stepped back. 'Mrs Portigo will be back soon, if you were looking for her or the children,' she said, turning for the door.

'What the hell should I want her for, or her kids?' Claude laughed.

He caught her skirt and roughly pulled her back to him. Taken off balance, she staggered. He snatched her into his arms and dragged her close against him, so that he could feel her body against his as she struggled. It excited him more than he had expected. He knew that he wanted her. And why not? He didn't have to go up and change just yet. And the day nursery was a quiet spot.

'Come on, lovey,' he urged, holding his head away from her struggles. 'You'll find I'm good fun – and generous, too. Come on now.'

He expected her to give in after only token resistance. She was no innocent, as it was easy to guess from how she'd looked when he came upon her. She had had the look of love about her. And she was only a servant and, in his experience, servants were usually easy to persuade.

Her resistance surprised and annoyed him. He exerted some force and brought her crashing to the ground, where he held her down with the weight of his body.

He had forgotten, however, that though they were alone in the day nursery, they weren't alone in the house. A flurry of skirts in the doorway caught his eye. He scrambled up.

'What on earth is going on?' his mother demanded.

'Nothing – I – er –'

'Claude, what are you doing in here?'

Claude said the first thing he could think of in his own defence. 'She invited me in,' he said.

'Invited you?'

'I didn't!' Morag cried. 'That's a lie!'

'She's a real little tease,' Claude went on quickly so as to capture his mother's attention. 'I was going up to change for the evening and she was sitting here, showing a lot too much leg. Well, Mama, you must admit, it was enough to make any man stop for a second look –'

'That's not true! I was just sitting here –'

'Claude, I think you'd better leave me to deal with this,' Mrs Aggerley said.

Only too glad to escape, Claude made for the door. But before he could go out, his sister Cecilia came in, still in her outdoor things. Raised voices had brought her up from the hall where she had been supervising the carrying in of the sleeping baby and shushing her older children so as not to wake him.

'What's all the noise?' she asked. 'I could hear you downstairs –'

'Oh, it's nothing,' Claude said. 'Just a little mistake on the part of your nursery maid –'

'What?' Mrs Portigo cried, made anxious at once by anything to do with her children. 'What has she done?'

'Now, now, Cecilia,' her mother said. 'Claude got up to his tricks again –'

'I did not!' Claude protested in loud tones. 'Hang it, Mama, would I bother with a little shrimp like that except if I was invited? I admit I gave in when she gave me the come-hither, but *I* didn't start it.'

'How could you?' gasped Morag, aghast at the lies he was telling.

'I *knew* she was up to no good!' Mrs Portigo exclaimed. 'I caught her out this morning, encouraging Cissie to be disobedient –'

'I didn't!' said Morag. 'I only made her –'

'She's deceitful, that's what she is!'

'Now, now Cecilia, don't get upset about it –'

'How can you talk like that, Mama? She's in charge of my children for long periods at a time! Do you think I want a bad influence getting control of them?'

'Oh, I don't know that she's exactly a bad –'

'I don't know that she's exactly good, either,' Claude remarked. This incident, now made public, could prove very

[67]

awkward. His parents had strict views about morals. If he couldn't prove that Morag was to blame, they might cut his allowance quite noticeably.

He had his sister as an ally in wanting to find Morag at fault. Cecilia Portigo didn't consider what a loss it would be if Morag was fired; she didn't remember how many hours of the night the nursery-maid sat up, how she worked over the children's clothes, how she played with them and kept them in order. All she remembered was that Morag had more influence with her children than she herself had, and that Claude was saying she was a bad girl.

'Look at her!' she cried. 'Anyone can see how she's spent her day off!'

'Yeah,' Claude said, studying Morag. 'You're right, Cecilia! When I happened on her, she was all aglow – and not with religious fervour, either!

Mrs Aggerley frowned. She eyed Morag. And it did seem to her that something was different about the servant-girl. She was flushed and untidy. 'Did you tear her collar?' she asked her son sharply.

'Gee, I wouldn't do a thing like that, Mama! Anyhow, I only just tried to kiss her, that's all –'

'But you were doing more than kiss her when I came in –'

'But we lost our balance, that's all that happened. I didn't touch her, Mama, honest. I leaned forward to beg a kiss, she leaned towards me, and we sort of fell over –'

'Where have you been today?' Mrs Aggerley asked Morag.

'I . . . went for a ride on the horse-car.'

'Alone?'

Morag shook her head.

'She was with a man. Anyone can tell that!' Cecilia cried.

'It's my day off!' flashed Morag, her head coming up. 'It's none of your business what I did!'

'Do you deny you've been with a man?' demanded Cecilia.

'Mind your own business –'

'Now, miss, that's no way to talk,' Mrs Aggerley said with annoyance. 'I'm responsible for your welfare. I thought it was

[68]

understood that followers weren't allowed here?'

'He hasn't come here –'

'Ah, so you admit you have a fellow?' Claude cried in triumph. 'Or is there more than one?'

'To think I've let her look after my children!' said Cecilia, bursting into tears. 'My little innocents –'

'What are you talking about?' Morag demanded, meaning the question literally.

'Don't be insolent,' Mrs Aggerley returned. 'Really, I begin to think we've been seriously misled about you –'

'I'm not having her touch my children again!' Cecilia exclaimed, her voice climbing as she let hysteria claim her. 'She's not to come near them! My little Cissie – she's not to be contaminated –'

'Cecilia, Cecilia –'

'She's got to go! I won't have her in the same house as my children!'

'I don't want to encourage immorality, that's for sure,' her mother agreed with a shake of her head. 'All the same –'

'Immorality?' Morag interrupted. 'Mrs Aggerley, I'm not immoral! Your son came in here when I was just sitting quietly, and when I got up to ask if he wanted anything he grabbed me –'

'That's an outright lie!' Claude said. '*She* made all the running, Mama! You can bet she's had some fun today and was out to get some more –'

'Morag, how did your collar get torn?'

Morag put her hand up to her neckline. 'It was an accident.'

'You look in a state. Your hair is a mess. What have you been up to?'

'Up to?' The words hurt her. They denigrated the wonderful experience she'd shared with Rob. 'Mind your own business!' she flared.

'You see?' Cecilia cried. 'She's selfwilled and immoral –'

'I will not be spoken to like that, Morag,' Mrs Aggerley said, her tone hardening. 'You will tell me who you spent the day with, and what you did.'

'I will not!'

'You'll do as you're told.'

'I won't.'

'There you are!' crowed Claude. 'She's been up to no good, or she'd tell you in a minute.'

'And to think she's been alone with my children for hours at a time! Who knows what she's been telling them –'

'Don't be silly!' Morag cried. 'I've only told them fairy stories –'

'The kind of fairy story about how I grabbed you? You know fine and good you led me on –'

'You're a liar!'

'Very well,' said Mrs Aggerley. 'That's enough. You'll leave this house, my girl.'

'What?'

The order was like a bucket of cold water thrown in Morag's face. Until then she had been bewildered, and then angry. But now she was at a loss. 'Leave?' she gasped.

'I will not have a girl in my house who is impertinent to her betters, deceitful, and of a loose character. Pack up and go.'

'But – but – you can't –'

'I certainly can. This is my house. I choose who I have in it.'

'But where would I go?'

'To the companion with whom you spent today.'

'But, Mrs Aggerley – he –'

'There you are! He doesn't want her – you can see by the way she says it – I'll tell you what happened,' Claude said. 'She picked up some fellow and spent the day with him –'

'Claude, I won't have such things talked of in my house,' his mother reproved. She looked at Morag with distaste. 'You're to pack and go – do you understand? I want you out of here within the hour.'

'But, ma'am – you can't do this –'

'Within the hour,' warned her employer. 'If you aren't gone by then, I'll have you thrown out bodily.'

Morag opened her mouth to beg for leniency, but Mrs Portigo rushed at her. 'Go!' she cried, pushing her towards the door. 'Get out of this room. You dirty it with your presence!'

Shocked and dismayed, Morag ran out.

5

ROB SPENT THE WEEK that followed in a state of utter perplexity. He told himself that the last thing in the world he wanted was a wife. He had his life before him; he had to find a good job, with better prospects than this hard labour at Dalgow's, and once he'd found that, he had to make a career for himself.

Saddled with a wife, everything would be more difficult. And yet, when he thought about Morag, his determination to be alone and untrammelled melted away. He pictured her in his arms. He mused over the idea of coming home to her every evening, of spending his nights with her. He relived that moment when she gave herself to him, utterly and generously, and knew that freedom, independence, were as nothing compared with that.

As day succeeded day, his longing to see her again grew stronger than any plans to be his own master. On Sunday he was up early. He bought a new stiff collar for his shirt, so that he would look smarter when he met her. On the way to Fourth Avenue from the ferry, he looked for a flower stall to get her a posy, but saw nothing that was worthy of her.

He waited outside the Aggerley house, on the opposite side of the street. At church time, the servants came up from downstairs, but Morag wasn't with them. They gathered on the sidewalk in expectation of the master and mistress, and fell into step behind them when the Aggerleys appeared. A young man accompanied them. That would be Claude, the younger son still at home, Rob knew. Mrs Portigo hadn't come out, so when the group moved off to make its way to church, Rob took it for granted that Morag had been kept at home to get the children ready for an outing. Morag would be allowed out then.

About an hour later a hired hackney carriage came up to the door. Mrs Portigo came out with her children and got in. Rob waited, expecting Morag to emerge belatedly for church. But she didn't come. He went down the basement steps and knocked on the door but Mr O'Malley, left at home to look after the house and expecting no callers, was out back putting petunias into garden baskets.

The Aggerley household returned from church about twelve-thirty. Rob was still waiting. As Mrs Aggerley mounted the steps in front of her brownstone, she saw him out of the corner of her eye. She somehow thought she'd seen him earlier.

She went to her room and divested herself of her chipstraw bonnet, her kid gloves and her fan. Before she went downstairs again, she glanced out. He was still there, across the street. His gaze was fixed on her house.

She went downstairs and rang the bell. 'Bertha,' she said, 'there's a young man on the opposite sidewalk. Fetch him here to me.'

'Yes'm.'

Rob was startled to receive the invitation. He felt it must mean that Morag was ill. She sometimes had a cough – perhaps it had got worse, perhaps she'd been taken to hospital . . .

'Well, now, young man,' Mrs Aggerley said when he was shown into her parlour, 'what do you think you're doing, keeping watch on my house?'

'I'm hoping to speak to Morag McGarth, ma'am,' Rob said, clutching his cap in his two hands.

'So,' she said, glaring at him. Secure in the knowledge that she was in her own home, and mistress of it, she went on: 'You ought to be ashamed of yourself, dragging that poor girl down!'

Rob stared at her. 'I beg your pardon?' he said, in a strange tone that should have warned her.

'She was given an excellent character by Mr and Mrs Henderson. If I had thought she was going to go to the bad like that, I would never have had her here. But it's to be laid at your door, and I hope your conscience will punish you!'

'My conscience is no concern of yours, mistress,' Rob replied, his thin face growing dark with anger. 'What are you telling me about Morag?'

'There's little you need to be told! I imagine you know only too well what's been going on between the pair of you.'

'Whatever it may have been, it's no concern of yours.'

'You mind your manners, young man –'

'You mind yours!' His tone threatened her. 'Where is Morag?'

'You want to drag her down further, is that it? You –'

'I want to see her. Be so good as to ring for her –'

'That would be no use,' Mrs Aggerley said in a tone of triumph, 'since she's left my house.'

'Left?'

'Do you think I could keep her here, with innocent little children in my care –'

'Left? Where has she gone?'

'I have no idea, and it will be the better for her if you don't catch up with her, I daresay –'

'You high-handed, narrow-minded bitch!' shouted Rob. 'Where did she go?'

Mrs Aggerley shrank back in her cane chair. She was frightened by the fury she had unleashed. 'I . . . I don't know . . .'

'You don't know? You *mean* that?'

'I . . . Of course . . . I have no concern with a girl of bad character –'

'Morag McGarth's character is beyond reproach! You ought not to be allowed to speak of her, if you can only think ill thoughts –'

'How dare you speak to me like that!' She gathered her courage. Her husband, after all, was downstairs in his study, and her son in the dining room waiting for the midday meal. 'I called you in to tell you what you had done –'

'And what have *you* done?' he raged. 'You've turned away a girl who never harmed anyone in her life, and who's a stranger in this city! I cannot believe you would do such a thing!'

'You take a great concern in her affairs –'

'By God, it's as well I do, for it seems you don't! I travelled over on the same ship as Morag. I'm the only friend she has on this side of the water. Where has she gone?'

For the first time, Mrs Aggerley experienced misgivings. Her daughter's insistent dislike of Morag and her son's hints that she was no better than she ought to be had lulled her conscience since the girl was driven out; but it now occurred to her that it was no sin for her to go out with a young man whom she had known for some months, and even if perhaps there had been some … well … indiscretion, that was no reason to throw her out on the street.

'I … er … I was told by my upper housemaid that she … er … intended to go to the minister of the Scottish church near Bowling Green.'

'Thank you for the information –'

'Young man, it would really be better if you left her alone. It's no advantage to her to have a follower out at elbows like you.'

'Mistress!' He drew himself up. Tall and muscular, he was impressive despite his lack of years. 'That is no way to speak to Craigallan of Glen Bairach!'

'Craigallan of Glen Bairach,' she repeated sneeringly, trying to justify her own behaviour. 'A penniless nobody, clearly.'

'One day,' he said, his mouth hard, 'you'll hear my name and you'll understand that this nobody was destined to be a somebody.'

He turned and stalked out, shaking with fury. The heartless treatment of Morag, the insolence to himself, had roused him to a pitch of anger that made him less than tactful when he arrived at the parsonage of the Scottish church. The maidservant, alarmed, protested that the minister had just sat down to his dinner.

'You'll have to wait,' she said.

He brushed by her and, guided by the smell of roast beef, walked into the dining-room. Mr McIver and his family were half-way through a hearty plateful of meat and vegetables. The minister half-rose as the tall young man in a threadbare suit surged in.

'Where is Morag?'

'Who?' gasped McIver.

'Morag McGarth – from Mrs Aggerley's house.'

'Oh, *that* girl –'

'Yes, that girl. Where is she? I want to talk to her at once.'

'She isn't here –'

'What?'

'Young man, your behaviour is –'

'Devil take my behaviour! What have you done with my Morag?'

'I have no intention of discussing it with you –'

Rob took hold of the minister by the lapel of his black frock-coat and yanked him from the dining table. 'You'll discuss it!'

'Angus!' screamed Mrs McIver, finding her voice.

Papa!' shrieked the children.

'Sir, sir . . .' the minister quavered. 'You're frightening my wife –'

'Tell me what I want to know.'

'I cannot discuss a girl like that in front of my family,' said Mr McIver. 'That is out of the question.'

'Come on then,' Rob said dragging him towards the door.

Outside, he released his grasp on the preacher, who led the way to a smaller room lined with books and chiefly furnished with a heavy desk and a fine old Bible on a stand.

'Now,' said Rob. 'Where is she?'

'She isn't here, young man,' McIver said, gathering his courage back.

'What have you done with her?'

'I? I've done nothing! I can do nothing with recalcitrants like that.'

'What d'you mean? She came to you for help, didn't she?'

'So she said. But she showed no repentance, even though I gave her a bed and a roof over her head. Such ingratitude I never did see –'

'You took her in? Thank you for that at least! So where is she now?'

'She ran away during the night.'

'Ran away?'

'I don't appreciate behaviour like that! I understood her to say that she wanted to be a good girl – and then when the time was near for her to stand up and confess her sins, she ran away.'

'What sins did you expect her to confess?' Rob cried. 'What in God's name have you been saying to the poor girl?'

'That is between her and me,' McIver said with some dignity. 'As a pastor it is my duty to wrestle with souls in error. But I will tell you that I was able to learn that she had fallen from grace . . .' McIver paused, looking at Rob with sudden understanding. This, presumably, was Morag's partner in disgrace.

'You and Mrs Aggerley are quick to judge her by your own standards,' Rob said, his chin jutting indignantly. 'Did it never occur to you that Morag is better than either of you?'

'How dare you, sir! She admitted to me that she had had experience of the flesh –'

'And if she had? Why do you cry out at that? You have children, I saw –'

'Sir, I am a married man!'

'I have come here to find Morag and ask her to marry me,' Rob said. 'If that's all that matters to you, put me on her tracks and your conscience can be at rest.'

'I can't tell you where she went.' To do him justice, McIver was beginning to feel very unhappy. 'I told her yesterday that before I could recommend her to any other employer, she had to make a full confession of her fault, in church this morning. She has a proud spirit, sir! A very wrong, proud spirit! Rather than go before the congregation and admit she had done wrong, she preferred to run away.'

'You don't know where she went?'

'No.'

'But you must have some idea! When did you discover she had gone?'

'Early this morning. She climbed out of the attic window, it seems, walked along the main house roof, and got to the ground by the apple tree. There's a lower bough broken.'

Morag had been unable to take her little tin trunk with her

because it was too heavy and would have made too much noise. She had taken nothing except a change of underwear wrapped in her apron. Her plan was to get to Fourth Avenue by the time the churchgoers would be setting out, and meet Rob there.

When she first arrived at the house of Reverend McIver, she thought her problem was solved. The minister was not a lenient man, but had given her shelter at once, on her promise that she would discuss her faults with him and lead a better life. Innocent that she was, she had imagined she would only have to describe the incidents at the Aggerleys' house for him to understand everything.

But in one conversation after another, he had probed and probed until at last he guessed what she refused to say – that she and this young man she admired so much had made love. McIver was experienced enough to see that she truly didn't know she had done anything wrong, and had explained to her that she had committed a sin.

Morag was stricken by his words, by the reprobation in his tone. At first, in the shock of new knowledge, she had submitted to his judgement. But as the days brought her nearer to the moment when she was expected to stand in front of the congregation of the church and admit her errors, her heart rebelled.

How could it be a sin? That glory, that splendour? If God didn't wish men and women to experience it, why did he create them with physical needs of that kind?

She couldn't stand up and say she had sinned. She didn't believe it. And it would be tarnishing that moment. It would be like a slug crawling over the picture she held in her memory.

On Saturday she made up her mind that she wouldn't do it. No matter that a minister of the church told her it was right – she knew it to be wrong. She would go to meet Rob, explain what had happened, and ask for his advice. She didn't expect help from Rob; he had little enough money himself, so she would never dream of throwing herself upon his mercy. No, she would never be a burden to him . . .

It was very early when she left the manse. She had torn her skirt

[77]

on the apple tree and almost lost a shoe that slipped off as she was clambering down from the branches.

She had about an hour's walk to do, and plenty of time in which to do it. So she didn't hurry. She felt listless and a little lightheaded. All week she had been harassed and badgered by Reverend McIver, besides being kept at work by the disapproving Mrs McIver as payment for her bed and board. She had had no appetite. Her chest hurt a little. She had made no complaints to Mrs McIver but now as she made her way towards the Aggerleys' house she wondered if she had a chill.

As she drew near Washington Square, a wave of faintness came over her. She saw the towers of the university wavering before her eyes. She was passing a shady tree; she stepped off the path and leaned against the trunk. After a moment she decided hazily that she had better sit down, and slipped to the grass in the shade.

She had no watch, and no idea how long she sat there. People hurried by – students of the university, ladies and gentlemen on their way to chapel, families out to take the air in the greenery of the lawns.

By and by she became aware that the numbers had increased. She frowned and shook her head to clear it. People were coming out of church! She sprang up. Her head whirled. She leaned against the tree to steady herself then hurried away. Rob would be waiting for her at Fourth Avenue.

In her dazed state she got lost in the alleys on the north of the square and turned the wrong way. It was some time before the angle of the shadows cast by the buildings made her look about, and discover she was heading east when she meant to be going north.

She turned in her tracks and began to run. Panting and with her forehead wet with sweat, she reached the block where the Aggerleys lived. She didn't dare walk past the house – she dreaded the thought of Claude Aggerley espying her and coming out. He had made sure she was dismissed, but she sensed he would be glad to happen upon her again.

She lingered for a time on the corner close to the entrance to the railroad station but was frightened off by a hard-faced girl who hissed: 'This is my pitch! Clear off!' Morag had no idea what she meant, but shrank back and hurried off. In any case, the spot was too far from the block on which the Aggerley house was situated; she ought to be closer if she wanted to contact Rob.

She stayed there a long time, sitting on some building blocks on a lot where a new house was to be erected. She had nowhere else to go. Besides, she felt unwilling to move. She didn't feel sick, exactly. But she seemed to have little energy.

She was roused by the sight of a carriage drawing up outside the Aggerley house. Mrs Portigo got down. Mrs Aggerley came out to help bring in the children. It dawned on Morag that it must be time for dinner, that Mrs Portigo must have come home from a day out.

It meant that the time was now probably about seven in the evening. Seven o'clock? It was terribly unlikely that Rob would be at the Aggerley house at this hour. To wait here any longer was useless.

What should she do? She had to find Rob. He was her only friend in New York. She had no one else to turn to. She must get to Staten Island. She recalled that the store for which Rob worked, Dalgow's, was at Grymes Hill Crossroads. She must go to the wharf and ask how to get there.

When she dragged herself to her feet it was to find that the bundle in which she had brought her apron and her linen was gone. She couldn't recall when she'd had it last. But she had to find it, for it had her money wrapped in the middle. The remains of her first month's wages – eight dollars and twenty-two cents.

Panic and anxiety almost made her rush away, but good sense intervened in time. She searched the ground round the rock on which she'd been sitting, but it wasn't there. She must have dropped it under the tree in Washington Square when she got up in a hurry. She assured herself it would still be there – who would pick up an old apron?

When she got back to the tree there was nothing on the ground beneath its branches. She thought for a moment she must have mistaken the tree, but though she looked under two or three others she still found nothing.

What should she do? Report her loss to the police? She'd no idea where the police station was. She'd seen the policemen on the streets, tall muscular men in long doublebreasted coats and flat caps with peaks from under which their hard, shrewd eyes stared out. They carried riot sticks at the ready. She shrank from the idea of going to them for help. She had the feeling they wouldn't think her loss was very important.

And time was getting on. She didn't know whether the ferry shut down in the early evening or stayed in action during the hours of darkness. She *must* get to the ferry. She'd be able to persuade the captain to take her on promise that Rob would pay her fare on the Staten Island side.

She looked about one last despairing time for her rolled apron. She was unaware that she was looking in the wrong place, that her apron and its little store of money had been expertly slipped from under her arm by the streetwalker on the corner near the railroad station entrance. The streetwalker was in a not much better state than Morag. She had a roof over her head but no money, so that even the cruelty of stealing from someone as obviously in distress as Morag had not deterred her.

It took Morag a long time to make her way to the docks. She had a vague notion of the way, because she'd made the journey from South Street Wharf with Bertha in the omnibus. But South Street Wharf wasn't the place to find a ferry to Richmond.

There was a crowd outside the Fraunces Tavern. To one of the more respectably dressed seamen she addressed a query about the ferry to Grymes Hill. He, hearing the word ferry, waved her on towards the Battery. She thanked him and hurried on.

Nobody knew where the Grymes Hill ferry was to be found. She lost a lot of time inquiring for it. Finally she reached the right jetty for the Staten Island boats, but by now darkness was coming on and the service was growing infrequent. There was no call for transportation to Staten Island after a certain time in the evening; the folk over there went to bed early, and the few high-steppers who were out late would pay for a boat to take them over privately.

One boatman had been watching Morag for some minutes.

When she received a rebuff from a ferryboat crewman because she couldn't pay to step aboard, he approached her. 'Listen, little lady, I can see you're in a fix. Want to go across to St George, do you?'

'I want to go to Grymes Hill . . .'

'That's beyond St George. You have to disembark there and walk on a couple of miles. Pretty late to be doing that, ain't it?'

'I have to get there,' she insisted.

'Live there?'

She coloured. It was light enough for him to see the blood rushing to her cheeks. She looked young and pretty and enticing.

'No, I don't live there, but I have to find someone in Grymes Hill.'

'Find someone? You mean you lost them?'

'I . . . I've never been there.'

'Not been long in New York, have you? I can tell by your voice. You've still got the lilt from across the water. Pretty, that is.'

Encouraged by the friendliness of his manner, she confided that she'd only been in the United States about two months, that she had to find the friend with whom she'd made the crossing because, just at the moment, she didn't have a place to stay.

'Is that so?' he remarked. 'Gee, that's tough! It's really important to you to get to the Island.'

'Yes, it's terribly important. But . . .'

'You ain't got the fare?' he hinted, for he'd seen her pleading with the crewman of the ferryboat.

'I . . . I lost my money. I don't know how it happened.'

'You're in a fix, and that's for sure! Look, tell you what, little lady. I'll take you across. How about that?'

'You will?' she cried. 'Oh, you *are* kind! It would be so helpful to me –'

'That's all right. I like to be helpful. We'll go in a minute.'

'Oh, I'm so grateful.'

'How grateful?' he asked.

'What? Oh, I . . . you mean, what about money? Well, my friend will pay you when we get there.'

'What, at Grymes Hill? I'm not walking no two miles to get the fare. No, no, that would be stupid.'

'Well, could I send it to you? I –'

'Oh, come on, don't be coy! You and me can soon come to an arrangement about paying for the trip. What d'you say, girlie?'

He slipped an arm round her as he said it, and she suddenly had a glimpse of what he meant. The frightening remembrance of the struggle on Leith Docks came into her mind. She ducked in terror and, taking to her heels, ran as fast as she could.

When she drew up, she was much farther along the waterfront. The district was poor, almost a slum. She sat down in a doorway to get her breath back. There was a tavern further up the street, from which noisy laughter, the strains of music played by a melodeon, voices raised in song, and a strong smell of spirits rushed forth. Men were about on the cobbled wharf – some lounging, some chatting, some on their way to a little amusement.

She stayed back in the shadow of the doorway, afraid to be seen. She hardly knew what she had to fear, but she sensed that she ought not to be about in this shady neighbourhood at night without an escort.

After about a quarter of an hour she crept out again. She made her own way down to the edge of the wharf. Men were busy loading a little steam boat with the mail and goods for the merchants of some island town. In the flickering light of an overhead lamp she read the address on a parcel: Messrs. Hobart and Dugdale, St George, Richmond Borough.

St George! Grymes Hill was two miles out from St George! This little steam packet was going to St George. If she could get aboard she would at last reach that promised land. But by now she knew it was useless to ask for a free ride. She would have to stow away.

She crouched down by a bale of piece goods waiting to be lifted aboard. The boat was tied up alongside the jetty. All she had to do was jump on deck. But she had to do it at a moment when everyone's attention was elsewhere.

She held her breath. At last she could see by the goods left on the wharf that this bale would be picked up soon. The men were hauling up a heavy box in a net by means of a pulley at the stern.

Morag rose, still keeping low, moved to the edge of the stone coping, and was about to step on board when luck deserted her.

The big box had just reached its resting place. The bo'sun called: 'All right, lads, break off for a mouthful!' and the men swung about to head for a jar on the capstan top. As they did so, they all witnessed a slight figure gleam for a moment in the light before disappearing behind the wheelhouse.

'A stowaway!' they crowed, and rushed in pursuit.

The first man to find her raised a cry of triumph. 'A neat little piece, my buckos!' he carolled. 'My, we're in luck!'

They all rushed up to see what he'd got. He was holding a struggling girl against his chest, a slender girl whose rich brown hair was a wild tangle as she fought to get free, whose slim legs were exposed by the way he had caught up her skirts.

It was late, they'd been working hard, and they'd drunk enough to make them feel they needed something to enliven their labours. With whoops of delight they carried Morag ashore to the lee of a warehouse where a pile of haulage nets made a comfortable bed. There they held her down, and had the fun they felt they deserved at the expense of this pretty little stowaway.

Morag, sobbing and screaming for mercy, thought at first they were going to kill her. When she learned that they had quite a different purpose, a terrible understanding came to her. Now she knew what the minister had been thundering about, when he preached in the kirk at home. This heaving, animal attack, this pawing and grabbing, this grunting of rum-sodden breath and this weight of sweat-soaked bodies – this was 'the sins of the flesh.' Either that, or it was the hell promised as a punishment.

She had rejected the Reverend McIver's insistence that she and Rob had done anything wrong. Now she understood what he thought it had been. Now she understood why he had spoken with revulsion. Shocked, destroyed, almost unconscious under the attack, she ceased to cry out. Weeping was no use. Nothing was any use any more. Everything was wrecked.

When they left her, falling back to find the rum pot and refresh themselves, she lay for a while half-fainting. Then she dragged herself up and crawled away, on her hands and knees at first, and

[83]

then in a staggering run. She kept going until she found some boats pulled up on the wharf for tarring. She crept in between and huddled there for safety.

She felt degraded, dirtied. She shivered as she though of the words she had sometimes heard or puzzled over in the Bible – words that were names for a bad woman. Such women were outside the bounds of society. Decent folk turned away from them.

And now she was one.

6

ROB SPENT A LONG day that Sunday hunting for Morag. He questioned the Aggerley servants at the area door, to see if she'd come back there. He went to every place that he had ever taken her to, in hopes she might have sought him out there.

In the end, he had to go back to Grymes Hill. It seemed a good idea. She might somehow have made her way there. She might even have been on a ferryboat going to St George while he was crossing to Manhattan.

But she wasn't at Dalgow's waiting for him. Next morning he went to St George before he started work, but the porters on the wharf hadn't seen her. Not that they would have noticed her especially as she stepped ashore, since she was only one of many pretty girls who had come to St George that Sunday, for the outing.

That night, he hurried to the ferry as soon as work was over and crossed to the Manhattan side. His first call was at McIver's, to see if Morag had returned there. The servant there shook her head.

Next the servants' quarters of the Aggerleys. No, they hadn't seen Morag. 'She's still missing?' Bertha said, pursing her lips and drawing in a breath. 'That's bad, feller. New York isn't a town for a little simpleton like her.'

'Don't you think I know it?' he groaned. 'I've got to find her.

Do you know if she had any money?'

'Oh yes. She had most of a month's wages,' she said in a reassuring tone.

That, at least, was something. He turned his attention to the cheap boarding houses, but there were so many of them, and there had been such a huge influx of immigrants that the population of New York seemed to be constantly on the move – from lodgings to shanty town, from shanty to rooming house, and so from there perhaps to a hotel or an inn or some job with living accommodation.

He couldn't accomplish much in the short time available to him in the evenings. He returned early on Sunday morning to start all over again, and kept up his search until very late. The result was that next day he was physically so weary that he could hardly stay awake. When Dalgow demanded overtime on Monday, to move some harvesting equipment, Rob refused.

'You what?' Dalgow said in amazement.

'I can't work tonight. I've got something important to do –'

'This is the important thing, buddy,' Mr Dalgow said. He turned to the foreman. 'Siddall, see to it.'

Siddall glared at Rob. 'Come on, we've got this reaper to load –'

'I tell you I can't. I've got to go to New York.'

'What the hell's going on? You've been there every night in the week and Sunday as well. You got a little hot piece there? You been tomcatting?'

'It's nothing like that. I've got to find someone –'

'It'll have to wait. The haymaking machinery's got to be loaded on to the wagon –'

'I can't do it. I've got to get to the ferry –'

'Listen, sonny, I've put up with a lot from you – lies and trickery and –'

'Yes, and you've been well paid for it!' Rob flashed.

'You think so, do you? Why, you young runt, I could hire a big husky brawler for the wages I pay you and get as much kickback from him with twice the work!'

'I pull my weight. Don't try to pretend you're not getting the work done –'

'What, the way you've been working today? Hardly strength enough to pick up an empty sack –'

'I've done everything you've ordered me to do,' Rob said.

'And now I'm ordering you to put your shoulder to that reaper and get it on the wagon.'

'I can't stop to do that. I've done my day's work. I'm going to New York now.'

Siddall put his hands in his pockets and stared at him. 'If you do, don't come back,' he said.

'What?'

'I got a guy asking for your job – willing to pay me five bucks for it for openers.'

'Listen, Siddall, I'll be back in good time. I'll get up early tomorrow and put in some extra time –'

'It's the time *now* we want,' Siddall said. 'You stay here and put your back into it – hear? I've been lenient enough.'

'Lenient? Is that what you call it? You never let up –'

'It's not my job to let up. My job is to get the work done –'

'Yes, and make a profit on it –'

'So what? I get the going rate –'

'It's extortion! I'd think a man would be ashamed –'

'Listen, bud, you're the one with something to be ashamed of. You're the guy who's on the run. So you'll do what I tell you.'

'Not this time, Siddall.'

Siddall knew the other men were watching, keen to see how this challenge to his authority would work out. They all paid him something for the privilege of staying in work. If this youngster could outface him, maybe they'd be able to do the same.

The foreman knew his danger. He had to make Rob knuckle under or lose his authority.

The fight was short and ugly. Rob won it, in that he knocked Siddall into a heap by a lucky blow under the ear. Siddall clambered to his feet, roaring with pain. 'Out! That's it! Pick up your gear and get out!'

'Now wait a minute, Siddall –'

'Get out! I can get another man with a snap of the fingers – one whose mind is on his job. Get your clothes and pack up. You were paid on Saturday so there's nothing owing to you! Go on, move it!'

Rob could see it was no use begging for mercy. Siddall had to follow through on his threats, for he'd been beaten physically. And anyhow, time was getting on. If he didn't get to Manhattan soon, there'd be no chance at all to make any inquiries tonight.

He had few items to collect before he left. He'd bought a new shirt and a new pair of boots, and had been planning to get a new suit before next winter, but so far he had only the jacket and pants he'd come in. He folded up the shirt, stuffed it in his pocket, tied the laces of the boots and slung them over his shoulder. And then, unsure whether he was glad or sorry to be leaving the job, he left.

He had a little money. Most of last week's wages, some from the week before. He crossed to Manhattan and spent the remaining hours of the evening looking for Morag, but when night fell he found himself a quiet spot near the Little Church Around the Corner. It was warm and sheltered, under the awning of a tobacco shop. He was up and away next morning before the shopkeeper stirred.

While this hot, airless weather continued he wouldn't need a bed to sleep in. Like many another immigrant, he found a quiet corner every night, like a stray dog or cat. He had money for food during the day.

But that ran out surprisingly quickly. Food was so dear in New York! It cost thirty cents for a piece of broiled beef and potatoes and two cents extra if you wanted coffee with it. He soon learned to buy bread and cheese, and when the money for even that was gone he took to searching in the trashcans in the alleys at the back of the fashionable homes. There was always something worth eating, especially after some big evening party. He learned to eat pieces of iced cake and little scraps of pastry with dark fish roe on it and grapes encased in caramel and lengths of strange vegetable which had been dipped in melted butter, now congealed.

One day a torrential rain storm warned him that tonight he'd need something more than a sleeping place in the open. It was time to try for employment, instead of spending his days in search of Morag. He hated to give it up even to that extent; it had become an obsession with him to find her.

But it wasn't easy to get a job. Ten days of sleeping rough had made him look bedraggled. He needed a good shave instead of a scrape with an unsoaped razor. His hair was shaggy, his boots were muddy.

A way to earn money presented itself unexpectedly. The thunderstorm had startled many of the horses on the streets of New York, particularly those waiting outside shops, warehouses or hotels.

Instinctively, Rob leapt to catch and hold the bridle of a horse that reared as a flash of lightning tore through the sky overhead. He held it, standing close to the beast, speaking soothingly to him.

When the owner of the carriage came out of the tailor's to see a ragged young man soothing his well-groomed bay, he smiled in thanks and tossed him a dime. Rob caught it automatically. He helped clear a way for the driver to edge his Stanhope out into the traffic stream, and was rewarded with another smile but no more cash.

A vanman delivering bales of cloth at the tailor's trade entrance called to him. 'Hey, boy, hang on to this nag, will you? She's nervy as an op'ry singer in this weather.'

Thus Rob discovered a way to make a few cents, enough to pay for a bed that rainy night. It took a lot of persistence, for some riders and owners were prepared to move off without any reward to their helper. But the press of vehicles on the New York streets was so great that it was always possible to find horsemen or drivers willing to pay for someone to keep their beast quiet, while they were indoors on some short visit.

He earned only enough for occasional sleeping accommodation and, now and again, a hot meal. There was nothing over for clothes, not even enough to pay for a visit to the barber. He knew he was beginning to look like a scarecrow. Commonsense told him it would really be best to leave the city, and look for work in the countryside where his skills with farm tools and animals might gain him a decent wage. But he couldn't go yet – not yet, not without finding out what had happened to Morag.

He'd learned that one of the spots where gentlemen liked to go was a certain hotel in Clinton Place, where there were gaming tables and dancing girls. Many a man liked to look in at Potterton's Hotel on his way home from the office of an evening, or take a client there for some amusement after a business dinner.

It wasn't a place for respectable women to be seen. That was why the breath was knocked from his body when Rob saw Morag McGarth lurking on the pavement outside.

It was late evening. Shadows were darkening the fronts of the redbrick houses. The oil lanterns hadn't yet been lit by the lamplighter. For a moment, from his post by the head of a pair of matched greys in the shafts of a parked dray, he couldn't believe he'd really seen her. He thought the light was playing tricks with his eyes.

Then she stepped into the light of a window overhead. She moved in front of a man coming down the sidewalk fanning himself with his silk evening hat.

Rob was shocked. Her manner was unmistakeable. She was offering herself for hire. He stalked away from the horses so suddenly they tossed their heads in suprise. As the evening-clad gentleman was still studying his accoster with his head on one side, Rob grabbed her. 'Morag! What the hell do you think you're doing?'

At the sound of that voice, a great wave of shame and guilt rose up and hit Morag in the face. Her senses reeled. She threw her hands up to her face to hide her crumpling features.

'Rob!' she moaned.

'Look here, young feller –'

'You stay out of it!' Rob raged. 'Come on, Morag –'

'Oh, Rob –'

'But just a minute, you! She's my –'

'She's nothing to do with you!' Rob cried. '*Nothing*!' He seized Morag by the wrist and dragged her away.

She didn't resist. She let herself be pulled along while her feet seemed to stumble without any volition. Her breath grew short. She was gasping when at last he pulled up.

'Now,' he said in a tone of fury. 'What in God's name do you think you're up to?'

'Rob,' she sobbed. 'Oh, Rob! I thought I'd never see you again.'

'I've been searching the whole of New York for you! Where have you been?'

She made a little helpless gesture round about. 'Here,' she whispered.

'Here? All the time?'

'N..no . . . I . . . I found this neighbourhood about a week ago.'

'A week ago,' he repeated, his voice like ice-cold iron. 'Have you been here every night for a week?'

'Oh!' It was a gasp of agony. 'Oh, no! No, I only do it . . . do it . . . when I have to get money. I . . . Rob, I haven't . . . I'm not . . .'

'Not a whore?' he demanded, beside himself with anger. 'Is that what you're saying? Because you could have fooled me, from what I saw a minute ago.'

'No! No, you don't understand! I haven't eaten all day, Rob. My money ran out yesterday at midday –'

'The money from the last time you picked up a client?'

She bent her head. Her tears dropped unchecked on her clasped hands. She said nothing.

For a long moment Rob stood staring at her. He was so angry with her he could have killed her. 'How many?' he asked at length. 'How many times have you done that?'

'Five . . . five times. Five times for money. The first time . . . they . . . I didn't know you could get money . . .'

'The first time? What do you mean?'

She turned away from him, her head bent even further, her shoulders hunched. 'Don't,' she begged. 'I don't want to think about it.'

'Morag,' he said. His voice changed. The anger died in him. He stepped up to her and put his arms round her. 'What happened?' he said gently.

She shook her head, not responding to his embrace.

'Tell me, Morag.'

'I went to the ferry to come to St George. I'd looked for you all day. There were some men . . .'

'Oh, Morag . . .'

'I . . . tried not to . . . There were four of them. I couldn't . . . Rob, I didn't understand what was happening at first.'

'Sh..h . . .' he said, holding her close. 'Don't. I shouldn't have asked.'

'I just felt so . . . sickened. I got away and then . . . I hid . . . and then next morning I knew I could never come near you again after what I'd done –'

'What *you'd* done? Dear God!'

'I know everything's ruined between us now, Rob. I know now how men think of women like me. It didn't matter until you saw me. It was only getting money for something I didn't care about any longer. But now . . .' She leaned against him and she was shaking with the sobs of her grief. 'Oh, Rob, why did you come looking for me?'

He made no reply. He held her with her head pressed against his chest, feeling himself shake as she sobbed, stricken with the same grief that overwhelmed her. They were in the entrance of a quiet arcade. One or two passers-by glanced at them with idle interest, but neither was aware of that. They were lost in the agony of this moment.

It took a long time for her to recover her composure. When at last she raised her face, it was a timid gesture, asking if he wished to speak to her again. When he smiled, an expression of such rapturous gratitude flashed across her face that he was almost crushed by guilt. She was grateful to him for his forgiveness.

But what right had he to give or withhold forgiveness? If anyone was to blame, it was himself. He had made love to her without stopping to think what it might mean to her. Because of that episode, she'd been made vulnerable to the disapproval of her employers and been turned away. Wandering about the city, how was she to subsist . . . friendless, lonely, innocent?

'You've got to put it all behind you, Morag,' he whispered, his lips against her hair. 'You've got to start again.'

'But how? I can't find work. I'm so untidy now, my gown's bedraggled and muddy, I can't find anywhere to live where I can get clean and neat . . .' She leaned against him. 'I'm so tired, Rob. I don't seem to have the strength to go on any more.'

He touched her face. She seemed hot and feverish. Sleeping out of doors as she had done, she must have caught some infection from the damp air, or she had a chill . . . 'We've got to get out of New York,' he announced, suddenly taking control both of himself and the situation. 'I can get work, Morag, but not here. I'm a farmer. I only really know about farming. Once we get out to the countryside, I'll be able to get enough money for us to live on.'

'Us?' she breathed. She stepped away from him to look keenly into his face with her dark eyes. 'You want me to go with you?'

'Of course.'

'Oh . . .' In that moment, she was enslaved for ever. No matter what he might do, she would always love and revere him with the deepest part of her soul. She could hardly believe that anyone would be so good, so noble and forgiving. Ater what she had done! He still cared for her, was willing to assume responsibility for her.

It didn't occur to her that he felt some guilt. All she saw was nobility and generosity. When, in the future, he might do things that hurt her, she would always say: 'It's because I don't understand all the reasons. Rob is so good and kind . . . I should know that better than anyone.'

'It'll be better for you, Morag,' he said. 'I don't think your health is suited to life in the city. The air's harmful. We'll go out to the green fields and the meadows, sweetheart.'

'But how? I've got no money, Rob. Have you?'

'Only a few pennies. But we'll get a ride from someone. Or we'll walk. I'm used to walking, and if we take it easy you won't find it too tiring.'

'Oh, I'll be all right,' she said, eager to fall in with any plan of his. 'When will we go?'

'Tomorrow. We'll get a night's sleep and tomorrow early we'll leave this damned place!'

She nodded, accepting his word as law. Hope had come back to her. Her life wasn't totally spoiled by what had happened – Rob was going to help her start again.

Rob had been sleeping in the graveyard of a church, but a

recent downpour had made the ground too wet. They sought out a doorway in the business section, the canopy overhead giving them shelter in case there was rain in the night and the stone floor promising at least dryness, if not comfort. Rob spread his worn jacket for Morag. She tried to refuse this luxury but he shook his head at her. He still had this sense of guilt – he wanted to make some amends.

They lay together in the darkness, talking quietly. Rob told her how he had come looking for her. At length there was nothing left to explain. He put his arms about her. Shivering, Morag drew away from him.

Memory was too strong within her. She couldn't allow anyone to touch her in that way – not even Rob, not yet.

'It's all right,' he said. 'It's just to be sure you're all right.'

'I can't, Rob,' she whispered. 'Don't . . .'

'All right.' He turned away from her, hurt at her lack of trust. In the night she had another of her bad dreams. She was crouching away from men who shouted and laughed, and instead of receding from her they drew nearer, grew bigger, until their long clutching arms were about to engulf her. She screamed, but no sound came. She sat up, struggling wildly against the air.

Rob was wakened by the violent movements, the muffled sounds. He caught her by the shoulders, calling, 'Morag! Morag! What's wrong? You're all right, Morag! You're all right!'

At last she struggled into wakefulness. In the darkness she huddled against him, shuddering. 'Oh, Rob, darling – I had my dream again! It was horrible . . .'

'It's all right. I understand. Go back to sleep, my lass,' he soothed, rocking her as if she were a child. 'It's all right . . .'

He kissed her gently, her lips and her cheeks and her eyelids, murmuring that he would look after her, that she was safe now. Gradually she grew calm, her nightmare distress ebbed away. She wound her arms about him, whispering her thanks, sighing his name like a benison to keep her safe. By and by she was returning his kisses, and the murmurs of gratitude changed.

'Ah, my love,' she breathed, 'if only you knew how much I think about you. You're the centre of my life, Rob.'

'My little lass, my darling,' he said. 'From now on we'll be together. Nothing shall ever part us again.'

'Oh, that's all I want – to be with you, to belong to you.' She held him close, hearing his heart beat against her own.

When they made love, the magic returned to her body. The evil things she had gone through were banished. In that moment of grateful passion that swept through her when Rob finally took her, she was made whole again. Afterwards they slept, arms about each other, her head on his breast.

In the morning, very early, they washed with water from a horse trough and tidied themselves as best they could. They set out towards the outskirts before the city was stirring. They had so little idea of the geography of their new home that they didn't know they were on an island. Rob knew, of course, that he had to take a ferry from Richmond to Manhattan, but he had always thought that Manhattan was the mainland. They trudged north on the western side of the island, avoiding the city of New York and keeping to the greener outskirts, fondly imagining they would reach the rolling prairies spoken of in the tales they'd heard, where the Indians used to hunt the buffalo and build their tepees.

At length they came to an imposing building with lawns about it. A signboard announced it as Columbia College. Rob approached an elderly man in a shabby black suit, to inquire whether they were on the right road for the farmlands.

'Farmlands?' the man said. 'You mean New York State?'

'Er . . . yes, sir, I suppose so.'

'Don't you understand, boy, that you have to cross the Hudson River to get to New York State?'

'No, sir, I didn't know that.'

'Huh,' said the professor, looking at him with scorn. 'Another newcomer to our shores, I take it, who doesn't take the trouble to acquaint himself with the very basic points he needs to know.'

'If you please sir,' Rob said, looking humble, 'we only want to know how to get out to the countryside where we might find work.'

'Well, no one is going to hire a scarecrow like you, that's for sure –'

Rob stiffened. 'I'm sorry I troubled you, sir,' he said, and was about to walk away.

'Wait a moment.'

'So that you can tell me what I already know, that I'm poor and ill-educated?'

'Don't get in a huff, sir!' the older man said with asperity. 'I'm going to answer your question. It's not in my nature to deny a request for information.'

'But I have to listen to your opinions as well, I take it.'

'Hoity-toity! Poor but proud, it seems!'

'I'm not going to stay poor all my life,' Rob said. 'I'm –'

'You think to make your fortune on the farms of New York State? A fantasy, I fear. Well, well, you keep north on this road, boy, and you'll reach the edge of the island of Manhattan. There are boatmen on the quays behind Balliter's Farm by the fort, who'll ferry you across to the mainland for a small fee.'

'Thank you, sir.'

'Here!' A coin twirled in the air, which Rob automatically caught 'That's to soothe that injured pride of yours and ensure that you reach the promised land.'

Rob hesitated. He would dearly have liked to throw the coin back. But good sense prevented him. He needed that money. He bowed in stiff acknowledgement and walked away.

The professor of law watched him. Really, young men were full of their own importance these days. The boy reminded him of one of his own more obstreperous students, Theodore Roosevelt; neither of them would come to anything, despite their boasting.

The eight mile walk took them until just past midday. They reached the quays on the rocky shore below Fort Tryon about half an hour later. There was no problem in finding a ferryboat to take them across the grey blue waters that poured out from the river through its narrow passage to the Atlantic Ocean. On the mainland they found a long wooden landing stage, with wagons lined up to send goods across to the Manhattan side. Fresh vegetables, flour, meat and poultry were waiting to be taken to the ever-open maw of the growing city of New York.

'This here's Westchester,' the boatman said with casual kindness. He'd heard Morag whispering questions to Rob. 'This here's mainland Americky. Landing stage is part of Morrisonia, a place I allus heard was named after some important family that built it – helped make the Constitution, so they say. Well, good luck to ye.'

'Thank you. Can you . . . can you tell us whether there are good farms around here?'

'Oh yeah. Lots o' big famblies got houses and estates – them that own the big stores in the city and stuff like that.'

'Any sheep farms?'

'Sheep?' The ferryman knew only about the sea. He looked doubtful. 'Never heerd much about sheep. Dairy cows, I think they got. And they grow stuff – wheat and barley.'

'I see. I come from sheep farming country.'

'Is that so? Well, boy, I can't tell you no more'n that. What kind o' country do sheep grow on?'

'Hill country, sir.'

'Huh! Plenty o' that around here. Catskill Mountains over to northwest, but I don't reckon you should go there – they're funny, the folk that live in the Catskills. Why don't you head on up to White Plains? I reckon White Plains is a good town with lots of farmers living around it.'

'How far is White Plains?'

'Oh, I reckon about ten miles or so. Not too far. You gonna walk?'

'Yes, sir.'

'Oh,' said the boatman, 'that's hard in this heat. Why don't you hitch a ride with one of them wagons? Goin' back empty, most of 'em. Plenty of space to take you.' He strolled a few yards along the jetty to address an elderly man on a high-seat platform cart. 'Hi, driver – you goin' north?'

'Could be.'

'How 'bout takin' these two young 'uns? The boy can march a good many days, I reckon, but the girl looks kind of tuckered out.'

The waggoner looked over his head at the two standing uncertainly on the jetty. The boy had his arm protectively around the girl's shoulder. He felt an impulse of pity. He had had daughters of his own – married now, and long gone, but he still liked a pretty young thing about him.

'Ask 'em if they want to go to Albany.'

'Hey, feller!' the boatman said, going back a few paces. 'This here waggoner's willing to take you to Albany.'

'Where's Albany?'

'Oh, it's on the Hudson River. Could take you up there by boat, but it'd cost you a lot more than hitching a ride with him. Nice place – even if it is full o' Dutchmen. Hey,' he added, struck by a thought, 'there's plenty of rich old Dutch farmers! You'd be sure to pass good farms on the way to Albany.'

'Thank you, sir,' Rob said respectfully. He was always quick to show respect to anyone who could be or had been useful to him.

'It's a pleasure. Look after the little lady, huh?'

'You can be sure of that.'

They hurried to the waggon. The driver was turning his vehicle and paid no heed until he had the horses back into the right position. Then he barely turned his head. 'Come on if you're coming,' he said.

Rob helped Morag up at the tailboard and clambered up after her. 'Hook her up,' the driver said over his shoulder, and almost at once slapped the reins to go forward. Rob closed the tailboard and fell down in a heap beside Morag as the wagon lurched forward.

They moved on at the quick, easy walk of the trained carthorse, over a dirt road packed hard by the summer heat. The sun beat down with relentless vigour. There was no shade overhead at first, where the land had been cleared for the wharves, but soon trees were branching above them. They skirted the village of Morrison, then headed out along a well-used road.

'Sir,' Rob said, getting up on his hands and knees to approach the driver's seat from behind. 'Sir, how far is Albany?'

''Bout four days' drive.'

'Four days?'

'Well, two days if I press on hard, but I don't see any reason for that. You in a hurry?'

'No, sir, but . . . I was hoping to get work quite soon. I . . . we . . . we don't have much money.'

'Who's asking you for money?'

'But I meant . . . for food and lodging, sir.'

'Well, you can always eat with me,' said the waggoner. 'And as to lodgings – I sleep under the canvas this summer weather. You can do the same, and welcome.'

'Thank you.'

'Thank you,' Morag echoed.

The waggoner turned and looked at her. 'That's all right, missy,' he said, and smiled for the first time.

They made twenty miles before he drew up. Their way had been over rolling country, dotted with farms. 'That there's Fishkill,' their driver informed them. 'Did I hear that boatman telling you about the Dutch families?'

'He said there were good farms owned by the Dutch.'

'He sure as hell is right. See that crop o' buildings south of the town? That's van Wyck's – family owned about half of everything around here. Tell you what, feller – if you want to light on a good place to work, why don't you take a look at van Huten's? We'll be on his land tomorrow about midmorning. Farmer Huten's got a good name, so far as I recall.'

'Do you think he's taking on farm workers?'

'You kidding? We're just getting on to harvest. The one time of the year you can be sure of getting a place is late summer. They may turn you off again come Christmas, but at least you'll have had four months' work.'

'You're right.'

'You used to handling a reaper? Huten's got all the latest machinery – big horse-team reaper, I think it's called a header, made by McCormick's. Six horse team, as far as I remember.'

Rob was baffled by this talk. As far as he was concerned, reaping was what you did with a sickle. He'd heard tell of horse-drawn contraptions used by the big land-owners in Scotland but had never seen one. As for a machine that needed six horses . . . it didn't make sense.

'I . . . I never handled one,' he said. 'But . . . I'm good with horses.'

'Yeah, well, the horses need a lot of care when they're hitched to a thing like that. I don't hold with it myself,' the waggoner said, slapping his team-leader affectionately on the shoulder as he freed her to graze by the roadside. 'Unnatural, to have horses pushing a rig instead of pulling it. The beasts don't like it an' I don't blame 'em. Well, come on, let's build a fire and have some grub.'

Pulled well off the road on the verge, they settled down like gipsies to make a meal. Morag took over the cooking. Their host provided fresh eggs and a loaf of bread, bought before leaving Morrisonia. He had onions and potatoes in the box under the driving seat. She made a quick soup, and a big omelette flavoured with herbs she found by the edge of the meadow. The waggoner ate quickly, produced a stone jug of apple-tasting liquor from which he drank deeply, then wrapped himself in a blanket and settled down under his vehicle. Morag ate less heartily, refused the drink, and soon curled up to sleep, tired out by the excitement of the day.

It took Rob longer to settle down. His mind was racing, picturing the machine he'd heard described. Six horses – to push the contraption. So it must be between ten and fifteen feet wide. Fifteen feet of sickle blades? The fields must be very big to need blades like that to cut the grain. And it stood to reason the blades must be sharp – perhaps steel edged. Certainly the whole thing must be reinforced with iron or the strain would shake it to pieces.

The heads of the wheat must be cut very quickly, so it stood to reason there must be some contrivance to gather them up – it wasn't like back home, where you cut with a hand-held blade low on the stalk, then stood the wheat in stooks to be dried before you took it to be threshed. Here, in this big, strange country, farming was on a different scale. You cut the wheat from its stalk and somehow put it quickly into some vehicle to take it to be threshed.

It made good sense. You had the grain, which was what you wanted – no pieces of straw mixed up with the heads. When you threshed, there must be far less wastage.

He was eager to see this machine. What had the waggoner called it? Not a reaper. A header. He wanted to see it, wanted to be part of the harvesting team that used it. He wanted to see grain more rich and golden than the thin oats he'd raised in Glen Bairach.

He fell asleep at last, to be haunted by dreams of groups of men working with great heavy horses pushing a gleaming machine of steel and wood, its cutting bars turning, turning, sending the golden grain flickering in the sun.

Next day they rose early and washed at a stream in the meadow. Breakfast was bread and sweet tea without milk. Rob helped harness the horses, talking to them soothingly as they were led from their comparative liberty to take up their task.

The countryside became more rolling as they travelled. About ten o'clock, there were wheat fields on either side. They seemed to stretch towards the horizon – a yellow sea, rippling in the breeze to shades of silver, and brass and gold, making a murmuring sound.

Rob stood up on the platform of the wagon, holding on to the back of the driving seat. His eyes drank in the sight. He had never seen anything like it. When Morag looked back later to that moment, she realised she had been watching Rob see the real love of his life – the golden mistress, wheat.

The cart slowed at a crossroads quarter of a mile further on. 'This here's Huten's Crossroad,' the driver said. 'You want to head on up to the farm to see if they'll take you?'

'Yes, thank you,' Rob said. He was already jumping down. He helped Morag. 'How far up the road is the farmhouse?'

'Just over the knoll.' The driver pointed with his whip. 'Good luck.'

'Thank you.'

'Good luck to you, little lady.'

'Thank you.' She held up her hand and he took it in his. She felt his palm, calloused by many years of holding the reins, fold about her fingers. She smiled at him in gratitude. 'Perhaps we'll meet again.'

He shook his head. ''T'aint likely. I don't generally take this road –'

'You mean you came out of your way?'

He shrugged. 'What's the difference? Hope you get fixed up at

Huten's. Now take care, won't you?'

He took off the brake, called up the horses, and moved on. They waited to see him go round the next bend then headed up the lane he had pointed to. The farmhouse came into sight in a few minutes.

'Oh,' said Morag, drawing back in awe.

It was the biggest house she had ever seen – bigger than the Aggerleys' in New York, bigger even than the orphanage where she'd been brought up. It was in fact two houses dating from about the mid-seventeenth century, which had been joined by skilful builders at the beginning of the nineteenth – part wood, part brick, with a quite imposing porch over a shallow flight of entrance steps. Before it was a garden of flowers and shrubs, lovingly tended, around which there was a white picket fence. The lane on which they were walking led directly to the gate then continued on round the fence, towards the back where no doubt the servants' quarters and the farmyard were situated.

Rob was stricken with apprehension. This was beyond all his expectations. But only a farm of this size could have the expensive machinery he'd heard described. He drew Morag's arm through his, marched on with resolution, opened the low gate, walked up the drive between the flower beds, and rapped on the door.

A woman in a dark dress and an apron opened the door. 'Yes?'

'Ma'am . . . we're looking for work . . . I wonder if you could tell us who we should speak to –'

'Go round in back,' she interrupted. 'That' the foreman's business –'

'Who's that, Senta?'

'Just some vagrant looking for work, Mrs van Huten.'

'Tell him to go . . .' The speaker appeared, coming out from the darkness of the hall into the band of sunshine let in by the open door. She was holding a lace scarf in one hand, a needle in the other. The words she was uttering died on her lips when she saw the newcomers.

'Oh,' she said. 'There are two of you.' Her sparkling black eyes dwelt on Rob. 'You're looking for work?'

'Yes, ma'am.'

'Cornelius! Cornelius! You there, husband?'

A heavy tread sounded on the wooden floorboards of the hall. A tubby, older man joined the woman. 'What is it, my love?'

'Did you say you were looking for extra hands for the harvest?'

'As usual, my dear.' He glanced at Rob. 'Is this a candidate?'

'I'm hoping to find employment, sir . . .'

'Go and see the foreman, boy. Round the back of the house, in the building to the left of the stables.'

'Wait a moment, Cornelius,' said Mrs van Huten. 'You know how crossgrained Dubec can be. Why don't we ask what this fellow can do?'

'If you like, Dorothea.' Van Huten waved the two of them in. They followed him into a large hall, panelled in buttonwood, rather gloomy but smelling of soap and beeswax. He went into a room at the back of the hall, a place cluttered with books and journals. There he took his place behind a big mahogany desk. His wife sat down on a cushioned chair.

'Well now, what's your name? Where are you from?'

'I'm Rob Craigallan, from Glen Bairach in Scotland.' Rob explained about his employment with the grain merchant, stressing how much experience he'd gained and omitting any mention of the fight that had sent him out into the wilderness.

'Been on the road quite a while, have you?' van Huten said, putting on a pair of silver-rimmed spectacles to inspect him.

'Oh now, my love, you know how tramping around in search of work wears out a man's clothes,' Mrs van Huten put in quickly.

Rob glanced at her. He saw that she was keenly interested in him. Her plump, pretty face was flushed with curiosity and, perhaps, something more. He was used to women finding him interesting. He addressed van Huten, but his words were for Dorothea his wife. 'It's not what a man wears that counts, is it?' he remarked. 'It's whether he's strong and fit . . .'

'You're a pretty strong fellow, I take it?' the farmer said.

'Yes sir. And interested in machinery. I hear you have a new heading machine from McCormicks.'

'You've heard that, eh? Well, well . . .'

'There, dear. That shows he's got a head on his shoulders.'

'Thank you, Mrs van Huten,' Rob said, flashing her a smile. 'I promise to take an interest in the work if your husband hires me on.'

'I think you will,' she said, on a lingering note.

He recognised it. She was envisaging him as someone to be friends with, to flirt with . . . 'You won't have anything to complain of,' he assured her.

'How old are you?' the farmer took it up again.

'Twenty, sir,' Rob said. He had guessed that to be too young was a disadvantage; he'd implied he knew something of machinery used for harvesting, and a boy of not yet eighteen would have had little chance to learn much about it.

'Twenty, eh?' said the farmer's wife. She smiled with satisfaction.

'And . . . er . . . the young lady?' van Huten said, transferring his pale blue glance to Morag.

'My sister, sir,' Rob said. He had understood at once that the chance of employment was gone if any other relationship was given to Mrs van Huten. He heard Morag draw in a breath, but didn't turn his head. But behind his back, his hand made a little gesture. Keep silent, he was warning her.

She said nothing. From that moment, she began to live a lie.

7

DUBEC, VAN HUTEN'S FOREMAN, had to admit that the new hand was eager to learn and that he pulled his weight. The resident gang on the farm was bigger than usual, for a reason which Rob was to discover; among these men, he stood out by his willingness to deal with any difficulties in the equipment.

He began by helping to get the machinery ready. He had never seen a heading machine before, and it fascinated him. The width of the swathe it would cut was almost unbelievable. Rob's chief task was to habituate the team to the vehicle. Since it was only used for a short time each year, the horses never had the chance to become docile in the traces.

Harvesting had been held up that year by heavy thunderstorms. At last Cornelius van Huten rolled some grains of wheat in his fingers, dug a thumbnail into a kernal, looked up at the skies, and announced from his thick lips: 'Tomorrow at first light, boys . . . Out on the fields!'

The excitement in the farm that night was almost palpable. The die was cast now. If the weather held, they would get in the fruits of a year's work. If the weather turned against them, they would be forced to hold up or, worse yet, harvest wet grain which might go mouldy in the barns.

Rob led out the heavy horses before dawn and put them in their harness. The strange-looking piece of equipment had already been left ready on the verge of the first field, so all that was needed was to urge the team to push. Rob walked in front, leading and soothing the team leader. The driver had his hands full, using the reins and manoeuvring the header by means of the low wheel at the back. To Rob this had seemed an impossible task when he first saw the Dane, Denstadt, get up on it, but he then saw him do it by redistributing his weight on the bar just above the wheel.

From then on, the harvesting team seemed to breathe, eat, drink, and dream dust. Twenty acres a day, over the van Huten lands. For the first time, Rob understood how much land Cornelius owned. His own farm back in Glen Bairach was small even by Scottish standards but he had seen the farms of the bigger landlords there. They dwindled to nothing compared with the van Huten acres.

Not all Cornelius's land was under wheat. Long settled on his estate, he had learned the value of crop rotation. So that when the men had spent ten days harvesting, they had only worked on a third of the farm.

Rob had been so busy and so exhausted with this new, confusing task that he had thought everything would end when they had come to the verge of the last wheat field. Not so. Now Rob understood how it was possible for one farmer to own so costly a piece of new equipment. Cornelius hired it out to the others in the area.

Without a single day's rest, the header team went on to the next farm, and the next. For a month, the header was never at rest while daylight lasted and the grain was dry. There were two teams of six horses, which each did half a day's work every day for that month. Rob's task was to keep them fit and happy. By the fourth day both teams had fallen into the servitude of the dreadful machine – pushing, pushing, always into the standing grain while the sickle blades revolved in front of them, sending chaff and chipped strands of straw into their nostrils. Rob began to love these great patient beasts; he talked to them, cosseted them, brought them great buckets of water at break time, though it meant carrying them over long distances.

He fell into bed every night drained of strength. But each morning he woke ready for the day. He was learning all the time –

about how to farm this great new land, and how money was made. He understood now that Cornelius was rich – not just comfortable in the way of an ordinary farmer, but really rich.

The men slept in the big stables building. The girls had quarters either in the house or in the long cool room above the dairy. The house staff consisted of a skinny housemaid, Senta, and Nellie the black cook. Morag had been taken on as a dairymaid. 'She's a wonder with the butter churn,' Rob had told Mrs van Huten. It was a complete lie; Morag had never touched a butter churn, for in the orphanage where she was brought up milk was delivered to the door in pitchers.

Luckily the dairymaid, Nancy, was unwilling to let her touch any of her precious equipment. It was part of her mystique that she alone could bring the cream so thickly to the top of the pan, that it was her expert knowledge which made van Hutens' cheese famous. But she used Morag as a cleaning girl – which Morag accepted without dreaming of complaint.

Within a few days, however, she was found to have talent of her own. Mrs van Huten came out one day to ask for some cool buttermilk, and carrying with her that same lace scarf she'd had in her hands when Morag first saw her.

'This stupid thing,' she sighed, sitting down on a hard wooden chair inside the dairy door. 'It's giving me such a headache. I'd throw it away only Mr van Huten gave it to me for an anniversary present . . .'

'May I see, madam?' Morag asked.

She took it from her employer's plump hands. There was a darn of thick cotton thread in the intricate pattern of the lace. 'Oh, Mrs van Huten,' she reproached her. 'You're making a big lump in the fabric!'

'I know I am! I can't see where the stitches ought to go. I tore it while I was dancing last spring at the Suderman's.'

'Look – you should use a finer thread and pick up stitches from side to side –'

'Could you do it?' Dorothea asked, with sudden hope.

'Well . . . yes . . . I think I could . . .'

'Then take it, take it, in heaven's name! Nancy, you must let

Morag have time off to do this for me.'

'Suits me, ma'am,' Nancy said with a shrug.

Morag mended the scarf with little difficulty. All it needed was patience and fine stitches. She took it back that evening, to be greeted with enthusiastic gratitude. Dorothea invited her to sit down in her boudoir and showed her one or two other items of clothing that needed repair.

From that, Morag soon became a house servant. She took charge of the repair of the linen, both household and personal, with special attention to Mrs van Huten's clothes. When the Harvest Supper began to draw near and Mrs van Huten decided she would like an old dress re-furbished, Morag did the needlework.

Although there had never been a maid with such a role in the household before, Cornelius was tolerant. He was dotingly fond of his wife, who was twenty years his junior. Pretty and plump, she was allowed almost anything she wanted.

They had two children, a son and a daughter. Both were absent from home, the daughter at a school in Albany, and the son, Julius, missing on some scheme of his own. It was partly because Julius had no interest in farming that his father had to employ a farm foreman. His lands were extensive, beyond the ability of one man to supervise. Julius could have been second in command to a fine estate but preferred to go off gambling and kicking up the dust in Philadelphia. As if that wasn't bad enough, the boy had stolen a hundred dollars from his father's desk before he left.

'By golly, if he weren't my son, I'd put him in jail,' Cornelius groaned when he thought about it. But he still had hopes that his nineteen-year-old heir would grow out of his wildness.

The evening of the Harvest Supper came. The big barn was decked with lanterns and plaited bands of straw. Nellie the cook had been preparing the food for days beforehand. There were pies of every kind, cakes and cookies, preserves and pickles, roast duck, leg of pork, glazed venison, quail, and all kinds of fresh-water fish, fried crisp and light in breadcrumbs.

Cornelius had a barrel of beer rolled into the barn, and bottles of rum and brandy. Neighbouring farmers supplied their own speciality – home flavoured spirits, raisin wine, apple brew. The party went on late into the night. Most of the guests slumped into sleep on the straw in the barn.

Dorothea enjoyed herself. She loved an occasion like this, when she could dance and sing and giggle with her friends. She knew she looked well in her freshly trimmed gown of taffeta and ruched ribbon, her rounded forearms gleaming amidst the loose flounces of beige lace, her white neck contrasting with the dark velvet ribbon at the throat.

Her husband tottered off to bed as soon as the musicians packed up for the night. Dorothea stayed in the barn, talking to those who lingered on. At last, reluctant and a little unsteady on her feet, she turned her steps towards the house.

She tripped on a loose cobblestone and would have fallen. Someone leaning on the fence nearby leapt to her rescue. 'My, thank you,' she gasped. 'I think I've had a little too much to drink.'

'We've all done well tonight, Mrs van Huten.'

'Why, that's Rob, isn't it?'

'Yes, ma'am.'

'Have you had a good time?'

He certainly had. He'd never seen anything like it in his life. The little gathering of neighbours he'd been accustomed to at home, the Highland *ceilidh*, had never stinted the drink – but the vast outpouring of liquor, the unlimited supply of food, the neat attire, the ribbons and laces of the women . . . all this was hitherto unknown to him.

'You'd better help me indoors, Rob,' Dorothea said. 'I might fall and hurt myself.'

'Yes, ma'am.'

He put his arm under hers and supported her – or at least, she leaned upon him and he showed himself willing to accept the burden. When they got to the house, the big back door stood wide open to the September night. He walked with her through the kitchen, to the back stairs in the stone lobby outside. She began to ascend the stairs alone, but leaned upon the banister. 'Oh, I'm giddy,' she said, fanning herself with a lace-edged handkerchief.

'Shall I help you to your room?' Rob asked.

'That would be kind, Rob.'

He came to her side. This time it was she who took his arm. He accompanied her to the door of the room she indicated. There he made as to leave her, but she leaned on him more heavily. 'Don't let me go, Rob,' she murmured, 'or I'll fall.'

With concealed reluctance, he opened the door and went in with her. He expected to see Cornelius asleep in a big double bed, but instead he found himself in a pretty little feminine room furnished with a small fourposter draped with pink silk.

'Where's . . . where's . . . ?'

'My husband?' she ended for him. 'Oh, we don't sleep together now. Mr van Huten's getting on, you know – he likes plenty of sleep. And I'm restless. I sleep badly.' She pouted, sinking onto a flounced chair. 'I don't know how I'm going to get to sleep now,' she said. 'It's been such a lovely party – I'm all tensed up.'

'Shall I ring for a cup of chocolate for you?'

'No, no . . . that wouldn't help.' She wriggled as if in discomfort. 'Unhook the back of my dress for me, Rob.'

With a little frown, he came up behind her. She leaned forward in the chair so that he could reach the hooks. His fingers felt clumsy against the slithery fabric. He unhooked the first six, and paused.

'Well, go on,' she said, 'that's no help.'

He undid the rest of the hooks. Her gown, stiffened at the front and sides with whalebone, fell forward entirely, to reveal an area of lace ruffles and cherry-coloured ribbons.

'Ah, that's better,' she breathed, leaning back in relaxation. She smiled up at him, knowing very well that as she reclined towards him he could see the deep hollow between her breasts.

Rob knew that if he was to get out of the room, it had to be now. If he stayed, they would make love – and that might lead to complications. But how could he say goodnight and walk out without offending her? She was so clearly inviting him to take her.

'Mrs van Huten –'

'Dorothea,' she corrected.

'Dorothea, it's getting late.'

'It's late already. Everybody else is asleep.' She turned to lean on the back of the chair and stare up at him. 'There's nobody going to know if you stay here, Rob.'

'Am I going to stay?' he asked.

'I think so,' she said. 'I think so.' And she held out her arms.

She was something new to him – new and delightful. Her skin was scented with fine perfumes, and her garments were of fine silk or lawn. The mere task of undressing her was erotic. When he carried her to the bed, she wound her arms about him and pressed her plump body against him so sensuously that his scruples vanished beneath a tide of quick passion. He didn't trouble to be gentle with her. He took her as she seemed to want to be taken... roughly and without finesse.

'My, what a strong fellow you are,' she whispered when it was over. 'I knew the minute I saw you that you'd be . . . interesting.'

'You mean you had this in mind from the outset?' he said, secretly shocked.

'Hadn't you?'

'Of course not, Dorothea! You're the boss's wife!'

'And he's old enough to be my father,' she pointed out, pulling his head down to plant a teasing little kiss on the corner of his mouth. 'I must have *some* compensation.'

'Isn't it a big risk?'

'Of what? Cornelius is too fond of me to think I could do anything wrong. And even if he knew, I don't see how he could say too much. He's stopped being a real husband – he'd rather eat too much and smoke too much than make love, so I feel I'm entitled to carry on my own life.'

Next day the work of the farm slowly got back into gear. Dubec was out in the barn watching the machinery being laid up for the winter. He turned on his heel to survey Rob when he came in. 'You don't look awake yet,' he remarked.

'I'm all right,' Rob said, although he still felt drugged and drowsy.

'Had a good time, did you?'

'I've never seen a party like that before,' Rob admitted.

'I wasn't talking about the party.'

'I don't know what else you could mean . . .'

'Aw, don't behave as if you think I'm an idiot! You think you're on velvet now, don't you?' Dubec gave a bitter laugh. 'You'll be cock of the walk for a while, buddy. But don't think it's for ever. It's just until the next pair of pants walks by.'

Rob stared at him.

'Didn't you know? You're only one in a long line.'

'I think you're under a wrong impression –'

'Have it your way. But remember what I say. It's great while it lasts – but it won't last long.'

Rob moved away to help dismantle the cutting bands of the header. His mind was in a whirl for a moment. A picture of Dorothea kept forming and dissolving in his mind. He had felt so rich, so rewarded by the gift she had given him. Now it seemed it was a gift many had received.

He thought about Dubec. Stocky, muscular, balding . . . She had gone to bed with *him*? For a moment he was angry. He, Rob Craigallan, wasn't on the same level as Pierre Dubec.

But I'm not looking through the eyes of Dorothea van Huten, he thought. She has to sort out a man from those who come to be employed at the farm. She couldn't be too finicky. And Dubec probably had a lot of attraction for a healthy physical appetite. The foreman was vibrant with animal sexuality.

That put it all into perspective. No use getting starry-eyed about Dorothea. There was nothing about love in all this. She wanted to have fun with someone, and Rob happened to be the partner of the moment. It could have advantages for him.

He wasn't prepared for so many people on the farm knowing what was going on. The farmhands soon let him see that they were watching. Nothing was put into words, but a smile, a nod, a turn of the head or the lift of an eyebrow – all these told him they were an interested audience. Morag was told of it by Nancy, the dairymaid. It came out quite matter-of-factly. 'She'll get rid of Dubec now she's got your brother,' Nancy remarked.

'How d'you mean, Nancy? Rob hasn't the experience to be foreman.'

'Oh, she'll let old Stilworth take that on. Stilworth knows what he's about. He hasn't much grip on the men, but he knows the land. He'll plan out the work with the boss. Mrs van Huten will suggest that your brother takes over as foreman to control the men, and the boss'll agree. He always does whatever she suggests.'

'But why?' Morag said in perplexity. 'Why should Dubec go?'

Nancy stared at her. 'Ain't you got eyes?'

'I don't understand what you're talking about.'

'The missis is sweet on your brother.'

'On Rob?'

'Sure is. You've only got to look at her when he's around.'

'But she's a married woman!' Morag burst out in dismay.

'What?' Nancy paused in the chore of scouring the cream pans and began to laugh. 'Sure she's married. That don't mean she can't have some fun.'

'But . . . Nancy! You're not suggesting . . .'

'I'm not suggesting, I'm stating. Honey, you can't be so blind that you haven't noticed? She's going round like a cat that's caught a mouse, and your brother's being very careful to keep out of the boss's way. It's a sure sign. By and by he'll learn that he don't have to worry. The boss don't seem to see what's under his nose.'

Morag couldn't believe it. Rob wouldn't get involved in anything so sordid. She left the dairy convinced Nancy was mistaken. But before that same day was out she'd seen enough – now that she'd been alerted – to understand that the dairy maid was right.

She and Rob had very little contact since they'd come to live at van Hutens'. Rob had to work hard out of doors, and she herself had been taken onto the house staff. Besides, they ought not to meet and converse too much – they were supposed to be only brother and sister, not sweethearts. Now Morag had to conceal the hurt she felt, for that hurt was inappropriate to a sister. Nor did she have the courage to seek him out and reproach him. She felt she might make everything worse.

She couldn't understand how he could do such a thing. He loved her. She knew that to be so. Why was he getting involved with Mrs van Huten? Morag viewed Dorothea from her stance of a sixteen-year-old girl. The farmer's wife was old . . . Forty. She was overweight too. True, she had a creamy skin and soft hands, dark flashing eyes and carefully dressed brown hair: she dressed well, wore a rich, exotic perfume. But she was *old*.

At first she was sure that the affair would quickly die. She couldn't believe it could go on. Yet the weeks went by and she could see that Dorothea continued to be pleased with herself. 'You know, I think it's getting serious,' Nancy remarked to her. 'She's always been one to like having a man around, but I've never seen her get so keen on anyone before.'

Morag spent quite a lot of time with Dorothea. Her employer loved clothes, and there was almost always some gown being re-made, some nightdress being re-trimmed, some bonnet being re-styled. Morag was kept busy with this work, which until now she'd enjoyed; she loved the feel of the fine fabrics under her hands, the needle slipping through them to take tiny stitches almost invisible to the eye. Besides her ability as a needlewoman, Morag had an artist's eye. She knew what would look good, what would work.

When Dorothea was planning for a visit to Albany, she called in Morag to make a dress for her. 'There's that length of velvet Mr van Huten gave me for my birthday,' she remarked, gesturing at the highboy in her boudoir. 'Get it out, Morag – it's in the thick brown paper.'

Morag fetched it and unwrapped it. The lush dark blue velvet unrolled from the paper. Despite herself, Morag exclaimed in pleasure.

'Yes, lovely, isn't it? It's just the thing for a winter evening gown. Husband is taking me to a dinner at the capital, something to do with those tedious agricultural politics. Still, I'll be meeting important people – *and* their wives. I want to look good.'

'So you will, in this,' Morag agreed.

'How do you think it should be made up, child?' Dorothea by now had so much faith in her that she didn't think to call in the local dressmaker who came to the farm from time to time to carry out commissions.

'Oh, it must be rather plain. Too much trimming on the skirt would pucker the fabric and besides, it's so lovely that you want it to fall in its own weight and to glow with its own colour.'

'Yes, but the bodice? The bodice has to be trimmed. I can't sit at a dining table with my chest poking up all dull and plain, when everybody else will be dripping with lace.'

'No, that's true. You want just a touch of pure white lace, Mrs van Huten, at neck and forearm, with pure white kid gloves and a pure white fan – not ivory, but pure white.'

'Yes,' Dorothea agreed, taking fire at the idea. 'I've got a white feather fan –'

'No, that's too airy for use with heavy blue velvet. You want something solid. White silk or satin.'

'Oh yes . . .'

'And matching ribbon laid plain in loops round the neck above the lace . . .' mused Morag, lost in her vision of the dress.

'I'll send for Mrs Bolton to bring ribbons and threads. I've got gloves already, and I'll get Mr van Huten to buy me a new fan when we get to Albany.'

'Yes, and in your hair, Mrs van Huten . . . A flat bow of the ribbon edged with white lace . . .'

'Good, good. I think it will look fine. You're a good child, Morag. Will you make the pattern for cutting out the dress straight away?'

'Yes, ma'am.'

'I'm looking forward to the trip,' Dorothea said, leaning back on her chaise longue and tilting her head, eyes half-closed. 'I do so love being in town! And I'll see Luisa, of course. We'll bring her back with us for Thanksgiving.'

Morag had never yet met Luisa, who had been away since she and Rob came to the farm. 'She's at school?'

'Oh yes, Miss Anhalt's Academy. Very expensive. Luisa's had advantages I never had, so we expect her to make a fine marriage. It's difficult to be sure, for she's only seventeen yet, but I think she's going to turn out pretty.' Dorothea sighed and sipped the blackcurrant cordial she was fond of. 'I'm quite looking forward to seeing her, and of course the dinner will be fine. But the travelling in November is wearisome, and . . .' She paused, a half smile on her mouth. 'I'll be glad to get back to the farm when it's over.'

Morag looked at her, and knew her employer was thinking about Rob. Something strange seized her – it seemed to clutch at her heart, so that for a moment she was gasping for breath.

'What's the matter, girl? Are you sick?' Dorothea sat up and stared at her. 'What are you changing colour for?'

'It's nothing, ma'am . . . I felt . . . faint . . . for a minute.'

'Hm.m . . . I hope you're not going to have bad health in the winter. I've noticed you have a slight cough. It will be very inconvenient if you're sick because I've got a lot of things I want made ready for the Christmas parties.'

'I'm quite all right, ma'am. It was just . . . something choked me for a moment.'

Jealousy!

She'd never experienced it before. She'd never before felt she was important enough to anyone to have rights over them. But with Rob, she felt that she came first. He had been her friend throughout the voyage from Scotland, had sought her out at the Aggerleys, had made her his own on that bright summer day and had come looking for her when she lost her job. It was thanks to Rob that she was here in this comfortable household, living well, working for a lenient mistress at tasks she enjoyed. True, Rob had to lie to achieve all that, but she had quickly rationalised that. He had spoken on the spur of the moment and now they simply had to accept the situation. She was used to having the others speak of Rob as her brother. It was much too late now to correct the error, but she didn't feel towards him as a sister. The thought that he might be Dorothea's lover rent her with agony.

She took a chance to speak with him alone by volunteering to take the midday meal to the men working in the straw yard. Rob was on top of a stack, tying down the straw against the coming winter gales. When he saw her below him with a plate wrapped in a napkin, he waved and clambered down.

She watched his lithe movements, and thought how he had filled out since she first saw him. Eight months had made a difference in him. He seemed taller, more broad-shouldered. His muscles fitted over his frame like well-made armour. His hair, a dark russet, gleamed, and his features were growing more definite, stronger – particularly the wide, thin mouth. He had always looked older than his years, she thought. Now he looked a man, although he hadn't reached legal majority.

'What are you doing out here?' he inquired as he accepted the food from her. 'Nellie in a pet again this morning?'

'No. I offered to bring it.'

'Oh, did you?' He sampled the slice of veal pie. 'That's worth bringing, I can tell you. Good old Nellie, she always sends me something special.'

'She's fond of you,' Morag murmured. And then, in a lower tone, 'So is Mrs van Huten.'

'What?' He looked up from the plate. 'Oh ... yes, I suppose she is.'

'Rob ...'

'What?'

'The others are saying that there's something between you and Mrs van Huten.'

'They what?' He looked startled. It was well acted. He knew the other hands on the farm were quite aware of Mrs van Huten's preference for him. 'That's just stupid gossip.'

'Is it, Rob? I've seen her looking at you ...'

'You can't make anything of a look, Morag.'

'But they're saying it's gone beyond looks. They're saying you ... she ...'

'That's rubbish,' he said, putting the plate down on a bale of hay and taking her hand. 'That's just envy and malice, Morag.'

She looked up at him, willing him to make her believe it.

'Sure, she likes me,' he went on. 'She's the kind of lady that likes a bit of romance in her life. You can't blame her, Morag – married to an old man like van Huten, while she's still young and full of spirits.'

'But it's just because she's married that it's so wrong,' Morag said in a stifled voice. 'And Mr van Huten's so nice! It's wrong

[117]

to . . . to do anything he wouldn't approve of.'

'But we're not doing anything,' Rob lied. He didn't want Morag to be hurt. He wanted to talk himself out of this accusation so that she'd be happy again. 'I admit we chat together and make little jokes – you must have noticed how she loves to giggle and tease, Morag. That's all it is.'

'But she's not like that with any of the other men –'

'How do you know?' he riposted. 'You don't follow Mrs van Huten around when she takes a look at the farm work, now do you? You're stuck indoors most of the time, bent over your sewing. I tell you, sweetheart, she likes a joke with anybody. The others are making a point of what she says to me because we're new here, that's all. They're a bit jealous because we've fitted in so well, I reckon.'

'You swear to me, Rob? That's all it is?'

'I swear it,' he said, mock solemn.

She took the empty plate back to Nellie, still thoughtful. 'You're lookin' down in the dumps, child,' Nellie said. 'You got that cough again?'

'No, I'm all right, Nellie, thank you.'

'You come to me later and I'll give you some strong beef tea. Nothing so good for the delicates as strong beef tea.'

'Thank you, Nellie.' But Morag knew deep within herself that beef tea wasn't going to help.

Rob had assured her that there was nothing between himself and Mrs van Huten. And Rob, of course, was all that was good and dependable. Why didn't she believe him? Because she'd heard him come out with lies, all readymade, to Mr van Huten when he was asking for a job. But this was different, she told herself. This was about what they felt for each other. He knew how important it was to her. He wouldn't lie about it.

When he said he was only joking and talking with Mrs van Huten, it must be true. He had never held her in his arms. She was sure that he could never take another woman into that strong embrace. She was his only love. If that wasn't so, she couldn't bear it.

So she had to believe him when he said he had no special feeling for Dorothea. She had to believe it, or she would die. She kept telling herself: He loves me, he loves *me*. He could never go to another woman.

Yet some intuition, some instinct, insisted that Dorothea had a secret which concerned Rob. Despite herself, she was on the alert for evidence. Every glance, every smile of Dorothea's was analysed and catalogued.

The time for the visit to Albany drew near. The carriage was taken out of the stables and polished. The horses were given a special grooming for their appearance in the capital. Morag packed for Dorothea under her directions. 'Put in my fur pelisse. No, wait, leave it out – I'll wear it tomorrow for the journey, it'll be draughty in the carriage.' Dorothea was in a happy muddle of expectancy. 'My, to think that tomorrow I'll be walking in and out of shops in State Street! It'll be like heaven. And yet . . .'

'Yet what, ma'am?'

'Part of me doesn't want to go!'

'Oh, the minute you get there you'll love it,' Morag said.

'Yes, of course. And after all . . . there's always tonight.'

'What, ma'am?' Morag asked. Dorothea's voice had dropped when she said the last few words.

'Nothing, child, nothing. Don't forget my blue evening slippers. They're not the right shade but I shan't have time to get any made for my new gown. And put in my Mechlin lace cap. I hear they wear caps out of doors even as late as November, in Albany.'

'Yes, ma'am.'

'There's always tonight.' Morag heard the words but refused to acknowledge their meaning. But next morning, when she came to help Dorothea to dress for the early start to the journey, she found under the flounce of the pink-draped bed a creased kerchief of brown cotton. It was the kerchief Rob wore around his neck in lieu of a cravat, when he changed from his work clothes to his suit.

Morag went through the motions of helping Dorothea get ready, waved her off with the rest of the house staff, and did all the chores of that day without remark. But she was scarcely conscious of what she was doing. Her mind was always with that brown cotton kerchief.

It was true. Rob was Dorothea's lover. But she'd always known that, really. She was wounded. He had lied to her. That was terrible, unbearable. But worse, he had been with another woman. He had taken someone else into that intimate closeness where she had thought she alone held sway.

Dorothea . . . He couldn't really care for Dorothea. Why, why had he done it?

She was so ignorant of physical appetites that she didn't understand how it could happen. Rob loved her – therefore he should be incapable of even wanting to touch another woman.

In Morag's view, there were good men and there were bad men. Bad men had treated her with cruelty and callous disregard. These were the kind who could go with any woman merely to satisfy an animal need, who would offer money instead of love.

Then the good men, like Rob, were quite different. Love came first with them. Did it follow, then, that she was losing Rob to Dorothea?

All day she wrestled with this terrible thought. And when the day's work was over and she went to her bed above the dairy, she lay for a long time thinking about it. She couldn't live if she lost Rob. He was the mainspring of her existence, the only thing that she could hold on to in a strange, shifting world. He had taken charge of her being – she had surrendered herself to him, willingly. If he turned away from her, she would cease to exist.

Slowly it came to her that perhaps she had been foolish. They had been at van Huten's since the harvest. Three months had gone by. In that time she'd scarcely ever been alone with Rob because of the masquerade under which they lived here. But Rob perhaps had missed her. Rob had longed for her and she had not been there. So when Dorothea, who was provocative and inviting, had made it easy for him to approach her, he had fallen into the trap.

Morag understood that she was at fault. She had been thoughtless. After all, she and Rob had been lovers. Had she really believed their relationship would continue if she made no efforts to be with him?

In the quiet dark she rose. She threw a shawl over her shoulders, tiptoed barefoot to the door and lifted the latch. She went down the open wooden staircase to the dairy, where the stone floor struck chill to her feet.

Outside, a cold wind was blowing. She went across the paved yard to the stables, like a wraith with her white nightgown billowing in the breeze. When she came to the room at the side of the stables which was the province of the farm foreman, she saw the light was on. She peered in between the gingham curtains. Rob was sitting in a cane rocking chair, reading.

She stood for a long moment, uncertain. Then, drawing a deep breath, she turned the door handle and went in.

'What the – ? Morag!' Rob leaped up. 'What's wrong? Are you ill?'

'No, I just wanted to see you, Rob.'

He had held out his hands to her as she came in. She put her own in his. He said, 'Good God, you're freezing. Come in, come to the stove.'

An iron stove stood in the corner where his chair and a table with a lamp were placed. She saw that the table was covered with journals concerned with farming.

He put her in his chair and brought a comforter from the bed which stood behind gingham curtains in an alcove. He wrapped her up and stooped over her, his hand touching her forehead to see if she had a temperature.

'Oh, Rob,' she sighed. Grasping his wrist, she leaned her head against his arm.

'What's the matter?'

'Nothing, nothing! I . . . Don't you want me to be here?'

'Of course I . . . It's just that you took me by surprise. Do you know the time? Why aren't you sleeping?'

'Why aren't you?' she returned.

'Oh, I often read late into the night. Mr van Huten lets me have these old magazines. Farming's different here in America, Morag. There's a lot to learn, to catch up with.'

'So that's what you do at night?' she murmured, with sad irony.

'Now, now,' he soothed. 'You've been imagining things again. We sorted out all that –'

'I just thought,' she said, 'since the boss and his wife are away, that you and I ... It would be safe ... Oh, Rob, don't you want me any more?'

'Morag!'

He was shocked. It had never occurred to him that she would take the initiative. What had come over her?

'We hardly see each other any more,' she whispered. 'I miss you so much, Rob. Everybody here is quite kind but ... it's you that's important to me and we're never together any more.'

'Well, it's difficult, isn't it? There are always people about –'

'There aren't people about *now*, Rob.'

'No ...' He was still so surprised that he didn't know how to carry off the moment.

Morag reached up and wound her arms about him, drawing him down towards her. 'Darling,' she begged, 'tell me you still love me. Make everything like it was before! I'm so lonely and unhappy without you – kiss me and tell me everything is still all right!'

Her great eyes, like forest pools touched by sunlight, stared up at him. He could feel her slender arms pulling against the nape of his neck. The shawl had slipped off her shoulders, showing the tucked cotton of her nightdress masking the swell of her young breasts.

It was impossible not to want her. He picked her up out of the chair and carried her to his bed. Then he put out the lamp so that no one passing by could glimpse at the scene within. He came back to the bed, to find Morag sitting up in the dark taking off her nightgown. He felt the thick cotton folds fall to the ground at his feet.

He was astounded. It was almost wanton. He had never imagined her capable of acting so totally without restraint or modesty. The action roused him more than anything in his life before. And when she greeted his approach with an ardour that was almost fierce, he let it carry them both to a triumphant love-making different from what they had known in the past.

She was sweet, eager, responsive. Her kisses were like fire on his body, on his face. The slim frame that sought his onslaught was alive to his every touch. She was different from Dorothea; Dorothea was clever and expert – Morag was passion itself.

They fell into sleep, arms about each other. When he woke, she had gone. He pulled himself up on an elbow hoping to see her still in his room, to coax her back to bed again before it was time to begin the day. But she had left him.

He sat up, bewildered. Had that really been Morag who had made love to him last night? Who had taught her such things?

She didn't know it, but she had changed his thinking about her by her act. Until last night, she had symbolised for him all that was good and pure. He had felt responsible for her, against his will. But the girl who had shared his bed last night was not the innocent child he had pictured. He remembered the days she had spent in New York after she had been turned out of the Aggerley household. She'd earned enough to live on by picking up customers. Was that where she'd learned to please a man? Was it from these strangers she'd found out the art of making the blood take fire?

He was perplexed. His body remembered the pleasures of the night and was grateful. But his mind kept going over the thought that she no longer belonged to him in the way she used to.

She had changed. What right had she to change? Where had she gone, that shy, innocent girl he used to love?

8

MR AND MRS VAN HUTEN returned three days later, bringing with them their daughter Luisa to celebrate Thanksgiving. Luisa was a surprise to Morag. Influenced by Dorothea's view of her, she'd been thinking of her as a gawky schoolgirl. But the young lady who stepped down from the high old carriage showed herself to be taller and more womanly in contour than Morag herself. It ocurred to Morag that the 'schoolgirl' was actually a few months her senior.

Luisa van Huten had a high opinion of herself. Her mother had always taught her to think she would do well in life; the daughter of Cornelius van Huten could hardly do otherwise. The family had been settled in the district since the mid-sixteen-hundreds and was well-respected. Moreover, Cornelius might be lax and easygoing in some things, but he was an excellent farmer. His lands prospered, his crops were sure of a good price, he seemed to know how to counteract attacks of blight or drought better than his neighbours.

At his wife's insistence. Cornelius had sent Luisa away to school this past year. Dorothea held that Luisa needed to have a little polish put upon her. She had to learn how to mingle with the better sort of people, for Dorothea was determined her daughter wasn't going to be buried in the country but would have an interesting life in the state capital.

So here came Luisa, stepping down from the van Huten's

carriage, little varnished boots sparkling under lace-edged petticoats and pantaloons, hands hidden in a ruched velvet muff, face peeping out from under a fur-edged bonnet with under-ruffles of picot muslin, ringlet curls jostling the fur of her cape. Her eyes were the light blue of her Papa, but where she had inherited her dusky-blonde hair was a mystery. Her face gleamed with health, her figure was rounded and well-nourished. Like Papa, she loved the good things of life – meat with rich sauce, sips of brandy when she could wheedle them out of the grown-ups, strong scent to sprinkle on her handkerchief, roaring fires at which to toast her toes.

In the flurry and happiness of having their daughter at home, the van Hutens had time for nothing else for the first few days. Morag, who was often with Dorothea and Luisa, was delighted; they were wrapped up in each other, fussing over pattern books and trying to do over each other's hair.

Morag was sure Dorothea never so much as thought of Rob. And when she had a moment to steal out and talk to Rob, he seemed quite unperturbed at the neglect from the lady of the house. She was secretly delighted. Her daring act of the night when she went to Rob's room had brought its reward. She had regained Rob's love.

So she was startled and dismayed when, at the Thanksgiving Day party, Rob flirted outrageously with Luisa.

Luisa certainly invited it. She had persuaded her Mama to let her put her hair up in a very grown-up style, and though her gown was extremely demure in appearance, it seemed very revealing. It had a low square cut neck which appeared to reveal a large area of soft white bosom. In fact, the neckline was filled in with a fine voile called illusion, so that the white flesh was really silk veiling. But the plump arms really were bare under short puffed sleeves. In Miss Anhalt's Academy, Luisa would have worn elbow-length white gloves with the dress, but in the more relaxed atmosphere of her father's farm, she discarded them.

Luisa had looked about her on settling down at home, and decided that the only male worth bothering about was the young foreman, Rob Craigallan. She had taken care to stroll in his direction when out for an airing, and to chat with him a few times. He was goodlooking. He spoke up well, and seemed to have some kind of education. More important, he was quick to react to her signals. He paid her little compliments, teased her, opened gates for her, offered his arm over muddy stretches of the farm's paths.

On Thanksgiving, Luisa decided to make Rob her partner. Everyone on the farm shared the great meal in the early evening, so at the big trestle tables in the barn it wasn't possible to be near him. However, when the tables were cleared to the side and the dancing began, Luisa deliberately walked up to him and tapped him with her fan. 'Can you dance the waltz?' she inquired.

'I learned at the Harvest Supper.'

'Come along then, let's show everybody how it should be done.'

'Just as you say, Miss van Huten,' he said with a mock bow.

Dorothea, dancing with Cornelius, eyed them with tolerance. After all, there was really no one else for the child to dance with. The other farmhands were older and rather rough for a girl from a young ladies' academy. There was no harm in it. Dorothea would take care that there was no harm in it.

Luisa, whirling round the stone floor of the barn in Rob's arms, was loving every moment of it. He guided her so well, and his arms were so strong. And when she caught his eyes, his laughing glance made something stir within her. She was aware of the spot at her waist where his right hand rested; it seemed to generate a warmth far stronger than the exhilaration of the dance.

As daughter of the house, she was duty bound to dance with as many of the men as possible, and as many of the neighbours. But she took care to chat with Rob in the intervals between the dances, to be near him when supper was served so that, though they weren't alone together, he was part of the group which surrounded her. She singled him out for attention; the local suitors were vexed or amused, according to how seriously they rated their chances of landing the van Huten dowry.

'My love,' Dorothea murmured to her as the evening drew to a close, 'I think you'll be well advised to have the last waltz with someone other than our foreman.'

'Quite so, Mama,' Luisa said with docility. She danced the waltz with Joe Bettinger from West Dale, an old man with a wife and three daughters. She knew her mother was a little vexed; it would have been more useful in the game of matchmaking if she had shown some favour – even pretended – for one of the young men.

As the guests were waved farewell, the servants set to work clearing up the debris in the barn. Rob was carrying away the trestles on which the tables had been set up. Morag paused on her path to the door with a pile of tablecloths. 'You were having a high old time with Miss Luisa,' she remarked.

'She's a high-spirited girl.'

'Did you have to play up to her so much?'

'What did you expect me to do? She came up to me and asked me to dance.'

'But you could have kept out of her way afterwards!'

'Why should I?' he said, irritated.

She wanted to say, Because you belong to me. Because it hurts me to see you behave like that with another girl, when you've trapped me into pretending I only have sisterly feelings. Because . . . because you ought to think of *me*.

But there was a look of vexation about him. She knew he wouldn't like it if she spoke of her own claims on him. She said instead: 'I don't think Mrs van Huten approved.'

He stared at this double-edged remark. It was sharper than anything she'd ever said to him. Gathering himself together, he laughed. 'Luisa is as stupid as her mother. None of it means anything.'

But it meant something to Luisa. Spoiled and with little to occupy her, she was very taken by the new young foreman. When she came home for the longer Christmas holiday she tried to be wherever Rob was. She, who had always hated exercise, took to walking out to look at the fields where Rob was ploughing, took to riding out where he was supervising the felling of trees.

Rob couldn't exactly avoid her. She was, after all, the boss's daughter. He thought of her as a child, in a way he had never thought of Morag. Perhaps it was because Luisa was childish –

easily put into a pout, seeking approval and attention all the time. She was easy to keep quiet – all you had to do was tell her she was pretty and give her an occasional kiss on the cheek behind a tree trunk.

The fact was, Rob preferred the mother to the daughter. Dorothea's interest in him had brought him advancement, given him benefits he'd never dreamed of before. He had a room to himself whereas the other hands bunked together. He had books and journals to read, carrying within their covers an unending store of information about the science of agriculture. Rob had never realised before that agriculture was a science. With all his heart he envied Julius van Huten, the missing son of the house, who was supposed to be at agricultural college but who was more often an absconder.

Julius himself reappeared just after New Year, supposedly repentant. There was a great reconciliation scene, Rob gathered. The prodigal was forgiven, and promised to settle down.

He was a plump young man, with a pale skin and large light blue eyes. He dressed rather well but took no care of his clothes. The day after he came back, he was up early, clad in a thick Loden coat so as to ride out for a survey of the farm. This was evidence of his change of heart; from now on he was going to be a good young farmer.

He was actually twenty, the age that Rob laid claim to. As the only man on the farm of about the same age, Rob was elected as 'friend' by Julius. This consisted of being at all times willing to welcome him into the room by the stables, so that he could drink and sit about at ease.

'I tell you, Papa is a tyrant for all his easygoing manner,' Julius said, pouring more Burgundy into his glass. 'Not a cent of pocket money is he going to give me until March. It's not fair.'

Rob had heard the rumours that Julius was being made to repay the money that had gone missing when he left home. But it made no sense to say so. 'I can't see it matters too much, if you're going to stay on the farm and work,' he pointed out.

'Huh! There's no help for that at the moment.' Julius came nearer to the stove, shivering. 'How I hate the country! If I had my way, I'd live in town all the time. Somehow it's never so cold in town.'

'That's because there's shelter from the other houses –'

'Thank you, Craigallan, I did actually manage to work that out for myself,' Julius rebuked him. 'I'm not a fool, you know.'

Rob got up and put another billet of wood in the stove. Julius said: 'In a huff, are you? You don't like being talked down to. I've noticed.'

'No one does.'

'But you don't bear it so well as the others. You're proud, Rob. What have you got to be proud of?'

'Little enough. But I hope to make something of myself one day. That's why I left Scotland.'

'Oh, yes, that's why you all come here. That's why my ancestors arrived on these shores in sixteen fifty-six. Do you know that they were comfortable merchants from Amsterdam? Can you imagine leaving a city like Amsterdam to carve a farm out of the wilderness? They must have been mad! The minute I get this farm handed on to me, I'm going to put in a manager and get back to the city.'

'You mean, let someone else run it?' Rob said, thunderstruck.

'Yes, why not? It's not uncommon.'

'But . . . it'd be *your* farm.'

'So it would. That doesn't mean I have to live on it.'

It was a new idea to Rob. In his limited experience, a man lived on his land and made a living from it. No one else could do it for him half so well as he did it himself. But yet . . . on a farm as big as van Huten's, it was in fact possible to pay a manager and still make a profit. There was a living here for many people; the owners and the farm staff and the hired teams that came in for threshing or drilling.

Walking back from church the following Sunday with his 'sister', he inquired: 'How old do you think van Huten is?'

'He's sixty-seven next birthday,' Morag told him. 'Mrs van Huten has asked me to make him a new waistcoat for it. Why do you ask?'

'Sixty-seven? And his health isn't so good, is it?'

'Well, he eats too much and suffers from breathlessness and pains in his arm, but that's only to be expected at his age.'

'That's what I mean.'

'Why does it interest you, Rob?'

'Julius was telling me the other night that when he inherits, he's going to take on a manager instead of living on the farm.'

'What?' She turned, pausing in her walk over the frozen ruts of the road to the farm. 'Oh, but that's for years ahead.'

'Perhaps. But perhaps not. You know, Morag, I could make a good job of being manager of this farm.'

She shook her head. 'Julius would want an older man.'

'I don't see why! If I'd been foreman here a couple of years, and proved I knew what I was doing?'

'No, I still think . . . I mean, there'd be lawyers and people like that, advising him. They wouldn't let him take on a manager unless he had years of experience.'

Rob thrust his hands into the pockets of his jacket. 'That doesn't seem fair,' he murmured. 'If I stay on here and keep doing a good job, the manager's post ought to fall to me.'

'Rob, we're not going to stay here for ever,' she cried.

'Well, I've no plans for moving on until I learn all I can.'

'But I can't go on pretending to be your sister, Rob –'

'Why not? It's worked all right up till now –'

'But I *hate* it, Rob! You and I . . . With things as they are between us . . . it's so . . . so wrong –'

'To be in love, you mean?'

'If we're brother and sister, it is terribly wrong!' she flashed, with a distaste and anger he had not suspected. 'You don't seem to think of that, Rob!'

He took her hand and patted it. 'But as we're not brother and sister, you needn't get in a state –'

'But how are we ever going to get married and settle down? We can only do that if we leave here.'

'Oh . . . well . . . plenty of time for that,' he said. 'We haven't got anything like enough saved up yet.'

The truth was, there had been a subtle change in his feelings for Morag in recent weeks. Since that night when she had come to him in his room, he'd asked himself once or twice if she was really

[130]

so much in need of him as he had always believed. If she could be like *that* with a man, she wasn't so innocent and helpless after all.

And about the farm, too . . . He saw her move about the house, trim and neat in her dark winter dress, her white cap and apron, her well-polished button boots. She had everything she needed, didn't she? She fitted in, was content, liked her work as linenmaid and needlewoman. What need was there for any change?

As for marriage, Rob had realised, from the talk about Luisa's prospects, that marriage could be a financial step. If he married Morag – as he ought to, he admitted, since it was he who had first seduced her – he would gain no monetary advantage. There would only be his savings and hers. It would take them about three years or so to get together enough to have a house and a scrap of land unless they went out to the pioneer regions: and he didn't want to do that when there was the whole of van Huten's waiting to be grasped.

It had come to Rob, as if in a vision, that Cornelius really had no heir. Julius would inherit, but Julius didn't want the farm. How much better it would be if Luisa married someone capable and keen, who would take over the management of the place.

In this scheme, Morag could play no part. She began to realise this as the months went by. Luisa came home as often as she could from the Academy, at which she was in any case almost finished. Her education would end at the cotillion ball with which the summer term terminated. Miss Anhalt already allowed her much freedom, as it was understood she was being courted by the young men of her neighbourhood.

This was in fact the case. All the available sons of neighbouring farmers were angling after the van Huten girl, for her dowry was considerable.

'But I don't like any of them,' Luisa pouted to Rob. 'I wish you had money, Rob. Then you could ask for my hand.'

'Yes,' he breathed. Oh, if only it could be! But there were problems that Luisa wasn't aware of.

There was Morag. Well, Morag wasn't hard to handle. He'd deal with that when the time came. There was also Dorothea. He wasn't so sure he could handle her. True, since Luisa began to come home more often, Dorothea had to be more careful; it wasn't any longer possible to summon Rob to her boudoir whenever the mood took her. Nor could she visit Rob in his own room by the stables, for her troublesome son Julius had taken to lounging there often.

This being so, Dorothea had to content herself with infrequent lovemaking. She'd been through spells like this in the past; things always worked out to her satisfaction in the end. But this time she was unhappy. Rob had become important to her in a more fundamental way than any of the others. He was brighter, younger, more interesting than any of the other partners she'd managed to find among her husband's employees.

She watched her daughter's infatuation with hidden amusement. Oh, if Luisa only knew! Her innocent romancing, her blushes and dreamy looks, the kisses no doubt stolen when no one was looking, the hand-holding and the treasuring of locks of hair – Luisa was welcome to all that so long as Dorothea kept what was of value to her, Rob's strength and power as a lover.

Rob was mistaken in thinking that Dorothea's hold was gradually loosening now that the whole family was around the house. Because of this misunderstanding, he made an even greater mistake.

After a long and serious conversation with Luisa at Easter, and hearing that Bernard Stettinius was about to offer for her, he went to his employer. 'Sir,' he said, taking off his cap as he stood before Cornelius's old mahogany desk, 'I've come to ask for your daughter's hand in marriage.'

Cornelius gave a gasp of astonishment. A purple colour came into his face. 'What? Luisa? You dare?'

'Mr van Huten, please hear me out. Luisa loves me, and won't accept any of the other fellows who are after her. I know this because she told me so –'

'Told you? What right has she to discuss such things with you?' Cornelius cried. 'A daughter has no right to talk about marriage to a hired hand –'

'Sir, I know it seems presumptuous,' Rob said in a soothing

tone. He'd learned how to handle van Huten since he first arrived at the farm. The old man huffed and puffed a lot, but he would listen once the first astonishment wore off. 'But look at it from Luisa's point of view.' This was an important point to make. Van Huten was devotedly fond of all his family, especially the womenfolk. 'She won't be happy if you force her into a marriage with anyone else. You wouldn't want it on your conscience that she was unhappy?'

'She won't be unhappy,' Cornelius protested. 'She'll settle down – they all do. Why, my Dorothea didn't want to take me, you know. But look at her now! Who could be happier in her marriage?'

'But things are different these days, Mr van Huten. Women are being allowed more say in choosing their husbands. Do you want it said of you that you're a tyrannical father?'

'Tyrannical? Me?'

'We both know that you're kindness itself, sir,' Rob went on quickly. Flattery never did any harm, and moreover, it was true. 'But if Luisa is married off against her will, unkind things are sure to be said. Besides, Mr van Huten . . . why should she?'

'Eh? Why should she what?'

'Be married off to someone she doesn't love?'

'I . . . I don't want to marry her to someone she doesn't love –'

'Then you agree she can marry me?'

'What? I said no such thing –'

'But if she's to marry the man she wants, that's me, Mr van Huten.'

'No, no, it's out of the question! Luisa has money coming to her. She comes of an old family. You're a nobody with nothing.'

'Mr van Huten, I come of an old Scottish family,' Rob insisted. 'I had a farm of my own in Scotland. Small, I admit, but I had land – I'm not a nobody. I have chieftain's blood in my veins. And though it's true I haven't any money here in America, I'm earning a good wage here on the farm. Isn't that true?'

'Yes, but Luisa can't live on the wages of a farmhand –'

'I'm not suggesting she should. Mr van Huten, if you agree to the marriage between me and Luisa, I'd put the money due as her dowry into buying a share of the farm.'

'What farm?'

'This farm,' Rob said, disguising his impatience. Of course it was all new to the old man. The thoughts that had been revolving in Rob's head for weeks were coming as a sudden assault on Cornelius's consciousness. 'Don't you see, sir – it would be to your advantage? You wouldn't actually have to part with any money as a dowry. It would stay here, invested in your own lands. Doesn't that strike you as a good idea?'

To tell the truth, it did. Cornelius liked Rob, thought him industrious and keen and clever. If only he had money, he'd be an ideal son-in-law. But it had always been Cornelius's ambition to marry off Luisa to the son of a neighbouring landowner and thereby enlarge the van Hutens' domain. His family had been doing this for generations. He saw no reason to change now.

'No, no, younker,' he said, not unkindly. 'I see you're carried away by love and all that – and no doubt that rogue Luisa has told you I can be persuaded to anything if it's what she wants. But look at it from my point of view. I've more or less promised my daughter to Stettinius's son. I can't go back on it just because of romantic notions. And it's more to my advantage to have a family tie with Stettinius than with some landless young landowner from far away across the ocean!'

'Luisa will never agree to marry Bernard Stettinius,' Rob said.

Cornelius eyed him, and was inclined to agree. Compared with the tall, spare young foreman, Bernard wasn't in the running. Short and bull-chested, he suffered from a slight stutter. A good young man, but not appealing. Whereas the young Scotsman . . .

'Luisa will do as I tell her,' Cornelius said, but he had his doubts about that.

He sent for her, and found that she was as stubborn and resolute as she usually was where her own self-will was involved. She loved Rob, she insisted. She would never take anyone else as her husband.

Well, why not, after all, mused Cornelius. The boy was hard-working and obedient. He still had much to learn about farming, but Cornelius had no objections to teaching him. It would mean, too, that Luisa wouldn't have to leave home. It would be nice to have her about the house. He'd missed her during her year at the Academy.

As to Stettinius . . . well, that would be a nine days' wonder. Why should Cornelius van Huten care what people said about his daughter's marriage? There would be gossip and some hidden ridicule, but that wouldn't perturb him so long as Rob proved a good husband and the farm prospered.

It would be more likely to prosper under Rob's future guidance than that of Julius. Mr van Huten had to admit to himself that his own son was a fool where farming was concerned. Time might still cure him, but in the meantime it might be comforting to have a son-in-law as devoted to the farm as Rob Craigallan.

'My love,' Cornelius said to his wife that evening, 'have you given any more thought to Luisa's marriage?'

Dorothea signalled to the housemaid to take out the dessert plates. She poured the coffee. 'I'm waiting for Bernard to make the offer officially,' she said. 'The engagement party can be held as soon as the contracts are signed.'

'Dorothea, would it vex you very much if Luisa didn't marry Bernard?'

She handed him his coffee. 'Not Bernard? Who, then? It's true, I've heard Stettinius is in some slight trouble with railroad investments –'

'Ah, he'll come to no harm with that,' Cornelius said. 'Money invested in railroad track is like money in the bank. No, no, I've nothing against the Stettinius family. It's only that Luisa tells me she doesn't like Bernard.'

'Doesn't like him? What's wrong with him?'

'Well, my treasure, he is rather unattractive . . .'

Dorothea thought of the husband to whom she herself had gone. More than twenty years her senior, already fat and short-sighted, wheezing with exhaustion even on their wedding night . . .

'There's nothing wrong with Bernard,' she said. 'I'll speak to Luisa.'

'I already spoke to her – this afternoon. She's quite set against Bernard.'

'You've spoken to her about it? My heart, that is the mother's place, surely.'

'I agree, Dorothea. But it was brought to my attention as being urgent, so I sent for her. Luisa will most decidedly not take Bernard.'

Now that really is too bad, thought Dorothea. I give her her head with foolish day-dreaming for a while, and she lets it run away with her. Surely she's always understood that in the end it has to be Bernard or someone of his standing.

'What do you mean, urgent?' she asked.

'Someone rather unexpected asked for Luisa this afternoon. I had to speak to her because of that.'

'Someone unexpected? Who do you mean, husband?' But already the truth had dawned on her. She sat back in her high-backed chair, so shaken that her trembling hand sent black coffee all over the snowy tablecloth.

'Robert Craigallan came to my office and said he and Luisa wished to marry. Apparently they've talked it all through. I was taken aback, my pearl. You've been somewhat remiss in allowing the situation to develop.'

'What?' she gasped. She was incapable of defending herself against the charge of neglect, incapable of speech. That they should *dare* . . . !

'It seems it's serious. I have spoken to both the young people and they are utterly determined. Luisa says she'll take no one except Rob, and Rob says he wants Luisa.'

'Wants? Wants? How dare he use such a word –?'

'Well, my own one, they are in love, I believe.'

She sprang up. 'Don't talk such rubbish! Love? I won't have it!'

Cornelius wasn't surprised at her anger. It was to be expected in a good mother who had brought up her daughter to make a good match. There was no denying, Rob didn't measure up to what his Dorothea expected for Luisa. He would have to talk her into it.

'My angel, let us discuss it,' he began. 'In a way, it might not be a bad scheme. He would be a good husband in many ways. I think he would give us better grandchildren than Bernard Stettinius –'

'Be quiet!' she screamed. She reached over, grasped his shoulder, and actually tried to shake him. 'Don't talk like that! I won't have it!'

'But, Dorothea –' He began to stumble to his feet, frightened by the passion she was showing.

'No, no! It can't be! I won't allow it! Luisa will never marry that man! No, never, never!'

'My love, my love! Pray, calm down. I didn't know you had your heart so much set on the match with Bernard. All right, all right. I'll tell them they must put the idea from them –'

'He must go!' Dorothea cried. 'I won't have him in this house! Send him away! Cornelius, promise me you'll send him away?'

'But, Dorothea, that would hardly be fair. He's done nothing wrong –'

'Done nothing wrong?'

'Except fall in love with Luisa –'

'He's not in love with Luisa!'

'But he is. He told me so.'

'I tell you, he's only after her money –'

'No, no. I think he's a good young man –'

'Oh, you're such a *fool*, Cornelius!' She spat the words at him. But she saw she'd gone too far when his puffy face creased in pain and surprise. She knelt beside his chair. 'Promise you'll get rid of him, husband,' she begged. 'I feel in my bones that he is not being honest with you over Luisa. I agree, she's moony over him at the moment, but it will pass, and as for *him* . . . he's being greedy, that's all. Send him away.'

Shaken, Cornelius nodded. Anything to restore the habitual tranquillity of his house. He couldn't bear to see his wife so upset.

When Rob was sent for, he feared the worst. The message came via the skinny housemaid Senta, who looked scared. Luisa had been got out of the way, being taken by her mother to spend the day with neighbours.

'I'm afraid, my boy,' said Cornelius, 'that the answer to your request is no. My wife is totally against it.'

'She'd come round in time, sir –'

Cornelius shook his head. The searing scene of last night was clear in his mind. Nothing he'd ever seen before had been like Dorothea's passion against the idea of the marriage. What a devoted mother she was, to feel so strongly about her daughter's good!

'She has asked me to dismiss you. I hate to see you go, Rob, for you've taken on the foreman's role with great success – although I didn't feel quite confident when first I let Dorothea put you in the job. Well, well . . . perhaps it's time for you to move on. I've nothing against you, you understand. I'll give you a good character. But I don't think you'll get another foreman's job anywhere in this neighbourhood – you're a mite too young, younker.'

Rob heard him out in silence. He knew it was useless to argue or plead. 'Does Luisa know?' he asked.

'No, she'll hear of this when she comes back this evening.'

'I think you might have let me say goodbye to her, sir.'

'No, boy. It's over and you might as well get used to the idea.' Cornelius looked sympathetically from behind his silver-rimmed glasses. 'God go with you, Rob. I'll have your money ready for you by midday. You can eat with us as usual before you leave.'

Morag was beside herself when Rob sought her out to tell her. 'Leaving? But why? What's happened?'

'It's not worth discussing. Van Huten has dismissed me.'

'Why?' She drew in a breath. 'Is it something to do with . . . Mrs van Huten? She was very upset this morning, I felt.'

'No, it's nothing to do with Mrs van Huten.'

'Then . . . is it Luisa?'

'It's nothing do with you,' Rob said roughly. 'I'm going, and there's an end of it.'

'But that's not the end of it!' she exclaimed. 'I must go too –'

'Nonsense! Why should you? You've a good place here –'

'But I can't let you go without me, Rob –'

'Why not? Brother and sister don't have to work in the same place.'

'But I can't stay here without you –'

'Of course you can. Good heavens, Morag, be practical! What

good does it do if we both lose our jobs?'

'I'll find something else –'

'There's no need. You stay here, where you're snug and safe –'

'But I can't be happy here if you're gone –'

'Listen, be sensible! You talk as if I'm going to the other end of the world! I'm only going to Albany – it's only fourteen miles!'

'To Albany?' she echoed, seized by a vague apprehension.

'You remember the carter who gave us a lift from Morrisonia? He was headed for Albany. There are lots of grain dealers there, chandlers and the like – dealing on the Erie Canal. I'll get a job there, I'm sure of it. I'll not be far off.'

'Oh, Rob!'

'I'll write to you,' he said. 'Come on now, dry your eyes and be a good girl. If you let Mrs van Huten see how upset you are, she'll start asking questions. There's no need to tell her my plans, by the way.'

Morag had no arguments to use against him. He seemed to have it all worked out. She was a little surprised at how calmly he took it all. To lose his job for no good reason, to part from Morag – she'd have thought it would distress him more.

She had no idea that Rob had half foreseen this already. He had even sounded out one of the waggoners who called at the farm about a possible post in Albany.

Luisa would be sent post haste back to school there, he was sure. He judged aright. Miss van Huten was back under the care of Miss Anhalt by the following day. Dorothea brought her personally, with dire warnings to the schoolmistress to guard her daughter with her life.

Miss Anhalt tried to do this. But, as the old saying goes, love will find a way. And Luisa was in love. The first time she saw Rob in the streets as the girls walked in crocodile to the library, she started with surprise, but recovered at once. Without being noticed, she accepted the note he had prepared.

Easter that year was mid April. The graduation ceremonies of the Anhalt Academy were to be in June. Before that date, Luisa slipped out of the school and went with Rob to her father's farm. They drove there in a hired carriage, sitting well back so that no one saw them until they alighted at the door.

Senta came stumbling into Mr van Huten's office with the news. 'Sir, sir – Miss Luisa's here –'

'Luisa? But she's not due until after the –'

'And Rob Craigallan is with her, sir.'

'What?'

'He says . . . he says he must speak to you, sir.'

Cornelius got up, but sat down again, his face suffused with sudden blood. 'Show . . . show them in,' he gasped.

The young pair came in, shoulder to shoulder but not touching. They looked tense but somehow triumphant.

'Well?' croaked Cornelius. He had meant to thunder in disapproval, but his breath seemed to have gone from him.

'Mr van Huten, I've come to tell you that your daughter is expecting a baby – my baby – and to ask for your permission to marry her.'

Cornelius van Huten leaned back in his chair. 'Dear God,' he panted.

His first thought was, 'What will Dorothea say?'

9

ROB CRAIGALLAN'S DEPARTURE FROM van Huten's Farm hadn't of course gone by without remark. Julius had enough interest in him to want to know why he had gone.

His father gave him an explanation, joined with an urgent request that he would keep it to himself. Julius saw no reason to be discreet; the dismissal of the foreman for daring to aspire to his sister's hand made a good story. Within a day or two he'd told it to his friends and it immediately filtered through to their servants and thence to the van Huten farm staff.

'You got to admit, he got more sass than that Pierre Dubec,' Nellie the cook said when she heard of it. 'Dubec, when he fall out of favour, he just pack up and go. But your brother at least try for a consolation prize!'

'I don't know what you mean,' Morag said, looking down.

'Yes you do, honey. Ev'body knew what was going on with the missus. You just don't want to admit it because he's your kin. I don't know why you so down about it. He couldn't help it if the missus took a fancy to him.'

'He isn't –'

'What?'

Morag glanced about, remembering that she wasn't the only one in the kitchen with Nellie. She'd been about to blurt out that Rob wasn't her brother. 'Nothing,' she mumbled.

'If I was Miss Luisa,' said Senta the housemaid, 'I'd be crying my eyes out now.'

'Yeah, I reckon she'll be soaking her pillow consid'able,' Nellie agreed, returning her attention to the bread dough. 'But a few days back in Albany'll cure her.'

'You think she'll get over it quick? By golly,' said Senta, 'I wouldn't get over it quick! That Rob . . . he make a good husband, I think! But if the Pappa and the Mamma don't approve, it's not good.'

'I think it's all a story that Mr Julius has invented,' Morag said, her head bent over the needlework in her lap. 'I don't think Rob is interested in Miss Luisa.'

'He tell you that?'

Morag made no reply. She tried not to take part in the gossip of the other farm staff: her own position was so dishonest that she couldn't bear to hear discussion of private feelings or affairs.

'He got to say that,' Nellie remarked, pushing and pulling at the dough. 'He got to make out he ain't put out by losing his throw of the dice. He a proud man, your brother.'

'Where's he gone, Morag?' Senta asked.

'He said he'd write when he was settled.'

'I reckon he should go a long way off. By golly, a fellow like that can get a good job anywhere pretty easy.'

'So long as the farmer ain't got no pretty little daughter,' Nellie said, laughing.

'Don't talk like that!' Morag cried, stung.

'What's the matter? Don't you know you got a handsome, comin'-on brother?'

Morag got up, gathering the folds of the gown into her arms, and fled. Nellie glanced at Senta and raised her scanty eyebrows. 'She too bound up in that brother of hers,' she opined. 'She oughta find herself a good man and git married pretty soon or she'll spend the res' of her days being auntie to his chillun . . .'

Now Rob's visit with Luisa set the whole household into a hubbub. Senta came into the kitchen to report it, trembling with excitement. 'He brought Miss Luisa *with* him! By jimbo, I think that's pretty dam' rash!'

Nellie, stirring a sauce over the stove, looked round for a moment. 'I wonder if Morag knew he was comin'?'

'*I* wonder what's going on in that study!' Senta remarked.

The scene there was certainly interesting. After the first announcement of the reason for their visit, Luisa burst into tears and collapsed on the nearest chair. Her father, always an easy target for weeping women, stumbled to her side.

'There, there,' he said, patting her clumsily on her shoulder, 'don't cry. I'm not going to lecture you. You've been a bad girl, it's true, but it's too late to tell you that.'

'Oh, Papa!' wailed Luisa.

'Mr van Huten, may I speak to you alone?'

'Eh?' Cornelius said above the noisy sobs of his daughter.

'I want to discuss the situation with you, and Luisa is in no condition . . .'

'Oh . . . Yes . . . You're right . . . Luisa, my love, I think you had better go up to your room and lie down. Now Luisa, come along – stop crying. Come now.' Cornelius rang the bell, which was answered with extraordinary promptness by Senta, to whom he confided his daughter. 'See her to her room. Get her some sal volatile. Make sure she lies down. Perhaps you'd better draw the shades to keep out the sunlight. There, there, daughter, there there . . .'

Senta, hopeful of learning what it was all about, put an arm round Luisa and guided her, still weeping, to the door. But Luisa had been well-schooled by Rob before they set out. He had told her to say nothing until he gave her her cue, and she had vowed to obey him.

When the door closed, Cornelius went slowly back to his chair behind the desk. He had been working on the accounts of the farm; he pushed them aside aimlessly. He was angry over what had happened and yet, curiously, it didn't seem worth being too angry. Rob loved Luisa and Luisa loved Rob. But for the opposition of her mother, Luisa might by now have been a bride, and the coming baby would have been a longed-for addition to the family.

Cornelius felt very old as he looked up at the tall young man in his study. 'Well, so what do you want to say to me?' he inquired in an exhausted voice. 'Are you going to throw yourself on my mercy?'

'That hardly seems necessary, sir,' Rob said. 'All I want is your permission to marry Luisa. The baby is mine – no one can deny that. But Luisa is still a minor. Everything will be easier if we have your permission.'

'Ah-hah,' Cornelius said, taking off his spectacles and rubbing his eyes. 'And you expect the dowry, too, I suppose?'

'No, sir. All I want is Luisa.'

The old man studied him. It might actually be true. There was an angle of the chin, a light in the eye, that made him look very high-minded. But long experience of men had made Cornelius slow to think they acted from high-minded motives very often.

Still, these two young ones were in love. And when a man's in love, he does silly things . . .

'I ask you to think back to the first time I spoke of this to you,' Rob went on, pressing his advantage. 'You seemed to have no serious objections.'

'But my wife was very much against it,' he countered, shaking his head.

'Your wife can hardly object now,' Rob said.

Cornelius had a feeling that she could. 'We had better let her know what has happened,' he said, stifling a shiver of apprehension. 'She's visiting the parson's wife. I'll send a message to her.'

By the time Dorothea arrived a strange alliance had formed between the two men. Cornelius wanted this scandal hushed up as quickly as possible and to him it was obvious that the only way to do it was to marry off the youngsters at once. Rob seemed totally honourable, eager to make good the damage to Luisa's reputation. Cornelius had even gone so far as to offer him a glass of brandy.

When Dorothea came in, she stopped dead on seeing Rob. 'What is he doing here?' she demanded.

'My dear, he's come on a very serious matter,' Cornelius began.

Dorothea swept across the room to knock the glass out of Rob's hand. 'Get out!' she cried. 'Get out of this house!'

'My love!' exclaimed Cornelius. 'Wait, wait! You don't know the story –'

'I have no interest in anything he is concerned in,' she said. She had opened the door and was standing by it, waiting for Rob to pass her on his way out. She looked as if she might spit at him when he did so.

'You *must* have an interest in this,' Cornelius said. 'It's about Luisa.'

'Luisa?'

'Wife, our daughter is going to have a baby.'

Dorothea turned slowly to stare at Cornelius. She drew in a ragged breath. 'The silly little bitch,' she breathed.

'*Dorothea!*' Cornelius was more shocked by that phrase than by anything else he had heard today. Dorothea had always been so sweet and happy and comfortable. To use such a word! And of her own daughter!

Rob looked from one to the other. It had suited him to let Cornelius do his talking for him, but now he took up his own cause.

'Mrs van Huten, to make everything right it's necessary that Luisa and I get married –'

'No!' It was a gasp of denial. 'No, I won't have it!'

'Dear heart,' Cornelius intervened, 'it really must be so. Otherwise we'll all be shamed.'

'No!'

'But what would you have? Do you want Luisa to be held up to public scorn?'

'No,' Dorothea said, gathering her wits, 'not that, of course. We don't want a disgrace for everybody to snigger about. She's got to be married, I agree, but there's no need for her to marry this blackguard. I can still find her a good match –'

'With whom, for the love of heaven?'

'Bernard Stettinius – who else?'

'But Dorothea, she's expecting a baby!'

'Who's to know that unless we tell them?' She glared at Rob. 'How far on is she?'

'Two months.'

Her mouth went thin. 'You didn't waste any time, did you?'

'Mrs van Huten, it didn't happen like that. Luisa was desperately unhappy, she turned to me . . .'

'Spare us the sentimental rubbish,' she said. 'If you wanted to make sure you got her hand, you should have waited until the baby was more in evidence. At the moment we can still retrieve the situation. Bernard need never know.'

'But he will know,' Rob said.

'Nonsense! Many a man has accepted a seven months baby as his own –'

'Not this time,' Rob persisted. 'Bernard Stettinius won't sign the contract with Luisa when he knows she's pregnant –'

'Do you think I'm going to announce the news to him the moment he steps in at the door?'

'No. But Luisa will.'

Dorothea gave a gasp of dismay. After that, silence held the room in thrall for several seconds. 'She wouldn't do that,' Dorothea said. But her voice held no certainty.

'She would. You don't understand, Mrs van Huten. Luisa and I are in love and want to be married. Luisa doesn't want any other husband. If you try to marry her off to anyone else, she'll prevent it by speaking out.'

'Dear heaven,' breathed Cornelius.

'You can imagine how difficult it would be to keep the disgrace a secret after that,' Rob ended.

'Yes. Yes! Oh, my treasure, listen to what he's saying! We must at all costs avoid a situation like that! Dorothea, after all . . .! He is the baby's father. It is only right that she should marry him.'

'No!'

'Wife, I don't understand you.' For once, some authority was coming into his tone as he addressed her. 'You want to make a public show of Luisa? For what? To fit in with your decision not to have Rob Craigallan in the family? That's carrying dislike too far, in God's name. Besides, I don't know why you've taken so much against the boy –'

'Oh, you don't understand!'

'No, I don't. What I understand is that these two must be very much in love to go to such lengths to be married. I have to say that though I don't approve, I see their point of view.'

'Don't give in, husband!' begged Dorothea. 'Don't, don't – you're making a terrible mistake! You don't know him! He thinks only of himself –'

'Your feelings as a mother are carrying you away,' Rob interrupted. His manner was a nice balance between hurt and forgiveness. He knew now that he was going to win this battle because Cornelius was on his side, and Cornelius was, in the end, master of the household. It was just as well to state the positions clearly now, for the future. 'I will be a good son-in-law to you, Mrs van Huten,' he said in a quiet tone. 'You will never have cause to complain of me. Once Luisa and I are married I will be a model husband.'

Dorothea glared at him. Then, with a sob of defeat, she wheeled about and rushed out of the room, to run upstairs and throw herself on her bed in a storm of tears.

The plans for the wedding were announced next day. It was to take place at the nearby church in the following week. Invitations were sent out. Nellie began to design the wedding cake.

Morag was set to the making of Luisa's wedding dress. The first shock of the news passed without anyone noticing how it had affected her. The whole household was taken up with its own excitement, far too busy and intrigued with the principals to look at the linenmaid. Morag learned the news from the dairymaid, Nancy, in the late afternoon of the day Luisa came home.

'You heard the latest?' Nancy remarked, thumping down a brimming pail of milk on the stone floor. 'I just heard from Senta. Miss Luisa's back – *with her fiancé.*'

'She's engaged?'

'Short engagement. Senta says Nellie's been told to get the food ready for next week. Parson Bletchley has been asked to take the ceremony, Senta says Thursday.'

'Who is Miss Luisa marrying?' Morag asked, catching hold of the edge of the dairy table. Something told her she already knew the answer.

'Ah, you're a sly one!' Nancy laughed. 'It's going to make a big difference to you, ain't it? They won't be able to pay you maid's wages once you're kinfolk. What'll you do – ask for an allowance?'

'No,' Morag said. 'No, I shan't . . . ask for anything.'

She got out of the dairy with the pitcher of milk she'd come for. She'd spent most of the afternoon sewing in the shade of the apple trees in the orchard. For her, the drama of the day had gone by unknown until now.

She went up to the dormitory room above the dairy, carefully carrying the milk. She set it down on the little bedside cupboard that held her few possessions. She stood there for a long time, gazing blankly out of the dormer window.

That night she saw a light again in the room given over to the farm foreman. She got out of bed, dressed quickly, and crept across the cobbled yard. She knocked on the door.

Rob opened it. He drew back to let her come in. 'I was expecting you,' he sighed.

'Rob, what does it mean?' she burst out. 'They say you're marrying Luisa!'

'It's quite true.'

'But . . . you told me she meant nothing to you. You said she was as stupid as her mother!'

He had an impulse to tell her to mind her own business. What right had she to come here demanding explanations? But in the lamplight she looked so young and vulnerable. Why hurt her when it wasn't necessary?

'Sit down, Morag,' he said. 'I'll tell you all about it.'

His story was convincing. In Albany, he'd found a job as he had hoped. Luisa saw him one day while she was out walking with the other students of the Academy. From that moment she sought him out constantly. Miss Anhalt found out and made an issue of it. Her reputation compromised, Luisa ran away.

'She turned up at my lodgings one night,' he narrated. 'She was in a terrible state – crying and carrying on. I couldn't turn her away, Morag. And next morning Miss Anhalt arrived and took it for granted that we'd spent the night together.'

Morag sat with her head bent, listening to the story. It sounded possible. Luisa was headstrong and selfish, perfectly capable of behaving just as Rob had described.

'To hush up the scandal, Mr van Huten has begged me to marry her,' he ended. 'Nobody else will have her once the gossip gets out about what she did. I can't turn my back on her, Morag. She loves me – she's ruined her reputation for me.'

'But Rob – what about us?'

He leaned over her and took one of her hands. 'That's over, Morag,' he said. 'You must see that I've got to do the decent thing by Luisa.'

'No! I don't see that!' she cried. 'Luisa can look after herself. She has rich parents and plenty of friends! Things will settle down; she'll live down her foolish actions. Why should you have to marry a girl you don't care about just to preserve her reputation?'

Rob was vexed. He'd thought she'd fall for the romantic tale at once. He straightened, moving away to stand tall and upright. 'I've given my word,' he said.

'Rob . . . you don't love her.'

'No.'

'Then how can you? How can you marry someone you don't love?'

'Lots of people do that, Morag. You and I – we were different, we were everything to each other for a while. But perhaps it was too much to expect from life.' He paused. He knew she suffered from this strange sense of guilt for what she had done. 'Perhaps you and I are being punished,' he murmured. 'Perhaps that's why we can't ever be together now.'

She huddled in upon herself. There was a frightening truth in what he was saying. Her puritanical upbringing, the stern morality of the local parson's sermons every Sunday, reinforced her feeling that she might be beyond redemption because of what she had done – her love for Rob, the lie she was living as his 'sister'.

He saw he had put an end to her protests. He pressed the point. 'You won't cause any trouble, Morag? Luisa has been through enough.'

'No, I won't cause trouble, Rob. I'll leave as soon as I can find somewhere else to go.'

'No!' To his own surprise, he was stricken at the thought. 'No, don't do that, Morag. After all, why should you?'

'Do you think I could stay here and watch you and Luisa?' she asked bitterly.

'Don't be headstrong, Morag. You know you're delicate. You might not be so fit and well if you went somewhere else. This is an easy place for you here –'

'*Easy*?'

'Promise not go until I've had time to talk it over with you,' he urged. For some reason, he was sure he'd be able to keep her by him at van Huten's.

Next day, when Dorothea sent for her and ordered her brusquely to discuss the wedding dress with Luisa, Morag was able to listen without an outcry. She went paler, but Dorothea was too wrapped up in her own bitterness to see that.

The wedding was attended by an inquisitive crowd, but there was no proof that anything had forced the sudden ceremony. Cornelius had advanced a sum of money for Rob to buy clothes; he seemed a total stranger to Morag as he stood at the plain altar in his frock coat and high collar. Luisa in her gown of pure white taffeta edged with ruched satin was as radiant as a bride should be. The dress had been made by Morag in six days of constant work, from sun-up to sundown. Little pinpoints of red here and there showed where she had pricked her finger and drawn blood, as tears blinded her eyes.

The wedding breakfast at the farm was sumptuous. Cornelius had decreed that his hospitality was not to seem stinted by any dislike of the marriage. Everyone got drunk enough to feel kindly disposed towards this ill-matched young couple. Even Julius, though he was prevented from attending the races at Albany, enjoyed himself.

'Good ol' Luisa!' he said, kissing her with patronising affection. 'Always thought you'd end up the wife of some stuffy old attorney . . . Well, well, at least you've done me a favour. Rob can take on all that boring stuff about the farm.'

Rob was only too willing. He could hardly wait to get the wedding guests out of the way so as to deal with the haymaking. The grass was tall already, and the summer thunderstorms would soon be here smashing it down, if he didn't get the men out on the meadows.

Cornelius was happy to let him get things going. The wedding celebrations had tired him. He seemed to have such difficulty in getting his breath these days, and this strange pain down his left arm came to him when he least wanted it. It wasn't rheumatics. It was different – keener, more menacing.

Perhaps God had sent him this strong young farmer to help him as his health deteriorated. Perhaps it had always been intended that his daughter should marry someone with less in the way of money and position yet ideally suited to the task of keeping van Huten's Farm in its place at the forefront of agriculture.

Julius bequeathed to Rob a whole roomful of books, stacked in shelves around his bedroom. 'Papa fondly imagined that if he bought me every book ever written about farming, I'd know more than he did,' he remarked with ironic amusement. 'If he only knew, I never opened one of 'em. Help yourself, Rob. You seem interested in that kind of rubbish.'

Rob took him at his word. He had all the books transported to the room by the stables, which he still used as an office. His main quarters in the house were the bedroom he shared with Luisa, and the study. Here he found all Cornelius's records of the farm work, painstakingly kept over fifty years, ever since Cornelius began to help his own father.

Here was a store of knowledge that couldn't be gained from books. Here was an account of climate, crop, soil condition, blight and insect pest, farming method. Night after night Rob pored over it, so much so that Luisa pouted and said she might as well not have married at all.

In any case, she had temporarily lost any appeal she had for him. She ate too much during her pregnancy on the grounds that she was eating for two, though no baby could be expected to want a diet of chocolate cake, cream shortcake, raisin cookies, rum punch, and other richnesses. The food went to form extra flesh, and as the baby made its presence known, Luisa rapidly grew ungainly and gross.

Rob found his interest in the farm. The wheat was soon ready to be harvested. The machinery was made ready. Neighbouring farmers came asking what the terms would be for the header team this year. Rob and Cornelius made a schedule of work. Harvest began, six weeks this year, six weeks of exhausting labour. Then came threshing, and after that, the transport of the wheat to the town for sale to the merchants.

This was all new to Rob. So far he had only been involved in the production of the crop. It was an eye-opener to him to see the kind of money involved in the buying and selling.

Cornelius was too unwell to get much enjoyment out of the bargaining this year. In former times this had been a big event for him – two or three days in Albany, chaffering and arguing, until his fine wheat was sold to the highest bidder among the dealers. It then went by means of the Erie Canal to the coast, at which point it was lost sight of as far as the farmers were concerned.

The wheat of New York State was soft wheat, spring sown, yielding plentiful crops on the heavy chocolate clay of the area. It was not unlike the wheat grown in Europe, so it was in demand there because, so it seemed. Europe couldn't grow enough for its own needs. Rob was amazed by all this: back home in Glen Bairach, men had grown grain for their own immediate use – to feed their livestock and, if there was a surplus, to sell to the local miller. The great wagons of grain reaching Albany and transferred in a gleaming golden spate to the barges of the Erie made something beat like a drum inside his chest. This was a harvest such as he had never dreamed of. It was transformed into a river of gold. It had strength, force. It gave life meaning.

As soon as the crop was gone and the harvest-home parties were over, it was time to get the plough-teams out. Experience in Scotland had taught him always to be beforehand with the work, for ground opened up to the frost was far easier to work in the spring; the tilling was more rewarding. All through the fall Rob walked and rode around van Huten's land, supervising the readying of the ground for the spring sowing. It was good to be ready to get the seed in as soon as the seeder could go on the earth – that way, the cold soil encouraged the wheat to 'tiller', to form many branching roots so as to produce many stems from one seed.

Thanksgiving came. Rob realised with a shock that he had been scarcely more than a year at van Huten's. Last Thanksgiving, he had danced for the first time with Luisa. This year she was hardly in a fit state for dancing, he thought, eyeing her across the barn. She sat, draped in shawls, looking like a great many-coloured tent. Dorothea was doing a sedate polka with Walter Waldmann – she almost looked younger than her own daughter.

She caught Rob's eye upon her and flashed him a glance of dislike. Since the wedding she had scarcely exchanged a single word with him. She had concentrated upon the role of devoted wife and nursemaid to Cornelius, which suited her well enough for the time being. She took little interest in her daughter's pregnancy. It had come to her with something of a pang that she didn't really like her daughter much, and never had.

In January, Luisa's baby was born – a fine healthy boy, named Cornelius in honour of his grandfather. The event gave satisfaction to the neighbourhood, who had done some counting and understood now the reason for the sudden June wedding. No one of course mentioned such things in the messages of congratulation that poured in.

Rob stared down at the baby with a strange feeling. It was because of this child that he was where he was. Without him, Rob Craigallan would still be a day labourer in a grain store in Albany. The little round face, the closed fists, the struggling legs were the result of his determination to direct the fate of van Huten's farm, to grow the acres of golden grain that gave the farm its importance. This little fellow had brought him a great deal in his tiny fists.

But the baby also lost Rob something. The birth of Cornelius brought about the departure of Morag. She, too, now understood the need for the June wedding.

She had reached the end of her tether. She was leaving van Huten's.

[153]

10

HER DECISION TO GO surprised the servants, with whom she still spent most of her time although now, as 'sister' of the son-in-law of the house, she might have claimed an upper status.

'Why you goin' *now*?' Nellie demanded. 'It the worst time of year, snow ev'where, and Boston got mighty cold winds, I hear.'

'My new employer needs me now,' Morag said, giving her attention to putting away cooking equipment.

'You been thinking of this all along, then,' Nellie said. She gave a little considering nod of the head. 'You been mighty unhappy a long time, it seems like.'

'I'm not unhappy, Nellie. It's just that it's time to make a change.'

'I don't see why –'

'It's best, Nellie. Miss Luisa is talking as if she thinks I might take on little Cornelius for her, like a kind of nurserymaid. That was my first job in New York, you see. She thinks I've got experience. And I don't want to do that.'

'But why not? You'd be comf'able, the Lord knows, and the little fella ain't no trouble. I never did see such a healthy boy.'

Morag shook her head. Everything was urging her to the decision to go. The free chit-chat among the servants about the shortness of Luisa's pregnancy, the candid acceptance that she'd had to get married, the almost admiring view of Rob's handling of the van Huten family – all of those had done away with her naive

[154]

belief in Rob's total honesty. Added to that was the way Luisa was trying to involve her in the bringing up of little Cornelius: while she'd been able to stay away from the family, hiding herself among the servants, it had been just possible to go on living in the same household with the young married couple.

But if once she was in continual daily contact – if she had to sit down to meals with them, get up at night to tend the baby in the room next to their bedroom – no, it was beyond her strength. Disillusioned, wearied by the struggle to keep her feelings to herself, she had decided during December to begin looking in the newspapers for a new place. With the turn of the year she began writing after them; she asked Cornelius van Huten for a reference which he, unwillingly, provided.

Her new post was as maid-companion in the household of a retired sea-captain in Boston. Captain Kauffman's wife had been stricken by some mysterious disease which progressively deprived her of the use of her limbs. He had advertised for a 'well-educated young woman, capable of some housework but able to fit it with conversation and pastimes of an invalid.'

Many young women had applied for the post, but two things had persuaded Captain Kauffman that Morag McGarth Craigallan was the ideal applicant. First, her letter; beautifully penned in faultless spelling and grammar, well expressed – an exact mixture of respect and self-confidence. The other was the reference from Mr van Huten, a name known to the captain; the farmer spoke of Morag in terms of satisfaction and affection almost. It also came to Kauffman's ears that the young woman was sister to Luisa van Huten's husband, although she herself made no mention of that point. He admired her for that. She wished to stand or fall by her own abilities.

He had written back to her in cordial terms. She would probably have accepted the job in any case, but three weeks' contact with the new baby had warned her that she must get away before she fell in love with him. Once he had wound himself around her heart, she would be bound to him for ever.

Luisa was vexed when she heard the news. 'But Morag–! I don't understand you! I was relying on you to take Cornelius off my hands.'

'I'm sorry if it puts your plans out,' she replied, hiding a frown at Luisa's phrase 'off my hands'. 'Perhaps I should have discussed it with you. I've had it in mind for some time to make a move.'

'But why?' Luisa couldn't understand it. Why should Rob's sister suddenly up and go? Just when she was about to be at her most useful?

'I . . . I think I'd like to try living in a town,' Morag said. 'Until I came here, I'd never lived so far out of town.'

'Well, I know what you mean,' sighed Luisa. 'It *is* dull here, heaven knows. I miss the pleasures of Albany myself . . . But I never thought of you as being a pleasure-seeker.'

'It's not the pleasures, Luisa. It's just that . . . I'm not used to the farming life.'

'What? But you and Rob were born and brought up on a farm.'

'Oh . . . yes . . . but not a farm like this.' How careful one had to be to keep the lie going! She must indeed get away. She couldn't go on in this web of lies any longer. She said with firmness: 'It's time I made a life of my own and stopped relying on Rob. I know it's inconvenient to you, Luisa, but you'll find a nursery helper without trouble, I'm sure.'

Luisa wasn't pleased to hear her real views on Morag's role dragged into the open. Sometimes this girl would come out with simple remarks that were very prickly. And sometimes Luisa had felt her eyes upon her, examining her conduct in a way she found uncomfortable. Perhaps it was as well she was leaving. Having relatives permanently in the house wasn't always a good idea.

Rob heard the news from his wife. He reaction to it astounded Luisa.

'Going? What the devil do you mean, she's going?'

'Goodness, don't shout at me, darling. Morag's going. She told me so this morning, when we'd bathed Baby.'

'Going? She can't go!'

'What do you mean, she can't? How can you stop her?'

'I'll damn soon change her mind!' He stalked out, leaving his mid-morning coffee undrunk on the table. He was in a fury. How could she be so underhanded? To plan all this, and get so far with it, keeping it a secret? It was so unlike Morag.

He found her in the big linen cupboard on the uppermost floor of the old house. It was a walk-in closet, lit by a small dormer window, and it was the nearest thing to a room of her own that Morag had at van Huten's. He came in, closing the door behind him. They had to stand close because there was scant room between the broad shelves laden with folded, ironed sheets scented with verbena.

'Now,' he said, taking her wrist in an angry grip, 'what is all this?'

'What, Rob?'

'Don't play the innocent. Luisa tells me you're talking about leaving.'

'Yes,' she said, looking at him with a direct gaze. 'It's all arranged. I wrote to Captain Kauffman yesterday, accepting his offer.'

"Captain Kauffman? Who the hell is he?"

She explained about the captain and his wife, and the advertisement she had answered. 'The salary's quite good – the captain calls it my "emolument",' she said with some faint amusement. 'I think he's rather an academic kind of man. I'm quite looking forward to it.'

'Morag!' He was aghast. She really wanted to go.

'I'm taking up the appointment at the end of the month. Nellie says it's a bad time for travelling, but I can go by train once I get to Albany.'

'I forbid it,' he said.

She looked away. It seemed to him that she even smiled a little. 'You can't,' she said. 'You have no authority over me, Rob. Don't forget, you aren't really my brother.'

'But everyone believes I am, and if I openly forbid this, you'll have to obey –'

'Don't do it,' she warned. 'If you do, I'll come out into the open and confess that we're not brother and sister.'

His grip on her wrist tightened. 'Morag, don't defy me!'

'It's not defiance. It's sheer weariness. I can't go on like this. It's all right for you –' and she let some of her bitterness show in her voice – 'you're the master of the house or almost so, you're a successful farmer, you're the father of a fine boy. But what is there here for me? Am I to live out the rest of my life watching you with your wife? Has it really never occurred to you that I found it . . . distasteful?'

'Oh, I know you've been made unhappy by it,' he said, although for weeks he hadn't given it a thought. 'But I always intended to make some arrangement for you –'

'What? Just tell me what, Rob?'

He was momentarily silenced. He let go his grip upon her and turned away a little. 'You wouldn't really go away and leave me, Morag?'

'That's exactly what I'm going to do.'

'But why did you do it without talking to me about it? That's not like you, Morag. I never thought you'd be deceitful.'

'What good would it have done to talk about it? You'd have said the things you've just said. But none of it would have made any difference to the fact that I'm here under false pretences, forced to look as if I feel nothing for you except sisterly affection. It's too much for me, Rob. And besides, it's wrong, totally, utterly wrong.'

'I don't see anything wrong in it,' he objected. 'We each live our own life –'

'Don't you understand?' she burst out. 'You live your life – mine is nothing! One day I'd be driven too far and blurt it all out – from exhaustion, from jealousy, from sheer desperation! I don't want that to happen. Despite everything, I don't want to wreck things for you, Rob.'

'But you went along with it at the outset –'

'I'd no idea then that you were going to marry Luisa! At first I thought the deception was wrong but not important. Now I think it's so important that it obsesses me – it' never out of my thoughts that I love you and you're married to Luisa –'

'Look, don't be too considerate of Luisa. She's happy enough –'

'But I am not!' She laid her hand on his shoulder and almost shook him. 'Don't you see? I'm thinking of myself! I know I can't survive another year like the one I've just lived through. I'll either go mad or do something unthinkable. So I'm going. I'm leaving on the twenty-eighth. Next time I go into Albany with Mrs van Huten I'll arrange about the train ticket.'

He was taken aback by the strength of her attitude. Until now she'd always been compliant, soft, yielding. He'd thought it was her nature, but he saw now that her love for him had made her so tractable. It was that same love that had turned her to steel.

The day of her departure was a Monday, an inconvenient day on the farm because, after the lull of Sunday, work had to be re-started. The frost was still too hard for much to be done on the land, so Rob had the men working on maintenance, on clearing the rubbish from the barns, making rope, greasing axles, oiling leathers.

Her luggage was brought down and put in the old Clarence carriage that Cornelius had bought to gratify Dorothea when he married her twenty-three years ago. The household was assembled under the porch to say goodbye, all except Dorothea who was annoyed at losing this good, useful dressmaker.

Cornelius van Huten kissed her kindly. 'I'm sorry you're going,' he wheezed. 'Come back and visit us often.'

'Yes, of course,' she said, although she knew she never would.

'Goodbye,' Julius van Huten said, shaking hands. 'I may drop in on you now and again. I like Boston.'

'I should always be pleased to see you,' she lied. She had never cared for Julius.

'Goodbye, sister,' Luisa said, kissing her on the cheek. She took the baby from Senta and waved one of his fat little fists for him. 'Goodbye, Aunt Morag.'

'Goodbye,' Morag said. She bowed and nodded to the rest of the servants, with a special smile to Nellie who had always been kind to her.

She got into the carriage. Rob climbed in after her and pulled the yellow-varnished door shut. The coachman – the Dane Denstadt – took off the brake and clucked at the horse. The carriage rolled forward over the frosted ground.

On the long drive to Albany Rob and Morag spoke very little. Now that she was actually leaving him, Morag saw her life stretch out in front of her as an empty wilderness. True, that was better than the minefield through which she'd been treading at van Huten's, but it had little enough in it to attract her. She would be among strangers – and she was always shy with strangers. She would be in a great city – and she knew nothing of city life, she was accustomed to the almost parochial atmosphere of a small Scots town. She would have to be companion to a sick woman, and there was no way of knowing how she would get on with Mrs Kauffman.

When at last they stepped down at the depot, she was almost tempted to cry, 'Let's go back! I don't want to go!' But she had her train ticket in her reticule, a letter of eager welcome from Captain Kauffman in her valise. And how would she explain her change of mind to those at the farm? They would find it strange indeed. She had to go forward. It would be best, in the end.

The train was standing at the track. Denstadt brought her trunk, Rob carried her valise. 'You'll write to me?' he begged.

She shook her head.

'But you must! I've got to know that you're all right!'

'I'll write once. That would be expected.'

'Morag, don't be so hard on me. Write to me.'

'What would be the point?' she pleaded. 'To keep going a relationship that can't have any good result? I'm going to Boston for one reason – to make a clean break between us.'

He hesitated. It took him by surprise, how much something within him ached at the thought of losing touch with her. 'At least I can write to you.'

'I wish you wouldn't, Rob. I shan't reply.'

He sighed. 'I'll write. Even if you don't reply, I'll feel you're still there.'

She made no reply. The porter looked at her expectantly, waiting to pick up the steps by the entrance to the car. 'All aboard,' he warned.

'Look after yourself,' Rob urged. 'Don't do too much. Get some advice about that cough of yours.'

'It's nothing. I'll be all right.'

'Oh, Morag!' He had her hands in a convulsive grasp. He was drawing her towards him.

'No, Rob, no,' she gasped, trying to draw free. 'Don't. You mustn't. You're a married man.'

'Can't I kiss my own sister goodbye?' he said with angry humour.

He wanted to feel her in his arms again. Some last despairing hope told him that if he kissed her as they used to kiss, it would rekindle her adoration. She would change her mind and would stay. He'd be saved this sense of aching loss.

He drew her hard against him and kissed her, deeply, passionately. In that moment she was everything in the world he wanted, and his kiss let her know it. She felt her head begin to swim. She put her arms about his neck and drew his head down, pressing her mouth against his, almost tempted to open her lips to the searching sweetness of his tongue.

Dorothea van Huten, hurrying into the depot to say goodbye, paused in shock at the sight of them. As the hour of departure drew near, she'd felt remorse for being so cold to Morag. Besides, coming into town to say goodbye gave her an excuse to do some shopping along State Street.

She'd come in a hired carriage alone, well wrapped against the cold in a cape of fox and velvet. When she stepped down at the depot she saw the van Huten's Clarence standing by the kerb, with Denstadt taking a secret tipple from a brandy flask. She was still in time – whoever was seeing Morag off hadn't gone back yet.

She swept quickly into the station, under the handsome wooden canopy edged with frozen snow. By the front of the train, she saw the couple embracing. The porter was calling, 'All aboard, please board the train . . .'

She stopped short, sheltered from view by an ornamental pillar. She watched.

Morag stirred in Rob's arms and drew away. "I must go,' she whispered.

'No, Morag – stay! Don't leave me!'

'I must, I must,' she said. She turned her back on him and hurried to the car entrance. The porter helped her mount to the iron deck.

Rob moved after her, his hands outstretched in useless appeal. 'Morag!'

The girl didn't turn back. Her face hidden by the turned-up collar of her dark short cape, she hurried into the car. The train surged forward as the porter drew up the step and swung aboard.

'Morag!' Rob called, moving along the train, trying to find her at one of the windows.

But she stayed out of sight until the train had long gone from the station. Rob stood at the outer edge of the station canopy, a tall, lonely figure in his dark suit, bareheaded in the cold. No one but Dorothea took much notice. Farewells were common enough at a railway depot. But not farewells like that. Dorothea stood unseen by the pillar and frowned to herself.

That had been a most unbrotherly embrace . . .

11

ROBERT CRAIGALLAN WAS A very lucky young man. He was in almost total control of a flourishing farm, in which he had a share as his wife's dowry. He was son-in-law to one of the best families in New York State. He had a beautiful son, round and firm-limbed, with the dark eyes of his grandmother and the reddish hair of his father.

Even within the family, he seemed to have little to complain of. Cornelius allowed him almost complete freedom of action, although they discussed farm planning between them. Cornelius was a sick man these days, steadily gaining weight and less able to get about. His doctor prescribed ten drops of iodine in milk night and morning as a medicine for his strange chest pain, but knew that it would do little good. The old man's heart was in bad shape.

The son, Julius van Huten, was no trouble. He was more often than not away from home. He had never had any interest in the farm and, now that Rob was there to take his place, Cornelius no longer reproached him with his neglect. In the old man's mind, the farm was now safe. Julius would own it at his death but Rob would manage it.

Luisa Craigallan seemed to be a good wife. She'd borne her husband a healthy boy, and if in the doing of it she'd grown a little blowsy, that was allowable. She liked to go into Albany to visit and to attend parties, sometimes escorted by her husband and sometimes not. They always appeared happy enough when they attended a ball together.

Dorothea, too, had apparently settled down. There was no gossip among the servants now about her goings-on at the farm. The reason was that she had found herself a discreet lover in Albany, a widowed politician called Struther Biddup, who suited her very well. It was in both their interests to have no scandal.

Everything seemed to have turned out for the best for Rob. Why was it then that as the months went by, life seemed to grow darker and more bitter?

He was worried about little Cornelius, in the first place. The baby's development seemed to him strangely deficient. He would smile and gurgle when you tickled him. He would crawl after a toy if you drew it in front of him. But he never turned his head if you called him; nor did he even try to repeat the words Rob tried to teach him. It was true he seemed to say 'Mama, Mama' or rather 'Mummummum' when he was happy, but he never even attempted to say that important word, 'Dada'.

On the child's first birthday, Rob sat down cross-legged on the nursery floor, determined to get the word out of him in response to the toy horse he'd bought him as a present. 'Say Dada,' he coaxed. 'Dada – say Dada, Cornelius. Dada! Dada!'

The baby sat on the rug in a shaft of cold winter sunlight, looking at him with his dark, quiet eyes. He stretched out his hand for the toy. 'Mmm..mummum . . .' he said.

'No, not Mama. Say Dada. Dada, Neelie.'

Cornelius wouldn't obey. He fell forward on his arms in his efforts to reach the wooden horse, crawled forward vigorously in his efforts to grab it, and squawked with fury when Rob held it out of his reach. Rob pacified him and started again from the beginning.

'You're too impatient,' Luisa remarked, watching from her cushioned chair by the stove. 'Lots of babies don't begin to talk until well into their second year. I asked Milly Finnemund about it. She says her eldest didn't say a real word until he was past two.'

'But he doesn't say *anything*!' Rob pointed out. 'Other people's babies are making all kinds of crowing noises all the time. The only sounds Cornelius makes are roars of protest and mumbling noises when he's pleased –'

'That's Mama. He says Mama when he's pleased.'

Rob threw down the toy and got up, dusting his pants leg. 'I don't know,' he said in disgust. 'I suppose you're right. I wish you'd teach him to say Dada or Papa, though.'

'I will, I will,' she said. Anything for a quiet life.

The baby's grandfather too was an anxiety to Rob. Mr van Huten was clearly failing. He still liked to talk farming with Rob, but the days were gone by when he would come out to look at the work. During the year that had just passed he came out in good weather in the buggy, well-cushioned against the jolting by pillows and rugs: but over Christmas and New Year he had seemed less and less well, hardly leaving his bedroom. It came home to Rob that if Cornelius died, he would miss him; his long experience of farming was irreplaccable.

If it happened he would face it. But he dreaded what the house would be like without Cornelius. Luisa was so stupid, so vain and empty-headed. And as for Dorothea, she had given Rob a terrible fright just after Morag left the farm.

'I dropped by the depot to say goodbye to your sister,' she told him, with a strange little smile. 'I was just a little too late. The train was just about to leave.'

'It's a pity you missed her,' he said.

'Oh, I don't know. I quite enjoyed the trip.' She paused and stared hard at Rob. 'I saw you kiss Morag goodbye. Strange behaviour between brother and sister.'

For a moment he was scared. What was she going to say? But he pulled himself together. All she had seen was a goodbye kiss. 'I was very distressed,' he said calmly. 'She and I have been through a lot together.'

'No doubt.' She appeared to consider the matter. 'Listen, Rob, I won't mention it to Luisa –'

'Mention what?'

'There's nothing to mention, really. Let's just say that you and I understand each other.'

'Of course we understand each other,' he said. 'We know what

[165]

we used to be to each other, but that's all in the past now.'

'In the past, yes. And now you're master of the house. I'm more or less left to my own devices because Cornelius is so sick, and I quite like it that way. Let's say I have a free hand, eh? Money to do as I like – is that agreed? No need to talk it all over with Cornelius, it would only worry him.'

'I see.' For a moment he was tempted to challenge her, but then he thought: Why bother? 'All right, Mother-in-law,' he said in a gentle, understanding tone. 'It's only right you should have some diversions. I've no objection to paying for them out of farm earnings – within reason.'

Her black eyes flashed. 'I don't have to submit to your judgement of what's reasonable –'

'Listen, Dorothea, don't let's quarrel. You want to go your own way – that's all right with me. Agreed?'

So there was peace between them, but he never felt easy with her. It wasn't just that she disliked him because of what had gone by. It was that she had seen him at that vulnerable moment when he lost Morag.

Morag had written, as duty bound, to say that she arrived safely in Boston. In a few lines she described her new surroundings: 'The house is a pleasant one with a yard in the back, the trees of which are heavy with snow at present but will make good shade in summer. Mrs Kauffman tells me she likes to sit there when the weather is clement. She is a very pleasant lady, bearing her suffering with courage. Her husband is very interested in things scientific. He conducts experiments in a shed out in back, the intentions of which I don't rightly understand but learned gentlemen come to the house to discuss them. There are concerts and plays in Boston but as yet I have no time to attend any. I look forward to a pleasant life here, and remember all kind friends at the farm with fondness. Please give my regards to all, Yours affec. Morag.'

Her phrases summoned up a picture of a world into which he had no entree. They made him feel lonely despite all the bustle of life at the farm. He wrote at once in reply, telling her all that was going on, trying desperately to keep her concerned with his life.

She didn't reply. In the year that followed her departure, though he wrote several times, she only replied once, for the birthday of the baby. She sent a beautifully made and embroidered short frock for him. 'This small token is to wish your son a happy birthday. I hope he is growing well, and that you and Luisa are in good health. My news is on the whole good; Mrs Kauffman seems to have improved a little which the captain is kind enough to say is due to my attendance and encouragement, but I fear it is only a remission in the disease. Boston is an interesting city, with many famous persons dwelling here, some of whom are frequently at the captain's residence. I hope the farm flourishes, with best wishes, yours affec., Morag.'

It was so formal and distant, unlike her own tone of voice. Rob read it and re-read it, saddened more than he would ever have thought possible. He longed to see her, to think of some excuse to go to Boston. But he had no reason. He went from time to time to Albany, and sometimes to New York, on business. There were the county fairs, at which his farm always won some prize for produce or crafts, but nothing would ever summon him to Boston. And, it seemed, nothing would ever bring Morag back to the farm.

An event occurred, however, which seemed to Rob to provide a reason to write inviting Morag to van Huten's. It was sad enough, but it was legitimate as an occasion for Morag to return.

The winter of Cornelius' first birthday lingered on in very hard weather into March. Heavy snowfalls immobilised the countryside. Blizzards cut one farm off from the other. In one of these blizzards, Julius van Huten went missing.

He had been to a bachelor party at a friend's house about eleven miles away. No apprehension was felt when he didn't return on the following day, for Julius was silently acknowledged as a heavy drinker who might well need a second day to recover from his hangover. When, late on the second day, Dick Criswell turned up expecting to find Julius at home, alarm woke in the household.

For Dick had left the party at the same time as Julius, and had expected to find him safe indoors by now.

'He's lost his way in the snow,' Rob soothed old Cornelius. 'You know what it's like at night, even with lanterns to light the way. You can easily miss the road. Don't worry about it, Father-in-law. We'll find him.'

Night was already falling. It was a bad time to go out searching. But they had to go, for if the old Clarence carriage had been trapped in snowdrifts the horse would by now be exhausted and perhaps even dead, and the two passengers might be in serious difficulties. Rob wasn't too concerned; Denstadt, the coachman, was a sensible fellow, well able to take care of himself in any weather. He'd make sure that they set out on foot with perhaps the horse as way-maker, to find a house where they could shelter until the carriage could be dug out.

Rob organised the men into pairs and sent them out, well-clad against the bitter cold and the snow flurries, with lanterns and with sticks to help them from blundering into deep places, and with food and flasks of brandy to keep them going and succour the lost ones. In the late evening, the wind rose and a blizzard began to whine over the land. One by one the search parties came back, frightened of losing their way, even close to van Huten's. One pair found shelter in a tool cabin on the far side of the estate, thus causing added fears until they struggled in at daylight.

No sign had been found of the carriage with Julius and Denstadt. Cornelius was still asleep when the men came back, worn out by a night of watching. Rob warned everyone to be quiet, not to clatter about, but alas, the noise of putting away the sled roused the old man.

'Mr Rob, he's calling for you,' Senta told him, running down from Cornelius's room. 'He's mighty restless.'

Sighing, Rob went upstairs. He was near exhaustion himself, having spent the early evening organising the search and the latter part of the night looking for the missing pair of searchers.

Cornelius was propped up in his great old four poster against a pile of lace-edged pillows. His flabby face was white; his pale blue eyes stared out in terror. 'Where is he? Have you found him? Is he alive?'

'Now, now, Father-in-law,' Rob said, 'we're still looking. We –'

'No, no, I heard the men in the yard –'

'That's only to get warm and be ready to start out again. I'll be out with them in half an hour.'

'You haven't found him . . .'

'Not yet, but the chances are he's not far off in the carriage, Father-in-law. He'll be safe enough, and Denstadt is with him –'

'What time is it?'

'Just after six.' The light outside looked stronger because it reflected against the brilliant white of the snow.

'It's later than that –'

'No, see – here's my watch.' Rob took it out of his pocket and held it out, but the old man couldn't read it without his spectacles. He shook his head from side to side in frustration. 'Go out!' he cried. 'Don't stand there showing me your watch! Find him, find my son –'

'We're going in half an hour – I told you –'

'Julius!' cried the farmer. 'Julius, my boy, where are you? Oh, dear God, don't punish him for his wickedness! He'll reform – he's still young –'

'Father-in-law, please be calm,' Rob began, for the mounting emotion was bringing a strange raddled colour into Cornelius's cheeks.

But it was already too late to check the damage. Cornelius gave a sharp cry, hunched his shoulders, and clutched at his fat chest. His breathing seemed to be suspended for a moment. When he drew in air, it was with an agonised gasp. His lips tried to form words, but they wouldn't obey him.

'Senta!' shouted Rob. 'Senta, fetch my wife!' He grapped at the smelling salts Dr Arbuthnot had left for emergency use, and took the glass stopped out of the bottle with trembling fingers. With one arm round him he held the bottle to the old man's nostrils.

Cornelius gasped and struggled to breathe. His hands grasped at Rob's arm as he battled to draw in air. The bulky old body was rigid with strain.

Totally immersed in the battle to help his father-in-law, Rob didn't hear the thudding of Senta's running footsteps, the slamming of the door as Luisa rushed from their room. As she came in her father's body became a dead weight on Rob's arm. The head fell back.

'Papa!' screamed Luisa. 'Papa!' She flew to the bedside, fell on her knees beside it, and seized her father's hand.

Rob let the smelling bottle fall on the counterpane. He put both arms round Cornelius and tried to heave him up from his pillows. It was impossible. The body seemed to weigh a ton.

He pulled away the arm from under the shoulders, straightened, picked up from the bedside table a mirror used when Cornelius was shaved. He held it in front of the old man's lips. For a long moment there was total silence in the bedroom as Luisa watched, frozen, for the verdict.

He took away the mirror. The surface was bright, undimmed.

'No!' cried Luisa. 'He's not dead. Oh, Papa! Don't leave us!' She grabbed the mirror from Rob and held it against the lips so that a smear of moisture dulled it. 'There,' she panted. 'He's breathing.'

'That's spittle, Luisa,' he told her. He took the mirror and laid it down on the bedside table. 'He's gone.'

'No, no –'

For answer Rob took one of the dead man's hands. He held it, felt the warmth already draining from it. 'Feel for yourself,' he said. 'Come, my love, don't upset yourself. We knew he was likely to go.'

'No, no,' she sobbed. But already she was accepting it.

Dorothea wasn't at home. She had gone to Saratoga Springs for Washington's Birthday, on the grounds that nursing Cornelius had exhausted her, and she needed a holiday to restore her. Since then she'd found one reason after another for remaining there and at present was provided with a perfect one by the long bout of bad weather.

The same bad weather made it impossible to summon the doctor to certify the death at present. In any case, the efforts of the household had to be bent to finding Julius. With scarcely even an interval to be sad for his father-in-law's going, Rob set out in search of his brother-in-law.

This time he sent off groups at marked tangents from the farm, with instructions to spread out and come back to the radial arm. His intention was to make a circumference round the house at regular distances, sweeping the area in between. Since they hadn't found Julius on any of the roads between van Huten's and the various other farms, it was reasonable to suppose the Clarence was a long way off the expected routes.

They found him at four o'clock that afternoon. The top of the roof of the carriage stuck up out of the snow like a square yellow patch. They had already been alerted to the possibility of its whereabouts by finding Denstadt about a mile away, frozen to death in the snow with the carriage horse's harness still grasped in his stiffened fist. The horse too was dead. The search party struggled towards the carriage, following tracks scarcely visible because of further snowfalls after Denstadt left it.

Rob was leading the search. When he saw the top of the Clarence he gave a shout, urging the weary men forward. A sound answered him.

Julius was alive. He was safe inside the carriage, dead drunk. His friends, packing him in at the end of the party two night ago, had loaded in a crate of brandy. Julius had stayed safely inside the carriage, drinking to keep out the cold, sleeping well-wrapped in his overcoat and the carriage comforter, while Denstadt died out in the snow trying to find help.

He was still drunk when they got him home. He was almost delirious with alcohol, laughing and cheering and embracing Rob. He seemed to have no idea of the danger he'd been in. It was impossible to tell him yet the news of his father's death.

For four days Julius was very ill, with what Dr Arbuthnot diagnosed as alcoholic poisoning. Frostbite and exposure had not touched him. Denstadt had taken all those hazards. Julius, as master, had not had to endanger himself; nor had he even thought of leaving the carriage because his mind was totally taken over by the brandy. He had done the safest thing without knowing it.

It had taken the doctor twenty-four hours to reach them after a man on a sled forced a way through to tell him what had happened at van Huten's. It then remained impossible to bury the dead because the ground was too frozen to accept a spade. The bodies were laid out decently in a cold outhouse.

It was now that Rob realised he could write to Morag and ask her to come back. He took the obligatory black-edged notepaper and penned a letter, very formal and full of the terms of effusive grief thought necessary for the occasion. Luisa at the same time wrote to her mother.

Dorothea came, as in duty bound. Morag did not. Many days later came a letter of regret: Mrs Kauffman was so unwell that Morag couldn't leave her and besides, the travelling conditions were very bad. She sent her heartfelt condolences and remained, as always, 'yours affec.' Rob noted yet again that she never signed herself 'Your affectionate sister.' He realised she wanted that pretence to be forgotten, intending in the end to cut herself off from him completely.

When the will was read after the funeral, its terms were as expected. Julius inherited the farm with an instruction to provide a good income for his mother and for his sister if she were to be still unmarried; if married, he was to allow her to choose any items from the household for her new home up to the value of a certain sum.

No mention was made of Rob. Cornelius had never had his will re-drawn since the day he first made it after the birth of his children.

'But you don't need to worry,' Julius said, clapping Rob on the shoulder with a plump hand. 'You know the place is yours, really. Now I'm free of the old man's reproaches, I'm off to the city –'

'I'd have thought you were tired of Albany by now –'

'Albany? That dull old hole? I'm going to New York! That's where all the life is, Rob! Pretty girls, good restaurants, theatres, parties, picture galleries, exhibitions, concerts, races . . . Friends I used to know at college have settled there. I'll go and stay with them for a bit then I'll get a place of my own.'

Rob frowned. 'Don't start throwing money about, Julius. Things are going to be hard for a bit, after this winter.'

'You'll manage, my friend. You always do. You know how to make the farm pay, I saw that from the outset. We'll have a gentleman's agreement, shall we? I'll go away and leave you to it, and you'll provide me with funds.'

'I want it understood, though, that you have got to be reasonable in your demands for money.'

[172]

'As reasonable as I can, old boy.'

Although Rob pretended to be uneasy, he was satisfied with the arrangement. He could keep Julius misinformed about the profits of the farm, thus curbing his extravagance. Although Julius would spend money like water, it was worth it, to get him out of the way and have the farm to himself.

He ventured to put the same proposal to Dorothea, rather more tactfully. To his surprise and somewhat to his dismay, she told him she intended to stay at home for a time. 'People have said some unkind things about the fact that I was away when Cornelius died,' she sulked. 'I need to restore myself in their eyes so I'll stay at the farm like a good, sorrowing widow.'

'Please yourself,' he shrugged.

At last the weather relented. He got the men out on the fields at once, getting the ground ready for seeding. Everything was late that year. The fruit trees seemed to be in leaf almost as soon as they were in blossom. The bluejays rushed about, nestbuilding in a frenzy. The whole world was busy.

Dorothea found it all quite interesting. She'd forgotten how enjoyable it was to take part in running a farm. It was inevitable that she and Rob should clash.

'Did you tell Pickering not to spread the wood ash?' he demanded, stamping indoors on an April afternoon with heavy mud on his boots after a sudden downpour.

'I decided we could use it better in the orchard,' she said, frowning at the mud on the hall floor.

'You decided? What the devil has it got to do with you? Now we've got the rain that anyone could see was coming, and the wood ash isn't being soaked in on the fallow –'

'There wasn't enough to be any use on a whole field –'

'That's what you think! Just a trace of wood ash on that old pasture would make it in good heart for ploughing –'

'It's too late for ploughing –'

'Everything's late! Don't you understand that we've got to –'

'I understand that we've got to keep the fruit trees in production otherwise we'll have no –'

'We're not in business to produce fruit!' he exclaimed. 'We're

[173]

grain producers, wheat producers –'

'Then why are you increasing the acreage under potatoes –'

'Because it's time to increase the area of rotation, that's why! If you'll just keep out of it –'

'Let me tell you, young man, I was helping Cornelius to run this place long before you ever came on the scene –'

'No doubt, and using the same old schemes of agriculture he'd learned from his father –'

'What's wrong with that? It worked well, as you can see by –'

'Dorothea, of course it worked well, but we can do better! In the books I've been reading, I see the *reasons* for doing things –'

'I know your reasons,' she flashed. 'It's to make yourself big! Don't think you can hoodwink me, Rob Craigallan! You wheedled your way into this family by using Luisa, and all you really wanted was to get control of the farm –'

'Cornelius trusted me –'

'The more fool he! Anyhow, the farm belongs to Julius now, and it's up to me as his mother to make sure you don't –'

'I don't need you to supervise me!' he cried. 'All you do is mess things up! Keep out of the way, Dorothea – go back to your kafee-klatches in Albany and your admirer Struther Biddup!'

She was shocked to find he knew about that. She'd thought it a perfectly-kept secret. Angry at being found out, she counter-attacked. 'You pretend to be so hardworking and upright! You think I don't know you through and through? The way you leapt into bed with me –'

'At your urgent invitation!'

She drew back, furious. 'You didn't hesitate a moment! You were waiting for the chance!'

'Don't delude yourself. I made love to you because I wanted to keep my job, and that's all!'

'You – you –' Dorothea's whole body was shaking with anger. 'I'll pay you out for that!'

She turned and rushed upstairs. At once Rob was sorry for what had happened; he'd always known that Dorothea would be a bad enemy and had been glad that her own good sense had held her in check. He should never have let the argument grow into quarrel.

He had no idea what she would do. She had various possibilities. The one that would hurt him most was if she were to get in touch with Julius and somehow persuade him to restrict Rob's activities at the farm.

In a way what she did troubled him less – but that was because his feeling for his wife was so shallow. She went straight from their scene in the hall to Luisa's upstairs sittingroom.

Rob heard the upshot when he had finished the day's work and was changing for dinner. Luisa insisted on this. She had learned the custom in Albany and said she couldn't bear to sit down opposite a sweaty man. Rob fell in with her wishes without argument. It pleased him to come up to his big bedroom and find hot water in the hip bath in front of the fire, and warmed towels on a wooden stand ready for him when he stepped out of the water, aired clothes laid out on the bed.

This evening, Luisa was sitting in a padded armchair, waiting for him. She was wrapped in a fine lawn dressing-gown trimmed with flounces and ribbon bows. At first sight he thought she wanted to make love. Her appetite in that respect was healthy and she often let him know her needs by coming into the bedroom when he was about to undress for his bath.

One look at her stormy face warned him that this wasn't a time for lovemaking. Her eyes were red with weeping. She hadn't dressed because she wanted to show him she was too upset to do so.

He stiffened. It had to do with Dorothea, of that he was certain. What form would the attack take?

'Mama says there's something between you and your sister,' she blurted out.

'What?'

'She says she saw you saying goodbye when Morag left Albany. Kissing each other. Not like brother and sister.'

'Luisa!' he said in protest. He hoped to put her off the scent by pretending utter innocence.

But she was too quick to be put off. She got up and came to him, staring up into his eyes. 'I always thought she was strange,' she said. 'She followed you around with her eyes . . .'

'No, you're wrong –'

'It's disgusting,' she spat out. 'Your own sister!'

'Luisa, stop this! You're talking wildly. Morag and I –'

'Morag and you were bound together by something more than sisterly affection. That girl idolised you – I see it now. I've heard such things whispered about –'

'What things? What are you suggesting?'

'I think you slept with her. Your own sister!'

'Luisa!' He took her by the shoulder and shook her. 'Stop this! You've let Mother-in-law infect you with her sick ideas –'

'Mama told me. She wouldn't have said such a thing if she wasn't sure. She saw you at the depot. She says you were shameless, right there by the railroad track in front of all the people.'

'Luisa, I swear to you by all that's sacred – by little Neelie – that I never went to bed with my own sister.'

'I don't believe you! I know you're capable of anything. Mama told me how you married me just to get the farm.'

'That's just her vindictive imagination –'

'And why should she be so vindictive?' she cut in. 'I wonder . . .'

'Don't start imagining things, Luisa –'

'I don't need to imagine. I see things, even though you think I'm stupid. Oh, I know what you think of me. You scarcely bother to hide it. You never discuss anything with me –'

'Because you show no interest, Luisa.'

'I'm showing interest now, though! I want you to tell me what was between you and Morag.'

He could see that he would have to give her some answer or the accusations would go on for ever. He knew Luisa only too well; with hardly anything to occupy her, she was apt to get fretful and emotional over little things. How much more so over something like this . . .

He forced her to walk back to the chair and made her sit down. 'I'll tell you all about it, Luisa. But you must promise to keep calm.'

'I'm promising nothing!'

'You'll only make matters worse if you get hysterical –'

'You mean there's something to get hysterical about?'

'Not at all. Certainly nothing of the kind you've been led to believe by your evil-minded Mama.' He drew a breath. 'Morag isn't my sister.'

'What?'

'She's no relative of mine. Her name is Morag McGarth, from Dunbar in Scotland. I came from the other side of the country. I never saw her until we met on the ship coming over.'

'She's not your sister?'

'No.'

'But you said . . .'

'I had to,' Rob said. 'We needed work. We'd had a bad time in New York, and we left the city without a penny, looking for a job. Your father wouldn't have hired me if he'd thought Morag was with me because she was fond of me.'

'You admit that, do you? You admit you were lovers?'

He hesitated. 'We were. Before I fell in love with you. I admit that, Luisa.'

'And afterwards? Are you saying you never touched her?'

'Never.'

She glared up at him. 'You must think I'm a fool! If you weren't still carrying on with her, why did she stay on here after we got married?'

He could see he had to satisfy her doubts. He said: 'I tried to persuade her to leave. You have to realise she . . . she's a very dependent sort of girl. She couldn't tear herself away although I kept telling her it was all over. In the end, when Neelie was born, I found her that job in Boston. I told her it was the end. She could see I meant it. That's why she left.'

Luisa studied him. 'You swear it? You got rid of her because you love me?'

'I swear it.'

Somehow this lie seemed a terrible betrayal. He told himself that night, after he and Luisa had had a tumultuous reconciliation, that it was necessary.

And it was what Morag wanted, wasn't it? A final separation.

12

THE HOUSE IN BOSTON where Morag lived was a handsome
place. Captain Kauffman had retired from the sea with enough
money to keep it in the state his wife was accustomed to, for
Gertrude had brought him his home together with some
investments in railroads and oil. The environment at the
Kauffmans' was pleasant and elegant, if not exactly luxurious.

Morag had settled in without difficulty. The captain was
disposed to like her from the outset, coming as she did from a
family whose name was known to him, but she endeared herself
to him almost at once by her interest in Gertrude.

'You've made all the difference in the world to us,' he told her
at the end of the first week. 'We've had all kinds of help in the
house – nurses, trained teachers, simple maidservants – but
we've never had anyone who made my wife feel so easy.'

Unused to direct priase, Morag coloured and looked away.
'It's only that I'm concerned to understand her,' she murmured.
'Her speech is difficult to catch, but once you get the knack it's
easy to be ready with whatever she wants.'

She'd been somewhat frightened at first by what she found at
the Kauffmans'. Mrs Kauffman was clearly very ill, with a
disease which no one seemed to understand. Morag gathered
from the house servants that it was progressive; last year at this
time Gertrude had been well able to walk about and even go out

for carriage airings. Yet now she was confined to a chaise longue, moving from there to bed at night and back again in the morning. Her ability to talk was growing less. Her doctors spoke of the sickness as being of a nervous origin but couldn't tell what course it would take nor how it had come about.

Morag gathered that the search for some sort of companion had been uppermost in the captain's mind for more than a year. The problem was that Gertrude, intelligent and lively, soon grew bored with the companionship of anyone less bright than herself. For that reason, the captain had ceased hiring nurses – who in the main came from a class of woman with little education – and had tried seeking out teachers. But Gertrude complained that they treated her like a child; she was quick to take offence, the more so as the sickness made her tongue less obedient to her thoughts.

Morag seemed a gift from heaven. She had a good basic education and a quick mind, so a strange relationship grew up: Gertrude took it upon herself to teach Morag. Unconsciously, Morag had provided the ideal solution. She had given Gertrude an interest in keeping her companion with her because there was always something else to be taught. On the side of nursing, Morag soon learned that Gertrude could make her needs known if one listened attentively; if one could be beforehand with whatever she wanted – a drink, a change of position, the drawing of a shade – little temper tantrums could be avoided.

By good luck, as Morag thought, Mrs Kauffman was better in health the first summer she spent there. This confirmed her place in the household. Captain Kauffman elected her their good angel; he increased her 'emolument', inisted that she occupy a better room, and began to introduce her to his eminent visitors.

They were mostly men, for Captain Kauffman was interested in things scientific. There was a 'club', which met once a week in the captain's study for discussion of some topic already selected. One of the group would read a paper, and the others would comment. Coffee and cake would be served.

It was at this point that Morag and Mrs Kauffman usually came in. Morag dispensed the refreshments, and after that, both women would sit silently by while the discussion went on.

Gertrude had a mind as keen as any of the men but no longer took part in the conversation because her speech defect embarrassed and annoyed her.

It was because of this problem that one of the group invited Gardiner Greene Hubbard to attend. A wealthy lawyer and pillar of Bostonian society, Mr Hubbard had a daughter who could scarcely speak. He had sought advice for her, and with some success.

'I do wish you'd let me bring you together with Mr Bell,' he remarked on his second visit. He was sitting back at ease in a big buttoned leather armchair, enjoying pecan pie.

'We have heard of him,' Captain Kauffman acknowledged. 'There was a most interesting article about him in The Home Journal –'

'Very superficial, I assure you,' Hubbard broke in. 'It did little justice to his remarkable invention. Have you seen his system of Visible Speech?'

Gertrude nodded and made to reply. Morag supplied the words for her. 'Mrs Kauffman looked at it, sir, but the problem is, Mrs Kauffman cannot hold a pen to make the necessary symbols, so it is of little help to her.'

Gertrude nodded again, to signify she agreed wholeheartedly.

'But we need not give up Mr Bell's abilities for all that,' Hubbard continued. 'He has a remarkable ability in improving the vocal chords. My daughter, Mabel, has been scarcely able to make herself understood since she was seven, but since we took her to Mr Bell she has noticeably improved. Mrs Kauffman, do consult Mr Bell.'

This idea simmered for a time. To encourage her, Hubbard brought his daughter Mabel to call. A young, pretty girl, she spoke in a halting style with a monotonous delivery, but understandable. Mrs Kauffman was impressed. But she was too shy, too self-conscious to go further with the notion.

Morag didn't press it. She prevented the captain from going on about it. 'The time will come when she'll be ready to do it, sir,' she told him.

With the coming of winter, Gertrude seemed to slip back

again. Morag sat by her chaise longue, reading to her from the scientific and literary journals she enjoyed, or working with her needle while the captain took over the reading. Morag was working on the short frock she sent as a birthday present to Rob's son; she intended to remember the baby's birthday this year and the next, as was befitting an affectionate sister, and then allow the contact to wither away.

She tried never to think of Rob. There was plenty to occupy her here in Boston. But from time to time her mind went back to him, usually when she received his letters. Rob wrote irregularly, at intervals of about two or three months, seeming to find some pleasure or relief in pouring out his plans to her. She sensed that he found little companionship in his marriage to Luisa, though he never criticised or decried her – and for this she was glad. He had known well enough that Luisa was wayward and self-centred when he married her; she was the wife of his own choosing.

The letter telling of Mr van Huten's death caused her some grief. She read between the lines and saw that Rob wanted her to come to the funeral, and she was tempted. She longed to see him, to find out how things were faring with him. But she knew it would be madness to go.

The severe winter provided her with the perfect excuse. She wrote back in formal condolence. Captain Kauffman said with sympathy, 'This is a bad winter for all of us, Morag . . . If you would like to go later to visit your brother, you know you are free to do so at any time.'

'Thank you, no, captain.' She hesitated. Perhaps it was necessary to provide some reason for her unwillingness to visit her brother. 'To be candid, Luisa and I do not get on.'

He raised his shaggy brows. 'You surprise me! I can't imagine anyone who would not get on well with you, Morag.'

At Christmas came another letter, announcing the birth of a daughter, Ellen Rose, called after Rob's mother. Morag wrote back in congratulation and later sent two caps for the baby, delicately trimmed with the narrowest lace, and made with stitches so small as to be invisible. She also sent a knitted jacket for Cornelius, now two.

After that she intended not to reply to any more letters. But in the July of that year she received one that shook her resolve.

'I scarcely know why I set this down to send to you,' he wrote, 'except that I feel I must speak of it to someone – and you are the one person to whom I can speak without holding back. Morag, I fear my little boy is mentally inferior. For some months now I have been hinting to Luisa that Cornelius doesn't seem to develop as other children do. He is strangely silent and withdrawn, never speaking, never responding to anything one says. I have sat with him for hours, trying to coax him to reply, but I believe he does not understand a word.'

The letter went on to describe the arguments with Luisa over the little boy, the temper tantrums he threw, the food knocked over and spat out, the toys wickedly broken, the flailing fists, the stamping and kicking. Cornelius had even taken to attacking his baby sister.

'Parson Bletchley thinks the boy is possessed of a demon, but I can't go along with such Old Testament ideas. However, the alternative view is that he is an imbecile, destined never to understand or communicate with any of us. Already I've heard the farmhands referring to him as the Dummy or the Booby – it hurts, Morag, to have my son spoken of in those terms.'

He ended begging Morag not to desert him, to write to him even if only a few lines. 'I miss you. You can't imagine how much I miss you, Morag. Let me have a few words to tell me you haven't forgotten me.'

Shattered, she sat in her room with the letter in her hands. Tears welled up in her eyes. Poor Rob. Some might say this was a judgement on him, for his deceit and scheming. But Morag had never liked the passage in the Bible about the sins of the fathers being visited upon the children. If God was just, how could he punish little children?

'Wh.what a m.matter?' Gertrude asked later in the day. 'You seem . . . v.very d.down in sp.sp.spirits.'

'It's nothing, Mrs Kauffman. Some rather bad news in a letter from Rob.'

'T.tell me wh.what ails b.brother.' Gertrude's speech had

improved a little under the instruction of Alexander Melville Bell during the spring months. The professor had come to the house regularly in the evening, after his day's teaching at the institute for teachers of the deaf.

'Rob's little boy is unwell,' Morag explained. She didn't want to talk about Rob. She had never grown accustomed to referring to him as 'my brother'.

'Ah, ch.children,' Gertrude said sadly. She had lost two children herself, before poor health made it impossible for her to have more. For this reason, she took a lively interest in the children of others, notably Mabel Hubbard, the lawyer's daughter. Mabel often came to the house these days – partly, in Gertrude's view, to happen upon the son of Professor Bell.

Alexander Graham Bell had substituted for his father the previous year as lecturer at the institute. A tall, strong-featured young man, he had been living quietly at the family's home in Ontario, haunted by the fear of the disease that had carried off his two brothers. But when his health was assured, he took up the profession he had already learned from and shared with his famous father, and he was now taking more than a slight shine to Mabel Hubbard. He claimed to be interested in painting; it was no coincidence, Gertrude pointed out, that Mabel was a talented painter.

Gertrude's thoughts ran on for a moment on the subject of romance. 'Young Mr B.bell c.coming t.tea 's'afternoon?' she inquired.

'I believe so.'

'B.bringing Ira Jones with him?'

'I dare say.'

'Ira b.becoming . . . r.regular v.visitor.'

'So I notice.'

'So you sh.should. He c.comes s.see you.'

Morag shook her head.

'He does,' Gertrude insisted. 'L.likes you a l.lot.'

'I think he comes because he's interested in Alexander's conversation. His plans to open a school of vocal physiology are very interesting.'

'C.could t.talk about p.plans anywhere,' Gertrude pointed out. 'C.comes here b.because of *you*.'

He's wasting his time, Morag thought to herself. She liked Ira, an earnest and clever young man, but if he had any special interest in her, it was useless. Some day she might forget her feelings for Rob, but not yet. Certainly her two years in Boston had taught her to feel less guilty about her own actions, and to take a less fundamentalist view between right and wrong; but though she now felt she might be forgiven for what was past, she couldn't shake off the notion that while she still loved Rob, she was still guilty. Rob was a married man. She ought to put him utterly out of her mind, and it was inexcusable that she could not. No young man like Ira Jones ought to be thinking of a girl who still longed for another woman's husband.

That afternoon young Alexander Bell called, as did Mabel Hubbard and her mother. Ira Jones did not in fact appear, which was just as well, for the conversation took a turn of tremendous interest to Morag.

Mabel began to describe the frustrations she used to feel as a little girl when she couldn't make herself understood by her family. 'People don't understand,' she said in her strange, slow way. 'They speak, you can't hear, they mouth at you . . . It is frightening . . . Sometimes you want to *hit* them.'

'But, l.like me,' Gertrude put in, 'you had once b.been able to h.hear. You knew . . . what the m.mouths were d.doing. Th.think how d.dreadful . . . n.not to know what m.mouths were opening and cl.closing *for* . . .'

'What?' Morag said.

'N.not know . . . D.didn't I s.say it r.right?'

'Yes, yes, we understood what you said,' Alexander replied. 'That's not why you exclaimed aloud, Morag. What's the matter?'

'Are you saying,' she asked, 'that a child who is born deaf would have no idea what speech actually is?'

'That is so. The children with whom I come into contact . . . Those are the ones who are hardest to help. Rage and frustration seem to drive them mad.'

'Professor Bell,' Morag said, leaning forward to hold his gaze, 'let me be sure I understand you. Are you telling me that the symptoms of profound deafness in a young child could be mistaken for derangement?'

'Certainly. And have been so taken, often and often.'

'Thank you.' She inclined her head and sat back. From then on she took little part in the conversation.

A week later Rob Craigallan received a letter in a hand he recognised with lifting spirits. Morag had relented, and replied to his letter! He took the mail into his study to read in peace and it was well he did so, for what she wrote made him spring out of his chair with a movement so convulsive he sent a pile of papers spilling across the floor.

'I don't wish to rouse hopes that may be ill-founded,' Morag wrote, 'but at Captain Kauffman's house a frequent visitor is a young professor of what is called vocal physiology. I don't pretend to understand exactly what that is, but he follows in the footsteps of his father, the great Alexander Melville Bell, inventor of Visual Speech. The young Professor Bell gives me to believe that a child who is born deaf would behave in the way little Cornelius does, that such a child would be unable to speak (because he cannot hear the sounds he should imitate) and therefore would be thought to be dumb. Anger and irritation at his limitations can make a child of this kind react strongly into tantrums.

'Do you not feel it might be worth bringing little Cornelius to Boston to be seen by Professor Bell? It may well be that the boy is not feeble-minded or defective, but simply deaf – to such an extent that he is closed off from the rest of the world. Professor Bell could tell in a short test whether this is so. Nothing could be lost by having this examination made, it seems to me.'

'Luisa, Luisa!' shouted Rob, running upstairs to his wife's boudoir. 'Luisa, where's Cornelius?'

Luisa came out on the landing to find out the cause of the outcry. 'What on earth's wrong with you, Rob? You scared me out of my wits!'

'Luisa, look – look at this letter! Morag says Cornelius may not be mad –'

'Morag?' Luisa cried, her eyes darkening with anger. 'You said you'd sent that girl away and forgotten her?'

'Luisa, don't begin all that again. Morag knows a doctor –'

'A doctor? What doctor?'

'A doctor who may be able to prove that Neelie isn't mentally defective –'

'How does Morag know anything about Neelie's trouble?' Luisa countered. 'You've been in touch with her?'

'Luisa, Luisa, that doesn't matter,' he urged, dragging her into the room. 'Listen, she says there's hope –'

Luisa wailed, bursting into tears. 'You promised you'd put her out of your life.'

'Oh, for God's sake! I have, I have! She's miles away in Boston, for the love of heaven! All right, so I send her a letter once in a while. You can't complain of that!'

'I do complain! You swore to me that you were never going to be in touch with her again –'

'I might not have bothered, if you'd been halfways interested in anything I do,' he replied, suddenly angry. 'You never listen to anything I say about the farm or the property –'

'Are you pretending you want me to? Look how you treated Mama when she tried to take an interest –'

'She tried to interfere. That was different.'

'She only wanted to play a part in running the place. You chased her out! You're to blame for the fact that I never see my own mother any more!'

'Oh, don't try to pretend that you miss her! You never had much time for her when she was here –'

'It's all your fault that she's off in New York with Julius throwing her cap over the windmill! And it's your fault, too, that Neelie's the way he is! It's a judgement on you! For all the wicked things you did –'

Rob drew back his hand to slap her. She flinched, then stared at him. 'That's right, hit me! It would be just like you!'

He took a firm hold on himself. 'Listen, Luisa,' he said, insisting on a fresh start to the whole conversation, 'there's a chance to prove that Cornelius isn't subnormal. This doctor in Boston –'

'Some acquaintance of your Morag's, is it?'

'It doesn't matter whose acquaintance he is. He's quite well known, Luisa. I remember reading about him in The Home Journal.'

For a moment, Luisa was silenced. She greatly respected The Home Journal, which was her exemplar of fashion and gracious living. If this doctor was mentioned there, perhaps he was worth considering. But then she came to the worst point of all. She would have to take Cornelius out into the world.

It was symptomatic of the little boy's disfavour in the household that he was called by his full name. 'Cornelius' had been used to him at first when he was in disgrace. But as the months went by and he was always up to some bad action or other, it became normal to call him that. No one at van Huten's Farm was fond of him. And Cornelius in his turn was fond of no one.

Buried away on the farm he was scarcely known to Luisa's friends. It was accepted that her little son was 'difficult', 'troublesome' – visitors didn't press to be allowed to see him. They brought their own pretty children and showed them off, but made no remark when Luisa dandled Ellen Rose and never mentioned her son.

The thought of taking him out to be seen by other people appalled Luisa. She was ashamed of having produced an imbecile child. Everyone knew it was a judgement of some kind. She couldn't put herself in the position of being stared at by others.

'Very well, *I'll* take him,' Rob said.

'You?' she challenged. 'You don't even like him!'

'He's my son, Luisa. If there's any kind of chance to prove he's not weakminded, I must take it.'

'You'd go to Boston with him?'

'Of course.'

'You only go so you can see Morag!' raged his wife. 'You can't fool me –'

The argument went on for days. At last he took her aside and made her sit down. 'Luisa,' he began. 'Hear me out. I have made up my mind that Cornelius must go to Boston to be examined by this Dr Bell. I shall go, either with you or without you. Please yourself. I shan't force you to come if you're too ashamed to do so.'

She hesitated, on the verge of precipitating another row. She thrived on them. It excited her to have Rob dark with anger, to see those grey eyes take fire. If he wouldn't love her, she could at least rouse his rage.

But this time she realised he had made up his mind. He wasn't going to argue or dispute. He would go. He had said so.

She certainly wasn't going to let him loose in the same city as Morag McGarth. Moreover, Boston was a fine place. There were great department stores there, with clothes better than she could buy in Albany. It would be something to crow over her friends about.

She let a long moment elapse before she spoke. She wanted him to think it had cost her dear to agree. 'Very well,' she said. 'I'll accompany you. But I refuse to take any responsibility for Cornelius's behaviour. If he shames us in front of everybody, you'll have to deal with him.'

Strangely, the little boy was as good as gold during the journey. His dark eyes followed the actions of everyone he met. He watched the countryside go by outside the carriage on the way to Albany, and only at the depot did he cause any alarm about a tantrum. When the locomotive came in, he turned in Rob's arms and buried his face in his coat, clutching his father's collar and making as if he would scramble away.

Much later, when the boy was being examined in Alexander Graham Bell's office, Rob understood what had caused that moment of terror. The vibration of the train's pistons had shaken the ground. Cornelius had been able to 'hear' it.

Rob had written in advance making an arrangement to see Professor Bell. They arrived at the school by appointment, were shown in, and Luisa launched into a long excusatory account of Cornelius and his behaviour.

'Shall we let the little lad speak for himself?' Alexander Bell put in gently.

'Speak? But he can't speak, Professor –'

'He can, in his way. Come, child.' He held out his hand.

Cornelius sat on Rob's lap, staring at Bell and the office with its strange equipment. He looked without emotion at the outstretched hand.

'He won't go,' Luisa predicted. 'He never goes with anyone.'

Bell pursed his lips and tugged for a moment at his luxurious beard. Then from his desk he picked up a tuning fork. He struck it against the edge of the desk and held it to the little boy's temple.

The result was extraordinary. Cornelius jerked back his head. Then he put up a hand to touch his neck behind the ear. He rubbed his neck, shook his head, and shivered as if he were cold.

Bell took away the tuning fork. He struck it again. The pure clear middle C seemed to fill the room. He held the fork against the other ear.

Cornelius stared at him, leaning away a little from the appliance.

Once more Bell struck the fork and held it to the right ear, the ear he'd tried first. Cornelius drew back in consternation, then turned his head to stare at the fork.

'He can feel the vibrations,' Bell explained. He threw down the tuning fork. Cornelius half put out a hand towards it, then stopped. Bell picked it up and took a step away. Once more he held out his hand.

To the surprise of both his parents, the child scrambled down from Rob's knees and ran towards the professor.

The first tests were carried on in the presence of the father and mother, but Bell said at the end of two days that he would like to do more extensive work. Luisa wasn't reluctant; she longed to go out and about in Boston instead of sitting in Bell's darkly furnished office.

Rob took the little boy to the school on each of the succeeding days, and collected him again in the afternoon. During the interim he amused himself by walking about Beacon Hill and the agricultural department of the university. Often he was tempted towards Milk Street, where the Kauffman house was situated, but he always turned away; Luisa would crow with triumph if she could say he had only come to Boston to see Morag.

They ran across each other one day by luck. She had come to

the old City Hall to deliver a letter from Captain Kauffman to a politician. Rob had wandered in to look at the building as a historical monument. They came face to face in the lobby.

She was so unprepared to see him that she dropped her reticule and the frilled parasol she was carrying. 'Rob!' she gasped

He had not written to her about coming to town. He knew it would enrage Luisa. When asking for Professor Bell's help, he had merely said that he had heard of his work and would be grateful for his opinion. As for Bell, he hadn't dreamed of talking of this new patient: that would have been against professional etiquette. As for the name, it is doubtful whether he even knew that Morag's supposed name was Craigallan. She was always referred to by her Christian name.

Rob stared at her. She seemed different. He had been accustomed to seeing her either in the dark 'best' dress of her first days in New York, or the check gingham thought suitable for maidservants. Even at van Huten's, when she had earned some status by being 'sister' to Luisa's husband, she hadn't changed her style.

Here in Boston, she was elegant and quite striking. She was clad in a close-fitting gown of polka-dot muslin over cotton satin, the skirt many tiered but slim, the bodice carefully boned to hug her figure. At neck, wrist, and round the hem there were flounces and bunches of ribbon, grey and cream, to pick out the colours of the muslin. Her rich brown hair was drawn back in three or four ringlets, held away from her face by a simple comb. On top of that she wore a tiny hat, scarcely more than a circle of lace over straw, held firmly by ribbon strings tied to one side. From under the ruched hem of her gown peeped little gaitered boots of grey suede. Her parasol was of white coarse lace. Her gloves were white kid.

Automatically, Rob took off his hat. It was the first time he had ever done so for Morag. 'If you knew how often I've looked for you in the crowds since I got here,' he said. 'But now I see you, I might have failed to recognise you except at close quarters.'

'You've changed too, Rob.' He had always looked older than his years; he was now twenty-one, looked twenty-five, and allowed himself to be thought that age. He felt it gave him authority.

His frame was filled out, his skin was bronzed by an outdoor life no matter how Luisa might deprecate that as ungentlemanly. At her insistence, he took care to have his clothes made at a good tailor. He was wearing a tail coat and striped pants, the almost obligatory town wear of the gentleman. His vest was fine taffeta of a small black and white check; his cravat was black satin stuck with a single pearl. He made no claims to lead the mode; he looked what he was, an out of town farmer of substance, at ease in his clothes but not much interested in them.

'What brings you to Boston?'

'Cornelius is with Professor Bell, undergoing tests. If the professor can prove he isn't retarded, it will be a source of new hope to us. I want to thank you, Morag, for putting the idea into my mind. I should never have thought of it without you.'

'How long have you been here?'

'Three days. On Friday we hear the verdict.'

'I hope with all my heart that you hear good news.'

'Thank you.' He hesitated. 'Are you heading anywhere?'

'N.no. I was on an errand for my employer.'

'May I offer to buy you tea? There are some very pleasant cafes –'

'No, thank you.' She drew back.

'Oh, please, Morag.'

'It wouldn't be proper,' she said. 'You are a married man.'

'But we are such old friends.'

'I notice you don't still claim that I'm your sister.'

'No.' He sighed and shrugged. 'I told Luisa the truth. I always intended to, of course. I reproach myself for delaying so long.'

'Ah,' she said. 'So that's why you haven't called at the Kauffmans.'

'No, it would be awkward. I don't want to cause any awkwardness for you there.'

'Thank you.'

'You're happy there?'

'Very much so.'

'From your letters I gather you have many friends?'

'Yes.'

'This young Professor Bell . . . he is a friend of yours?'

'Yes, but not particularly so.'

'Ah,' he said, oddly relieved. Then, as an afterthought: 'Have you any particular friend?'

She lifted her chin a little. 'None that I care to discuss in the streets, Rob.'

'I'm sorry.'

'I must go,' she said. 'I'm expected at home.'

'No, wait –'

'Excuse me – Mrs Kauffman will be wondering where I am.'

'Well,' he said, with some reproach, 'may I meet you somewhere tomorrow? I suppose you have some free time?'

'I have free time. But I don't think we'll meet. We have no reason,' she said, cool and calm. 'It would look odd indeed if we were to have a rendezvous. No, Rob, it's better that we don't meet.'

'Don't you want to?'

'No.' She was lying. The mere sight of him made her pulse beat heavily in her throat. But she was determined not to let their relationship renew itself.

'Don't you even want to know what happens about my son?'

She hesitated. 'You can write to me about that.'

'And you'll reply?'

'No.'

There was dismay in the grey eyes he bent on her. 'It's strange,' he said, 'I always used to think you were someone who needed to lean on me. Now, when I want to lean on you, you're too strong to allow it.'

'You have a wife to lean on, Rob,' she said, and held out her gloved hand.

When he tried to press it for too long, she withdrew it at once. With a slight and polite inclination of her head, she walked away. He watched her go down the shallow steps, the ruffled hem of her train dragging gracefully on the treads. She put up her parasol against the hot sunshine. The shade lost her features to view. In a moment she was lost among the passers-by.

Although she had tried to give the impression she would wait until she heard about Cornelius, anxiety got the better of her. She said to Professor Bell when he called with Mabel the following evening, 'Alexander, I believe you are being consulted by Mr and Mrs Craigallan about their son, Cornelius.'

He raised his thick brows. 'You know them?'

'Yes, very well. It was at my urging that they came to you.'

'Indeed. Well, you did them a great favour. It may just be possible to save their boy from a life of misery.'

'Have you completed your tests?'

'Not yet.'

'But you can tell whether his intelligence is below normal?'

He hesitated. 'I ought not to speak of it.'

'Come, Alexander, don't be stuffy,' Mable urged. 'You can see Morag is closely interested in this case. Is there any harm likely to come from telling her the story?'

'We-ell . . . In fact, perhaps the opposite. As far as I can gather, the mother is a remarkably silly woman, little likely to be any use to the poor boy. He has a hard enough life ahead of him without a mother who thinks first of herself.'

'You're going to give them bad news?'

'Bad enough, I think. The lad is profoundly deaf. He has very little idea of sound, even by conduction. I have had Dr Deneuve examine his ears thoroughly; there is some deformity of the auricle and the lateral sinuses have defects. He is unlikely ever to be able to hear speech, although with training he may be taught to detect larger sounds by vibration: for instance, he can be brought to know when an orchestra is playing or when a cart is going by.'

Morag looked at him, her eyes wide with pain. 'And will he speak?'

'He can be taught to speak so that those close to him, those who know him, may be able to understand him. But with those outside his family circle he will have to rely on written conversation or sign language.'

'He is much worse than I,' Mabel Hubbard said in pity. 'Poor boy.'

'Do his parents know all this?'

[193]

'I have to tell them tomorrow. I don't look forward to the occasion.'

His worst fears were realised. Luisa had hysterics, and had to be given smelling salts and a small glass of brandy. 'Sign language?' she cried when she could speak. 'Like an Indian? Like a savage?'

'Mrs Craigallan, the savagery is in ourselves if we think harshly of those who have to use signs.'

'Oh, that's only a high minded way of looking at it! You know as well as I do that most folk think the deaf are funny or a nuisance. As for the dumb; I've always been afraid of them.'

'But surely, ma'am, you're not afraid of your own son?'

She shivered. 'Sometimes I've thought he is very wild and odd.'

'But that's only because he's been unable to make anyone understand him, or been prevented from understanding, himself, by his inability to hear. Now you recognise the cause, surely you see there's nothing to be alarmed about?'

'The point is, what happens now?' Rob said, taking the matter on quickly.

'He must begin lessons at once. He is bright, eager to learn, and any delay will only impair his character.'

'Can you supply us with a teacher?'

'Supply you? In what sense do you mean that?'

'Well, sir, I believe you train teachers of the deaf. If you could recommend someone who could come and live at van Huten's –'

'No, no,' Bell said, holding up a hand. 'I'm afraid that is impossible.'

'I don't follow you, sir. You just said my son needed lessons –'

'But I have no teachers to spare! Dear Mr Craigallan, I am only at the beginning of the task of teaching teachers how to help the deaf. The work is vast, the numbers needing help are very great. I cannot spare a teacher to go to the country and work with only one child.'

'But you say Cornelius needs immediate teaching –'

'I do indeed – and he can get that here in Boston.'

'In Boston?' Luisa echoed, aghast. 'You mean, stay here and let everyone know our son is a deaf mute?'

'It's nothing to be ashamed of, ma'am –'

'How can you talk such nonsense! I could never hold up my head again –'

'Luisa, it's not your head we have to worry about,' Rob interrupted.

'But he's only a little boy! Surely if we wait a year or two, there will be a teacher available to come to the farm –'

'I wouldn't advise that, Mrs Craigallan,' Bell said with firmness. 'The longer you wait, the more difficult it becomes. And more damage will be done to the boy's character. You have no conception how frustrating it is to a lively child, not to be able to communicate with the rest of the world. He may get into all kinds of scrapes, out of rage and impatience.'

'You would enjoy living in Boston,' Rob urged to his wife. 'You often say the farm is dull –'

'What enjoyment can there possibly be, living cooped up with a deaf and dumb child? I should be ashamed to ask friends to call! It would be horrid!'

Bell frowned at her and rose from his chair. He moved towards the door, signifying that the consultation was at an end. 'Perhaps you and your wife will discuss the matter and let me know what you decide,' he suggested. 'I have teachers here at the institution who could teach Cornelius after school hours until he reaches the age of normal entrance to the school. I repeat, the sooner he begins lessons, the better. I hope you'll let me have your views after the weekend is over.'

'Thank you.' Rob shook hands and ushered Luisa out. Cornelius was brought to join them by a young male assistant from the speech laboratory farther along the corridor. Rob couldn't help noticing how eagerly the boy held on to the young man's hand, and how unwillingly he allowed himself to be picked up and carried out of the building by his father.

At the hotel, Luisa and Rob argued for hours. Luisa was adamant. Nothing would induce her to come and stay in Boston with Cornelius. In the first place she would find it shaming to admit she had a child with defects that were almost like imbecility. In the second place, though this was unstated, she didn't want to leave Rob. She had a feeling that some young farm girl would capture his attention if she wasn't there.

'I'll live in Boston if you will too,' she suggested.

'You know that's impossible.'

'I don't see why? You could put in a manager at the farm.'

'Not the kind I'd trust with my farm,' Rob said. 'Even if I could find someone suitable, it would be six months or a year before I could train him in the ways I want the production to go.'

'Oh, nonsense –'

'It isn't nonsense, Luisa. Contrary to what you may imagine, agriculture isn't a matter of throwing seed on the ground and letting it do the best it can. I'm trying to study which seeds germinate best, which give the highest return –'

'You mean you think more of the farm than you do of me and Cornelius.'

'That's not so. But the farm is our livelihood. It has to support us all – including Julius, don't forget. His demands aren't low. To add a new household in Boston to our present expenses . . . Why *can't* you move to Boston and look after Cornelius? It's your duty to do so, as a mother!'

'It's my duty to do what I think is best for the whole family, and my opinion is that we should go back to van Huten's and forget the whole thing until Cornelius is old enough to be sent away to school as a boarder.'

He put arguments in front of her but it was never any use. On Monday he had to tell Professor Bell that they had decided to return to their home and wait for either the chance of a resident teacher to come to them, or for Cornelius to be old enough to go to school.

Bell sighed and shrugged his shoulders. 'You're making a great mistake,' he said.

'There's nothing we can do,' Rob said.

When they were leaving, and Luisa had gone out, Bell called him back. 'What exactly is the problem?' he inquired. 'Is it your wife's unwillingness?'

'I'm afraid so.'

Bell turned away. 'In my work,' he said, 'few things have

depressed me so much as the lack of kindliness shown by the hearing towards the deaf. In a mother, it seems almost a sin.'

Rob could think of no excuse. He bowed and went out.

Alexander Graham Bell wasn't easily deflected. He went out at once to speak to Morag. 'Your friends the Craigallans have given me their decision,' he said. 'They have decided, against my advice, to take their child home and let him wait another three useless years for tuition.'

'What?' Morag cried, shocked. 'But surely – that's totally wrong?'

'Indeed it is. That idiotic mother of his can't face the idea of living in Boston with her poor damaged child. She is ashamed of him.'

'But what does her husband say?' Morag asked.

'He can do nothing with her. He sees it is wrong, but he is powerless.' Bell hesitated. 'You led me to think you had some influence with the woman. Could you speak to her?'

'Oh no! No, that is impossible.'

'But I thought . . . Didn't you say you were close to the family?'

'Not that close,' she replied, with concealed bitterness. 'If you can't persuade her, I don't think I could.'

'I wish you would try, Morag,' he said. 'It is very serious. The boy's future is in the balance.'

She shook her head. 'I dare not interfere.'

But when he had gone, his words stayed with her, echoing and re-echoing in her mind: 'The boy's future is in the balance . . . I wish you would try, Morag.'

She went in search of Captain Kauffman, who was in the garden reading to his wife. 'Would it be convenient if I went out for an hour or so?'

He looked up from the book. 'Must you? Gertrude was just saying that she would like to go indoors and settle for the evening –'

'No, no,' Gertrude intervened. 'I c.can m.manage a while l.longer . . . Go out, Morag. You g.go out t.too little.'

Morag called a hackney carriage and went quickly to the Corner Book Store. Here she wrote a note and asked the hackney driver to deliver it at Rob's hotel. He was to come back with an answer: 'It's important,' she said, 'I'll pay you well.'

Within fifteen minutes he returned. On the note she had sent was scribbled: 'I'll be with you as soon as I can.'

Rob had to call a maid to take charge of Cornelius while he went out. Luisa was away on a shopping expedition – 'her last chance to buy something decent' as she put it, before they left Boston. The maid was quite willing to sit with Cornelius, who was playing quietly on the floor with a set of bricks given to him by the new friends he'd made at the school.

'My dear!' Rob said when he found Morag at the bookstore. 'Is something wrong?'

'With your family – I think so, Rob! Come, let's walk. I can't stay out long, for Mrs Kauffmann needs me. But I felt I *must* speak to you.'

He offered her his arm and they began to pace along the side-walk. The late afternoon sun beat down, dust rose from the wheels of the carriages and carts on the busy roadway. Shoppers were still hurrying among the big stores. Rob instinctively turned away from them, for fear of seeing Luisa. They walked down towards the harbour. Here a slight breeze from Massachusetts Bay brought a tang of salt.

'Alexander Bell came to the house earlier this afternoon,' she began. 'He's very distressed at your decision about Cornelius.'

'It isn't my decision!' Rob roared. 'It's his mother's! We've been arguing ever since we left his office. She's gone out in a temper, to spend as much money as she can to punish me.'

'Are you telling me that you can't handle Luisa?'

'What can I do? She equates deafness with mental deficiency. She's ashamed to have it known that Cornelius is deaf and dumb. She wants to take him back to the farm and keep him hidden, until he can be sent at a boarder –'

'Good God, Rob! That's years ahead! What's he to do meantime? Cower like a frightened animal in a hole while he might be learning how to get ready for a decent life?'

He shivered at her words, turning to stare down at her. 'You're not sparing of your contempt, Morag.'

'Nor should I be! Didn't you keep telling me, on that voyage from Scotland to America, that you had the blood of Highland chiefs in your veins? Didn't you tell me you'd left your home to escape injustice? And is this what it comes to here in your new life – that you'll inflict injustice on your own son?'

He made no reply for a moment. Then he said: 'I want him to have tuition. I want to keep him here in Boston. But his mother will not stay to look after him. He's too young to be put in school in the ordinary way.'

'You can't stay here with him yourself?'

He hesitated. 'I've thought about it. It's been in the back of my mind ever since Luisa declared she wouldn't stay unless I did too. But the difficulties are enormous. There are financial considerations, and the welfare of the farm. Morag, you know yourself, at this very moment I should be at van Huten's, supervising the harvest . . .'

'I see.'

'Don't say it in that tone. It's not just that I want the farm to prosper, that I enjoy having it in my control. I have responsibilities besides Cornelius. Julius doesn't care about the farm but he spends the money. Dorothea, too, must have her allowance. Luisa's dowry is invested in the farm. It *must* do well.'

'All that is quite true –'

'I always hoped my son would take over from me. But it's quite clear now that Cornelius never will. He'll never be able to learn how to handle a plough or a header; he won't be able to call to the horses. He won't be able to give instructions to the farmhands. He won't be able to haggle over prices with the grain dealers. In a way, it might be kinder to him just to let him grow up as a carefree boy in the countryside.'

'Wild boy, you mean? And what happens when he's a man? Is he to be a wild man? Is he never to be fitted to make friends, to court a girl and marry?'

'I don't know what to do, Morag!' Rob cried. 'I just don't know what to do!'

'You must find a way to look after your son,' she said. 'I refuse to believe you'll let Luisa's selfishness beat you! I'll despise you for ever if you do.'

'Oh, it's easy enough to take up an attitude of reproach. Tell me what to do.'

'What? Is this Craigallan of Glen Bairach? Helpless and confused?' She laughed without amusement. 'So far, Rob, you've been quick to find a way out of your troubles.' She turned away from him. 'I must go back. I promised to be home in an hour.'

'No, wait – tell me what you think –'

'I've told you all I have to tell you. I know from what Alexander said that it's possible to improve your son's chances. You must find a way to make that happen.'

'Morag –!'

'Goodbye, Rob.' She was already walking quickly to the corner, where a passing cab drew to a standstill at her raised hand. Rob hurried after her to help her in. 'Goodbye,' she said, pausing to look at him seriously with her great deer-like eyes. 'I'll be waiting and watching to know what you do.'

'I'll write to you –'

'Only if you have something good to tell me of Cornelius. If you take him home to hide him away, I never want to hear from you again.' She sat back. 'Drive on,' she called to the cabman.

13

WHEN LUISA RETURNED TO the hotel, Rob was waiting to argue with her again. Morag's words and attitude had spurred him into renewed effort. In the short time before his wife came into the hotel room he'd had time to think of a plan.

'Luisa, Cornelius must stay in Boston –'

'But I've told you –'

'Whether you agree to stay or not,' he went on, over-riding her protest. 'He must stay here under the guardianship of some reliable person –'

'Some person? But who?'

'We can ask Professor Bell. I believe he could help. If not, we must find someone.'

Luisa was recovering from the shock of his words. Her brain was flashing into activity. She could almost see the name Morag forming on her husband's lips. Rather than let him speak it, she leapt into action.

'We could ask Aunt Remegen,' she suggested.

'Aunt Remegen?'

'You remember her. She always comes to everything – she was at our wedding, and Ellen Rose's christening, and Papa's funeral. Not Cornelius's christening – she had colic. But usually she never misses. Aunt Remegen – in the lavender mantle edged with black braid, and the close bonnet. She gave Ellen Rose a silver rattle, remember?'

'Oh, that one . . .' There were always crowds of distant relations at all the gatherings. They came to get a good meal, to cadge a little money, to remind their more affluent cousins and nephews that they still existed.

Aunt Remegen came to his memory as a small, plump figure in – as Luisa had said – several shades of lavender and a worn little bonnet. Her face sagged in kindly creases. He remembered that she had cradled the little Ellen Rose in her arms with soft, vapid affection but had given her up again quickly when offered a glass of negus.

'She's very old,' he said.

'Not so very. Older than Mama, of course, but she gets about. She always turns up at everything.'

'So I recall. But she couldn't look after a little boy, Luisa.'

'I'm not suggesting she should. You'd have to rent a little house here for her, and provide her with a servant to see to the house and take care of Cornelius. But Aunt Remegen would be the head of the household. She'd jump at the chance, I promise you! Ever since Uncle Remegen died she's been living in Utica and she hates it.'

'I don't know whether I –'

'It's no use asking Mama,' Luisa swept on. 'She wouldn't entertain the idea. She's happy with Julius in New York. It's got to be someone who's in need of a home, of a little income to make it worth the removal.'

'She's a kindly old soul, I seem to recall . . .'

'Very kind. That silver rattle for Ellen Rose – she must have had to scrimp and scrape to afford it. She's not grasping, Rob. She'd be content with a little place and enough to get by on. And then, you see, she'd enjoy bringing Cornelius home for holidays with us, at Christmas and so on. It would give her a new interest in life.'

Aunt Remegen could hardly believe her luck when her wealthy relatives descended on her in Utica with their proposal. She had lived for years with a distant cousin, sharing expenses with her in a house belonging to the cousin and thus subject to tyrannical laws, such as no card games, no alcoholic beverages, no lights on after nine in the evening . . .

Her enthusiasm died a little when she learned that Cornelius was to stay in Boston because he needed tuition from special teachers. 'He's not . . . er . . . unruly? Doesn't throw himself about? I don't know that I could control a child if he were difficult . . . nor should I care to have to witness any mopping and mowing . . .'

Rob looked down at her with weary protest. 'Aunt Remegen, he is two and a half years old and perfectly normal except that he cannot hear – and therefore cannot speak. Under expert guidance, he is likely to improve greatly. All we ask is that you provide a home for him in Boston, where his teachers can come. You can have a maid to look after him. You need have little to do with him.'

'Ah . . .' She thought about it. 'May I have a carriage?'

'Aunt Remegen, don't be absurd,' Luisa said with a little stamp of the foot. 'You're being offered a nice little house, a little income, a place to be away from Cousin Rebecca, all the interest of Boston society, holidays with us at the farm whenever school is not in session . . . If that's not enough, we'll find someone else.'

'No, no – pray, don't be angry, niece! It's only that I can't get about so easily these days . . . But I shall be able to afford a cab when I want one, shall I not?'

'I'm sure you won't find yourself short of day-to-day cash,' Rob assured her. 'What do you say, Aunt Remegen?'

Luisa undertook to instal her in the new home. It gave her a great deal of pleasure to dash back and forth between the farm and Boston until fall was almost over. She furnished the house with items not needed at van Huten's, or those pieces she'd always thought old-fashioned and cumbersome. Thus, when Cornelius took up his abode there, the house seemed strangely familiar. Aunt Remegen, too, was known to him – a strange little lady who liked to lean down and put her plump cheek against his, and always smelt of dust and lavender.

Morag received a letter from Rob reporting his solution to the problem. Now and again, in her free time, she walked past the little house in Hull Street. She saw it begin to come to life, took note of the little widow lady who bobbed about inside supervising the hanging of the drapes and the polishing of the door knocker.

So . . . Cornelius had been saved from the world of silence. She took some pride in the thought that she had helped bring it about.

But at home with the Kauffmans, there was less to make her happy. Mrs Kauffman hadn't done well during the heat of this year's summer – quite contrary to last year's result. She seemed to be losing ground visibly. The doctor said in despair that he could do nothing. The captain and Morag built their lives around her, so that she should never be alone.

When the end came, it was night. Morag was sleeping on a cot in Gertrude's room, exhausted by a day of great activity and anxiety. She heard her employer's wife make a muffled sound, then heard a violent, undirected movement. There was a thud as Mrs Kauffman tried to get out of bed.

'Gertrude,' Morag cried, leaping up.

She could hear Gertrude trying to say something. She could only guess at it but she thought she was calling for her husband.

'Captain!' Morag cried, running to the door in her nightdress. 'Captain – quickly!'

But he was too late. When he reached his wife's side, she was gone. One poor useless hand was stretched out towards the door, hoping to feel his touch before she died.

The captain was completely broken up by his wife's passing. Morag had to take charge of everything. His many friends rallied round. All the arrangements were made, the funeral was held, the mourning was ordered, the letters of acknowledgement were written.

In November Kauffman asked for Morag to come to his study. He was pacing about when she came into the room. 'Morag, I won't beat about the bush. I can't bear Boston now that Gertrude is gone. I'm going back to sea. I only became a landlubber because she was so sick and longed for my company.'

'I quite understand, captain.'

'I'm going to sell the house. There are many of Gertrude's belongings still in her closets. You are free to take any of them for your own use. Those that you don't need or want, perhaps you'll dispose of to your own profit or to some worthy cause. I don't want to see them again.'

'Certainly, sir.'

'One of my worries is . . . what will become of you? You could go back to your family at van Huten's, I suppose?'

'I shan't do that, captain. I shall find another post.'

'If you require a reference, you may depend upon it that you shall have the most glowing one.'

'You are very kind.'

'I'm joining ship at Norfolk for the first week in December. Can you be ready to leave the house by then?'

'Of course.'

She'd expected a move of this kind from him. He had been restless and depressed since the funeral. She'd decided that she would move out to a boarding-house until she could find a new post.

Thanks to his generosity, she went with a good wardrobe of clothes, a small sum of money from the sale of such things as silver hairbrushes and perfume bottles, and three months' salary. She already had some savings. She was in no hurry to leap into other employment. She wanted to go where she would be happy.

Besides, now she had leisure, and could spare the time to see how things were going at Mrs Remegen's. She took to walking past the house on her daily airing. And what she saw depressed her.

Aunt Remegen had no control over the servant she had hired. She was a good enough girl, buxom and energetic, but she liked her own way. She soon saw that her mistress was weak-willed, forgetful, and nervous; it was easy to tell her that she hadn't been given the money to pay the butcher when it was already resting comfortably in her pocket. As to cooking, Lola's abilities were limited. She made no efforts to prepare food that would please a little boy. Cornelius began to have stomach upsets and, being unable to say so, was sick more than once over his bedspread or his clothes. Lola grew more and more impatient with him.

Morag saw them out together; Mrs Remegen insisted that Lola must take the boy out for exercise twice a day, as if he were a puppy. Morag could see he was growing paler and losing weight.

It was easy to strike up an acquaintance with Lola. She was gossipy and noisy. Morag took care to come across her on her evening out, invited her to a meal at a respectable restaurant, and let her talk.

'What I can't understand is why they're bothering,' Lola declared. 'He's never going to be any use, now is he? My sister's sister-in-law had a little girl like that – sat in a corner rocking herself, more like a sack of potatoes than a person! I say to the missus, I say, "All these folks coming in and out, all they do is tramp mud over my clean floors."' Lola shook her head. 'But she don't pay no heed. Just lets 'em come. I don't think she knows no more than I do what they're up to. Her head's full of whist and picquet.'

Morag's original intention was simply to keep an eye on the situation. But the more she got to know Lola, the more she became convinced that someone would have to take a hand. Lola ought to be replaced by a quieter, more intelligent girl. Aunt Remegen ought to be reminded that she was here to supervise Cornelius, not to join card parties.

What should Morag do? Write a letter of complaint to Rob? But it was clear that Rob had to deal with Luisa over these matters. Any change might bring about another row.

The solution, when it came, seemed so simple that she couldn't understand why it had taken so long. She said to Lola: 'Are you particularly devoted to Mrs Remegen?'

'Devoted? How d'you mean?'

'Would you just as soon work somewhere else?'

'I'd just as soon be married to Jack Wickhouse, if I were to be making a change!' cried Lola. 'I'm only slaving away, working my fingers to the bone for that silly old hen, because we haven't got the money to start out in life. He's a shoemaker in Peabody; he could set up on his own if only we could get eighty dollars together.'

'Lola, how would you like eighty dollars?'

'What eighty dollars?' Lola said, going even redder than her already high colouring.

'The eighty dollars I'm going to give you.'

'Why should you give me eighty dollars?'

'I want you to do something for me. I want you to tell Mrs Remegen you're leaving to get married, but that you can recommend a good housemaid to take your place.'

Lola was baffled. 'And who's that going to be, may I ask?'

'Me.'

'You? But you're a lady . . .'

'Not a bit. I started off as a housemaid when I first arrived in New York, and I've always been in employment of some kind. Now I'm seeking a post, and the one you hold seems ideal to me – an easy mistress, no one else in the house except a little deaf and dumb boy –'

'You may think it's easy! It's hard work –'

'Perhaps it is. But the point is, Lola – it's a good steady job. I'd be settled for life if I got it. Now you – you want to go away and settle in Peabody. So I'm prepared to pay you for your trouble if you'll go.'

Lola was suspicious. It took two weeks to convince her she was really going to gain eighty dollars and a husband, and lose nothing.

Mrs Remegen was stricken when she said she was leaving. It meant she would have to start interviewing girls to replace her, and that was so tiresome! Some were pert, some were aggressive, and some were sly – how could one know a good worker? And they nearly all had forged references.

'I can tell you of a good girl,' Lola said. 'A friend of mine. Been in some good places, too, I can tell you. A fine home in New York, and a rich farm out towards Lake Erie, and a good house here in Boston.'

'Why is she out of a post then?' Mrs Remegen put in, thinking she was scoring a point.

'Her last employer died. Shall you see her? You'll be sorry if you don't.'

Mrs Remegen quickly agreed. Anything, to ease the problems of replacing Lola.

The girl who came was dressed in quiet dark clothes, of rather good quality. She had a pale clear face, big dark eyes, and a gentle voice. Her references were exceptional – and genuine.

'But surely you want something better than a housemaid's post?' Aunt Remegen objected, handing them back.

'I wish to stay in Boston, ma'am, and it's not so easy to find a post as companion. If you would take me, I should be happy to serve you. This seems a quiet household.'

'When could you start, Miss . . . er . . . McGarth?'

'Whenever you wish, ma'am.'

Thankfully, Aunt Remegen hired her, but because in the course of a few months of sharing the house with Lola Arnold, she'd become accustomed to summoning the maid by calling 'Lola!' Aunt Remegen kept up the habit. It never fully entered her consciousness that Morag had a name of her own.

And when, one triumphant evening months later, Cornelius at last managed to utter an approximation of the name of the girl who'd shared so much of his short life with him, the strange monotonous sound was enough like 'Lola' not to be differentiated by Aunt Remegen.

But what Cornelius was trying to say was 'Morag.'

Rob had seen the announcement of Mrs Kauffman's death in the newspapers and had written to Morag inquiring what she intended to do. He received no reply. When he could arrange matters so as to get away from the farm and visit Boston, he found the Kauffman house closed up. At that time, when he dropped in on Aunt Remegen to see his son, Lola Arnold was still housemaid. There was no trace of Morag. He even inquired of Alexander Bell, if he knew where Mrs Kauffman's companion had gone. Professor Bell could only say he thought the young lady had gone away on a holiday.

For some weeks Rob watched for the mailman, hoping Morag would write. But the months went by and nothing came.

Times weren't so good on the farm. He had plenty to take up his attention. The price of wheat was slowly going down from the usual two dollars a bushel that had become as accepted as the rising and setting of the sun, and no one at first quite knew why. The newly organised Department of Agriculture, not yet ten years old, was trying to gather statistics to explain the change, but in Rob's opinion, it needed no government department to account for it. The reason was production from the new lands to the west.

In the few years since the end of the Civil War, the tide flowing west had been phenomenal. The Department of Agriculture proudly reported that the 'centre of wheat production' was moving westwards with irresistible impetus; whereas in 1850 the biggest producers were thought to be in and around Columbus Ohio, they were now some miles west of Springfield Illinois.

That in itself need not have perturbed the eastern growers too much. Wheat grown on vast open land is easier to raise, but it still has to be transported to market. The eastern farmers had for a long time held the advantage there; they were near the cities, where the dealers met, and near the ports from which the grain was shipped to Europe.

Now the railways were heading west, almost as fast as the ground was broken by the pioneers. The railroads provided freight cars which brought the wheat pouring into the primary markets. Because wheat was cheap to grow on the rich, new land, the western growers could afford the freight charges which brought their produce to market. Thus the price of wheat was slowly being forced down.

Every cent that came off was a cent off every bushel that Rob and his fellow farmers grew. At a yield of between ten and twelve bushels an acre, they were losing six cents on every acre they worked, although their costs were just the same to bring forth the harvest. And the decline continued.

The eastern farmers felt a sense of grievance. Their land was 'old', they had to practise crop rotation if they were to keep it in good heart for the wheat, but the other crops brought in nothing like the same profit. If the land was put to potatoes or other vegetables, there were difficulties in harvesting; no machinery yet invented could pick up potatoes or gather beans. If it was turned to hay, there was a market, especially if the farm were near a city with plenty of horse transport and a great need for fodder. But hay was even more subject to weather problems than wheat. Two or three heavy thunderstorms could reduce the grass to messy pulp, impossible to harvest. Cold weather retarded the storage of nutrients in the stem; too much heat dried it out too much. The New York State Farmers' Brotherhood held conferences on their problems. 'What we want is a mileage levy on wheat brought in from the west!' they cried. Or, 'We must prevent the dealers in wheat from buying in advance at a price they agree among themselves! They're taking the bread from the mouths of our wives and children!'

'What we really want,' Rob declared in a speech he was invited to give at the November convention, 'is better seed grain! Gentlemen, no raiser of sheep in my homeland would leave it to chance as we do with our grain. Sheep-breeders, cattlemen, raisers of hogs – they plan the fertilisation of their livestock. We must plan the direction in which our grain develops, not go on with this foolish hit-or-miss method. Which of us can prophesy the yield on his acreage with any certainty? I say to you, we must be able to buy seed we can rely on, or improve the seed we keep each year for sowing. We must *not* put back into the ground seed from grain that has been unsatisfactory.'

'But that's a programme for years of experiment,' they protested. 'In the meantime, we'll all be forced into bankruptcy by those sod-busters out west!' They thought Rob a visionary, wasting their time with airy-fairy notions while ruin stared them in the face.

Yet, strangely, this 'visionary' survived better in the wheat market than they did. His crops of both wheat and grass seemed less affected by hessian fly. Although leaf rust struck his fields as it did everyone else's, less of his crop was lost. The term he used for his plants was 'resistant' – they were resistant to infection and attack. For this reason he was sometimes referred to behind his back as Resistance Rob. The trouble was, when other farms made a deal with him for some of the seed he raised and kept for his own use, they very often didn't get results as good as those on the van Huten farm. It was annoying, more so as he sometimes seemed to imply that the reason for the shortfall was the buyer's carelessness.

Rob would from time to time ask Luisa to economise. He wrote to Julius and his mother-in-law in New York, explaining that the farm income was a little down again and would they be so good as to keep their expenses within reason.

Julius never believed a word of it. 'He's feathering his own nest,' he would mutter, and when ready cash wasn't available, bought clothes and wine on credit.

Luisa would respond to Rob's urgings by an economy drive which was rigid, but it soon wore off. Another occasion for a dinner or a party would come along, and then, despite Rob's protests, she had to show the expected van Huten hospitality. Aunt Remegen would bring Cornelius to visit his Mama on his birthday, or for Easter, so there would have to be cakes and gifts and a celebration.

Cornelius found the farm very strange. He was brought here, among these great animals and pieces of equipment which he vaguely remembered, and waved away to amuse himself. No lessons, no teachers sitting with him watching his every move. Then there was this little girl he didn't remember at all, for when he went to Boston, Ellie-Rose was still a babe in arms.

Ellie-Rose had evolved her own name for herself, in the way that children do when they begin to talk. There had never been any doubt that she *would* talk; from her earliest weeks she had gurgled and cried and demanded attention. She was in every way normal – pretty, active, good natured with just enough naughtiness to make her a character. Luisa was fond of showing her off to her friends; she would deck her out in ruffled frocks, lace caps, numerous starched petticoats. Ellie-Rose would enjoy all this for a time and then toddle off, her fat little feet in their shiny buttoned boots thumping on the ground, to find some mischief that would reduce her finery to tatters.

Ellie-Rose enjoyed Cornelius's visits. He was the ideal companion. He never argued with her, would do as she told him without complaint, never cried if he was hurt. They communicated in some mysterious way. Cornelius had been taught to sign by his teachers from the Bell School, and in his turn had taught Ellie-Rose, but Luisa had been horrified when she saw them 'talking' to each other in this fashion.

'No, no!' she shrieked. 'One dumb child is enough!'

'But Luisa – what's the use of paying to have Cornelius taught to communicate by sign language if you won't let him use it?' Rob protested.

'Let him use it with strangers! I won't have it in this house!'

'You will let him use signs. I warn you, Luisa, if you stop him from speaking to us in even this limited way, you'll force him into total isolation.'

She said no more and pretended to fall in with his wishes. But he knew she hated to see the flashing fingers 'talking' for the children. And they too were aware of her disapproval. Ellie-Rose never used the signs when she could make herself understood by Cornelius without.

Their father would take them up in front of him on his horse to ride round the farm. Cornelius would sit clutching the mane, staring about him eagerly. Ellie-Rose always had the place against Papa's jacket; she would hug one of his arms and squirm about from time to time to look up into his face. One of the things that made her irresistible to Rob was that she so plainly adored him.

The farm was a more silent world to Cornelius than Boston. He would watch the grain rippling in the breeze, feel the wind on his cheeks, but there seemed to be no sound connected with them. He could feel the heavy tread of the farm horses and the rumble of the carts, but the swish of the header couldn't reach him, nor the clink of pails in the cowshed.

In Boston there were many sounds he could be aware of. He could feel the organ in church, trembling in the floor under his knees. He enjoyed church; he would sit watching the people in rows, opening and closing their mouths in unison while the organ made the wood of the pew thrill under his fingers. He supposed the people were saying something to the organ; as yet he couldn't work out the words. He was not yet taking lessons in lip reading.

One of his teachers, Miss Gower, had taught him a prayer in sign language. 'God bless Mother and Father, Aunt and Morag, and make me a good boy, for ever and ever, Amen.' There were signs for God, for 'be kind', for Mother and Father, and for Aunt.

Morag's sign was 'lady'. Then came 'good' and 'boy', and a gesture that implied infinity or greatness. Amen was mouthed, no sound coming out of his lips.

Cornelius had been repeating this prayer under Morag's guidance every night for some weeks when he suddenly touched her arm. 'Who is God?' he signed.

She was taken aback. After a moment she told him, using the signs she had learned as he had learned them: 'God is in church.'

'How can God be kind to Mother and Father and everyone?'

She told him what she herself had been taught but no longer believed with quite such unquestioning fervour. 'God is a father who lives above us in the sky and looks after everyone.'

He considered that. 'Father lives at the farm,' he observed.

'Yes.'

'*You* look after me.'

'Yes.'

'Are you Father too?'

'No, Cornelius.'

He thumped the bedspread for her attention. 'You are Mother?' he urged, his face conveying that this wasn't a question so much as a statement he wondered about.

She shook her head. She felt her throat go tight. She put an arm round him and laid him down in the bed. 'Good night, Cornelius.'

He caught her hand. 'You are Aunt?' his fingers asked her.

'No, darling. I'm lady.'

'But everybody in skirt is lady.'

'Yes.'

He held on to her. 'I am Cornelius?' There was a sign they had all agreed as his name sign, an abbreviation of the alphabetic signs he would learn more fully when he began to read and write.

'Yes,' she said.

'Who are you?'

Morag had already learned the extended two-handed alphabet, in preparation for the time when he would want more from books than looking at pictures and learning a sign. She held out her hands and with them wrote 'M-O-R-A-G.'

He copied it at once. His actions were always much quicker

[213]

than hers and with him the signs became a little blur, with two pats of the hands against each other, one at the beginning and one at the end. From then on, that was his unspoken name for her. It became very dear to her, that little double thud of his hands against one another.

She knew that her life in the Remegen household couldn't go on for ever. One day her presence here would become known to Luisa. The time limit she set in her own mind was when Cornelius learned to write and had to send duty letters home. He was bound to mention Morag. Written down, her name was unmistakeable, and there could scarcely be another girl in the state of Massachusetts who bore it.

By then she hoped to have steeled herself to the necessity of leaving him. She knew now she'd made a mistake in coming to Aunt Remegen. She had almost come to regard Cornelius as her own child, the one she might have had if things had gone right between herself and Rob. That was why it hurt so much when he asked who she was, and why his affection for her was so important. More than once she told herself she ought to pack up and go, that she was being unfair to them both by staying in the same house with him. But he needed her. Who else did he have?

14

THERE WAS A GREAT scare in the van Huten family when Julius announced he was getting married. Dorothea turned up at the farm, tight with rage and contempt. 'You should see her!' she cried. 'She has no breeding at all, and I'm sure her hair is dyed! He met her at the race track, of all places!'

Rob felt that she might be prejudiced, but as he listened it did seem that the lady of Julius's heart was less than perfect. He had spent money on her like water. She was even buying a trousseau, in preparation for their honeymoon trip to Europe.

'I don't see a single item of clothing on her back that cost anything like what he's given her!' Dorothea declared. 'I think she's an adventuress. But he won't hear a word against her.'

The reason for her visit was to urge Rob to make inquiries. Rather unwillingly, Rob went to New York, and within a week he had learned, with the help of a private detective agency, that the lady Julius hoped to marry was already wed. The money he had given her went into the pocket of her husband; they were apparently a well-known pair of confidence tricksters.

Was Julius grateful at being rescued from this misfortune? Not the least. He refused to speak to Rob afterwards and was less than friendly with his own mother for her interference; so much so that she felt it expedient to remove herself from their New York apartment to Saratoga Springs.

Perhaps if she had been with him, the next disaster might not have struck. The first news of it to reach Rob came with the family lawyer, who arrived on horseback, panting, from Albany. 'Mr Craigallan! I must speak with you!'

'Come in,' said Rob, eyeing him with apprehension as he ushered him into the study and called for refreshments. 'It must be something important to bring you here in such a state, Mr de Peert?'

'Important? Monumental! Mr Craigallan, I have received instructions from Mr van Huten to transfer the deeds of the farm to a Mr William O'Donovan.'

Whatever Rob had expected, it wasn't this. He gaped at the lawyer. 'Transfer?'

'By wire, this morning.' De Peert held out the paper. Written on it in the copperplate script of the telegraph clerk was the message: 'Please transfer deeds of ownership van Huten's Farm, New York State, to the name of Mr William O'Donovan of Suite 41, Grand Central Hotel, New York, effective from receipt of this instruction.'

Rob read it with incomprehension. 'It's a fake –'

'No, I wired at once to Mr van Huten to ask if he had sent any such instruction and received this.' He handed another telegraph message form. This one said: 'Please comply with my former instructions urgently. Mr O'Donovan arrives to claim the deeds on the 22nd.'

'But . . . it's impossible!' Rob declared. 'He never told me he was selling the farm!'

'Mr Craigallan . . . There's no mention of price in these instructions.'

'No, I see that, but . . .' Rob's voice tailed off. 'What are you saying?'

'I don't know what to make of it. There is no mention of negotiation, of inventory, of any kind of deed of sale. *In toto*,' de Peert said in a plaintive tone, 'I am unused to receiving instructions by telegraph, especially on so large a matter.'

'Yes.' Rob took hold of himself. 'Sending a telegram is strange, isn't it? As if it was very urgent . . .' He stared at the message form. 'He's in desperate need of money – is that it? Debts, perhaps? But

[216]

surely he could make some arrangement with creditors? He wouldn't sell the farm.'

'I repeat, Mr Craigallan – there is no mention of sale. The instruction is – "transfer". I am to arrange a transfer, not a deed of sale.'

'This has to be stopped,' Rob said. 'I must go to New York at once –'

'Indeed, sir, and that is my reason for coming here post haste – to invite you to go with me. We must speak with Mr van Huten before this extreme step is taken. You note that this new owner – this unknown Mr O'Donovan – is due to arrive claiming the deeds in two days time.'

'He won't find that easy!' Rob declared, calling to Sternbach to saddle his horse.

They found Julius at home. He opened the door to them himself, rather fearfully, it seemed to Rob, unwilling to appear until he had asked through the wood who was there. 'What are you doing here?' he gasped.

'We're here to find out what the hell is going on,' Rob exclaimed. He brushed by Julius into the handsome livingroom of his Tenth Street apartment. 'What did you mean by those idiotic telegrams?'

'Idiotic?' Julius echoed. 'It's a matter of life and death –'

'Mr van Huten, I cannot quite understand how that can be. Legal matters are not undertaken in that fashion –'

'But they are! You've done what I instructed, I hope?'

'No, sir, certainly not!' de Peert said stoutly.

'Well, my God, you'd better!' Julius shouted, his plump cheeks trembling. 'Or I'm a dead man!'

'Don't be absurd, Julius –'

'I tell you, if de Peert doesn't draw up those papers by the stated time, I'll have a squad of Bowery Boys waiting for me outside the door. Broken limbs are the least I can expect –'

'Bowery Boys?' de Peert said.

'I believe they're gangsters,' Rob said. Dimly he was beginning to perceive a reason for Julius's wild message.

The story was brief and silly. Julius, stung by the criticism he'd had over his mercenary betrothed, had decided to recoup the money he'd thrown away on her. He had bought from a 'friend' an infallible system for winning at cards. At first, he had done well with it. He retrieved most of the sum he'd wasted. It then dawned on him how marvellous it would be to confront Rob with a substantial amount in cash, to throw it down in front of him, and say: 'There, you're always on at me about asking for money – here is a little to help you in your farming problems . . .'

But his luck turned. He couldn't believe it, and was sure he'd win back what he'd lost. He recklessly gambled on and on. 'I always knew I could win it back,' Julius moaned, plaintively. 'And I would have done, if I'd been able to go on longer. But O'Donovan closed down on me. He insisted I pay what I owed. So I . . . I . . .'

'You put up the deeds of the farm?'

'Well . . . I expected to win before ever I had to surrender them. You do see, don't you? I mean, if the system worked in the first place, it was bound to win again once I'd rectified the mistakes I was making –'

'Dear God,' groaned Rob. Then, pulling himself together, he turned to the lawyer. 'Gambling debts aren't legal, are they?'

'I believe not,' de Peert said. 'Although it is not a category of law I have ever had to dabble in –'

'No, no,' cried Julius. 'Don't try to wriggle out of it! You don't know these people – they'll half-kill me –'

'We'll get you out of New York,' Rob soothed. 'It'll be all right.'

But it was too late. Julius had gone before a notary public and signed a declaration that he formally and willingly assigned the property known as van Huten's Farm to William O'Donovan in recognition of services rendered. He produced a copy. 'O'Donovan has the other,' he said.

Rob watched as de Peert examined it. 'Is it legal?'

'Oh yes, quite legal.'

'Can we contest it?'

'Certainly, but it might be difficult to overturn. It is witnessed by the notary public's clerks, I have no doubt. They are probably men of character. Unless we can prove duress . . .' He raised his eyebrows at Julius. 'Were you dragged there? Was there a threat of violence?'

'Not in the office. But I knew the Bowery Boys were standing at the corner.'

'This is utter nonsense,' Rob said, trying to stay calm. 'You can't give away the roof over our heads, the total source of income of the family. It can't be legal.'

'Fight it if you like,' Julius said, huddling away on his chair. 'I certainly shan't.'

Rob called on William O'Donovan, who received him cordially. 'Craigallan,' he said. 'Van Huten mentioned you. You manage his farm for him, I understand.'

'Manage it?' Rob was brought up short. 'Yes, I suppose that's what I do. I've come to say, Mr O'Donovan, that his turning over the property to you isn't possible. It's not really his to dispose of. It's a family farm –'

'I think it is his,' O'Donovan said, turning a heavy signet ring round and round on a finger of his left hand. 'I talked it over with him thoroughly before I accepted it as guarantee for his wagers. I'm not a fool, Mr Craigallan.'

'No,' Rob agreed. He hesitated. 'Let's be sensible. You don't want a farm.'

'Quite right. I already have a buyer for it.'

'*What*?'

'He wants to take over, I hear, in time to get the seed in. Is that right? I'm not up in that kind of jargon. I'm a city guy. My attorney tells me the sale can go through without let or hindrance as soon as I have the deeds, and I expect to have them by the twenty-second.'

'You'll be disappointed!'

'Going to fight it, are you?' O'Donovan got up. He was a bulky man, scented with bay rum hair tonic, and exhaling the aroma of good cigars. 'You can take it to court if you like,' he said. 'But it won't be settled quickly, boy-o. Have you got the money for lawyers' fees?'

'Don't worry, I'll get it –'

'You will? And when you lose, what will you do then, after you've left yourself without a cent?'

'I won't lose,' Rob said. 'I can prove –'

'You can't prove a thing without van Huten's testimony, and he's a funk. You know it and I know it. Besides, the land belongs to me. He lost it to me, and I won't let it go, don't think it, bud!'

'You'll have to, if the court rules –'

'Aw, grow up!' O'Donovan said scornfully. 'Do you think I would risk going to court, without having a friend on the bench? Face it, Craigallan – I've got you in an armlock. I'm sorry if it means you'll lose your job –'

'My job?' Rob shouted. 'It's a damn sight more than that! I've got years of my life invested in that farm. And my wife's money –'

'You got that on paper?'

'Luisa's money – yes – there was an agreement with her father.'

'Okay, if it's a legal claim, you'll get whatever's due to you from the money the farm brings. I'm an honest man, Mr Craigallan. That's what they call me – Honest O'Donovan.'

'I'm not going to wait till you give me a hand-out –'

'What you going to do? See a lawyer? Go ahead, talk to one of the New York smarties. He'll tell you that it's better to show sense and not waste money fighting me.'

That was in fact the advice Rob and Luisa received. O'Donovan was a man who never went to court if he could avoid it, but if he did, he was sure to win. The corruption in New York politics was so wide-spread that the appointment of judges lay in the power of political bosses; O'Donovan was right when he said he would have a friend on the bench.

Unable to give up without some kind of a fight, Rob instructed his attorney to ask for a meeting with O'Donovan's lawyers. There was a long wrangle. During those weeks, the bitterness in the van Huten family left a bad taste in the mouths of all of them – Luisa was furious with her brother, and with her mother for exercising no restraint over him. Dorothea was more perturbed over her future; her income came from the farm through Julius, and now Julius had sold away his birthright. She would be penniless.

[220]

Julius said very little. When, at one of the family conferences, he mumbled that he didn't know how he would live, Rob replied, 'You'll have to get a job.'

'A job?'

'Yes. You've heard of work, I take it? It's how most men earn their living.'

'But . . . I don't know how to do anything . . .'

'Except drink and gamble and throw money away,' his sister said acidly.

'You've got to get a job,' Dorothea said. 'You've got to support your mother.'

Julius looked at them all in helpless defeat. 'I don't know what I'm going to do,' he said. 'I just don't know . . .'

Luisa sometimes turned her fury on Rob. 'I don't understand you!' she flared. 'You're still carrying on here as if it was going to go on being our home! Why on earth are you making the men work?'

'We must get the seed in, Luisa. If we don't, we'll lose a whole season's wheat –'

'And what difference does that make to us? It won't be *our* wheat.'

'I know that, but . . .' He had a duty to see that the grain was there at the end of the season, waiting to be loaded from the farm wagons on to the trains for Erie and thence to the ships for Europe. That was what his life was about – to make sure that the wheat lay in great heaps in the granaries and elevators after the harvest . . .

The new owner, coming to survey the property, was grateful to him for his work. 'It's mighty decent of you,' he said. 'You'll find I know how to show my gratitude . . .'

'How much gratitude?' Rob said, half in bitter amusement and half in genuine interest.

'Well, shall we say – a couple of hundred dollars?'

It was better than nothing. Rob had little to bring away from his time as mainspring of the van Huten's farm. He had saved a little from his salary as manager, but not much, for Luisa had expensive tastes. There was Luisa's money, now paid back by

O'Donovan's lawyers from the proceeds of the sale. Other than that, he had a wardrobe of good clothes, experience of good living he could no longer afford, a wife and two children.

It was his firm resolve that, no matter what happened, little Cornelius must continue to have tuition in Boston. His pride forbade him to let Julius van Huten spoil his son's chances.

'We can all go and live in Boston,' Luisa suggested, brightening at the thought.

'And I would do – what?'

'Oh, you'll find something.'

'I've already found something, Luisa.'

'You have?' She ran to him, throwing her arms round him in delight. 'Oh, I knew you would! Why haven't you told me about it before?'

'Because I wasn't sure you'd be pleased with my decision.'

She drew back. Her light blue eyes, so like those of her dead father, stared at him with suspicion. 'What?' she said blankly.

'I've been thinking for a while now, Luisa . . . farming in New York State is on too small a scale –'

'Too small? What can you mean? Van Huten's is one of the biggest –'

'Yes, yes, I'm not disputing that. But have you ever really looked at all the machinery that's coming in? The big harvesters, the threshing machines . . . the new binders . . .'

'Spare me a lecture on the marvels of mechanics,' she put in.

'But don't you see, Luisa? Machines like that can be used best on big fields – huge fields. The longer they can go without having to turn and come back, the greater their efficiency. It seems to me that the future of wheat lies out in the plains. That big expanse of flat terrain –'

'The plains?' she gasped. 'Now just a minute –'

'I've been thinking about it for a long time, ever since it became clear that we'd have to move out of van Huten's. We could start again out on the Great Plains –'

'No! Never! I'm not going out to the back of beyond –'

'I'm not suggesting we should go out to the government land,

Luisa. I know that would be asking too much. You're no pioneer woman – I don't see you helping to build a cabin or getting water from a stream. But I've been looking at the ads. in the farming journals –'

'No,' she broke in, her voice rising. 'Understand once and for all, Robert Craigallan! I am not going to move out to the Great Plains!'

'But it wouldn't be so bad,' he insisted. 'I've written about a farm for sale in Kansas – five years under cultivation by a Belgian farmer, in Barkworth County, not far from St Joseph. It's a good farm, Luisa – bought from the railroad – you know what the ads. say about railroad land, they always choose the best areas. Six hundred acres, Luisa – we could get a fine living off six hundred acres –'

'No! It's been bad enough sometimes here, cut off by snow in winter, everything having to be sacrificed for the work in spring and fall. I'm not going to go through it all again miles away from anywhere!'

'But I tell you, it's not far from St Joseph . . .'

'How far?'

'About fifty miles.'

'Fifty miles?' She laughed, angry and contemptuous. 'You must think me a fool! And what kind of a town is St Joseph, anyway? Some hick village with a post office and a church? *No*, Rob. I'm not moving west. When I leave van Huten's, I'm going to civilisation.'

'Luisa!'

She'd been about to leave the livingroom, but turned back at his tone.

'I've decided to buy that farm. I wrote the day before yesterday, making an offer for it. If we reach agreement, I hope to be out at Brown Bridge in time for the harvest.'

'Well . . .' She wasn't as angry as he'd expected. She smoothed down a pleat on the front of her silk skirt. 'What are you going to use for money?'

'Why . . . your dowry.'

She shook her head. 'Not on your life. That money's going to be invested in something I can depend on. I want a nice little income for the rest of my life.'

They argued for almost half an hour. At the end of that time, he had shaken her view of investment enough to make it seem likely that she'd let him have the money. He'd promised that he'd always make her a good allowance, that he'd even sign a contract to that effect, and that moreover he'd see to the future of her mother. That had been a worry to Luisa; she wasn't unduly fond of Dorothea but it would be embarrassing if her Mama was reduced to penury.

'I'm a good investment, Luisa,' he urged. 'Look how I improved van Huten's. I'll do the same out at Brown Bridge. You'll see.'

She nodded. 'All right. But if you go, you go alone.'

Rob was shocked. Husband and wife belonged together. He stared at her in disbelief.

'Why not?' she asked in a sharp voice. 'You're not going to claim you can't live without me, are you?'

'But you're my wife –!'

'I'm not likely to forget that! If you hadn't been so determined to get your hands on the farm, I might have married Bernard Stettinius –'

'Don't let's go into all that again –'

'And don't let's pretend that you feel anything for me. You've often enough let me see that you think I'm a fool. I know you only wanted the farm. Well, now you've lost it and you want another one. But this time I'm not part of the bargain!'

'Luisa, this is no way to talk –'

'I'll invest my money in this outlandish place you want to farm. All right – it's probably a good investment. But that's all I'm going to invest – money. You go to Brown Bridge, Rob, and I'll go with Ellie-Rose to Boston.'

He drew in a breath. He'd been about to fall in with her suggestion, but the idea that she would take Ellie-Rose with her was like a stab at his vitals. He didn't know how he could face life without the child. She was the one person in the world who totally loved him, who never argued nor found fault.

'Ellie-Rose comes with me,' he said.

'Nonsense. A farm miles from anywhere? It's no place for a child.'

'To the contrary – it's an excellent place for a child. Healthy and open –'

'And who'd look after her, pray tell? While you're out on the plains tilling the soil? Eh?'

'I'll have a housekeeper, of course,' he said impatiently. 'If you're not there, I'll have to hire someone. That follows, doesn't it?'

She hesitated. To tell the truth, she didn't greatly care about having Ellie-Rose with her. The child would pine for her father, and become unmanageable: she was apt to throw a temper now if Rob was away for a time. And they'd all be a bit cooped up in aunt Remegen's house in Boston. There were only two bedrooms and the attic room: if Luisa and Dorothea joined Aunt Remegen, it meant that Cornelius would have to be moved up to the attic, thus getting rid of the maid, and Luisa would still have to share with her mother, or persuade Dorothea to share with Aunt Remegen. True, Ellie-Rose could be put in with Cornelius in the attic but that could only last for a short time. A little boy and a little girl couldn't share the same room for ever.

Yet she suddenly had an urge to punish Rob for all the unkind things he'd said during the past weeks of argument, to pay him back for having trapped her into marriage when he didn't really care for her. She said, 'Ellie-Rose comes with me. That's final.'

'No, Luisa, you know she's fonder of me than of you –'

'She'll get over that.'

'Why should you be so stubborn about it? It's not as if she's the apple of your eye.'

Luisa shrugged. 'I have to think of Ellie-Rose's wellbeing. How about her education? Her religious upbringing?'

'There's a school at Brown Bridge, Luisa! For God's sake, it's not uncivilised. There's a Protestant church and a meeting house. There's a store and a hotel –'

'Huh! Three buildings and a shack.'

She remained adamant all through the settling of the purchase of the new farm, all through the signing of a legal contract that ensured her an income from the proceeds of the farm. The servants began packing the furniture and personal belongings at van Huten's. Little Ellie-Rose watched with keen interest: they were moving away, going somewhere new. It would be fun.

Two days before the vanmen were to come for the furniture, Rob stole Luisa's jewellery. It was in a velvet-lined box in her dressing table. She had taken it out so that the dressing table could be wrapped in sacking for the removal to the salerooms. It stood on a little travelling chest near the bedroom door. Rob looked at the box, picked it up, looked inside, closed the lid, and walked out of the room with it.

Luisa didn't miss it till next morning. She had put on a dark taffeta dress as being suitable for her last full day at van Huten's. Friends and neighbours would be calling to say goodbye. She wanted to make a good impression. She decided to wear a cameo that had belonged to Grandmama. When she couldn't find the jewel box, she nearly had hysterics.

'Don't cry, Luisa,' Rob said. 'I've got your jewel box.'

'You have?' She looked up, wiping tears from her eyes. 'Where is it then? I want to put on that pin –'

'I'm not giving it to you.'

'What?'

'I've put the box in a safe place, but you'll never find it unless I show you where it is.'

'But . . . but . . . why?'

He stared at her. 'You want your jewellery back?'

'Of course I do! Some of those pieces are valuable! The pearls have been in the family for nearly a hundred years!'

'Indeed.' He was tall and calm. 'All right, you shall have them back, safe and sound – on one condition.'

'You . . . you dare to make conditions about returning my own property to me?'

He gave a sudden smile. 'I'm taking the temperature of your maternal devotion. If you love Ellie-Rose more than your pearls, you'll give them up for her sake. If, on the other hand, you want your pearls back, you have to let me take Ellie-Rose to Brown Bridge with me.'

'What? But that's – that's –'

'Blackmail. Yes, I think that's what it's called.'

'But you can't *do* this.'

'I already have.'

'I'll call in the constable,' she cried. 'I'll have you charged with theft!'

'Do,' he agreed. 'That would be a cloud of glory in which to leave van Huten's, wouldn't it? It doesn't exactly fit in with your romantic view of your farewell scene.'

She ran at him and began to hit him with her hands. 'You're unspeakable! There's nothing you wouldn't stoop to –'

He held her off, turning his head away from her flailing palms. 'Don't be silly, Luisa. If we're going to have a rough-and-tumble, you know I'll win. Calm down. All you have to do is say Ellie-Rose can come with me, and you can have your precious jewel-box.'

'Only a man like you would dream of doing a thing like this –'

'And only a woman like you would give in and get her pearls back.'

She sank into a chair, dishevelled and red-faced. 'I hate you,' she said in a low voice.

'I suppose you do. Well? Which do you prefer? Ellie-Rose or the jewellery?'

It was a foregone conclusion. Luisa couldn't give up the ornaments that made her life worth living. She still had some good clothes and with those and her jewels she expected to make a good appearance in Boston society for a year or so. By then she hoped to have made enough friends in influential places to ease her position.

The servants and farmhands at van Huten's had either been retained by the new owner or had found new posts. Only the black cook, Nellie, had made no move. As Rob was packing to go, she knocked on his door. 'Mister Rob?'

'Yes, Nellie?'

'You got anybody to look after you at this new place?'

'No.'

'You want I should come with you?'

He was surprised. He looked at her, wondering why she should offer. 'I can't afford much in the way of wages, Nellie.'

'Am I askin' for wages, Mister Rob?'

'But . . . are you sure you want to go so far? It's a long way west, Nellie.'

'I been travellin',' she said. 'War forced me on the road when the fightin' started, so I came north. You think I'm near my home *here*?'

'Brown Bridge is even farther away.'

'But I'd be with frien's . . .'

He nodded. 'If you think you'd like it, Nellie . . . I'd be grateful.'

'When we goin'?'

'Tomorrow morning.'

'You takin' Miss Ellie-Rose?'

'Yes.'

'I'll jes' see she's got all her special things. She'll want her wooden doll, I reckon, to talk to on the journey. It's a long way?'

'Yes, a long way, Nellie.'

With a smile and a shrug, she went to help Ellie-Rose collect her treasures: Wilhelmina, the wooden doll, four pebbles with funny shapes, an old fan inherited from her Mama, and several picture books.

The journey seemed interminable. The train surged for days over the endless plain of midland America west of Chicago. At first Ellie-Rose was interested and amused, but by the second day of travel she was suffering nausea and was bored. Nellie soothed and dandled her, and Rob read to her from her books.

At St Joseph they disembarked. They hired a wagonette and driver to take them to Brown Bridge. Rob was awestruck by the unending expanse of tawny grass that began almost immediately outside the town, but he wouldn't have dreamed of letting it show.

The driver was laconic. 'You taken Lafleche's place?'

'Yes. You know it?'

'I seen it.'

'What's his crop like?'

'Dunno. Ain't been out that way since spring.'

'Heard anything about it?'

'Nope.'

When they came after two hours' drive to the beginning of the Brown Bridge spread, Rob watched the fields on either side of the dirt track with a keen eye. The wheat was sparse, rather short, pale in colour compared with the stalk he was used to on the New York wheat. He wondered what seed Lafleche had been using. The outgoing owner had promised to leave all his records, and Rob looked forward to settling down with them in a day or so.

The Lafleche house was impressive and yet saddening. It had been built in the style of what was called the soddie – the original builder had cut up sods of prairie grass and in the space left by his cutting, he had set his foundations. With the sods he had built walls and roof. There was little or no timber on the plains. The almost total absence of trees was one of the things that made it all seem alien to Rob.

This house was bigger than most soddies. Lafleche, Rob learned later, had gathered a large family. Outside it was like a great grey box. Inside, Mrs Lafleche had whitewashed all the walls and had windows made with glass, not big but at points where the light was good. The floor was beaten earth covered with tiles, which must have been imported from a long way at great expense. There was a good stove and a fine range in the kitchen-livingroom, with rooms opening off warmed by piping run through holes in the walls. In back of the kitchen was the root cellar, with four steps down made of wooden treads. The cellar was neat and well-stocked with shelves. Later, Rob understood that the cellar could be used as a living-room in the heat of summer.

There was a windmill to bring up the water, with, nearby, a pond, now a circle of baked mud on this early fall day. Round the pond stood spindly trees and bushes. Behind that were the outhouses – the cowshed and the stable with a store overhead for hay and straw, a lean-to with a brazier and bellows for shoeing and mending equipment. Folds and pens held the livestock – six hogs, four cows, and the horses in the paddock.

The wagonette's driver helped them carry in their belongings. 'You got furniture?' he inquired.

'It's coming by freight.'

'Uh-huh. Next freight's due next week. This time o' year, freight's all to hell, with the grain trucks being moved about to get 'em in the right places.'

'I expected that,' Rob agreed. 'We'll manage.'

'Well, good luck. Lafleche ain't had no luck here but mebbe you'll do better.'

'What happened to Lafleche, then?' Rob asked, with a sudden prickle of anxiety.

'Missus ran away. Couldn't stand the plains. Came from some place . . . France, I think. Didn't get on with the language, and one of her kids died. She up and took the rest back home.'

'Oh, I see. It wasn't to do with the farm?'

'You could say it was, kind of. Lafleche, he couldn't seem to come to terms with the weather here. Kept saying, "It ain't like back home" – as if it would be!'

Rob paid him off. Nellie was already unpacking skillet and food. Ellie-Rose was running from room to room exploring. He suddenly felt alone, lost, unwanted. What was he doing here, out on this vast alien plain so unlike any landscape he'd ever seen or imagined?

Next morning he saddled a horse and rode round his acres. He came home thoughtful. This was a poor harvest, reflecting badly on Lafleche; it had been neglected, planted in unprepared ground. But it must be cut soon; he must find out where the harvesting crews could be hired.

His neighbours began to call while he was out. They continued to come in a steady stream, from miles around, bearing welcoming gifts and offering information or advice. They would come and help cut the wheat, they told him, as soon as the header was free; it was at Soon West for the moment. In three days, perhaps four. In the meantime, did he need anything? They had looked after the beasts since Lafleche left, they had mended a window that got broken, they had brought back a straying pony. Would he like his little girl to come and play with their children? Where was Mrs Craigallan?

On Tuesday of the following week he was walking back from starting the header on the ridge field when he saw in the distance the big horse-drawn van bringing the furniture from the railhead. He quickened his step. It would be so good to have a chair to sit on instead of an old box, and a table to eat from instead of a board.

The vanmen waved as he came up. 'Brought your stuff,' they grinned. 'Brought you something else as well.'

'You have? What?' He was puzzled.

'Your wife.'

Too startled to speak, he hurried into the house. A woman was kneeling on the floor of the main room, talking to Ellie-Rose. It was dark indoors after the sunshine outside. He blinked and frowned, trying to gather himself together to face Luisa. Why had she come? What disaster had induced her to travel out to Brown Bridge, to share the hardships of this new life?

The woman who turned and rose to greet him was Morag.

15

She'd heard the vanmen call out, heard the answering voice. Her arms were held out to him as she rose to meet him. She saw him hesitate as he looked into the dimness of the room.

Then they flew together like magnet and steel. She pulled him against her heart, saying his name over and over. She'd thought never to see him again – had intended it – yet here they were, clinging together without pretences.

They were brought back to their senses by Ellie-Rose pulling at skirts and pants leg. 'Papa! Papa, the lady just arrived! Papa, she knew my name! Papa, she says she's brought me a present!'

'Ellie-Rose,' Rob said, stooping to scoop her up and whirl her round, 'this is Morag! Someone I thought I'd never see again!' He turned back to look at Morag over the child's fair head. 'How did you *get* here?'

'I came on the train to St Joseph –'

'That's not what I mean, and you know it. What are you doing here?'

'What did you bring me?' Ellie-Rose broke in. 'Is it a dolly? Is it a toy?'

'Let's find out,' Morag said, holding out a hand to her. They went into the side room where Nellie had put her luggage, and knelt to open her travelling box. On top lay a rag book, thick with pages, each bearing a picture made from patchwork with the word beautifully embroidered in big clear letters. Ellie-Rose seized it with a scream of delight, to collapse on the floor and croon over each thing that she recognised.

'Mrs Remegen told me where to find you,' Morag began when she rejoined Rob in the living room.

'Aunt Remegen? You know Aunt Remegen?'

'I should do. I've been living in her house for the past two and a half years.'

'But . . . I was told you'd left Boston!'

'Who told you that?' she said, surprised.

'Professor Bell. After the death of Mrs Kauffman, I came looking for you. Bell said you'd gone travelling.'

'No.' She smiled. 'I told him I thought I would take a holiday, which I did, but I never left Boston. I stayed there because I wanted to see what happened to little Cornelius.'

'I don't understand! Aunt Remegen never mentioned you!'

'She did, I'm sure. But she could never remember my name. She called me by the name of the girl I replaced – and I didn't correct her.'

'But Morag – all this time?' He seized her and almost shook her. 'You were there? And I've been so angry with you for disappearing from my life!'

'I felt that was best, Rob. All things considered, I felt you and I ought not to meet.'

'But you promised to keep in touch, Morag! You promised!'

'Did I?' she said, puzzled. 'I don't recall that.'

'You did! You said that if I didn't do something to help Cornelius, I needn't ever write to you again. I took that to mean that if I did, we could write to each other –'

'I see.' She sighed. 'I never meant that, my dear. I truly meant us never to see each other again – until Luisa came storming in last week angry with everybody because you'd gone out to the Plains to start again.'

'Luisa came storming in? Of course, she'd find you there. Good God, Morag – what did she say? She's always been so jealous of you.'

Morag untied her bonnet and sat down. 'It was quite a scene,' she admitted. 'For weeks I'd been on tenterhooks. It was clear something very bad had happened to the van Huten family but when I tried to get it out of Mrs Remegen, she just pressed her lips together and shook her head. Even now, I don't quite understand what the trouble was.'

'Oh, in a nutshell – Julius gambled away the farm.'

'It's unthinkable! After all that you'd done . . .'

He coloured. 'Don't, Morag. I'm trying to begin all over again out here . . .'

'Yes, yes – forgive me. That wasn't meant as a reproach. It's just that it's all come as such a surprise to me. I could glean nothing from Luisa –'

'What did she say? When you appeared at Aunt Remegen's?'

Morag smiled ruefully. 'Credit where credit is due – she gave one cry of astonishment and then held her tongue until she could get me alone. Then she told me I was deceitful and sly, to be battening on her family by living in Aunt Remegen's house. She implied I'd harmed Cornelius's character with my immoral ways. She made it clear I had to go immediately. I'd always known the day would come when I'd have to leave. I'd saved a little for that very reason, but I'd always thought I'd go somewhere to start again all on my own. Instead, I waited until the house had settled down, then I went to Mrs Remegen and winkled your whereabouts from her. And here I am.'

Rob had drawn up a chair opposite. He took her hands. 'I still can't believe it! I thought . . . I've been thinking all this time that you were miles away from me . . . perhaps married . . .'

'Oh no!'

'I can't believe you've never been asked, Morag.'

She shook her head. It was an implied untruth, for Ira Jones had asked her twice. But though she imagined she had put Rob Craigallan out of her heart, she still couldn't imagine herself in anyone else's arms, and so she always had put Ira off with gentle words.

'If only I'd come to Boston to see Cornelius!' he mourned. 'But Luisa was always so unwilling – she preferred him to come to us, where no one could see us with him –'

'And he loved it,' Morag put in. 'He used to look forward to his visits so much, Rob! Afterwards he'd tell me all about it – how you'd taken him out to look at the crops, what trees you'd planted, whether there were new calves or piglets. He's a wonderful boy, Rob!'

He nodded, but with some hesitation. 'I can't seem to understand him –'

'But that's only because he hasn't learnt to speak yet –'

'No, I don't mean that. I always had the feeling that he was watching me when he was around – analysing me, judging me.'

'Maybe so. I don't think anyone knows what goes on in his head yet. There's so much still to be done for him, Rob. I only hope and pray that Luisa . . .'

'That Luisa won't be a hindrance,' he ended for her. 'It's a fine thing to say about his own mother, isn't it?'

'It's just that she . . . she lets fear of the unusual take over. Once she gets used to him, sees how bright he really is . . .'

'She'll pay as little heed to him as possible,' Rob remarked. 'But at least there's the consolation that he'll soon be going to the school for the deaf. That's part of my agreement with her – a legal agreement, would you believe that? I had to set it down in writing, that she was to ensure Cornelius's education.'

'Oh, it'll be different when she's been there a while,' Morag insisted. 'She'll get fond of him. After all, he is her son.'

'She'd rather forget that. But as a condition for making provision for her mother as well as Luisa, I got a firm agreement about Cornelius. I'm reasonably satisfied about it.'

'You'll go to see them, though?' she asked.

He shook his head. 'Things were said between Luisa and myself . . . it's over, Morag.'

'That can never be. You're married, you have two children.'

'Marriages end, Morag, no matter what vows are made in church.' He shrugged. 'If mine ever existed, it ended soon after Ellie-Rose was born.'

'Yet it was of your own choosing –'

'No, no, I told you at the time – I couldn't do anything else because of the circumstances –'

'Come, Rob, we're not children any more. Luisa was expecting your baby when you got married.'

'Exactly! What else could I do? I had to marry her.'

She studied him, her great dark eyes tolerant and understanding. 'However it began, it's a tie you can't undo. She's your wife, the mother of Cornelius and Ellie-Rose. The children will keep you together despite anything you may have said to each other in anger.'

'No, I can't imagine anything that would make her want to see me again, ever. She's got what she wants now – town living, the chance to be somebody in society. All that's lacking is money, and it's up to me to supply that. I've made an agreement and I shall stick to it. But that's the only tie that binds us now – a legal contract about money.'

'Feelings don't die like that,'Morag murmured.

Rob gazed at her with a surge of regret for the lost years. 'Oh, why didn't I hurry you in front of a preacher that day we first set out from New York City?' he burst out. 'We could have been man and wife all this while –'

'No.' She shook her head, sighing. 'I wouldn't have allowed it. I was still all mixed up then, obsessed with thoughts of guilt for what I'd done. I thought I was "unworthy".'

'Unworthy!'

'Oh, I still carry the scars of that time, Rob. But while I was living with Mrs Kauffman I heard so much deep conversation, I had access to so many books, that I began to think more clearly about the past. Now I feel that I've forgiven myself.'

'There never was anything to forgive! It wasn't your fault –'

'Not at first. But I let things go on once we were at van Huten's. I was weak and silly. I hope I've grown up a bit since then, enough to know what I'm doing.'

'What *are* you doing?' he asked, pressing her hands between his. 'Why are you here, Morag?'

'I came because I thought you might need me.'

'But how long will you stay?'

'As long as you want me.'

'That will be for ever,' he said.

They had to break off there, for Ellie-Rose came running in

demanding attention, reminding Rob that he had a farm to run. He left Morag and Nellie in charge of seeing the furniture brought in – it was strange to both of them to see items that had graced van Huten's now placed about the sod house with its plain, rough walls. Rob meanwhile went out to see how things were going with the cutting.

When he came back at dusk, Nellie had contrived a celebratory supper. Nellie understood that there was something to celebrate for she, like all the other staff at van Huten's, had learned the truth about Morag after the row in which Luisa had forced it from Rob. That scene had meant raised voices, overheard by Senta; Senta, agog with what she had heard, told it to the others. 'Morag wasn't his sister! No kin at all!'

Nellie had nodded to herself that day. 'That li'l girl nearly tole me all that once,' she remarked. 'Poor li'l girl ... I sure hope Miss Luisa never runs up agin her in the future. Miss Luisa, she a good hater.'

Ellie-Rose was allowed to share supper, though it was past her bedtime. From those beginnings, she regarded Morag as some kind of good fairy who arrived to bring presents and ensure pleasant surprises like an extra hour in the evening and chocolate cake for supper. When Morag tucked her up at last, she pulled her down towards her by a lock of dark hair. 'I'm glad you've come,' she murmured, half asleep. 'Don't go away, will you!'

Morag and Rob stayed up a long time, catching up on all that had happened since their parting. When at last it was time to go to bed, there was no hesitation: he put his arm about her and led her to his room, and she went with her head against his shoulder.

It was taken for granted by all who met Morag in the coming days that she was Mrs Craigallan, the wife Rob had mentioned as being in Boston. He never introduced her so, he never contradicted anyone who called her thus. Most people were on first name terms in the district. The hard life, the need for co-operation, put people on a closer level than in towns.

Rob's first harvest was poor. He'd expected that and wasn't disappointed. When he examined the kernels that flowed from the thresher he saw that they were thin and skimpy. Lafleche's records – such as they were – showed that he supplied his own seed wheat from preceding harvests, and Rob quickly realised that the previous owner had never come to terms with the conditions in which he was farming.

Lafleche had come from the great plain of Flanders, where 'soft' wheat was grown easily and productively. There the soil conditions and the weather were totally different from Kansas. Rob could see that these facts had never come home to Lafleche. The Belgian had imagined that he would grow wheat here as he had done at home, only on a larger scale. Climate, wind-factor, insect pests and unknown blights had taught him nothing.

That first harvest and the succeeding winter showed Rob he too had a lot to learn. He had read all Julius's discarded textbooks, had attended lectures under the auspices of the New York Farmers' Brotherhood, and kept up with agricultural research reported in the journals. But that was all theory. Practice was different.

The land was a hard mistress. From the farm, the ground slipped away on a slight incline, but there were no valleys, no sheltered hollows. Beyond the shallow pond, the road from the post office at Brown Bridge went by, beaten hard like brick in summer, churned to a morass of mud in fall and then frozen into a bumpy helter-skelter by Christmas. Across the road the rolling prairie began – leading the eye on and on to a horizon like an edge of steel when the weather was good, but often blotted out by dust in summer, and snow or rain in winter.

Brown Bridge was the nearest centre of civilization. Here Rob collected his farming journals, which came by post. His neighbours thought he was a little eccentric, spending money on these thick magazines. But gradually he began to gain a reputation for knowing things; he knew the name of the local agent for the Department of Agriculture, who had to be contacted for advice on a new plant disease, and who could find out for him the price of wheat in any port of Europe.

They couldn't quite understand his obsession with different seeds. 'Wheat's wheat,' Bob Partridge remarked to him one day when he met him coming out of the post office with a new sample just arrived from Springfield. 'It's in the hands of the Almighty how much you get from it – He controls the weather and the yield.'

Rob frowned at him. 'Know your Bible, do you?'

'Sure do,' Partridge rejoined, surprised.

'Remember the story of Jacob and the herds?'

'Huh?'

'Jacob's bargain with Laban – "all the speckled and spotted cattle, and all the brown cattle among the sheep, and the spotted and speckled among the goats; and of such shall be my hire" Remember?'

'Of course I remember,' Partridge said. 'And the Lord arranged it so that Jacob received "much cattle, and maid-servants, and men-servants, and camels, and asses" – Genesis Thirty, verse forty-three.' The young farmer eyed Rob. 'I don't hear nothing about wheat in that.'

'It's how Jacob got all the cattle and so forth that should interest you,' Rob observed. 'He arranged for the cattle to breed so that they'd have specks and spots. He knew a thing or two about animal breeding, did Jacob.'

Partridge looked uneasy. 'Well, yeah . . . No harm in that . . . The Lord helps them that helps themselves.'

'Didn't it ever occur to you that you might be able to breed wheat so that it would be more suitable for this district?'

'Breed wheat? Say, you've got some funny ideas, Craigallan.'

'We'll see,' Rob said.

His neighbours watched with interest while he tried a patch of this seed, a patch of that. It was certainly true that his first year of farming, he got a far better return on his land than Lafleche ever had, but that was only because he had more sense than Lafleche, and hired better help.

Rob had to make money. Each fall a sum of money had to go to the bank in Boston for Luisa and her mother. He never failed, although it meant careful living for himself and his household at the Lafleche Farm. They ate well, because Nellie was a superb cook and laid up preserves and supplies in summer for the sparse winter months – quail in jars, dried peas and beans from the vegetable patch which she tended with such care, elderblow wine, sorghum molasses, melons even in winter, picked late after the frosts had come.

But there were inevitable expenses. Certain supplies had to be bought. Flour had to be milled, even from one's own wheat. Although Morag devised clothes for the growing Ellie-Rose from her own gowns cut down, sometimes piece goods had to be bought. The men had to be paid, the harvest crews had to be hired, tools had to be renewed.

And the price of wheat was still going down.

Scared and worried by the continuing, mysterious fall in income, the farmers sought remedies from the government. They banded themselves together in societies and lodges – The Patrons of Husbandry, The National Grange, The Agrarian Supporters.

In Northern Kansas, the society formed locally had odd aims, to Rob's mind. Long speeches would be made about odd aims, to Rob's mind. Long speeches would be made about these aims. Rob would listen without comment. He had joined the society for the social activities and because so many of his neighbours and their wives supported it. It gave Morag the chance of meeting other women at the gatherings, which took place about once a month except in the winter months when travel was so difficult. Besides, it would have looked odd if he had stood out.

Coming back from an overnight event one morning in April, he and Morag saw a lonely figure by the side of the road about a mile beyond Brown Bridge. A brief spring shower had just fallen; the boy had an old hat pulled well down over his ears and his coat collar turned up against it. As was the custom, Rob pulled up to offer a lift.

They were surprised to see a black face when the youngster turned at their hail. There were few blacks in Kansas as yet. Their cook Nellie was still something of a rarity.

'Hullo there,' Rob said. 'Going to Breezedale?'

'Yeah, that's my ultimate goal.'

Ultimate goal? What kind of talk was that from a negro? Rob grinned. 'Well, we're headed for Lafleche Farm, about eight miles on the way. Want to hop aboard?'

'Thank you, that would be great.' The boy swung aboard.

Skinny and lithe, he settled down crosslegged behind them on the planks of the buckboard.

'Looking for work?' Morag asked, thinking that perhaps they could give him a day or two's employment and let Nellie have the pleasure of company.

'No, ma'am, I got a job,' he said. 'In fact, I'm workin' now.'

'Working at what?'

'I'm an agricultural student.'

Both Rob and Morag turned to stare at him, in undisguised amazement. A black? Studying at college?

'Sounds weird, don't it?' he said. 'Well, I've been mighty lucky. Folks who owned my Ma and Pa were really good to me. The Carvers. Take my name from them – George Washington Carver.'

'That's some name!' Rob said, laughing.

'You're in college?' Morag commented. 'There isn't an agricultural college anywhere around here, is there?'

'No ma'am, I'm in school in Minneapolis.'

Rob frowned to himself. The whole thing began to sound like a fairy story. Minneapolis was miles away, better than five hundred miles to the north. But of course a negro boy trying to build up a confidence trick on the basis of being a worthy scholar would be apt to choose a school a long way off, so as not to be easily checked out.

Morag, who never thought harm of anybody until she had to, was expressing interest. 'You're a long way from home, then,' she said with sympathy.

'And travelling light, too,' Rob remarked, thinking of the satchel slung from the boy's shoulder.

'Yessir, that's the best way to travel,' said George Washington Carver. 'I got a spare shirt and my notebooks and pencils in the bag – that's enough for the job I'm on.'

'What job is that?'

'Collecting statistics for the Department of Agriculture, ma'am.'

'I thought you said you were in school?' Rob said, thinking to catch him out.

'Yessir, so I am. This is kind of part of my studies, but I get paid for it too. A two-way bargain, you could say.'

Morag began to ask about the city of Minneapolis – what was it like, did it have a library, were the shops good, were the winters as long there as in Brown Bridge?

'Longer, ma'am. Still got snow round Minneapolis. You seem to have a good thaw hereabouts. Got the wheat in early, did you?'

'We had the drills out the first week in March,' Rob said with satisfaction.

'Yeah, I can see the shoots have come on fine. Had one check, though, didn't you?'

Rob looked over his shoulder at him. 'Yes. Ten days ago – temperature went down twenty degrees overnight. How did you know?'

'You can see by the blade. Unchecked growth always has a smoother edge on the leaf-blade.'

The boy met Rob's startled glance. His brown eyes seemed to say: Yes, you thought I was a fraud. But I know what I'm talking about.

They chatted on through the jolting journey to the farm. Sometimes they talked about generalities and the little things that interested Morag. Sometimes they talked agriculture. And the more Rob heard, the more he was forced to the conclusion that this strange youngster – who seemed scarcely more than fourteen, but had to be older if he was in college – really had academic qualifications.

When they reached Lafleche Morag insisted that he come in to meet Nellie and have some home cooking. Nellie was delighted. 'Well, that's the colour skin I didn't ever reckon to see here 'bouts!' she beamed.

'Happy to know you, ma'am,' said George politely. He allowed himself to be pushed into a chair and regaled with coffee, rabbit stew, and new-baked bread.

Nellie tried to keep him overnight, for the sake of talking over 'slave' times. It seemed George's parents had been slaves – the father killed in some wartime skirmish, the mother kidnapped by marauders and never heard of again. George had been taken with his mother, but Moses Carver had been able to buy him back a few days later when the marauders found the baby too much trouble.

Later, when Morag was showing the boy the domestic livestock, Rob said to Nellie: 'Is he on the level? He says he's a student.'

'He tole me he got Mr Carver to let him enrol in a one-room school 'bout ten miles from Diamond when he was ten. That Mr Carver, he musta been a unusual man. Not many whites would let their negro boys 'tend school.'

Intrigued, Rob went out to join Morag and George. They had strolled in the cool spring afternoon to the edge of the wheatfield. The negro boy had stopped to finger a green shoot and was shaking his woolly head.

'See something wrong?' Rob inquired with irony.

'I see you had a few nibbles from the chinch bug, Mr Craigallan.'

'A few. That's usual.'

'I dunno,' Carver said. He was still kneeling, parting the little shoots and staring down into the axils. 'The larvae count's unusually high this year –'

'Not on my land!'

'No, as it happens, not on your land,' he agreed. 'But I'd say the prognosis this year for the bug is a kind of see-saw.'

There was an authority in his manner that Rob found impressive. He said sarcastically: 'You're an expert on wheat pests, are you?'

'Nossir, not really. But that's the job I'm on at present. Department of Agriculture needs a tally of damage by bugs and other pests for its Report on the Visible Supply of Grains for this quarter of the year. I did a special prelim. course on insects of wheat plants before I came out, and I got these reference texts –' He delved in the pocket of his shirt, and brought out folded papers bearing printed illustrations of the insects and a brief description of the damage caused by each. Rob took the creased sheets and spread them out, while Carver went on to remark that he'd seen a lot more damage in other parts of Kansas than he had here.

'You've been around, then?'

'Oh, yeah . . . Northern Kansas. I started from St Joe and I'm going back there at the end of the week. From there I go by train back to Minneapolis, where I post off my reports.'

'And where are they?'

'In the satchel. Sorry, sir, I can't show them to you. They're confidential. But it's just a lot of crosses and ticks in the relevant columns – kind of dull, if you don't understand the picture they're showing.'

'Are you saying there's going to be a chinch bug epidemic?' Rob inquired, with an inward groan.

'Mebbe not an epidemic. But I'd say you'll have trouble this year, sir.'

Morag turned the conversation to more optimistic topics, then tried to persuade the boy to stay overnight. 'Nellie would enjoy it so much if you'd stay –'

'I can't, ma'am. I'm real obliged, but I got to finish my "territory" and get back to my railhead by a certain time.'

He withstood all her persuasions. Finally she said, 'Well, if you have to go on to Breezedale to do your next survey, at least let us give you a lift on the way. The postman will be along any minute. He'll take you into Breezedale.'

'Thank you, Mrs Craigallan. I 'preciate it.'

When at last he boarded the post cart, they went out to watch him leave. Nellie was waving and calling good wishes after him. Morag was deliged at Nellie's pleasure.

But Rob was thinking about the lad's forecast.

Chinch bugs . . . Why should there be a problem with chinch bugs this year, particularly? Fine harvests for three years, seed wheat of prime quality, a good hard winter to kill off most of the pests. Yet it was true that chinch bugs liked a good hard winter.

Still, what did agricultural students know! Especially a black one . . .

16

ROB WAS HITCHING THE tugs to the whippletree of the buckboard when Morag came out into the dawn light. The strong prairie breeze moulded her heavy skirts against her limbs so that, in unintentional coquetry, she showed off the lines of her slender body.

Rob paused in his work. He felt a surge of happiness. She belonged to him. And all the land around them belonged to him. The green spears of wheat, stretching away to the horizon, were his. The little square house, so plain on the outside yet so comfortable within, was his. He felt as if he owned the sky and the clouds and the air he breathed.

Optimism rose in him like a spring of well-water. Everything would be good today. He would sell the crop at a break-even price – might even make a profit. All he needed was enough to see them through till next harvest.

Morag's unexpected decision to come with him to St Joseph seemed a good omen. 'Ready?' he called. 'Time's wasting.'

She came to be helped up to the worn leather seat. There was something eager and happy about him today, she thought; his lips were touched with a smile, as if he had had happy news. And yet he didn't know, couldn't know. She herself wasn't sure yet. That was why she'd decided to ride in with him to St Joseph to see Dr Hayes and have confirmation of her hopes.

'You're looking smart,' she said, settling herself, studying him. 'That's your good suit.'

'If I'm going to impress Pruman to give me a good price, I've got to let him see I'm no Rube from Rubesville.' He squared his shoulders in the well-cut broadcloth, relic of the life in New York State when Luisa had been so picky about his clothes.

'You impress *me*,' Morag told him.

With a shrug and a grin he climbed into the buckboard and took up the lines. 'Gid-up,' he called to the lead mare, who stirred unwillingly as the leathers flicked her back. 'Come on, Mandy, Pruman's waiting to give us seventy-five cents a bushel in St Joe.'

Morag slipped her hand through his arm and hugged it. 'Seventy-five cents! You'll never get him up to seventy-five, Rob – not even you.'

'Well, seventy-four, then.' He slapped the lines against Mandy's plump flanks. 'Come on, girl, we want to arrive while Pruman's still anxious to get out to lunch.'

'Why's that, Rob?'

'If he's hungry and wants to get along the street to Ruby's Restaurant, he'll be more likely to close the deal somewhere around my figure.'

'That *sounds* shrewd, Rob. I hope it works.'

'Yeah,' he said. He hadn't much faith in it, really.

The increasing warmth of the April morning was all around them as they drove from Brown Bridge towards St Joseph. Endless horizons rose and receded before them, clothed in the young green of the growing wheat. To Rob's eye, it looked strong and bright. Yet into his mind an unbidden picture came: the negro boy leaning down to finger a green shoot and shaking his head.

The drive to St Joseph was a long one over a hard road. Morag had some moments of apprehension as the buckboard lurched over the dried ruts made from last winter's mud. She ought to have realised the trip could be a mite hazardous to her in her condition; but she was eager to have Dr Hayes's assurance that she was right; and it was so long since she'd seen a woman other than Nellie, or a shop, or a dress pattern. This was such a good opportunity to buy a few things, to see if Ludental had any soft knitting yarn, to look at the Sears Roebuck catalogue.

She'd have to be careful about the money, though. No matter what Rob said, to cheer her up, he wasn't likely to get anything like seventy-five for the wheat. Mr Derricks had got only sixty-eight at the beginning of last week; he'd dropped by to report this gloomy news. It was going to mean another hard year.

When they trotted into St Joseph's main street it was late morning. Rob dropped Morag off in front of the store before going on to put up at the livery stable. 'See you at Ruby's for lunch,' he called back. Morag watched him round the corner then hurried on up the street to Dr Hayes's door.

As Rob opened the door of Cy Pruman's office, the grain dealer was leaning on his counter reading a newspaper.

'Morning . . . Mr Craigallan, isn't it?'

'That's me. Good morning, Mr Pruman.'

'How you doing? How's your good lady?'

'Fine, fine. You don't seem busy?'

'Nah,' Pruman agreed, folding his newspaper. 'Most folks've made their bargain for this year.' By 'this year' he meant the year of the harvest lately past. He reckoned not by the months on the calendar but by the twelve months from one crop to the next – August to August, when the new wheat came into the storehouses. He dealt year-long, but April was a slack month. 'May wheat' was when business picked up – 'May-wheat', when the crop was showing big enough to be assessed.

He studied this young farmer with covert interest. Craigallan wasn't one of those whining sod-busters who came in regularly, begging for an advance on next year's crop or hoping for help with transport charges. A proud feller, you could see that not only by the good clothes, but also by the carriage of his head and the calm set of the keen features.

Craigallan was an object of interest to Pruman. He was the last to sell August wheat this year. He'd held out and held out against the low prices, preferring to store his crop and pay the storage charges rather than take the seventy cents, the sixty-nine and sixty-eight cents that was the going rate from Chicago.

Proud – yeah, and stupid. Hadn't he understood that the price wasn't going to go up? Coming in now last thing, when he thought the market would be emptied and the price would be rising. Pruman had news for him. His lips twitched faintly under cover of his thick beard and moustache. ''Do for you?' he inquired, rubbing his watch chain between finger and thumb.

'I reckon it's time to make a deal for my wheat,' Rob said. 'What's the offer now?'

Pruman flicked over a sheaf of papers as if he were looking for the answer, although they both knew he had it ready on his lips. What else was he here for, but to know the price of wheat? 'Sixty-two cents the bushel,' he announced.

Give Rob his due, he didn't jump or shiver or cry out. He simply went stock still – cold and still as marble. 'Sixty-two? Jim Derricks got sixty-eight the bushel – at the beginning of last week.'

'Sure, a week ago that was the price.'

'You're telling me wheat has fallen six cents a bushel since the first of the month?'

''Fraid so.'

'But why? I . . . I can't believe it would fall six cents in only seven days . . .' Rob was ashamed of the bewilderment in his voice, but he couldn't prevent it. It was a trick, a joke – it couldn't be true. Six cents down in seven days? And down from a price that, even then, meant bankruptcy to more than one grower. Down from what everyone had thought was the deck of the market – sixty-eight a bushel.

Rob had reckoned that as the deals for August wheat were completed and May wheat wasn't being dealt, there would be a short-term deficit. A farmer who'd been able to hold on to his crop could come in then and sell at the short-term price-rise before May wheat was assessed. It had been a gamble, but then – what else was farming but a gamble? Against weather, against the withering winds of the plains, against crop disease and insects, against loneliness and isolation on the prairie, against the demands of the great cities who needed bread . . .

'It's a "bear" market in Chicago at the moment, Craigallan,' Pruman explained in a patronising tone. 'You know there's a "bear" clique in the Board of Trade at the moment – they got control around New Year, now they're *really* pulling us down. I couldn't believe it myself when they started offering under sixty-eight last week. I don't take any pleasure in telling a man he's got to take poor prices, you know that.'

Rob said nothing. He didn't trust his voice yet.

'How much you selling?' Pruman inquired.

Rob took off his hat and ran a hand through his hair in exasperation. 'That wheat cost me nigh on a dollar a bushel to raise, Pruman!'

'I know, I know – it's a sin, ain't it? But what can I do? The price broke again this morning, from sixty-two fifty to sixty-two. I got a wire here –' He picked up the top paper from his sheaf of information and held it out.

Rob glanced at it. 'As at 10.15am offer 62 repeat 62 down 50, signed Levasseur'. Levasseur was some clever young man on the floor of the Board of Trade, hired to let Pruman have fast information about any change in trading. 'Might go down again before they close around lunchtime,' Pruman murmured, watching Rob.

'Below sixty-two? That's impossible!'

'Once the "bears" get control you just can't tell. They're real hard, those guys. You see, there's plenty wheat. Fine harvests for three years: every bin is full everywhere in the world. They can buy as low as they please, and if folk don't want to sell at the price, what the hell? They don't need the wheat. So you're at their mercy, seems like. I'm sorry, Craigallan. You held off too long.'

Rob frowned. 'How can they fix the price like that? What right have they got?'

'What right? The right of having the money to buy it, that's what.'

'But they don't buy it,' he replied in rising anger. 'They've just started to "buy" May wheat. There isn't any May wheat. All that exists is green shoots on the plains. How can they buy that? At sixty-two or any other price?'

Pruman smiled at his indignation. 'They buy it because farmers sell it. Farmers anxious to be sure they can get such and such a price for wheat that's still growing rather than wait and mebbe see the price go below sixty cents a bushel. You know as well as I do, Craigallan – dealers buy wheat because farmers sell it, and dealers deal in "futures" because farmers need to have some kind of insurance of a market.'

'The Grangers are against futures. They'll put a stop to all this.'

'Yeah, yeah, I heard the speeches,' Pruman nodded. 'Saw a copy of the rules for the new club in Cleburne. Their constitution's the same old thing, wicked transport rates by the railroads, wicked storage rates by the silo owners, wicked deals by brokers on the Board of Trade. I'll tell you this, Craigallan.' He leaned forward to tap Rob's fine broad-cloth lapel, 'You'll never live to see the day they change any of it.'

'Something's got to be done! Prices are hiked up or dragged down – and for whose benefit? Who gets a dime out of the swing of the market except those swindlers on the Board of Trade?'

'That's not my affair,' Pruman said in a soothing tone. 'So long as I can sell off the wheat I buy, at a price I know is generally agreed, that's all I want. Now let's get to it – how much exactly are you selling?'

'I'm not selling.'

Pruman, who had picked up a pen and was opening his ledger, paused in surprise. 'What?'

'I'm not selling at those prices.'

The dealer waved his pen impatiently. 'What you going to do, then? Keep the wheat in store? I'd think the storage charges must be through the roof already – and then what? You've got August wheat on your hands and already the price is going down for May wheat. What's the point? Going to keep it till the rats solve your problem by eating it? Going to preserve it as an antique?'

'There must be a way to make a better deal than sixty-two –'

'Look, Craigallan, the price is sixty-two. Every dealer in Kansas is on that price –'

'Then I'll go outside Kansas –'

'You will? Where to? St Louis? Chicago?' Pruman was sneering now at this uppity farmer who dared to question the system.

'Yes, Chicago – why not! That's where all the prices are fixed, isn't it?'

'Grow up! You, go to Chicago?'

'Why not? There's a train from here – the track goes all the way to Chicago, I hear!'

'But what's the point? The price is sixty-two in Chicago.' Pruman shook the telegraph form under Rob's nose. 'All you'll do is add the train fare to your costs –'

'At least I'll find out who I'm selling to. I'll see who it is that's got the power to take six cents a bushel off me, push me into debt for the whole of next year –'

'You're out of your mind,' Pruman said. 'Why don't you just toe the line like the rest of the sod-busters?'

Because I'm not like them, Rob said to himself as he stalked out. He was shaking with anger. The smooth assumption that he was helpless, ignorant, had touched him on the raw. Damn the man and the business he controlled! Buying and selling the life-blood of the farmers while he despised them for opening their veins to him. Well, Rob wasn't going to humble, he wasn't going to be bled.

The price was sixty-two in Chicago, Pruman had said. Maybe so. If he had to, he'd sell at sixty-two but in Chicago, not to Pruman while he sneered at him from behind his beard as he signed the contractual note in his ledger.

He walked up the street with long strides. Morag ought to be in Ruby's Restaurant by now, waiting for him. He looked through the glass panel of the door but she wasn't to be seen. Annoyed, he strode along the sidewalk and finally espied her in Ludental's Dry Goods, fingering knitting yarn. She turned with a wide, happy smile as he came storming in.

'Rob, I've been choosing –'

'Come on, I've got something to tell you.'

'Why, what's the matter?' Her heart had come up into her throat at sight of his dark angry face.

'Hurry up, I have a train to catch.'

She had to run to keep up with him as he stalked out and back along the street. 'What train? What are you talking about –'

'I'm going to Chicago. Pruman's price is way down on what I hoped to get –'

'But why – why go to Chicago?' She snatched at his sleeve, trying to make him stop, out of breath with hurrying and with surprise, her head beginning to swim as it often did just at present.

'I'll sell to a dealer there. I'm not selling to Pruman.'

'But will the price be better –'

'Perhaps not. I want to go and see what goes on. I'm sick of being told what price I can get for my crop. I'm sick of being told Pruman's terms as if they came down from Mount Sinai.'

'But the fare to Chicago –'

'Damn the fare! I'm going, and that's that. You take the buckboard back to Brown Bridge – you can handle it can't you?'

'Yes, but –'

'But what?'

'How will you get home from here?'

'I'll hitch a ride from somebody. Don't worry about me.'

'But . . . how long will you be gone?'

'Couple of days, three maybe.'

'You've got nothing with you – not even a spare shirt –'

'For God's sake, Morag! I can buy a shirt in Chicago.'

She knew it was useless to protest further. She thought with wry disappointment of the purchases she'd hoped to make for the baby – small hopes of being able to afford them now, if he insisted on throwing money away on this wild goose chase. And the news she'd been looking forward to giving him – best to hold her tongue now. He'd be taken aback, perhaps even annoyed. She knew this restless, forceful mood of his.

'What time's the train?' she asked.

'There's one at noon.' He walked on, giving her quick instructions over minor matters of business he'd intended to deal with in St Joseph. 'There, got all that?'

'What shall I tell Brick?'

'Tell him to keep on with the work on that irrigation channel. He and Joe should watch out for any wilt in the crop, and if it's only small patches, spray at once. Confound it, Morag, you can keep things in hand for two-three days!'

'Yes.'

All the time he was buying his ticket and while they waited for the train to come clanking in from Omaha, she was trying to screw up courage to tell him her news. But he dropped a kiss on her cheek and swung aboard before she'd formed the words. ''Bye!' he called. 'Get yourself something as a treat – a dress length or something. See you soon.'

She turned away without waiting for the train to go out. Her cheeks were burning that he should think he could appease her with a length of gingham in the face of this behaviour.

The journey to Chicago took until early next morning, with a long wait at Rock Island. He disembarked feeling grimy and creased, annoyed that he'd put himself at a disadvantage by an uncomfortable night on a train. He sought out a hotel at once, took a room and ordered a hot bath while his suit was pressed. At eight o'clock he came down to the hotel dining room for breakfast feeling vastly improved both in spirits and appearance. To confirm his self-approval the waitress brightened at his approach; he'd always found the reaction of a woman to be a good measure of his effectiveness.

This was a voyage of discovery. He was in Chicago, the 'capital city' of the Plains, the home of millionaires and entrepreneurs and big dealers in produce. What he'd already seen on his way from the depot had awed him. All the buildings were so new and smart, rebuilt after the fire and not yet begrimed with dark soot from the factories. The people in the streets were so well-clad, so neat – not like the patched and dusty denizens of the prairies.

When the waitress brought his final cup of coffee he asked the way to the Board of Trade. 'Is it there you're heading?' she replied with her head on one side. 'You haven't the look of a broker.'

'I'm just a sightseer,' he told her. 'What's the best way to reach it?'

''Tis on the corner of Jackson and Lasalle. If you walk three blocks east from the door here, you'll see the crowds of clerks heading to the business quarter – just you fall in behind them and you'll be there. But I believe they don't open for business before nine-thirty.'

A sharp wind was blowing from the lake. He buttoned his jacket, regretting that he'd left Brown Bridge without a surtout – but yesterday in Brown Bridge the day had promised to be warm. The men around him were suitably clad, some in overcoats and some in frock-coats of thick face cloth with velvet collars. Hands were upraised to hat brims, to hold them steady against the breeze.

The street was crammed with delivery wagons and market carts edging their way to the stores, competing with vehicles headed to the Rookery where the business section began. In the centre of the street only a narrow way was left for the trolley-cars. Cabs plying for hire were few, and difficult to attract because of the flood of traffic. A couple who had come out of the hotel were on the street on the outside of the slow line of carts, fruitlessly calling to cabbies.

'Mind out, Marjorie, you'll get your gown dirty,' the man warned. The woman, concerned, drew her skirts aside as a heavy cart went by. She spied a cab ahead and cried shrilly, 'Grab that one, Sam!', pointing as she did so.

Her upraised arm allowed the wind to capture the folds of her cloak. The horse in the shafts of the wagon lurched away in alarm at the flapping blue satin. The wagon ground to a sudden halt. The packing cases on the wagon trembled and swayed above her.

Without stopping to think, Rob darted into the road. He grabbed her and carried her six feet farther up the street. They stumbled down in a struggling heap. The packing cases fell as if in slow motion, tumbling, descending, bumping against other boxes, to land on the road.

'Sam!' the woman was screaming. Sam!' She seemed to think she was being attacked and robbed.

Sam whirled. He backed away as the boxes fell between him and the wrestling pair. He shouted, 'Keep still, Marj, you fool!'

One more box toppled. It broke open to spill its contents in a noisy cascade – wrought iron gates.

'Jesus Christ!' breathed Sam.

People were hurrying forward to offer help. The vanman clambered down from his seat. 'You all right, ma'am?' he asked in scared anxiety.

'Yeah . . . yeah . . . I reckon I'm in one piece.' Marjorie suffered herself to be led back to the sidewalk, straightening the boned front of her bodice, smoothing down the ruffles of her skirt. She glanced over her shoulder at Rob. 'You okay?'

He was following her, rubbing his shoulder where he had hit the ground. 'I'll live.'

'Hey, feller, that was quick thinking.' Sam was holding out a hand to him. 'My name's Sam Yarwood, and I owe you for what you just did.'

'What happened?' Marjorie asked, looking dazed and frightened now.

'Just a badly tied load, that's all. Are you all right now?'

She shivered and leaned close to Sam, who put an arm round her. 'Sam,' she whispered, 'I think I almost got killed.'

'It's all right, honey. Everything's all right. There, there . . .'

Helpers had fetched the cab Marjorie had been trying to hire. She was helped in. Sam turned to Rob. 'You didn't mention your name?'

'Robert Craigallan.'

'Live in Chicago, do you? I'd like to drop by later, say thank you.'

'Well, no, I'm on just a short visit, probably going back to-morrow.'

'New in town? Mebbe I can help you.'

'Well, I was just going to the Board of Trade to see what goes on there in the wheat market. I grow wheat.'

Sam was surprised. The man didn't look like a farmer. His interest was doubly caught. 'If you want to see the Pit in action you've come to the right man! I'll be going there in a while. Hop in, I'll take you.'

'Oh no . . .' Rob was indicating Marjorie, already leaning back in the cab looking pale.

'We'll drop her off first. Come on.' Sam urged Rob in beside her and followed, calling an address to the driver.

The drive was quite short. Marjorie was handed down at a house in a rather seedy neighbourhood, where she was welcomed in by an anxious lady in a bright yellow wrapper.

'Take care of her, Joanie. She's had a shock.'

'Sam . . . Sam, don't leave me.'

'I got to, honey. I got business to tend to. I'll see you tonight, okay?' Sam directed her into the arms of Joanie and hastened back to Rob, who had watched it all with interest. 'A great gal, Marjorie. I think the world of her. Good fun at any hour of the day or night – know what I mean?'

Sam sat back, searching in his breast pocket for a cigar case. 'Smoke?'

'No thanks.'

Sam grunted and lit one for himself. 'So you grow wheat, eh? What you doing in Chicago, then?'

'I just thought I'd like to see the men who've cut six cents a bushel off my price this week.'

The older man puffed thoughtfully for a moment. 'Losing money, are you?'

'Faster than the spring thaw.'

'Can't understand why fellers work the land. Hard work for low returns, it seems to me.'

'It wasn't so bad until this year,' Rob protested. 'Now all of a sudden prices have taken a tumble.'

'Yeah, well . . . What else can you expect when the "bears" have got the market in their paws? But there's money to be made even in a bear market. That's what I mean about working the land. The only money in *that* seems to be selling the crop. In the Pit, you can buy it back and re-sell it, if you want to. A lot more flexible. If you take out a short hedge in a bear market you come out of it on an even keel. Seems to me to make more sense than –'

'Just a minute, just a minute,' Rob exclaimed, listening to this quick chatter from around the side of the big cigar. 'You're talking a foreign language. Did you just say you could buy back and re-sell on a *falling* market, and still make money?'

'Sure. You think half the Board of Trade's been making a loss since last September?' There was jovial scorn in his tone. 'Course not. But better still is if you know prices are going to rise. That's what I like – the coming in of a bull market. Just on the turn there – you can really make a killing.'

'I don't understand it. I can see that the grower can make a profit if the price of his crop goes up – but why should it make *you* happy?'

'Say, you really do need a guide to show you round. You're never going to make money if you have to wait for rising prices, boy – not while there's so much wheat in the silos.'

'You don't have to tell me,' Rob said bitterly. 'I've got last August's crop still on my hands.'

'What? You haven't sold it?'

He shook his head.

'Why the hell not?'

'I felt sure the price would go up now, at the six months point between harvest and harvest. I thought if supplies were low, the price would rise.'

'Damn it, boy, the price isn't going to rise.'

'No.'

Sam gave him a fatherly smile. 'Don't look so depressed. It's not as bad as all that.'

'It is for me. I'm losing better than thirty cents on every bushel I raise.'

'As much as that?' The other man raised his bushy eyebrows. 'We-ell, now, it's difficult to make up a gap like that. I can show you how to make money, but not thirty cents a bushel.'

Rob made a movement of denial. 'I haven't any money to play the market, Mr Yarwood.'

'Call me Sam. Everybody does.'

'Well, Sam, the only hope is if prices go up next year.'

'That's not likely. From what I hear, there'll be even more grain in the elevators next near.'

'I don't know if that's exactly right,' Rob said. 'I was told there might be trouble from the chinch bug this year.'

Sam had been about to tell the driver to stop. At Rob's words he sank back in his seat. 'What was that?'

'I beg your pardon?'

'What did you just say?'

'I don't know. What did I just say?'

'About the chinch bug.'

'Oh, that? A fellow was talking to me – an agricultural student.'

'From an agricultural college, you say?'

'That's right. Sticks in my mind – a young black fellow, but really smart.' Sam's face changed at the words, but Rob insisted, 'No, he knew what he was talking about. The Department of Agriculture had hired him – a vacation job, you see – to collect statistics. It was to go in some report – I don't remember what it was –'

'The Report on the Visible Supply,' Sam breathed.

'Yes, that was it. This youngster said that the larvae of the chinch bug are active, more so than usual. If he's right, it could mean a big drop in production.'

'God above,' Sam said, 'do you know what you've just said?'

'No, what?'

'Stop, dammit, stop!' Sam hollered at the driver. And to Rob, 'You've just given me the bull tip of the decade! Wheat likely to be damaged by the chinch bug, supplies likely to be down –'

'No, no,' Rob interrupted. 'That's not what I said at all!' He liked the affable Chicagoan, didn't want to mislead him. 'This young fellow Carver showed me some damage on the stems and that led him on to say there might be an outbreak this year. It's true, we haven't had a big breed of them for a while and they tend to come in cycles, but there's no real proof that they're coming this year –'

'But, for Chrissake, man, don't you see it doesn't matter? Suspicion is enough to send the prices up! If the crop's damaged by chinch bugs and there is less wheat, the price goes up.'

'Well … yes … of course.' Rob was struggling to keep track of the conversation as Sam paid off the driver and hustled him back along the sidewalk. 'But then if the bug dies off, or the wheat withstands the attacks, the crop will be much the same as last year and the price will fall –'

'But that's *then*. I'm talking about now. If it were known that the crop might be reduced by pests, the price would go up *today*. *Today*, do you see?'

'But the price would only go up if people knew what the agricultural report is going to say.'

'*You* know it, don't you?'

'Yes, but –'

'And you told me, didn't you? And I'm not above telling a few of my friends who need to know what the supply of wheat is going to be.'

'You mean,' Rob said, drawing in a breath, 'you could start a rumour?'

Sam grinned, taking out his cigar to wave it. 'You catch on fast. Come on, we've got business to do.'

'But Sam, you can't – I mean, is that possible? On the say-so of a casual acquaintance? What if nobody believes you?'

'They'll believe me. Everybody listens with both ears and their eye-teeth, when it comes to rumours on the floor of the Pit. I've seen money made on speculation that the French Revolution is going to break out again. You don't know, Rob – you just don't know! Come on.'

Arm in arm they walked back down La Salle Street. It swarmed with life. Brokers and commission men were moving quickly into the big building of clean new stone. Clerks, messengers, brokers' clients and depositors paused now and again to exchange information, to make guesses about the forthcoming day's business, but always breaking their groups to hurry on towards the mecca of their life – the Pit of the Board of Trade, the world's greatest grain market. Streams of dark-suited men came from Fifth Avenue, Dearborn and Clarke Streets, from Adams and Monroe, swept on inexorably towards the new offices, not yet officially opened but already like home to them.

Sam guided Rob past the stairways on either side of the entrance hall. They went to the corridor where the brokerage firms had premises. Sam threw open a door marked in gold lettering: 'Vinnison, Charle and Co.' and walked quickly into the customers' room.

It was a strange scene. Even though business hadn't yet started on the 'floor', Vinnison Charle were busy. The wall opposite the door was given over to a long blackboard with figures chalked in columns, facing which there were rows of chairs. Most of the chairs were occupied, with worried-looking men with sheafs of papers taking notes, thumbing through pocketbooks to refer back to a previous day's trading. The columns from which they were checking had headings: 'Oats', 'May wheat', 'Corn'. There was a continual background of sound – muted discussion, the click of the telegraph machine in the corner, the squeak of the chalk as the marker changed quotations. Cents, even fractions of a cent were rubbed out and altered constantly.

Sam nodded around to acquaintances but hurried on without pause. He opened the door of the inner office. Here two men of about his own age were conferring, one seated behind a heavy desk, the other perched on its corner.

'Vinnison . . . Charle . . .' Sam nodded greeting. 'Here's a friend of mine – Craigallan.'

''Morning,' said the thinner of the brokers, with a faint ironic lift of an eyebrow. 'Saw you at Kinsley's last night, living it up. Not been home yet?'

Sam pushed the teasing away from him with a brisk movement of his pudgy hands. 'Listen, Vinny – I want you to buy wheat for me this morning.'

Vinnison nodded in casual interest. 'Hedging?'

'Naw, this is big, Vinny. Who's going on the floor?'

'Well, I'm going myself –'

'No, no – that'll attract attention once you start to buy. I want this done quickly and quietly.' Both men were paying attention all of a sudden.

'Something on, Sam?' Charle asked, coming from behind his desk.

'I'll say. I'm going to give the market a bull turn today.'

'Tchah! What's the point of trying that? There's nothing doing on the price this morning.'

'You'll see,' Sam chortled, his tone rich with glee. 'My pal here – he's got inside information! The Visible Supply Report is going to give everybody a shock when it comes out –'

'How d'you know that, Sam? Anyhow, it may not come out today–'

'Mebbe it won't. But Rob has a hint of what it's likely to contain, and with a little judicious spreading that hint's going to make the price move up. I guarantee it.'

'Move up? Well, could be. It's gone too low, and that's for sure. How much d'you think it'll rise?'

'A whole cent.'

Both brokers gave him a stare of incredulity. 'Don't be dumb, Sam. The price can't go up by that much –'

'It went down by that much last Friday.'

'But that was when the bears sold enough to depress –'

'All right, so I'm going to buy enough to bring it up.'

Vinnison glanced at Charle and cleared his throat. 'How much you buying, Sam?'

'A million bushels.'

Three men drew in their breath – Vinnison, Charle, and Rob. There was a moment of utter silence in the dusty room. Then Vinnison said: 'You'll back it that far, Sam?'

'Sure.'

'It must be good information.'

'Rob takes it seriously. Don't you, Rob?'

'Well, I . . .'

'Do you or don't you?'

Rob remembered Carver's earnest black face, his intelligent brown eyes, and lean pointing finger. 'Yes, I think it should be taken seriously,' he said.

'See?' Sam said in triumph. 'So I don't want you going on the floor, Vinny. Send somebody junior to get it rolling. Later, when we've got the contracts, you go up to take over. I dare say you'll want to mop up a bit on behalf of other clients.' He swung suddenly. 'Are you in?' he said to Rob.

'In?'

'On the deal.'

'How?'

'D'you want me to buy for you?'

'Buy? I've got wheat to *sell*!'

Sam made a sound of impatience. 'Listen, boy, you did me a couple of big favours this morning. I owe you. You heard me. I'm going to buy a million bushels. You can have as much or as little of the deal as you want.'

'But I haven't any money –'

'You just said you had wheat to sell, didn't you?'

'Yes, but I meant I had real wheat –'

'Physicals,' Charle said. 'We don't deal in physicals here, but I can arrange it for you if you like.'

'Well, if the price is really going to go up by a whole cent a bushel, I'll be doing better here than I could have in St Joe –'

Sam gave a snort of laughter. 'Don't you understand what I'm telling you? If you sell your physical wheat at sixty-two, you'll have a stake for investment. Whatever you get for your crop, you can invest in my deal. You buy on margin – d'you understand margins?'

Rob shook his head.

'Well, you put down a percentage of the cost of what you're buying. You don't have to pay the whole price until the actual contract changes hands. But I'm going to sell again before that contract falls due: in fact, I'm going to sell before the close of business today, when the price will have gone up by one whole cent a bushel. Understand?'

'Yes, I see what you're intending to do.'

'It's called futures, son. You've heard of futures?'

Futures ... Those wicked dealings that the Grangers wished to see abolished. Yet, as Sam expounded the system now, it didn't seem wicked. It seemed intelligent, quick witted, exciting.

But – invest his own money in it? A whole year's work was embodied in the money he would get for his crop. If Sam were making a misjudgement, the money would be gone. And then what would they live on for the coming year? How would he pay the men's wages, buy seed, keep the plough and the reaper in repair?

'I'd better not, Sam,' he said, half unwillingly. 'I ... dare not risk the money.'

'There's no risk. It's a cert.'

Rob looked from him to the brokers. They made no affirmatory sign. 'I never did a thing like this,' he demurred.

'Would I give you a bum steer?'

'No, but you could be reading the signs wrong.'

Sam laughed. He threw out his arms. 'Do I look like a loser?'

Rob shook his head.

'Are *you* a loser?'

Vinnison intervened. 'Don't persuade him against his better judgement, Sam. And in any case, if we're going to do business, we'd better brief my clerk.'

'Who're you sending?'

'Cavely. He's a sensible young fellow. What are your instructions?'

'I want him to buy contracts for a million bushels – quietly. When that's done, let me know. I'll take over then. Okay, Vinny?'

'Right.' Vinnison went out by a door giving on to the street, to take his way relatively unobserved to the upper floor where his clerks awaited the opening of business. He had two young men who dealt for him on the floor; of these Cavely was the quieter and the more quick-witted.

Sam took Rob by the arm. 'Come on, I'll show you how it goes.' He led him up a shallow staircase to the visitors' gallery, where rows of chairs were set out close to a balustrade from which the onlooker could see the activity on the floor. There were a few men there, and one old lady with smelling salts in her hand. Sam set two chairs a little apart and took his place, pulling Rob down beside him.

The scene below was extraordinary. Messenger boys ran to and fro intoning names in a monotonous chant. Traders had formed little groups by the pits where the dealing would take place. The group at the wheat pit was no bigger than the others, although the men on its steps were watching the big clock for the beginning of business at nine-thirty. Rob saw a slender, fair-haired young man come in and take up his place by the rim of the wheat pit. 'That's Cavely,' Sam said in a low tone. The young clerk sauntered over to one of the sample tables, where wheat was on view in bags, to show its quality. He ran a finger casually through the grain in one of the bags, picked up a pinch, and ran it into his other palm. Then, throwing it down, he took up his accustomed dealing spot, on the top of the steps on the south side of the Wheat Pit. He was trying to disguise a nervous eagerness for the beginning of trade.

There was a little cage on the edge of the Pit. Here sat the official reporter, whose duty it was to keep track of the dealing. His eyes were on the clock on the opposite wall. Below the clock was a great circular dial whose hands were fixed at the point where wheat had closed at the end of yesterday's business: sixty-two cents, level.

The hands of the time clock moved to nine-thirty. At that precise moment the first offer was called by public outcry. 'Sell ten May at sixty-two. Ten May at sixty-two.'

The call was met at once by another voice. 'Give seven-eights for May. Seven-eight.'

A clamour broke out, drowning any distinct bid. It was like a burst of lightweight thunder, men's voices rising in wave upon wave up to the high vaulted ceiling. It dazed Rob.

'What's happening? Why are they so wrought up?'

Sam grinned. 'That's their usual state. It gets louder and louder until about ten minutes before close of dealing, and then it dies away. Now that first call was Lewis offering to sell wheat at the current price – ten contracts of five thousand bushels each, so he was offering fifty thousand bushels in all. There was a bid at seven-eight – that means sixty-one and seven-eighths, one-eighth of a cent under yesterday's closing price. Some fool may take it, but not yet. Everybody wants to sell at sixty-two or higher. Once they catch on that Cavely is buying on a large scale the price will edge up by – let's say – one-eighth. But I hope he'll have got my contracts bought in before that happens.'

Although Rob was listening, his eyes were on the scene below. It was like a battle. Men rushed at each other, grabbing at lapels or waistcoats as they called and shouted and bellowed. The buyers threw their hands out and closed the fingers round nothing, pulling it towards them in symbolic capture. The sellers held up fingers to show how many contracts of five thousand bushels they had on offer. By some strange telepathy, the eyes of buyer and seller would meet, nods were exchanged, and each clerk would note down the bargain on a pad. Over all, the official reporter kept guard.

Rob watched Cavely moving quietly and briskly in the Pit, throwing up his head to catch a movement of fingers, making the traditional mime for a 'buy', and nodding agreement.

'He's bought about twenty thousand by now,' Sam whispered in Rob's ear. 'I'm going to leave you now. If I'm seen up here watching, they may guess he's buying on my behalf, and I don't want that known – yet.'

He got up. Rob caught his sleeve. 'Sam.'

'Yes?'

'Let me in on it. Mr Vinnison said he could arrange for the sale of my crop –'

'Yes, but listen, son. It's still a gamble. I'm sure in my own mind that it's going to work but remember – I can't guarantee it.'

Rob stared up at him. He suddenly understood. *This* was where the power was. To own your own land, to bring your crop to harvest – there was satisfaction, triumph even, in that. But the real power lay in the manipulation of the harvest. It lay with these men in the Pit below him and in the offices around the building. Their dealing determined the price of wheat, the life or death of a farm and its owner, the supply of bread in distant countries. He wanted to take part in this. Even if he lost the money from the sale of his crop, he must take part. He must learn how to be one of them.

'Ask Mr Charle to arrange for the sale of my wheat. It should bring in better than five thousand dollars.'

Sam slapped him on the shoulder. 'You'll get it back plus about a hundred dollars profit if the price of the wheat goes up by one cent on that dial – and I think it'll make that much, Rob, mebbe more.'

'More?'

'Could be. There's a tide, you know. It ebbed too damn far last week. Let's see how far it floods back today.' Sam turned away. 'I'll fetch you by and by.'

Rob stayed where he was, entranced by the strange, wild scene below him. There was a frenzy in it that he'd never suspected in the business world. He kept his eye on Cavely. After an hour's hard dealing the fair-haired man seemed to retire for a moment, held in talk by a messenger. When he returned, Rob watched avidly. Now, presumably, Cavely would begin to sell. Sam had said that was the plan. But no, Cavely was still buying.

Puzzled, Rob moved uneasily on his chair. He felt a touch on his arm. Sam was at his side; he had been home to bath and change, and now was looking smooth and crisp in black tail coat and fine-checked trousers. 'Come on,' he said, 'this is where we begin to do our stuff.'

Sam led him down to the corridor of the Board of Trade. Men were still passing in and out under the big neo-Roman portico, some coming to begin the day's business at mid-morning because today had been expected to be a day of light trading. Idlers stood about, some smoking, some glancing through the newspapers.

Sam worked his way towards a spot not far from the doors. A youngish man in a checked jacket and grey trousers, very dandified, was checking a sheaf of reports clipped to a notice board. Sam took up his stance about a yard away from him and said to Rob in a startled voice: 'And you mean he actually showed you the damage on the stems?'

'What?' Rob said, taken aback.

'On your own land, was it? Or a neighbour's?'

'I don't know what you –'

'All right, all right, I understand you want to be cagey about it. Could be hard for you if your crop's condemned. But look, son, information like that is useful to me.' As he said these last words, Sam gave Rob a huge wink with the eye turned away from the well-dressed young man.

Rob caught on at last. 'I understand, Mr Yarwood,' he said, sinking his voice as if unwilling but making sure he was still audible. 'But you must realise that the man I was talking to was taking statistics for the Department of Agriculture . . .'

Sam smothered a delighted grin. The young man had stiffened and tried to move nearer. 'What did you say is the name of this pest?'

'Chinch bug. It winters on the wild grasses, you see,' Rob explained. Unconsciously he had made a return to his Scottish accent, to make himself sound more rustic. 'Around now it moves to the wheat stems and burrows into the sap. Makes the plants wilt, ye ken. A hard winter like the one just gone by – that makes them hatch oot a' the stronger in March or April.'

'But that's only around your own neighbourhood, after all.'

'I dinna ken if that's the case. The winter was hard in Ohio and even harder in Minnesota.'

'Say, did this guy have information from around there too?' As he spoke, Sam drew Rob further away to have a private chat, or so it seemed. Their eavesdropper, foiled, hesitated for a moment and then plunged into an office that opened on to the corridor.

Sam chuckled. 'Disley Warbuth,' he said. 'Biggest gossip on the Board of Trade. He'll have that all around his friends before the hour is out. And they'll all want to buy, because they'll think – for at least the rest of today – that wheat is going to be more scarce this fall.'

Rob shook his head. 'I can't believe people will buy and sell on a rumour like that.'

'You'll see. Want to come with me to talk to Vinny?'

'I'd rather go back up and watch.'

'Hooked, eh? Okay. Business closes in about two hours. I'll fetch you then for a little celebration at the Calumet Club.'

Rob nodded and turned away. He wanted to be back in his place, to see what would happen now. He could still scarcely believe that Sam would be proved right. But it was so. At first almost indistinguishable, there was a change in the tide. The clerks on the floor began to buy. One man after another began to draw imaginary packages of wheat towards his chest; those who were selling began to call out higher prices – and got nods of assent. The hands on the big dial moved from sixty-two to sixty-two and one-eighth.

In a series of little jerks, that hand travelled from sixty-two to sixty-two seven-eighths in the next hour. Then, at noon, a hubbub broke out. Men left the floor to crowd round a board under the gallery. A heavy murmur rose, different from the buying and selling roar. Those still dealing turned to listen.

It was the Report on the Visible Supply for April, posted unexpectedly by the Department of Agriculture. A dry announcement of what stocks were held, where, and how they were to be replaced. What had caused the break in trading was the laconic footnote: 'Pest control officers report some evidence of damage in North Kansas, South Nebraska and Western Iowa due to chinch bug. Data insufficient for forecast of control measures.'

That was enough to verify all the fears roused by Disley Warbuth's tale. Messengers began to hurry to the rim of the Pit with notes for the clerks. 'Buy wheat, there may be a shortfall.'

Before Rob's incredulous gaze the dial's hand moved forward: sixty-three, sixty-three four-eighths, five-eights, sixty-four cents. Sixty-four an-eighth. Sixty-four three. Sixty-five. Sixty-five an-eighth. And on. And on.

The temperature in the Pit rose. The noise level became almost unbearable. Men surged from one rim to the other, grabbing each other, shouting their bids and offers, writing down the prices and names then tearing off sheets from the pads which were trampled underfoot as they hurried on to the next piece of business.

Then at last, for no reason that Rob could tell, business slackened. The outcry began to diminish. Dealers began to head for the door. The day's business was over except for some fevered participants who had missed the tide. There was a drift away. Some few stood about, staring at their notepads, making quick calculations.

Then a gong struck. The official reporter rose and left his booth. The traders shrugged, put notepads in their pockets, straightened loosened ties, buttoned their jackets. The few visitors in the gallery rose. The old lady put her smelling salts in her reticule and shut it with a snap. She marched towards the stairs.

Weary as if he had run a mile, Rob got up and followed. He had made, not a hundred dollars, but six times as much. A hundred dollars if the price went up by one whole cent; so as it had gone up to sixty-eight there must be six hundred profit. It dazed him. In one morning he had made as much as would have cost him more than a month's labour on the farm.

As he picked his way slowly down the staircase Sam Yarwood came bounding up to meet him. 'Well? What d'you say? The Department of Agriculture came to our aid like a winner! I knew we'd make money but I never thought it would take off like that. Six cents advance in one day! The whole of last week's dive put back in one morning! I tell you, we've made history!'

'It doesn't seem possible to me, Sam, I don't understand it.'

It's nothing to do with understanding. It's instinct and courage that counts when it comes to a thing like this. And I've got both, boy, I've got both! Come on, let's celebrate.'

He dragged him off by the sleeve, happy, ebullient, on the crest of a wave. They walked quickly through the thinning press of traders. Rob scarcely knew where they were headed nor noticed the thin sharp rain now falling. Only when the sombre opulence of the Calumet Club enfolded them did he rouse enough to speak. 'I don't know how to thank you, Sam.'

'Thank me? It's the other way round. Now, what are you going to drink?'

Rob hesitated. Sam solved the problem by ordering champagne. The waiter smiled discreetly. Mr Yarwood had brought off another good stroke of business, it appeared.

During the meal Rob listened while Sam talked on enthusiastically about their morning's work. 'You ought to leave the money with me, Rob,' he suggested. 'Let me handle it for you. There ought to be some activity tomorrow in the Corn Pit, after today's rumours about wheat.'

'No, no . . . I've got to have time to think about it all, Sam.' He half-shook his head. 'Besides . . . I haven't actually had the money.'

'It's on its way. Charle will drop it in by and by. He's just doing the bookkeeping.'

They were sitting over cigars and port when the broker came in, tall and spare and moving with jerky eagerness. He handed a cheque and a note of contract to Rob.

Rob read it through. He had expected the price of his own wheat plus a profit of a little under five hundred dollars. The extra amount was one thousand and fifty dollars. 'But . . . but . . . This is double what I am owed!'

Sam snatched it from him and crowed with delighted laughter. 'Good for you, Charley! Don't you see, Rob? Charle waited to sell your wheat until the price had gone up to sixty-eight!'

'But how could he invest money for me when he hadn't sold the wheat to provide the investment?'

'You'll learn, Rob, you'll learn. You can't invest without collateral, but you don't have to have it in actual cash – and you had me, didn't you? Any friend of mine is a friend of Vinnison and Charle. Not bad, eh?'

Not bad? Over a thousand dollars. And he had done nothing for it, except to put his trust in George Washington Carver and his opinion about the chinch bug. 'Damned if I know what to say . . .'

'Then say nothing. What's a thousand or two between friends? Look, I've got a couple of things to do this afternoon, but why don't we celebrate this evening?'

'I . . . ought to get back to Brown Bridge . . .'

'Got a little woman waiting for you, have you? But see here, Rob, you don't get to Chicago very often, I s'pose?'

'This is my only visit so far.'

'Well, don't rush away without getting a bit of pleasure from it. A great place, Chicago. Tell you what, I'll pick you up around seven – you're at the Wentworth House?'

'Yes. But I ought to get the train back to St Joe.'

'There's a train in the morning. And don't you want to buy some gew-gaw for the little lady? You wouldn't want to go back empty-handed.'

Rob recalled of Morag as he'd seen her yesterday in Ludental's store – fingering the knitting yarn wistfully, no doubt trying to work out whether they could afford it. He'd take her something fine, something really pretty – a luxury she'd never think of buying for herself.

He agreed to be picked up at the hotel at seven so that he'd have plenty of time to stroll round the big stores. Sam pointed him in the right direction. He found the shops dazzling. He'd seen such places from the outside in New York when he first came to America. He'd been in smaller stores when he was made to tag along after Luisa on her trips to Boston. But the stores of Chicago seemed to spill out luxuries like some great market in the Arabian Nights. It took him more than an hour to come to terms with the vast choice spread out before him, he realised he would have to make up his mind or be late back at the hotel to bathe and change. He happened to be in Potter Palmer's store; he quickly bought a new shirt to change into, a new cravat, and a silk handkerchief to peep out of his breast pocket.

For Morag, in a rush of lavish generosity, he bought a hair ornament – a tortoise-shell comb edged with diamante and with three roses of creamy white silk attached. 'That's straight from Paris, France,' the salesgirl told him with approval as she packed it into a cube of gilt cardboard and tied it with gold tape.

When Sam arrived, he wasn't alone. He brought Marjorie, now fully recovered from the drama of the morning; and with Marjorie came a friend, Celeste. Both girls were decked out in gowns of looped, frilled and ruffled satin – Marjorie in coffee-coloured trimmed with apricot, Celeste in heliotrope edged with pink. Now that Rob had strolled through the big stores, he thought that these gowns were a little loud, but he was pleased to see that each had a pretty nonsense in her hair, a concoction of feathers and flowers and paste jewellery; he'd made a good choice for Morag.

Morag vanished from his mind again during the celebratory dinner that followed. Sam reserved a table in a discreet restaurant; fine food had been ordered. Wine flowed with each course, and afterwards there was brandy. Then there was a visit to a theatre where a chorus of pretty girls danced and sang, twirling parasols and showing their silk-clad ankles below frothy skirts. Around midnight, they made their unsteady way back to the Wentworth House.

By now Rob had quite accepted that Celeste was his partner. It took him a little by surprise when, at his room door, he found Marjorie with her arms wound round his neck. 'But... aren't you Sam's girl?' he murmured against the curls of her scented hair.

'Yeah... but he quite likes a change. You can go with Celeste if you like, though. But it'll cost you if you do.' She snuggled closer.

'With me, it's for love, honey. You saved my life this morning. I want to repay you.'

It was a munificent repayment. Clever, eager, generous, Marjorie provided both an experience and an education. As he was made to hold off again and again by her soft, quick caresses, desire reached a point where it was like some exquisite torture. When at last he could hold back no longer there was a delirium utterly new to him – a climax of triumphant delight never known in his nights with Luisa nor his now familiar pleasures with Morag. He lay beside Marjorie, left on some unfamiliar shore by a tidal wave, while she leaned over him in teasing laughter. 'Good, was it, country boy? I wanted you to get a real reward.'

There was more . . . much more. Marjorie was generous, without constraint. And, before the night ended, he had the best reward of all, the exultation of making Marjorie tremble and moan and plead in the final act of their love-making.

'Gee,' she murmured afterwards, her face a strange mixture of astonishment and utter satisfaction. 'You're not bad yourself, country boy . . .'

He caught the train to St Joseph with only moments to spare. Sam shoved him into a cab outside the hotel calling: 'Don't worry about the bill, I'll take care of all that. Stay in touch, Rob. I never forget a guy that's done me a favour.'

At first on the long journey home, Rob was keyed up, restless with memories and fantasies of the night just over. But by and by he dozed; his body relaxed, his mind drifted back to normal. When he woke his attention turned naturally to the prairies outside the train windows. He looked with interest at the wheat. His farmer's brain began to check for comparison with his own. He was Rob Craigallan of Brown Bridge again.

When he alighted in St Joseph he didn't look around for an acquaintance who might give him a ride. He had money now to hire a horse. He rode back, pleased with himself and with the whole episode in Chicago. The cheque for six thousand dollars nestled cosily in his wallet. Five and a half thousand earned by the sale of his wheat, at a good price. Five hundred from a little audacity. And there was more where that came from.

The never-ending prairie breeze carried the sound of the horse to Morag as she pinned out the wash on the line outside the kitchen. She ran to the kitchen door, calling to Nellie: 'He's here!' Then, untying her apron, she hurried round to the front of the house to meet Rob.

When he swung down and caught her in his arms, she clutched him with anxious fingers, almost afraid he would melt away again like the early morning mist. 'Oh, darling! I've been so anxious! How are you? How did you get on?'

'Wait till you hear.' He put an arm round her and led her into the house. Nellie, her black face beaming, had tactfully waited there to greet him.

'We'll have that coffee, Nellie,' Morag urged, going into the living room. She was sure Rob must be thirsty and hungry and exhausted. Yet there was an air of wellbeing and satisfaction about him.

'Did you sell the wheat?' she asked as she pushed him down into the best chair. 'I've been thinking, Rob – even at sixty-two we can manage if we pull in our belts –'

'Pull in, nothing! I sold the crop at sixty-eight.'

'Sixty-eight?'

'The price went up,' he explained. 'While I was in Chicago. Mind you, Morag, even at sixty-eight we've made no kind of a fortune. It's still a loss of something like thirty cents a bushel when you think of what it costs to raise. But...' he smiled, 'I did a good stroke of extra business.'

He produced the cheque. She read the copperplate handwriting, then raised her grey eyes to stare at him in disbelief. 'That's five hundred more than you'd get at sixty-eight cents a bushel?'

'Yeah. I got some good advice for a deal on the Board of Trade, Morag. I bought wheat while the price was down and sold when the price went up – and made a profit.'

'Five hundred?'

'That's it. Five hundred extra to the main price!'

She was wrinkling her brow. 'I don't . . . I don't quite understand. How could you deal on the Board of Trade with our wheat? I thought by now they'd be concentrating on next year's harvest.'

He was surprised at her knowledge of the trading routing. 'Yes, well, they're dealing in May wheat –'

'And you were buying and selling May wheat?'

'Yes, I used the price I got for our last year's –'

'What you're saying is you did a deal in futures?'

There was something in her tone that made him frown at her. 'Yes, I did. And made an easy profit.'

Morag sat down in the chair across the hearthrug. 'Forgive me if I've got it wrong, Rob ... But I thought the Grangers were so set against the deals in futures? I mean, they keep on making speeches urging members to get a bill through the Senate –'

'I don't know how you come to know so much about the Grangers!' he interrupted in annoyance. 'You're generally off with the women swopping recipes or quilting pieces when the men are talking.' Why couldn't she be pleased about the money? He'd expected her to cry out in delight. There was no need to be critical about it. She was too apt to try to set him right, always on about principles and conscience and stuff like that. Why couldn't she be like Marjorie and tell him he was great?

Morag saw the thoughts racing across his face. There was that dark, brooding look in his eyes. I shouldn't have made an issue of the money, she thought. And yet it was important, because she and Rob had been to many of the Granger meetings.

'The Grangers *are* against futures?' she persisted.

'So they say. I wonder if they've thought it through –'

'Rob, they're thinking of asking you to be a Vice-President for this county. I can't see it's right to be doing deals in futures –'

'When did you hear that?' he broke in. 'I haven't been approached.'

'Well, Mrs Johnson said her husband had been talking to some of the other men about it –'

'For this coming year, you mean?'

'Yes, but Rob – you can hardly take office with the Grangers if you don't support their aims –'

He got up in irritation. 'Nobody's going to know I did one deal on the Board of Trade, are they?'

She was silent.

'You aren't thinking of telling anybody?'

'No.'

Nellie came in with the coffee, carefully served in the best china. 'I brought some of your favourite cookies,' she said, putting the tray before him.

'Thank you, Nellie. At least you're pleased to see me home.'

The old cook glanced from one to the other. 'Ev'body pleased to see you home, Mister Rob,' she murmured. With that, she went out very quietly.

Her gentle words brought Rob up short. What were they arguing about? Morag didn't understand. You couldn't expect a woman to understand about business. And now wasn't the time to be explaining such a complex matter.

'I've brought you a present,' he said, suddenly remembering. 'It's in the saddlebag.'

He fetched the box and gave it to her. Divided between awe and delight at its elegance, she opened it. She lifted out the hair ornament. A fine comb of tortoise-shell edged with sparkling little stars and with three creamy roses glued to it . . .

Nothing could have been less suitable to the life she led. There was never an evening occasion at which she could wear this. Her only evening dress wasn't fine enough and besides, it would outshine anything that any other woman would be wearing, making her look outrée.

All at once she was swept by a wave of tenderness for him. It was so pretty, so useless. He had wanted to please her and this had been his choice. But she too had a gift. She would save it for later, for some more quiet moment this evening: time enough to tell him about the baby when he had poured out all his news about Chicago. For now, she must show him she appreciated his gift. Laughing with pleasure, she put the comb into the thick coil of hair at the back of her head. 'How does it look?' she asked, turning to present her profile for his consideration.

'You look great, just great. I never saw you prettier.' There was a glow, a warmth about her now that caught at his heart. He swept her into his arms and as he kissed her the tortoise-shell comb fell out of her hair and on to the floor.

Later, as evening came on, they walked out together to look at the fields. Joe and Brick were coming in from the day's work. He greeted them, heard their views on the wheat.

'Say, boss, there's some sign of damage on the stems over to the northwest field,' Brick remarked.

'Extensive?'

'Seems to be spreading. I saw more s'morning than I did last week. Chinch bug, I reckon.'

Morag sighed. 'I hope we're not going to have an outbreak this year.'

'I hope not,' he agreed.

No need to tell her that if wheat was damaged and the crop reduced, the price would go up and he knew how to benefit from that. He sensed that he knew now how to benefit from the price of wheat no matter what happened. He had only to ask Sam Yarwood for advice.

He started out past his field hands towards the expanse of prairie where the grain was pushing up. He knew now that he was no longer shackled to the burden of risk – bad weather, plant disease, low prices. He knew that the power of wheat lay elsewhere. He had had a glimpse of how that power could be gained. Sam Yarwood had given him the key to his fetters.

17

THEY NAMED MORAG'S BABY Gregor, after Rob's grand-father. Morag had no family names to offer; she had never known who her parents were.

The birth was hard for her, for she'd been unwell through the preceding winter with a recurrence of the cough that had long troubled her. The little boy was delicate, sleeping little, gaining weight too slowly.

Doctor Arnolf shook his head over them both. 'I don't think they're fit to go through another winter here in their present shape,' he said to Rob. 'You ought to send them south, to a milder climate, until the spring.'

'But we can't afford that,' Morag protested when Rob told her the doctor's view.

'We can afford anything that's good for you and the baby,' he replied.

He could afford it too. With the help of Sam Yarwood, Rob had done well with speculation on futures during that year. There were futures in corn and other produce as well as wheat; though Sam was chiefly in love with the drama of the wheat pit, he was able to give Rob tips for making money elsewhere.

As a result, Rob had bought in the land next to his own when Bob Partridge gave up and moved away. At this moment he was negotiating for a half share in a grain elevator to be built at St Joe. He preferred not to spread knowledge of this among his neighbours; most of the farmers were keen members of the Granger movement, utterly opposed to speculation and the 'cornering' of grain storage facilities. In fact, while Rob dickered over the setting up of a private elevator in St Joe, he was joining in a move to erect one as a co-operative in Falls City. He thought this would break even, but in the new outlook he'd gained he saw that the storage tanks would be better placed at a good railhead like St Joe.

Morag didn't want to go to Florida. She objected that Ellie-Rose would miss her.

'Do you think I won't?' Rob rejoined. 'We'll all miss you, darling. But you've got to think of Gregor. He's not doing well here. A few months in the South will make a world of difference to him.'

It was because of Gregor that she gave in. Dr Arnolf lectured her on her duty as a mother, glaring at her over his spectacles and wagging his finger at her. 'Your husband will be well looked after,' he pointed out. 'You have a cook and a maid – how many womenfolk does he need?'

'But Ellie-Rose –'

'Ellie-Rose can live without you for a few months.'

He proved to be right. Ellie-Rose moped and went off her food for a few days but Christmas was coming; at school there was much cutting out of stars from gold paper and learning of lines for the Nativity play. So Ellie-Rose forgot to be unhappy.

Rob missed Morag more than he thought possible. The house, now faced with imported stone on the outside and well-furnished inside, seemed empty without her. But Ellie-Rose kept him amused. Now eight years old, she was full of chatter about school, she was currently in love with her teacher, Miss Udall.

Then as winter receded there was ploughing and the never-failing thrill of planting the wheat. Rob was still looking for the ideal seed. He was in constant correspondence with another farmer, C. G. Pringle, with whom he exchanged samples of his own grain. He watched the kernels being transferred from the supply wagon to the seedbox of the drill, each field carefully noted in his records with the type, the amount, and the date of seeding. Partridge's land he put under clover, to get it back in good heart; this was regarded by his neighbours as self-indulgent eccentricity, bound to end in bankruptcy.

The first tinge of green came on the fields. The seed was germinating. The ground was still cold; he looked at the thermometer on the outside of his outermost barn every morning and evening to record the temperatures. He wanted to know what extremes the seed would endure, what temperatures produced the best root systems.

Ellie-Rose would come out with him to look at the thermometers before he took her to school. Sometimes she would painstakingly write in the figures on his record card in her round childish hand. She was interested – but only because he was interested. She was much more pleased to see the first signs of life in the silky sophora than the first shoots of the wheat, for when that silvery foliage began to appear again it meant the sun was gaining power.

Rob dropped her at the school in Brown Bridge before going to the telegraph office to see if there was word from Sam Yarwood. They were in the midst of a deal at the moment. The clerk handed him the message slip: 'Bernard sends regards, all well at home.' 'You sure got a lot of friends and relations, Mr Craigallan,' he remarked.

'Sure have,' Rob agreed. He and Sam used a simple code involving terms such as 'Best wishes' or 'Grateful thanks'. It didn't do any good to let anybody know their private business. From time to time Rob would make a trip to Chicago or New York to see what was happening in the market, with Sam as guide, but in the main he let Sam do the dealing. In return, he supplied Sam with inside information about crop prospects; through his membership of the Granger movement and through his contacts with agriculturists and experimenters on the Department of Agriculture's staff, Rob was better placed than most to know how the wheat was growing.

He was looking through a Canadian journal for an article about freight charges on the C.P.R. and its effect on the price of Manitoba wheat when he heard a wagonette draw up on the dirt road outside.

'Mariette!' he called. 'Somebody's coming!'

The maid came from the back of the house, straightening her hair under its plain cap as she went. She knew Mr Craigallan liked her to present a good appearance. Rob closed his magazine and rose to greet the visitor.

Mariette came in, looking flushed. 'Mr Craigallan, sir . . . it's a lady. She says she's –'

'Hello, Rob,' said the visitor, and swept in in a rush of taffeta-trimmed merino and Parisian perfume.

It was Luisa.

'Pleased to see me?' she cried. 'It's such ages, isn't it? I must *say* . . . This place isn't as I feared –' She surged across the room to kiss him on the cheek. 'Darling, say something!'

Rob recovered from his shock. 'You can go, Mariette,' he said to the maid, who was gaping in the doorway.

'Mariette?' Luisa said. 'French maid? Very nice.'

'She's Czech,' Rob said. 'What the hell are you doing here, Luisa?'

'That's a nice thing to say to your wife!' She pouted, swept some papers off a chair, and collapsed into it. 'My *dear* . . . The *journey* . . .' She began to untie her bonnet strings. 'It seemed to go on for ever! Just go out and see that the man is taking care of the luggage, will you? And tell Cornelius to stop skulking about in the hall –'

'Cornelius?'

'Of course. You didn't think I'd leave him in Boston, did you? Go ahead, now, Rob.'

As if sleepwalking, he obeyed her. In the hall he found a ten-year-old boy in knickerbockers and a Norfolk jacket, standing lost and scared, watching the driver put a trunk on the threshold.

'Cornelius?' Rob said.

The boy didn't turn. Rob went up and touched him on the shoulder. With a start Cornelius faced him. They stared at each other.

'Hello, Cornelius,' Rob said.

'Hey-o Fadder,' the boy replied in a flat, leaden voice.

Rob wondered whether to embrace him or offer his hand. The

problem was solved by Cornelius gesturing to the luggage. 'Wi'
you pay a mah?' he suggested, which Rob, rightly interpreting as
'Will you pay the man', took as a hint not to be emotional.

Luisa had left Boston last year. She was bored with life in the
little house, wearied by her efforts to get into good society. Julius
had sent for his mother in the spring, saying he could now provide
a home for her if she wished to join him. Dorothea, overjoyed,
packed up and went. She wrote to say that Julius was making a
very pleasant living these days.

Julius had been lucky. He met Mrs Laracky. She was an
earnest New York matron given to good works, who took it upon
herself to save him from the Demon Drink. When she had dried
him out after a prolonged soak, she found to her surprise that she
had on her hands a young, well-educated fellow with blue eyes
and charming manners. She promptly fell in love with him.

But only in the most platonic way, be it understood. He
became her protégé. To keep him out of mischief, she gave him
the task of refurbishing a house her husband had bought her, so it
was through Mrs Laracky that a new talent in a hitherto unheard-
of career was launched on the world. Julius van Huten became *the*
man to consult about house decoration.

There were many nouveaux riches in New York who wanted to
make a splash in society with a big house and lush entertaining. It
became *de rigueur* to call in Julius van Huten. Since his clients
were rich, Julius's fees were high.

Luisa heard of all this from her Mama and went to join her. It
was a gorgeous life. Julius knew all the best people – at least, the
richest. There was something faintly Bohemian about his
household. Luisa collected a lover, developed mannerisms of
speech that owed something to that young star of culture Oscar
Wilde, and had a good time.

But Luisa had never really got on with Julius. As her senior by
some three years he'd always bullied and patronised her. He now
took to criticising her taste in clothes, told her she was the wrong
shape for the Pre-Raphaelite draperies, and made no secret of the
fact that her lack of literary taste embarrassed him.

Then her friend Herbert dropped her in favour of a gipsy

dancer. There was a 'flu epidemic in New York. She had a furious row with Julius. All of these events brought forcefully to her memory a murmur she'd heard from one of Mrs Laracky's rich friends – that Rob Craigallan had done some very neat dealing the last time he was in New York. She had seen him then; they had bowed distantly to each other in a public room at the Metropolitan Hotel in November. It then occurred to Luisa that he was a husband whom no woman in her senses would leave lying around.

En route for Brown Bridge she made a detour to pick up Cornelius from Aunt Remegen. When his tutors protested, she waved them away. 'The boy is going to be re-united with his father,' she said. 'That's more important than lessons.'

'What's the point of this, Luisa?' Rob inquired when she had given her version of this need for a family reunion. 'You're not planning on staying?'

She was, but for the moment she felt it wise to say she was on a visit.

'You could hardly have chosen a worse time. I'm in the middle of getting the seed into the ground –'

'Always the same old Rob,' she crooned. 'You always were obsessed with things like that.'

'That's the way it is. There are only a few weeks when the soil and the temperature are absolutely right.'

'Well, I won't interfere, darling. I just wanted you to get to know your son, that's all.' But that wasn't by any means all. Luisa was twenty-eight years old and confident of her physical attractions. She was sure that before too long she could make Rob want her.

There was no time like the present. As she unpacked her trunk in the 'guest room', she spread out the nightdress and negligee she'd bought before leaving New York. They were of soft pink edged with black lace, very flimsy. She'd tried them on. Her curvacious body glinted through the folds very pleasingly. Luisa had learned a lot from Herbert, the lover who had left her for the dancer.

She intended to wait until the house had settled down for the night and then, clad in her soft silks, tap on Rob's door and say she couldn't sleep in these strange surroundings. If she couldn't get him into bed with her shortly after that, she'd enter a nunnery.

Alas for her plans. One of the farmhands came galloping up on a heavy horse soon after nightfall. 'Mr Craigallan, Mr Craigallan! Quick, quick – there's been a collapse!'

Rob ran out of the house, leaving his dinner on the table. 'What's that, Brick?'

'Out by Heddon Corner – the ground's caved in – might be old prairie dog holes but the spring flooding's weakened everything. Come quick, boss, the drill team's down there and we can't get 'em up!'

Rob reappeared for a moment to grab a coat. Luisa, running into the hall to find out what was the matter, was just in time to clutch his sleeve. 'Where are you going?'

'To get my horses out. You go on with supper, Luisa.'

'But when will you be back?'

'Pretty soon, I hope. Don't worry about me. Nellie will get me something to eat if I'm late.'

'But why must you go?' she complained. 'Can't you send your men –'

'Those horses are about the most valuable thing on this farm. More important, the seed's *got* to be sowed. Without the drill team, I'm stuck. I've got to get them out. I'll talk to you later, Luisa.

He was gone. She went back into the living-room where the two children still sat at table: Ellie-Rose confused and edgy in face of this woman who had been a far-off Mama in New York until now, and Cornelius silent and watchful.

She packed them off to bed as soon as they'd eaten. She herself undressed in luxurious expectation, sprayed herself with scent, and lay down on her bed to read until her plan could be put into action. The hours went by. She heard Rob's voice from time to time, out among the barns.

She fell asleep at last from sheer weariness. She slept late, for it had been a long day's travel to Brown Bridge. When she woke, bright light was edging the drapes at her window. She half sat up, feeling for the bell pull, and then realised she wasn't in New York.

Yawning, she clambered out of bed and put on the pretty negligee. 'Nellie,' she called, coming out of her bedroom into the living-room.

'Yes, Miss Luisa?' Nellie appeared in the kitchen doorway, sleeves rolled up and a wooden spoon in her hand.

'Can I have some coffee?'

'Sure 'nough. You sleep well?'

'Well enough. Where is everybody?'

'Mister Rob, he out on the fields – got the team out 'long about one in the morning. The chillun, they out in the barn – Mister Rob tole Miss Ellie-Rose she can have a holiday from school to play with her brother.'

Luisa nodded dismissal and sat down on a chair near the stove, running her hands through her tangled hair. She'd brushed it out loose last night instead of plaiting it. She was so unaccustomed to the different sounds of wheels on the road that she didn't look up when a buggy stopped outside. She was debating what to wear today; the weather was springlike, she ought to put on something bright and light.

The door from the hall opened. She looked up. A woman carrying a baby about five months old came into the room.

A dreadful, intense silence gripped each of them like a vice. They stared at one another.

A glance was enough to tell Luisa whose son Morag was carrying. That reddish brown tuft of hair, those grey eyes ... 'My God,' she gasped.

'What are you doing here?' Morag whispered.

'What am I doing here? What are *you* doing here!'

Morag shivered and said nothing.

'Where the hell did you spring from? Nobody mentioned you yesterday –'

'I've just got back from Florida –'

'Florida! You live in *Florida*?'

'No, I live here.'

Morag was totally at a loss. She had flown into the house thinking to surprise Rob by her unannounced return. She had written to him as usual last week but never mentioned she was

[284]

setting out for home. She'd pictured the cool spring weather glinting over the prairies, Rob's teams out plodding their patient way along the furrows. She longed to see them again. She'd been gone from him too long.

Luisa in her nightgown and negligee looked as if she was perfectly at home in the house. Her half-awakened appearance, her tangled hair and rumpled silks ... Morag looked down, trying to avoid what the evidence seemed to tell her.

Luisa had got up and come to glare at her from a few feet away. 'You scheming little bitch,' she muttered. 'I believe you rushed here the minute I chased you out of Boston.'

Morag didn't bother to deny it. The baby stirred in her arms, tugging at a strand of her hair.

'So,' Luisa said. 'You've been busy, eh?'

'Luisa, don't talk like that. Rob and I ... we thought you had turned your back on ...'

'Yes, and there are things you can do behind my back, aren't there. Hah!' she laughed in fury. 'And Rob always tried to persuade me you were something he'd got rid of, finished with! I never quite believed him – and it seems I was right.'

'You've got to believe me, Luisa. I thought your marriage with Rob was over.'

'Over?' Luisa suddenly saw a way to hurt her now. 'It's not by any means over, if last night was anything to go by.'

She saw that her blow had struck home. Morag went even paler, and held the baby closer against her shoulder. She half-turned; perhaps she meant to run out.

At that moment the sudden clatter of feet came from the hall and the children ran in, full of inquiry. 'Who's come in that buggy – Mommy!' shouted Ellie-Rose, and threw herself at Morag, bursting into tears of relief at seeing her. She hugged Morag's skirt, hiding her face, weeping out her confusion and alarm. Here was Mommy, who would explain about this stranger from New York.

Nellie, loitering in the kitchen wondering what to do, felt that perhaps this was the moment to provide a diversion. She'd heard Morag's voice, heard Luisa's shout of anger – and gone cold with apprehension. Things could hardly have turned out worse. She knew how sharp and cruel Luisa's tongue could be.

She put the pot of fresh coffee on the tray, where the cup and saucer, the cream and sugar, were already arranged and went bustling into the living-room. 'Here's your coffee, Miss Luisa,' she said.

Luisa turned her head momentarily but then paid no heed. She was watching her own daughter clinging to another woman for comfort. 'Ellie-Rose, get away from her,' she commanded.

Ellie-Rose didn't even seem to hear.

'Do as Mama tells you, darling,' Morag said, stooping to detach the desperate little hands from her skirt.

Ellie-Rose let her hands be unhooked. 'Why didn't you come back before?' she accused, backing away, wiping tears off her cheeks.

'Because –'

Morag broke off. A ten-year-old boy had come in from the doorway where he'd been hesitating. He came to stand in front of her, staring up at her, full-face. His expression was a mixture of recognition and doubt. Her heart seemed to lurch. She hitched the baby into the crook of her arm and with her fingers signed: 'Cornelius?'

The boy gave a strange sound, like a sob. He held out his hands to her. 'Mo-ag?' he said.

It was a strange moment. All the children seemed to be attached to Morag by invisible ties. Luisa saw it as if it was part of some gigantic plot to show her she wasn't wanted. With a shriek of fury she picked up the nearest thing to hand and threw it at Morag. It happened to be the pot of scalding coffee that Nellie had just brought in.

18

'NOW, NOW, YOU MUSTN'T upset yourself like this,' soothed Dr Arnolf. 'Of course it's serious. But he's young and you took prompt action. Mrs Craigallan, my dear lady, you really must try to be calm.'

Morag paced up and down the hotel room, clasping and unclasping her hands. 'But his whole face is blistered, doctor. Even up into his scalp . . .'

'I know, I know. It's distressing. I can't understand how such a thing could happen, Mrs Craigallan. You're generally so careful about things like that. I remember when Ellie-Rose got the nail through her shoe –'

'His temperature is so high, doctor! I'm so afraid.'

'That's shock. I admit I wish it would come down, but he's a strong little boy. You've done well with him, Mrs Craigallan. A pity all your good work of the winter is cancelled out by this dreadful mishap.'

'I wish I'd never come back,' she said, wiping away tears from the rims of her eyes.

'It's understandable you should feel like that. But in a day or two you'll feel different.' He patted her hand and made for the door. 'Now, you're to put the ointment on your own scalds night and morning. Don't attempt to wash your neck and shoulder until the burning sensation is gone. I'll look in again on the baby after supper.'

'Thank you, doctor.'

'I suppose your husband can't come and stay in St Joseph because he's busy with the sowing? Pity, pity. Never mind, we'll look after you, Mrs Craigallan.'

She nodded her thanks and closed the door on him. The only sound in the room after that was her own broken breathing and the gasping whimper of Gregor, half-sleeping and half-unconscious. He lay in the middle of the bed, carefully wedged with pillows so that he couldn't move in his writhing efforts to escape the pain of his burns.

The contents of the coffee pot had gone over mother and child. Gregor, squirming round to stare in terror at Luisa when she shouted, had received most of it in his face. The rest had gone over Morag's neck and shoulder.

Nellie was galvanized into action. She was the only person in the room with her wits about her. She turned Morag about bodily and hurried her out of doors, where the buggy was still standing while the horse cropped a few blades of new grass and the driver waited to unload the luggage.

Nellie quickly got them all to St Joseph. Dr Arnolf happened, by good fortune, to be in his office. Tut-tutting in dismay, he treated the baby, spreading salve on the blisters and convering them with gauze. Privately he wondered how the child was going to be fed – his lips were blistered by drops of boiling coffee. But aloud he only uttered words of reassurance.

Morag wasn't misled. She knew her baby was very sick. She sat by the bed in the hotel room, listening to him wail with pain in his sleep, praying that he might not die from the thing that had been done.

When Rob walked in, she was scarcely aware of any reason for his coming. Her whole attention was on Gregor. She didn't prevent Rob from leaning over the bed to look at his son, however. 'Dear God,' he breathed in terror. After a long pause he asked: 'What does Dr Arnolf say?'

'Not much. I think he's waiting to see how things go.'

'I don't know what to say, Morag. I wouldn't have had this happen for the world.'

'You didn't do it.'

'I should have sent her packing! But she . . . she brought Cornelius. I couldn't just turn her around and send her back to New York.'

'No.'

'I'll get rid of her, Morag. She doesn't really want to stay out here, no matter how she may fool herself for the moment.'

'Yes.'

'Morag, don't be like this with me! Morag, my darling, don't! I'll sort it out. Everything will be the way it was.'

For a moment she made no reply. He almost thought she hadn't heard him. Then she said: 'It's over, Rob. We'd better face it.'

'No! No, why should you say that? Just because Luisa takes it into her head –'

'She's your wife, Rob. Do you really believe she'll ever leave us in peace, now that she knows?'

'She will. I'll make her! She's got to understand –'

'She sees well enough that we've been living a dream, a dream that had to end some day – and "some day" is now.'

'It wasn't a dream! We shared a good life, Morag – we have a marriage in every sense except –'

'Except that it isn't legal, that I've no rights and you can't prevent Luisa from turning me out.'

'I can and I will! Luisa's the one who has to go –'

'Even if you eventually persuade her, what's to happen meanwhile? Think what it's doing to Ellie-Rose, to Cornelius . . .' She went to the window, her back to him. 'I think it would be better to face it now. Better for all of us – for you, for the children, for me, for Gregor.'

Since Nellie told him of the scene that morning, Rob had been in despair. All the way to St Joe he'd been rehearsing what he'd say to Morag. He'd been hoping to get rid of Luisa before ever Morag returned, although even that solution would have presented problems, for Ellie-Rose would have been bound to prattle to Morag about the visitors. But Morag's unexpected return had brought about what he most wanted to avoid – a confrontation.

Nellie had warned him the baby was badly hurt. 'He goin' to be real bad, Mister Rob. I watched Dr Arnolf's face. He was scared.' But that hadn't prepared him for the little head wrapped about in gauze, like some Hallowe'en mask, with holes for the nose and mouth. In that moment he could have killed Luisa.

But now his main thought was to help and reassure Morag. 'You're upset,' he said to her. He came up behind her and was going to put an arm about her, but then the smell of the salve Dr Arnolf had put on her scalds made him hesitate. Her neck was red, and where she had loosened the collar of her gown, he could see the weals on her shoulder.

'Morag, this is not the time to be trying to talk out our problems. You're sick yourself, and all your mind is concentrating on Gregor. Once he begins to pick up –'

'If he does –'

'He will, Morag, he will! I know it! He –'

'He'll be scarred,' she whispered. 'She's put a mark on him.'

'She didn't mean it,' he said helplessly. 'You know what she's like, Morag. She didn't mean to hurt the baby.'

Gregor woke with a wail of misery. She pushed Rob aside and ran to the bedside. 'S-sh, baby,' she crooned, 'Mommy's here. Everything's all right.' She fetched an eye-dropper from a bowl by the bed, dripped a few spots of moisture on to his tongue. All the while she murmured softly to him. Comforted by the sound, his cries fell to a whimper.

She looked at Rob. 'I'm very tired,' she said. 'You'd better go now.'

'Morag, I swear to you I'll sort it all out –'

'Will you?' she said, in a sudden flash of anger. 'By sleeping with her again?'

'Sleeping with her?'

'You went to bed with her last night. She told me so.'

'That's not true, Morag! On my honour – it's not true!'

Words seemed to tremble on her lips, but she caught them back. She'd been about to say, 'Once before you told me she meant nothing to you.' But what was the use?

'Please go, Rob.'

'I'll be back tomorrow.'

'Very well.'

Next day the baby was actually sleeping, a real sleep, unspoiled by moans of pain. Dr Arnolf was in the room. He said cheerfully: 'Well, he's past the crisis. Temperature's nearly normal. Splendid, splendid . . .'

Rob shook hands with him in gratitude. 'Thanks, doc, that's the best news I've ever had.'

'Still a way to go, you understand. Perhaps by and by he ought to go to Chicago to see a specialist. I don't know how to handle skin damage in a baby that young. I'll look up somebody who can advise you better.'

He bustled away, clearly relieved at the way things were turning out. Rob sat down to talk with Morag, but she seemed unwilling to chat.

'Luisa asked me to say she's sorry,' he began.

'Very well.'

'Have you any message for her?'

'None.'

'Darling, don't hold back like this. We've got to talk.'

'We've said all we have to say.'

'Nonsense! You're just giving up on our happiness – I can't let you do that. We've got to fight, Morag –'

'You fight,' she said in an exhausted voice. 'I'm too tired.'

'Oh, please – *please*, Morag! I can't bear it if you're like this.'

Suddenly she put a hand on his arm. 'You have to bear it,' she said, quiet and cool. 'Because that's the way it is now, Rob.'

'Are you punishing me? Go ahead then – be angry, shout and scream at me – but don't just go away from me.'

She actually smiled. 'That would disturb Gregor,' she said. 'And he needs to be kept quiet.'

'Oh, Morag –!'

'You know,' she broke in, 'I've never really liked the prairie. I never felt it was a friendly place.'

'We'll go somewhere else, then. It doesn't matter. I'll sell up –'

'And we'll all go and begin again somewhere else, is that it?

You and I and our baby, and Luisa and Ellie-Rose and Cornelius.'

'I'll work something out.'

'I don't think you will, Rob.'

When he left her he was as depressed as if he'd heard bad news of the baby. On the two succeeding days he skirted personal problems, reporting to her instead about the seeding and about Ellie-Rose's school project for Easter. She listened quietly, rising from her chair now and again to check that Gregor was sleeping. Rob began to feel more hopeful. She'd had a bad shock; she'd just needed time to regain her equilibrium.

He learned his mistake the very next day. When he dismounted from his horse at the hotel the old man who lounged on the porch looked at him with surprise. 'Didn't expect you today, Mr Craigallan.'

'Why not?' Rob said, not much interested.

'Seeing your wife's gone East, I mean.'

'Gone?'

'Yeah . . . You didn't know?' The old man's eyes were avid at his dismay.

'When – when did she go?'

'Last night, on the midnight train. In Chicago by now, I reckon.'

Rob hurried to the depot to inquire but all he could learn was that Mrs Craigallan had boarded the train with her baby. Her ticket had been taken for New York, not Chicago. She'd left no forwarding address, no letter of explanation. Although in the succeeding weeks he asked Pinkerton's Detective Agency to find her, he could get no information.

The gossips of Brown Bridge were agog. If the woman now living at the Lafleche Farm was Mrs Craigallan, who was the one who'd lived with him these past five years and borne him a son last fall? Whose kids were those that lived there now? Was one of them a dummy?

Rob stared them down. He had nothing to say to them, nothing to explain. He was forced to share his home with a woman he disliked – for short of physically throwing Luisa out there seemed no way of getting rid of her. He never went to bed with her. All her wiles were wasted on him. Instead he visited a fancy woman in Breezedale, the next township beyond Brown Bridge. He made no secret of it.

'If you're doing it to insult me, you needn't bother,' Luisa flared at him, 'because I don't care!'

'I wish your unconcern would go so far as to take you back to New York,' he replied.

'Don't think you'll get rid of me so easily. You'd go running straight back to that little slut of yours.'

'You bet I would,' he said. He didn't tell her he'd lost Morag. He wouldn't give her that satisfaction.

For compensation he turned to the children. Ellie-Rose had always been his treasure, but now he began to get to know Cornelius. The boy proved to be worth knowing.

His inability to speak had made him concentrate on other things. Devoted tutors in Boston had opened the world of books to him; far younger than most boys, he'd been introduced to the study of botany, biology and mathematics. Isolated for the time being at Lafleche, he began to devour the contents of Rob's bookshelves. 'He's a bookworm,' Ellie-Rose complained to her Papa, but good naturedly – for she'd begun to get fond of Cornelius.

He had come back out of the mists of memory as a boy she used to know in some other place, where she'd ordered him about. Now he couldn't be ordered about; he was a *person*, sometimes rather formidable: a real elder brother in almost every sense, except that he couldn't laugh and joke with her.

But that has its advantages. Some of her girl friends had brothers who teased them unmercifully. Cornelius never teased. He was almost always perfectly serious, perfectly straight-forward. Because it took him some pains to communicate, he didn't waste his time on foolishness.

Ellie-Rose learned again to speak with her fingers, to touch Cornelius on the arm and speak directly to him. He was good at lip-reading, and caught on to almost everything at once. His great problem was in making an easy reply. His voice was dull and metallic, without cadence. Some words he couldn't form at all. He knew he sounded odd, although he had no way of comparing voices. He was shy of strangers.

Ellie-Rose talked about her brother to her teachers. There were two at Brown Bridge, a woman who took the juniors and a man, Biddulph Dainton, who took the seniors. Bid Dainton took the trouble to ride out to Lafleche to see this unusual brother. 'He's exceptionally intelligent, Mr Craigallan,' he remarked to Rob, having asked him to stop by when he was collecting Ellie-Rose. 'You ought to continue his education.'

'It means sending him away,' Rob said. 'I don't know whether to send him back to Boston –'

'You'll blame yourself if you don't. He's – how old?'

'Nearly eleven.'

'That's old enough to go to school as a boarder. He would benefit by it.'

'He used to board with a relation. But boarding school might be better now.'

'Talk to him about it. He's got ideas of his own. I get the impression he's got things he wants to do.'

It hadn't occurred to Rob to ask his son's opinion. He went along with the general view that parents made the decisions and children did as they were told. But Cornelius wasn't like an ordinary child. 'Mr Dainton thinks you'd do well if you went away to boarding school,' he began with his son. 'What do you say to that?'

'If I could study here,' Cornelius said in his slow, careful way, 'I would rather stay. But Mister Dainton says . . . he can't do much for me. I think it would be best to send me to Boston.'

'To Aunt Remegen?'

Cornelius shook his head and smiled his quiet smile. 'You know . . . in all the time I lived with her . . . she never learned to talk to me?'

Ellie-Rose cried a little when Cornelius left. 'I like him,' she said. 'It won't be so much fun now he's gone.'

'But he'll be back for vacation,' Rob reassured her. 'He seems quite keen on that. I asked if he'd like to stop over with Aunt

Remegen but he said no, he'd rather make the trip out here.'

Cornelius wrote to Ellie-Rose and his father regularly. His letters were strange – fluent and quick, quite unlike the boy Rob knew. With a strange pang Rob realised that in that slow shell there was a lively, bright spirit, doomed never to be able to make itself really known.

What money could do for him, was done. Rob could afford to see to that. Although the farm wasn't doing well, there were other sources of income. Rob invested in grain storage, in flour mills. He could afford to hang on while other farmers went to the wall in the face of the continually falling prices, and the attacks of disease that cut down the yield and caused harvested grain to go bad.

He no longer troubled to conceal his spreading business activities from his neighbours. He no longer cared whether they agreed with his actions or not. He was no longer exactly of their kind; in a way they had alienated him when Morag went away and they gossiped about Luisa. He felt no kinship with them. All that kept him on the Great Plains was the wheat – the great rippling sea of gold that was the basis of wealth and power now he knew how to handle it.

'Don't you ever want to do anything else?' Luisa whined. 'At van Huten's we used to have parties, dances . . .'

'Have a party if you want,' he replied. 'See who'll come if you send out invitations!'

'But why do they take it out on me?' she cried. 'I'm your *wife*! Morag was the kept woman!'

'Yeah.' He surveyed her. She was wearing one of her best dresses, a concoction of voile and lace that might have looked very well in New York. 'The funny thing is, to everybody else it looks the other way round.'

Luisa had been determined to stick it out at Lafleche. She'd realised that Rob was a man of growing wealth, a man to be reckoned with. But the winters were unbearable with their hard frosts and snow flurries and the need to wear four layers of clothes. And the summers were little better, full of dust and flying needlegrass that brought your skin out in a rash. And the harvest . . . Dear God, the harvest, when men thought of nothing but the grain, when life seemed whittled down to anxiety over getting the wheat cut and getting a good price for it.

If there had been a town nearer than St Joseph, or if there had been more 'culture' there, she might have grown content with the lot she had chosen. Even after she had accepted the fact that Rob was never going to be a real husband to her, she might have found some consolation in a really glittering social round. But one day she looked in the mirror and realised she was past thirty. If she stayed on at Brown Bridge, she would be an old woman in no time at all.

Her brother Julius opened an escape route to her. He wrote to say that Mama wasn't well, that he couldn't look after her and was considering sending her to Lafleche Farm to recuperate. Luisa replied by telegraph: 'I'm coming to nurse Mama.'

It was a good excuse. She was an angel of mercy. Nothing less would have taken her from her post of duty by her husband's side. 'I'll take Ellie-Rose with me,' she suggested. 'She's growing up, Rob. It's time she saw a bit of civilisation.'

Rob lowered his newspaper to gaze at her. 'Luisa, don't start that again. Ellie-Rose stays here until she goes to college. Understood?'

'I'm only thinking of her good –'

'No you're not. You're thinking of holding some kind of hostage. Don't bother. You can have what money you need to set up house in New York. There's no need to be a wheeler-dealer about it.'

She hurried to him and dropped a kiss on the top of his thick russet hair. He winced away from her. She said blithely, 'You're not so bad after all, Robert Craigallan.'

It was a relief to have her out of the house. Nellie took over the role of housekeeper, and for companionship he had Ellie-Rose. He tried not to think of the day when she'd have to go away to college.

When Cornelius came to the farm that year, he stood with his father running specimens of grain through his fingers. He watched Rob's lips earnestly as he explained why there was this strange little distortion in some of the kernels.

'This is the second year. We had the same thing last year, only

[296]

to a lesser degree. It's some sort of bunt. It's not so bad here on Lafleche, but some of the farms have lost nearly fifty per cent of the crop. The plants appear with yellow blades and the seed-head has black mush instead of kernels.'

'Too little nitrogen in the soil?' Cornelius inquired haltingly.

'Too little what? Oh, nitrogen . . . That contributes, it seems. Everybody else has got worse results than I have, because they don't rotate crops and the soil is too "mean".'

'What does the Department of Ag-ri-cul-ture say?' Cornelius went on, enunciating with painful clarity.

'Oh, the Department of Agriculture – Yes. Well, they haven't got to the bottom of it yet. I gather they're trying to assemble specimens from all across the wheat belt. Meanwhile we still don't know what to do for the best.'

His son nodded. He turned a few seeds of wheat round and round on the palm of his hand. He seemed deep in thought.

During that vacation he took to riding about the neighbour-hood on a pony lent to him by Rob. Each time he came back he would show his father a little envelope of either seed or a blackened seed-head, with the district and the owner of the farm carefully noted.

'What's it for?' Rob asked.

'I . . . thought I'd do some . . . in-vest-ig-ation when I get back to college. In the lab. We have a series of good mi-cro-scopes there.'

Rob left him to it. The boy was interested – that was good. A great pity there seemed no way of putting him in charge of a farm one day. His difficulty with speech made it impossible.

That winter Rob spent several weeks in Chicago. He and Sam Yarwood had two or three schemes in operation. Rob could see a big expansion in farm machinery. 'It's going to be steam from here on in,' he declared.

'I s'pose you know what you're talking about. But I can't see how you can get a steam engine out on farmland.'

'Of course you can, Sam. A traction engine. Garr, Scott and Company have got a steam threshing machine in production already. I'll allow that it costs a fortune and hardly anybody wants it at the moment, but don't you see – it can be shipped by

[297]

rail to the nearest depot and then it can trundle along the roads to the harvest fields –'

'Scaring every horse within miles on the way,' Sam put in.

'That's a thing we'll have to live with. Sam, I tell you – those big fields out there are crying out for something that doesn't get tired, that can work at night if need be –'

'At night? Are you out of your skull?'

'If the weather threatens to break, it would be such an asset to work through the night and get the crop in! I tell you, the wheat belt is spreading all across the country. Bonanza farms on a scale we haven't thought of yet are going to want machines. So I'm going to put some money into the making of steam equipment.'

Sam shook his head but helped him to find an investment. There was a young inventor in Cincinatti looking for a patron; Rob guaranteed his research for two years for a share of the eventual profits.

At Christmas Cornelius came to Lafleche Farm for the holiday. He had a leather folder with him. On Christmas Day he took Papa into his study and invited him to sit down. 'This is your Christ-mas pre-sent from me,' he said. He held out the leather folder.

Laughing, Rob took it. When he opened it he saw a sheaf of papers, with sketches of seeds and embryos and analytical notes. He glanced up at Cornelius. 'I'm to read this?'

'Please. It won't take long. I come back in one hour.' The boy went out, closing the door carefully behind him. Early in life Cornelius had learned to close doors quietly because, unable to judge noise, he'd often been rebuked for banging them.

Rob settled down to turn over the papers. At first he couldn't make head nor tail of the notes, but slowly he began to catch on. When he came to the conclusions at the end, he was almost prepared for them.

Cornelius came back as Rob was looking over the last page or two again. 'What do you think?' he asked.

'It's a bit suppositious,' Rob said, reading.

'What?' Cornelius touched him on the arm, to remind him to look up when he spoke.

'It's got a lot of "Let us suppose" and "If this is so" –'

'It's a piece of pri-vate re-search,' Cornelius said, and though it was impossible for his flat voice to show emotion, Rob sensed his disappointment.

'What you're saying is that the wheat is suffering from a fungus disease that attacks the roots during early formation –'

Cornelius nodded vehemently.

'And that it might be warded off by dressing the seed wheat with copper sulphate?'

'And use of potash on the soil – to build up resistance – but that is not prac-ti-cal on large acre-age, Papa.'

'You're damn right it isn't. At least not with present equipment. It would have to be done by hand. I can't believe copper sulphate is the answer . . .'

'I may be wrong in choice of chem-i-cal. *Something* ought to react against the dis-ease.'

'Your theory is that enough of the chemical would stay on the kernel to clothe the shoot as it comes out, and so keep the disease off until the shoot is strong enough to get nourishment?'

'That is my the-ory. Papa, try it. It would not cost much to try. It could not harm.'

'I'll think on it, son.'

Cornelius put his head on one side. 'I think you will try it,' he said with a smile.

When the ploughs came off Rob's land after their first opening of the ground, winter was on its way. The farm hands always had make-do chores to keep them occupied. There was harness to mend, rope to make, bins and shelves in the granaries to clean out and repair, sacks to sew. The men hated sack-sewing, they'd do almost anything to avoid it.

So this year Rob provided them with an alternative. He bought timber in St Joe and had it shipped to Lafleche. Then he had Brick supervise the construction of a big wooden vat.

Brick, now upper foreman of the spread, privately thought the boss had at last taken leave of his senses. This vat was too big for any purpose that Brick could envisage; it wasn't even as if it was being made for the milk-shed, to hold the milk from the housecows when they came on flow. It was being made outside – next to the pump.

The men joked and swore as they wrestled with the making of the vat. They weren't trained barrel makers; old Winstall was the best with a saw and a hammer, so Brick took advice from him most of the time. By the end of January, allowing some time for bad weather holding up the job, they'd made the vat.

Worse was yet to come. From the boss's son there came a metal box, by special delivery. In the box was a big bottle, of the kind the hands were more used to seeing full of cider. This was labelled: 'Solution, $CuCo_2CuOH$'.

Mr Craigallan ordered the vat to be pumped half full of water. To this he added a measure of this new stuff called (by the men) Cuckoo Brew.

He then instructed Brick to bring the sacks of seed wheat. The seed was tipped out into the vat. The men stood round, staring in disbelief and groaning at the thought that there wasn't going to be anything to put in the drill-boxes this year, unless he brought in new seed. Yet it was too late to be buying now, and besides, there was a seed famine in Kansas this season because of the wheat-bunt outbreak.

The seed was left in the vat for twenty-four hours. Ellie-Rose, coming back from school to find the farm smelling of this strange mixture, laughed and pommelled her father on the shoulder. 'What are you doing, Papa? Making porridge?'

'You can laugh! This is your brother's idea. The boy's a fool – I should never have listened to him.'

Ellie-Rose pursed her lips. 'If Cornelius suggested it, there's something in it.'

Next day the grain was ladled out of the vat with a sieve nailed to a long pole. This was the most difficult part of the whole exercise; the draining method was totally make-shift, the sieve kept falling off the end of the pole and having to be re-nailed; the men grew weary at the strain on their arms. But by and by the seed wheat was all out of the vat, laid out on the floor of the biggest barn to dry.

Winter weather is not a good time to be trying to dry out wet

seed. A few days of warm spring sunshine would have helped –
but by the time the warm spring sun was shining, Rob wanted
that seed in the soil. He had his men shovelling and turning,
shovelling and turning, in a continual ritual that went on even by
lamplight.

It took a week, before the seed was dry again and would run
through the fingers – and therefore through the holes in the drill
boxes.

The ground was workable, the frosts had given up their grip.
Rob sent the drill-teams out. When the shoots came through in
April, he watched with an eagerness he tried to mask behind
imperturbability. He saw with delight that there were few of
those yellow tips that denoted bunt. He rode round the fields,
expecting each day that some sign would show, some hint that the
disease was going to come back. But the shoots stayed green and
straight.

By the beginning of May it couldn't be denied that Rob
Craigallan's wheat had not been attacked by wheat-bunt. His
neighbours came to stroll along the road near his house, between
the verges where the prairie phlox was blooming, to stare at his
fields. Copper sulphate . . . Maybe they should try it; but from
what the hands said, it sounded awful hard work.

'You know,' Rob said to Ellie-Rose, 'it might actually be that
your brother is a very smart fellow.'

'I always told you he was, Papa.' Ellie-Rose had always
believed in him. And so, years ago, had Morag. It was thanks to
Morag that Cornelius had got the education which taught him to
use his brains.

Where was she? Why couldn't she be here to see what
Cornelius had done?

19

FOR THE FIRST TIME in four years, Rob didn't lose actual money on the wheat crop he grew. The following year he did even better, thanks to an idea of his son's about dressing the seed – instead of steeping it in vats he had it spread out in heaps in the barn and sprinkled with copper carbonate, then turned and re-turned until it was all touched by the chemical. The result was the same – a good, bunt-free crop.

But the third year, something new came into the district, a kind of stem rust. Cornelius, by this time seriously studying plant virology, shook his head. 'It is bound to hap-pen. A one-crop area with almost no crop ro-ta-tion, no feed-ing of the land . . .'

'Dammit, I feed my land! I rotate my crops!'

'Yes, Papa, but your wheat is in-fected from other farms. You suf-fer less da-mage because your plants are health-i-er, but it is in-ev . . . in-ev . . .'

'Inevitable?'

'Yes.'

'I wish I knew what the devil to do.'

'Have you ever thought of going over to win-ter wheat?'

Rob shrugged impatiently. 'The winter here isn't suitable for wheat to survive –'

'Even if you used a "stronger" wheat?'

[302]

'I've tried it,' Rob confessed. 'I've grown experimental plants of fall-sown wheat. It doesn't do.'

'Have you heard of these new wheats from Russ-ia?'

'I hear Carleton of the Department of Agriculture is interested in them.'

'Papa, in the steppes of Russ-ia, the cli-mate is very like ours. They can grow win-ter wheat.'

'But I hear their harvests are poor –'

'That is be-cause their farms are worked by ig-no-rant peasants. A man like you, with in-tell-i-gence . . . if you could try out an over-winter-ing wheat . . .?'

Rob wrote to the many friends he now had in the realm of seed-breeding but they were all like him – dubious about the possible results with foreign seed, and short on information.

George Washington Carver, the black student he'd met years ago, was now settled at Tushagee, Alabama. They corresponded, but George had little interest in wheat. Soil exhaustion was his subject: 'The soil in your area *will* become impoverished,' he opined, 'but not yet – and when it happens I recommend you leave wheat and turn to legumes.'

C. G. Pringle, a pioneer seed-breeder, was more helpful, but dubious about the acceptance of other strains by the smaller-scale farmers. 'In any case,' Pringle wrote to him, 'in my estimation the increased gluten content of what we might call a "hard" wheat would offer tremendous problems to the flour mills. The equipment is not suited to dealing with kernels of that kind . . .'

Rob was not too perturbed about the flour mills. He owned shares in a milling group. He could arrange for one of the mills to alter its equipment to accept a high-gluten kernel. But in the hit-or-miss state of seed breeding in the United States, the risk wasn't worth taking. It would cost a lot of money to sow an area with winter wheat, grow it and harvest it, send it for milling into flour – and then find all was in vain because the wheat wouldn't adapt.

Yet there were these insistent rumours of a 'hard' wheat – *Triticum durum*. The Department of Agriculture was cautious, however. If they were to encourage farmers to try a new seed and it was a flop, the head of the Secretary for Agriculture would be demanded on a platter.

All the same, Rob couldn't get it out of his head that if he could get hold of some of this experimental seed and try some sample plantings, he would get in ahead of everyone else in the race to find wheats that would beat the diseases plaguing the Great Plains. Moreover, with advance notice of what was about to happen, he could make a killing in wheat futures.

Ellie-Rose was her father's confidante in all these musings. She was at finishing school in Bloomington, but came rushing back to him at every opportunity, flatteringly preferring him to the beaux who hung around her in town. She found them all so shallow compared with Papa. It was more interesting to sit talking with Papa and Cornelius about the crops, or to ride with Papa around his domain.

On a duty visit to her mother on Long Island, she met a young man at an Independence Day party. 'May I introduce myself?' he inquired, nervously straightening his cravat. 'I'm an acquaintance of your brother's – we met at agricultural college . . . Pete Sumikiss.'

'How do you do?' She held out a white-gloved hand, over which he bowed in politeness. When he raised his head, his eyes met hers – and he was captivated for ever.

Ellie-Rose was a pretty girl. Not a beauty, exactly, but with a sparkle and a force of character about her that made her very attractive. She had dark-blonde hair, blue-grey eyes, a mobile mouth, and a figure on which the current ridiculous fashion of the bustle looked delicious. Her tiny waist was accentuated by the folds and draperies of the skirt and by the falls of lace and ribbon on the bosom. For evening, it was now permissible to wear a low neckline; Ellie-Rose's creamy neck and throat sailed out of the dark blue lace of her evening gown like ivory, giving just a hint of the white skin of her bosom.

Pete Sumikiss had never seen anyone so exquisite. It had taken him all evening to pluck up courage to speak to her. And because he was a friend of Cornelius, whom she respected, she was kinder to him than to many a would-be admirer. She agreed that he might call again next day. She went out sailing with him on the following Saturday, with a party of friends. Pete was in seventh heaven. To be allowed to join the circle in which this angel moved . . . ! She was so much above him, so beautiful and clever, her family was clearly of some importance and had money . . . Starry-eyed, Pete hung about her.

She suddenly became interested in him when he began to talk about his job. It was all he had to talk about – his life had been uneventful, his family was obscure, of Finnish extraction. He thought it typical of Ellie-Rose's intelligence that she was interested in the Department of Agriculture's research station at Springfield, Illinois.

'Why, Pete – that's not far from my school! I'm at the Ladies' Academy in Bloomington!'

He felt that was an invitation to call on her there. He spent as much time as he could with her during his vacation on Long Island and then, when he had to return to Springfield, he wrote to her, having, of course, first asked her permission to do so.

Pete was no poet. He couldn't have written a love letter if he'd wanted to. But he wouldn't have dared write to Ellie-Rose in those terms. Not yet, at least. He wrote to her about his work.

To his delight, she invited him to call on her when she returned to school in Springfield in the fall. The other girls ribbed her about this shy, awkward beau of hers – he was tall and fair and had a skin that got sunburnt too easily. Ellie-Rose's friends couldn't understand what she found so fascinating.

They would have been surprised if she had told them. Pete was involved in experiments with samples of steppes wheat sent back by his boss, Mark A. Carleton, who was now on an extended trip to Russia.

Ellie-Rose wrote to her brother: 'Your friend Pete Sumikiss tells me he's busy on Actual Growth Trials. Is he the kind of researcher to be given important work or is he a dogsbody?'

Cornelius was intrigued. He saw Pete from time to time and had listened to – or at least watched – the outpourings about Ellie-Rose's intelligence and kindness and sympathy. It seemed a little odd to him. He'd have thought Pete too dull for Ellie-Rose. But he replied to her letter with an assurance that, at least where plant research was concerned, Pete was to be reckoned with.

For weeks Ellie-Rose tried to get an invitation to look at Pete's work. But it was too confidential. He was desolate at having to refuse her anything, but no one was allowed to see the trials.

'Well, at least tell me how they're going!'

'I can't even do that, Ellie-Rose. You know . . . well, I don't have to tell you, your father being a wheat-grower and all – a change in the method of growing wheat could be almost revolutionary. Naturally the government is reluctant to release its findings until in the first place it's sure what the results are, and in the second, there's enough of the new seed to meet the demand.'

'So there is going to be a demand?' she asked quickly.

'Oh, I think so. I think there's a belt of wheatlands where the new seed is going to make all the difference.'

'When will you have enough seed to sell to the farmers?'

'About two years, I think,' he said, too fond and foolish to be wary of her.

She asked to see the seed. He shook his head: no, he wasn't allowed to bring it out of the lab. 'What, not even a few grains?' No, not even a few grains. He brought out a leather purse from which he took a key. 'That's the key of the safe where the new samples are kept,' he said, proud to demonstrate the importance of his position. 'Do you realise, Ellie-Rose, that if our research is justified, those samples are worth far more than their weight in gold?'

She put on an expression of admiring wonder. The truth was, she understood the value of the seed wheat far better than he did. Her father's conversation had shown her what a fortune could be made with it.

She'd said nothing to her father about Pete's work, so far. When she went home for Thanksgiving, she had no difficulty bringing the talk round to the problem of finding plants that would withstand the prairie climate and the diseases that now seemed almost endemic among the wheat grown at present.

'I'll tell you what, girlie,' neighbour Duhamel said. 'I'm thinking of selling up and getting out. Ain't had nothing but one disaster after another for the past four years – and yet the price don't go up through scarcity because those damned bonanzy farms further west keep sending grain to market.'

'Now, George, don't talk nonsense,' his wife said, emboldened by several glasses of Mr Craigallan's wine, 'where would we go? You've got to hang on.' She looked hopefully at Rob. 'You found a way to prevent wheat-bunt that time, Mr Craigallan. You'll find a way to prevent rust.'

'No,' Rob sighed. 'What's needed now is a plant that's *resistant*. No amount of care in cultivation is going to prevent blight coming while we use the same seed. I've tried, God knows, and so have others. But none of us seem to hit on just the right hybrid.'

The other farmers and farm-hands at the party didn't understand about hybridization or the laws of Mendel. All they knew was that for once Mr Craigallan seemed at a loss. If a man like that was beaten, what hope was there for the rest of them?

Late that night, when the guests had gone and Ellie-Rose was sharing a last nightcap with her father, she said: 'Would it really make such a difference to have better seed?'

'You know it would,' he said, surprised. 'You saw last year's crop – on *my* fields I had a fifty-two per cent loss. And I came out ahead of the others. If it happens again this year, I'll make a net loss. A *net* loss, chicken! It would be good sense to sell the place, if anybody'd buy it. But who wants a Kansas wheat farm that's stricken with wheat-rust?'

It seemed to her so unjust. There was the new seed, sitting in sample bags in the safe in Pete's laboratory. And here was her father, having to admit defeat on the acres of Lafleche Farm. What sense did it make?

She teased Pete about the seed but he refused to take her seriously. 'It's only silly old sacks of grain,' he told her. No way was he going to take her into the Research Station. She began to be angry with him. He was so dense, so self-satisfied!

She began to have an obsession about it. All she had to do was get hold of his keys. He kept them in a leather purse in the inside pocket of his jacket. She could feel them when, from time to time, he hugged her and stole a kiss.

She was due to go home to Lafleche for Christmas. Pete begged to be allowed to take her to a theatre in Springfield before she continued her journey west by the night train. He himself had to go east to spend Christmas with his parents. It was a last chance to see each other for two weeks, for the Ladies' Academy didn't reassemble until mid-January.

'I'd love that, Pete,' she said.

She arrived in Springfield from Bloomington in the early afternoon. He met her and brought her with her valise to his lodgings. His landlady had no objections to a young lady visitor so long as the proprieties were observed, and, of course, this young lady was known to her as Miss Craigallan, daughter of a man of substance in Kansas and student at the Bloomington Ladies' Academy.

Pete had to go back to the laboratory to complete some notes, for the place would be closing down almost completely for three days over Christmas. Ellie-Rose spent the afternoon shopping in Springfield's main street. She knew the town quite well; Papa had brought her here several times for the State Fair in August. There were even Indians to be seen, moving about in their soft shoes, wrapped in blankets against the December cold, silent and withdrawn. Papa had made a friend of one of the Indian families at the State Fair a couple of years ago. She remembered a long discussion about Indian methods of raising corn and wheat, all for the benefit of Mr Pringle who wanted a report on such matters to help him with his seed-raising.

Pete took her to see Kester Wallack in a play of T. W. Robertson, an English author whose ironic style quite eluded him. Ellie-Rose seemed to enjoy it, although she was restless and inattentive. After the play he took her out to supper, for the night train didn't come in for another two hours. Pete felt fairly daring, eating a meal in a public restaurant so late at night. To give himself courage, he drank rather more than he was accustomed to. Perhaps that was why he let the time pass unnoticed.

When they got to his lodgings to collect Ellie-Rose's valise, it was very late. 'Ssh,' he implored as they went up to his rooms, 'Don't wake Mrs Vernon – she'd be mad!'

'All right, let's tiptoe . . .' She picked up the front of her stiff silk skirt and tiptoed up the stairs, showing to his dazzled gaze a pair of dainty black high-heeled shoes and silk clad ankles.

'Oh, Ellie-Rose,' he gasped as they closed the door of his room behind them. 'Oh, you really are so wonderful!' Emboldened by the events of the evening and the wine he'd drunk, he engulfed her in his arms.

He really expected her to rebuff him. It would have been only what he deserved, because he was behaving caddishly. But, to his incredulous delight, Ellie-Rose melted into his arms and returned the kiss.

They sank down on the settee with their arms about each other. Her pretty little hooded fur cape fell away from her hair. He kissed the thick, rich tresses, then her neck and her eyes. She lay back, drawing him with her. They hadn't lit the lamp; the room was lit only by the rays of a street lamp outside.

Pete was not so drunk that he didn't know what was happening, but he seemed unable to prevent it. He wanted to be honourable and upright and decent. But he also wanted Ellie-Rose – more than anything else in the whole wide world. And Ellie-Rose seemed to want him. That was the glory of it.

On a tide of desire he made love to her, inexpertly but with passion. For a moment he was brought to his senses when he realised she was a virgin – of course she was a virgin – and he was . . . he was being allowed to take her. But her arms wouldn't let him go and after a moment of ecstatic anguish she was his – *his*.

Afterwards he held her and caressed her, mumbling his thanks, his apologies, his excuses. 'It's all right, it's all right,' she whispered. 'Don't talk like that, Pete – it's all right.'

He kissed her in gratitude, and she helped him to undress her, and they went to bed together. He could scarcely believe that this gift was being given to him. By and by he made love to her again, and then he fell asleep – drugged with happiness and exhaustion.

Ellie-Rose lay awake at his side in his narrow bed, arms behind her head. So this was what it was like, the great dividing line that ruled off the married women from the virgins, the bad girls from the good. She had crossed it, but little difference it seemed to have made to her. There had been no joy, no sweep of passion. She had endured it all, pretending to find pleasure in it because once she had let it begin to happen it seemed cowardly to turn back.

Soon she could tell by Pete's deep breathing that he was sound asleep. She stole out of bed and found his jacket. From it she took the purse with the keys. With that in her hand, she fell asleep on the sofa.

The first sounds of activity in the street roused her. She dressed quickly and went out to find a locksmith. While she waited, he made copies of the keys. She was back in the room where Pete still lay asleep within half an hour. She put his leather purse back in his pocket. Then she woke him.

He opened his eyes, saw her, blushed to the roots of his hair.

'Pete,' she murmured, 'I've got to go now. Your landlady will see me if I stay any longer. And there's a train for St Joseph in about fifteen minutes. Help me get to the depot.'

'Oh, Ellie-Rose!' he blurted. 'About last night – I can't tell you – We'll get married as soon as –'

'S-sh. Put some clothes on and carry my valise to the depot.'

He was too embarrassed to dress in front of her. She went out to the landing, where he joined her a few moments later. He looked rumpled and at a loss.

They walked briskly to the station. 'Thank you,' she said. 'You'd best get back now. Your landlady will be bringing up your breakfast and you won't be there.'

'Oh, heavens, yes – Mrs Vernon –!'

'Goodbye, Pete.'

'Goodbye, Ellie-Rose. I'll write to you – come and see your father –'

'No, no, don't let's rush into anything. I'll see you after Christmas.'

He kissed her in helpless confusion and hurried away. She went into the waiting-room and sat there until the train to St

Joseph came in. She let it go out again. Then she went in search of Thomas Fishing-Bird, the Indian she'd met with Papa.

Thomas Fishing-Bird was an old man with several sons. He made a living carving model canoes for visitors to the state capital. He was honoured at the visit of the daughter of Mr Craigallan, and pleased when she said she could put him in the way of earning a little money.

'A friend of mine has given me his keys,' she said. 'He has gone away for Christmas, but has left some packages he needs in his room at the Research Station. Can you send one of your sons to fetch them so that I can send them on to him?'

'That would be very simple,' he said. He took the keys from her, and saw that she had put labels on them, to correspond with the metal tags on the originals. 'It must be a son that can read,' he said. 'I will send Willie.'

Willie listened unspeaking to her instructions. 'You'll find some sacks in a big cupboard or safe in a room. On the door of the room will be a notice: Actual Trial Laboratory. This is the key for that room.' He nodded. 'The sacks will have labels – metal tags, I think.' She glanced at him and he nodded again. 'Please bring only one sack. The tag will have these words, or something like them: *Triticum durum*, and the date. You must bring the sack with the most recent date.'

Willie put the key in his pocket. He said, 'Write down the words.'

She found a blank page in her engagement book and wrote out, in her clear firm hand: '*Triticum durum*.'

Christmas at Lafleche was quiet that year. Cornelius had gone to spend it with a former tutor, Ira Jones. The weather was bad. Few visitors called at the farm. Nellie had put up a tree in the living-room as usual, and it was beneath this that Ellie-Rose laid her gift for her father. It was an envelope with a sheet of paper inside. She watched with trembling eagerness as he opened it.

'Look in the barn,' he read. He glanced at her. 'What does that mean?'

'Come and see.'

She led him out into the cold, blustery wind of Christmas

morning. They fought their way across to the nearest barn. Rob always made sure that everything in his barns was neatly put away or stacked, so the little sack of grain sitting by itself in the middle of the floor was at once noticeable. He went to it, shaking his head in perplexity.

With his pen-knife he cut the strong twine that fastened the neck. And he did so, he saw the metal tag with the laboratory's code stamped into it, and the words: *Triticum durum*. With a little gasp of interest he pulled the sack open. He thrust a hand in and ran the fingers through the grains. He knew at once what it was.

'Where the devil did you get this?' His voice was shaking with excitement.

A strange, terrible regret seized at the heart of Ellie-Rose at that question. 'Don't ask, Father,' she said, 'don't ask.'

20

ALTHOUGH IT WAS VERY late in the year, the ground was workable; there had been frosts in early December but over Christmas this mild, blustery spell had supervened.

Rob was out the day after Christmas, by himself, sowing the Durum seed as an experimental crop on a plat of land a long way off from the house. From the house, and from the road, now known as Lafleche Road, it was impossible to see the wheat growing.

But grow it did. Strongly, triumphantly. The cold spell in January and February seemed to make no difference. It began to show in March, green and sturdy. It seemed to check in April during a dry spell, but took off again in May. Through June it reached maturity and turned colour. By the end of the first week of July it was ready for harvesting.

Rob harvested it himself, in the old-fashioned way, back-breakingly, with a sickle. He didn't want any of the precious seed damaged by the header blades. He knew he didn't get as full a return on the sowing as he would have, had the seed gone in in September. The plants didn't get a proper chance to tiller. They needed time in the cold soil to feel their way out into root systems. But he knew that with this harvest to use as seed wheat, his next year's harvest would be triply rewarding.

He made arrangements through the summer to have a flour

mill ready to take these strange, flinty kernels when he sent them to market. The master miller at Prime Power Mills in Mineapolis disparaged the sample he sent; 'It's like trying to grind bedrock!'

'You'll find a way to handle it,' Rob urged. 'I tell you, this is the wheat we're going to grow! In ten years' time it'll be all over the wheat belt.'

'I don't see it. You'll practically have to bribe the millers to take it. It's got no "give".'

'Russell, by my reckoning this seed is going to give twenty bushels to the acre –'

'Nah!' sneered the miller. 'You're kidding yourself.'

'I tell you, it's going to yield far higher than any of the "soft" wheats we're growing at the moment –'

'Yeah, well, so what? The soft wheat is what the millers like. They'd rather pay more for fewer bushels of soft wheat. I don't see how it's worth your trouble to grow this hard wheat.'

'You'll see,' Rob said. 'You'll see. In the meantime, I want to put one of our milling engineers on this problem. I want my next year's harvest to go through the processing and come out as bread flour –'

Russell still felt it wasn't worth the bother. But Mr Craigallan was the boss; he owned fifty-one per cent of the shares of Prime Power Mills. If he wanted the engineers to find ways of milling this peculiar wheat, the engineers had better get busy.

Rob knew that the new seed wheat would begin to find admirers among the wheat belt farmers. A seed that would stand up to the climate, was at present disease-resistant, and yielded high, was bound to find takers. In the next few years, the wheat yield in the Great Plains was going to go up. The futures market would be deeply affected. So Rob had a conference with Sam Yarwood.

Rob had learnt a valuable lesson since first he came to Lafleche Farm. It was important to own the land on which you raised your crop: his bitter experience with van Huten's had taught him that. But to own the land wasn't enough. You could own a good farm and still go bankrupt. It was the wheat that was important. That brought in the money. On the stock market, 'grain paper' had a greater credit value than land and had the same value in New York, Liverpool or Buenos Aires. If a farmer owned storage facilities for wheat, and the mills where it was turned into flour, he could keep wheat over from one year to the next and sell it when the price suited him. It was a financial weapon.

Rob began to be consulted by state officials in the wheat belt about farming policies. He was invited here and there to speak at dinners, to address conferences. He was able to give time to these activities because, once he'd established the routine of his new winter wheat, there were almost no problems. He invested in the newest machinery. He left Brick and Joe in charge of looking after the farm.

He was so busy that he had almost no time for Ellie-Rose. She was away at school at first, and then when she was nineteen she divided her time between Lafleche Farm and Cornelius's apartment in Boston. She seemed restless and unsettled.

For a time one of her young men, Peter Sumikiss, kept turning up at Lafleche. Rob was quite perturbed. 'Not thinking of marrying that poor dope, are you?' he asked.

'No, I'm not. What makes you ask?'

'He seems to treat me as a sort of father-in-law. I don't like it!'

'It's just that he's . . . trying to show his respect for you, Papa. He admires you.'

'I thought it was you he admired?' Rob laughed. And then, with a shrug, 'Well, if you don't want him, get him to stop hanging around, I can't be doing with him!'

Pete couldn't understand why Ellie-Rose wouldn't marry him. It seemed to him that they were duty bound to get married, after what they had done. He referred to it in awed tones, and never seemed to see that it annoyed Ellie-Rose. Of course he didn't blame her at all for never allowing a recurrence of that extraordinary event. He could never really understand how it had happened in the first place.

It didn't dawn on him to connect her with the strange theft at the lab. The whole thing was most odd. He'd come back after the Christmas break to find a sack of Durum seed missing. There was no sign of a forced entry. Enquiries brought nothing to light. In the end he privately came to the conclusion that one of the cleaners or janitors had taken the grain to feed to poultry at home. It was no use pursuing the matter any further. Luckily, there was enough seed Durum for investigation otherwise.

When at last Durum wheat began to make its way on to the market as a crop, it was too remote from Pete's work for him to think that someone had gone in first with foreknowledge of the new seed.

On Ellie-Rose's twentieth birthday her father took full note of her discontented frame of mind. She'd come to Lafleche, as she always did. Schooldays were behind her now. She was 'out', as the saying went – out in Society. He expected her to be choosing a husband soon, among the rich young men of the eastern seaboard.

To that end, he'd decided to build a house in New York State. That was her birthday present. He showed her the architect's drawings on the front and back elevations and waited for her cries of delight, but to his surprise, they didn't come.

'Don't you think, Papa,' she murmured, bending over the drawings, 'that this is really rather vulgar?'

'Vulgar?' He was taken aback. 'I don't see how! It's just like the place the laird used to live in, back in Glen Bairach.'

'But that was in Scotland,' she protested. 'It fitted into the landscape there. You can't just transplant it to New York.'

'Why not? If Vanderbilt can build a Renaissance palace and Brokaw can put up a French chateau, why can't I have a Scottish castle?'

'Because you've got more taste, I hope!' she flashed.

If Ellie-Rose thought the idea vulgar, Luisa thought it delightful. She could just see herself presiding over a castle. Her daughter's half-contemptuous remarks about it didn't perturb her; these days people with money had to show off a bit – it was expected. And there was no doubt, from all she could gather, that Rob had money.

Luisa still thought of herself as having her life before her. So far she'd never had quite the success she hoped for. Living with brother Julius was quite agreeable and certainly she met interesting people, but it was always in her mind that the apartment was Julius's domain.

When Rob came east to supervise the building of Craigallan Castle, he took a suite at the sparkling new Waldorf Astoria. Nothing he had ever done impressed Luisa more. Ellie-Rose shared the suite with him, and her mother was a frequent visitor, bringing with her such friends as she wished to impress. 'I'd like you to meet the son of a dear friend, Beecher Troughton,' she cooed to Ellie-Rose.

'How do you do?' Ellie-Rose said coolly, allowing him to touch the tips of her fingers.

'How do you do, Miss Craigallan.' His admiring dark eyes drank her in. 'I've been longing for an introduction.'

'Is that a compliment, sir?'

'Miss Craigallan,' he said earnestly, 'there isn't a thing one could say about you that wouldn't be a compliment!'

Ellie-Rose couldn't help being pleased by his open flattery. When she saw him at a ball the next evening, she allowed him to claim more than his fair share of dances.

'You're being awfully silly,' Maisie Lukerwood warned her. 'Beech Troughton's got a rep.'

'But he's so amusing, Maisie.'

'That may be, Ellie-Rose. All I can tell you is that my Mama won't leave me alone in the room with him.'

Ellie-Rose was bored and restless. She'd spent all the summer getting rid of Pete Sumikiss once and for all, and now the New York season was about to begin she was ready for someone amusing, someone entertaining. Beech Troughton was made for the part. He was determined to make this bright, lively girl fall in love with him. And though Ellie-Rose wasn't ever sure that what she felt was love, she found Beech irresistible.

Luisa watched the friendship grow between these two and congratulated herself. A match between them would unite Luisa with one of the best families in New York, an old banking family. And it would be a triumph if her daughter hooked him away from the patronising Kitty Highclare, who took it for granted she would marry him.

Rob was too busy with business matters and the building of the house out at Carmansville north of Morningside Heights, so no one was able to warn Ellie-Rose what she was getting into. It's doubtful if she would have heeded the warning in any case. The time had come, it seemed to her, to let herself lose her head over a man.

Ellie-Rose wanted to find out what it was like to be in love. She wanted to be in someone's arms and lose herself in the delight of his kisses. When she looked back at the night she'd spent with Pete Sumikiss, it seemed to her absurd, empty, worthless. If that was 'making love', why did poets sing of it? Why did women pine for it? Why did it drive people to drink and madness? With Beech it might be different. She wanted to find out.

Their first encounter as lovers was carefully stage-managed by Beech. He took her home after a ball at Mrs Schermerhorn's, having previously made sure her rather formidable Papa was out at Carmansville for a few days. In the lavish hotel suite, he accepted her polite offer of refreshment. She rang for coffee; while they waited for it to be brought, she left him glancing at a magazine while she went to take off her dancing slippers and her tiresome hair ornament.

When the door of her bedroom opened and closed quietly she guessed at once that he had come in. In a way, she'd almost expected it. 'Need any help?' he asked lightly. He came close to her and helped unpin the two tea roses and the gilt star from her hair.

She was looking into her mirror. Over her shoulder she saw his dark head bend and she knew he was going to kiss her bare shoulder. She waited. It all seemed to happen in slow motion. The touch of his lips was like a wound.

It had to be now! It had to happen – she was going to give herself to him and find out, once and for all, whether there was any such thing as love. She turned in his arms and kissed him, opening her lips with a muffled gasp as his tongue darted like a snake into the warm cavity of her mouth.

He was very expert. He stroked and teased and laughed as he took off her garments one by one. He carried her to her bed and laid her down. He gazed down at her, studying the strong, firm body. She held out her arms to him, smiling.

He wasn't sure whether he was surprised or not to find he wasn't her first lover. He'd had a feeling she wasn't totally innocent, like most of the other girls in his circle, yet he could never have described her as experienced. He found her eager and sweet, ardent, responsive. The hours seemed to speed past in ever-growing wonder at his good luck in rousing such emotion in such a wonderful girl. He crept out just before the cold dawn of September, congratulating himself on his perceptiveness.

They met often, either at her father's suite when he was away or a bachelor apartment Beech kept up on Central Park West. He would call her by telephone, suggesting a rendezvous. She seldom refused. She had given herself up to him for the moment, allowing him to rule over her in a way that no man ever had before.

Perhaps it was in some way to recompense herself for losing her little-girl relationship to her father that Ellie-Rose became so reckless. She somehow blamed him; she had given up so much for him – even her virginity so that he should have the seed wheat he wanted so much. Of course, her father didn't *know* that. But she felt he should have sensed the sacrifice she'd made for him. She felt he was ungrateful, although he didn't even know how grateful he ought to be. She felt he had failed her.

The time came when Beech wanted to try for something even more delightful than the relationship they already had. 'Wouldn't it be great, Ellie-Rose,' he murmured, 'if we could spend some time together without having to cover it up? Without having to rush away so as to turn up somewhere else for dinner or breakfast or whatever?'

'It would be nice,' she agreed, smiling up at him. 'But it's not possible.'

'Yes, it is. I know a dinky little hotel, out by the sea at Oyster Bay. It would be ever so quiet now, with the season practically over. What d'you say?'

'What do I say to what?' she countered.

'What d'you say we go there for the weekend? You can say to your Papa that you're spending the weekend with your friend

Maisie Lukerwood in Brooklyn.'

'And what do you say to *your* Papa, Beech?'

'Ah, well . . .' he shrugged and laughed. 'Fellows don't have to account for their time the way girls do, honey.'

'It seems unfair, doesn't it? There ought to be as much freedom for women as for men . . .'

'Oh, now, don't talk tosh! But what d'you say, darling? It's a great place – miles away from everybody. It hasn't even got the telephone. Shall I send them a note to reserve us a room?'

'Yes,' she said, with sudden decision, 'why not?'

How easy it was. Her father didn't dream of doubting her word. She felt a moment of guilt over the breakfast table when he nodded from behind his morning paper at her announcement. 'Good idea,' he said. 'Next weekend I'd like you to come out to Carmansville to look at how the house is getting along. It might be time to start thinking about how you want the inside decorated.'

'I thought you'd already got that fixed?' she said. 'Baronial beams and claymores . . .'

'Oh yes, in the downstairs rooms. But the bedrooms need to be comfortable.' He was quite unaffected by her irony.

Ellie-Rose and Beech had arranged to travel separately to Oyster Bay. It was an easy trip by boat. There were few passengers, for by now, as Beech had foretold, most of the Long Island holiday traffic was finished.

A porter at the quay picked up her portmanteau and led the way to the Sagamore Hotel. There was no point in hiring a hackney; the hotel was too near. The jetty was long and wooden, smelling of salt and tar. The town charmed her – wooden houses brightly painted, their storm shutters folded back, and a little street with shade trees and a town hall and a clock tower. At the end of Main Street a fine eighteenth century house dominated the scene. There was a wooded hill behind the town, turning gold and red and orange in the fall sunshine.

There were one or two other couples in Oyster Bay, taking advantage of this fine sunny weekend; they looked like honeymooners or, perhaps, like Beech and herself, lovers. There were three other guests at the hotel – an elderly couple and their son.

Beech had registered for them both under the name of Mr and Mrs Walker. Walker was his middle name. It had made Ellie-Rose start, the first time the waiter called her Mrs Walker, but she covered it up well, though perhaps the waiter was used to such hesitations.

The weather was so fine that she asked to go out for a pre-dinner walk. Amused at her little-girl enjoyment of the sea-shore, he fell in with her wishes. They walked along the beach, getting their shoes full of sand but laughing and teasing each other. They threw pebbles into the waves; they picked up and compared shells. Slowly it grew perceptibly colder and they realised the sun was going down behind the horizon.

As they sauntered back, arm in arm, they came to a little house at the outer end of the town, whose ground floor window had been made into a display cabinet. In it on a background of white satin lay a muff, of steel grey velvet ruched and stitched in folds, trimmed with tiny seed pearls and buttons of white fur.

'Isn't that pretty!' cried Ellie-Rose. 'What a pretty thing to find in a little place like this!'

'Oh, I daresay there's a lot of customers here in the season,' Beech pointed out.

Ellie Rose looked at the gilt lettering on the sign above the window. 'Modes et Travaux' she read out. 'My, my – a French modiste! No wonder it's such an elgant muff. Oh, I do love it, Beech! It would go so well with my fall costume. Buy it for me, darling.'

'Oh, you can buy one to match exactly in New York –'

'Ah, don't be mean. Buy it for me to show you love me!'

'I'll give you the money –'

'No, no, come in like a good little husband and buy it for Mrs Walker.'

The bell above the door tinkled. From a curtained alcove at the back of the quiet little shop, a woman appeared. She came towards them on the polished floor, her shoes tapping on the wooden planks. There was something about the way she held her head that seemed familiar to Ellie-Rose, even though the light in the shop was dim. 'Can I help you?' she inquired.

That voice . . . The slight lilt of the tone, somehow well-known.

'Er . . . thank you. My wife would like to look at the muff in the window.'

'Yes, sir. One moment, I'll fetch it.' She moved away to the window, drew back the silk drape that formed a background, and brought the muff to them. 'I'm glad you've been attracted to it,' she said. 'An exclusive design, after a style I saw in a French fashion book. Would madame like to try it?'

Ellie-Rose put her hands in it. As she did so, she became excruciatingly aware that she had no wedding ring on her left hand. The other woman made no remark on that point, nor seemed to notice that Ellie-Rose had coloured deeply.

'The velvet is pure silk imported from France. The seed pearls are genuine. The white fur buttons are ermine. The lining is Indian silk. How does madame find it? Is it roomy enough?'

'Oh . . . yes . . . quite roomy,' Ellie-Rose said. She found it difficult to say a word. For as the modiste chatted about the muff, Ellie-Rose had realised who she was. The voice had come back to her with long echoes of the past.

This was Morag, who used to live with them at Lafleche Farm; Morag, whom Ellie-Rose had called Mommy. And for some reason that made no sense at all, Ellie-Rose felt ashamed at standing in front of her with her lover.

21

OVER THE YEARS THE memory of Morag had faded from Ellie-Rose's mind. Now and again some present-day event would call back the terrible drama of Morag's final departure – the sound of a baby screaming in pain, the clatter of a suddenly dropped metal object, the thudding of hooves as horses took off at speed.

At those moments she would have a sudden, frightening pang of loss. In a flash of memory she would see a young woman running from a room, a stain of black coffee spreading on a tiled floor, Nellie's face as she hurried after the woman. She remembered the anguish of the hours that followed Morag's going. She and Cornelius had clung together, frightened and bewildered, while Mama wept hysterical tears on the bed in the guest room. There was no one else in the house: Nellie had gone with Morag to Brown Bridge, and Papa was out at the far side of the farm with the drill teams.

When Papa came in soon after midday, Mama had grabbed him and sobbed out a muddled tale. Then Papa had ridden off fast, towards Brown Bridge and Morag. Ellie-Rose, prompted by Cornelius, had asked what was happening. Mama had snapped, 'Mind your own business – it's all too dreadful for young ears.'

In the following days, Ellie-Rose had begged Papa to bring Morag back. That never happened. She never came back. It had taken a long time for Ellie-Rose to work out the cause of that disappearance – several years of growing up and trying to catch nuances of adult gossip and cross-questioning of an unwilling Nellie.

By the time she was sixteen, Ellie-Rose had worked it out. Mama in New York was her real mother, Papa's legal wife. Morag, who had lived with them and whom she had loved, was that wicked thing, a 'mistress'. She knew about mistresses from the history lessons at school: kings like Louis Sixteenth had mistresses. But ordinary men weren't allowed to step outside the bonds of convention like that. It had been extremely wrong of Papa to allow Morag to live with them. Everyone seemed to think so.

And then there was the baby. Ellie-Rose only just remembered the baby. If it was wrong for a woman to live with a man outside the ties of matrimony, it was even worse to have a baby. Clearly, Morag must have been a very bad character. Yet everything that Ellie-Rose associated with her was good; gentleness, patience, interest in all her schoolgirl undertakings. . . . all the things she'd never had from Mama.

She was utterly certain that this dressmaker in the little shop at Oyster Bay was Morag. She hesitated, wondering whether to say anything. Meanwhile Morag was explaining that the muff could be made to order in other colours if madame would like that.

'No, no, my wife liked that one. How about it, dear?'

'Never mind,' Ellie-Rose said. 'Let's get out of here.' All of a sudden she wanted to get away.

'No, really, Ellie-Rose, I want you to have it.'

Morag, hearing the name, stiffened. Ellie-Rose? There wouldn't be two girls in the world with that name. She stood bending over her work table, her hand on the silks and velvets, and drew in a deep breath. Should she introduce herself to the girl? But what could she say? 'I was your father's mistress – I lived with you at Lafleche Farm.' Hardly the thing to say to a young bride.

When she turned back she was quite composed. Ellie-Rose glanced at the velvets but said she preferred the grey. 'All right,' Beech said, 'we'll take it. How much?'

'I'm afraid it's rather expensive,' Morag replied. 'Forty-five dollars.'

'Whew.w . . .' whistled Beech. 'That's stiff!'

'Let's never mind, then, Beech –'

'No, no, you fancied it. I want you to have it. See here, I don't have that much money on me. We'll take it, and I'll send –'

'I'm sorry, sir,' Morag put in gently, 'I can't sell on credit terms. There's so much transitory trade here, you see.'

'But I'm –' Beech broke off. He'd been going to tell her he was Beecher Troughton, son of the banker. 'All right then, can you deliver it to the Sagamore? I'll pay you then.'

'Thank you, sir. What name, please?'

'Beecher Tr – I mean, David Walker.'

When the young pair had gone, Morag sat down at her work table, breathless, her head swimming a little. The encounter had startled her. She knew of course that Rob had made money. She'd followed his career in the newspapers. And in the society columns, she read little paragraphs about Miss Craigallan at the ball of Mrs Schermershorn, at the opening of the Water-Colourists' Exhibit, at the races with Mr and Mrs Dupont. But there had been nothing about her engagement or marriage. Here she was, with a young man who referred to her as 'my wife'. Had they run away? Was it an elopement?

She put the muff in a box with her trade name on it – Cecile, Modiste. Then, donning her pelisse and bonnet, she set off for the Sagamore. The desk clerk gave the box to a bellboy telling him to take it up to the Walkers' room and bring back the cash. When he'd gone, the clerk smiled at Morag. 'Bought her one of your pretty things, has he? You can tell he's got money to burn.'

'It's a muff. He was more keen on it than she was.'

'Oh yes, that's quite common.' He winked. 'Trying to set her mind at rest by giving proofs of affection, eh?'

'I . . . er . . . don't quite know what you mean.'

'Well, it's pretty plain, ain't it? They're not here under their real name.'

'You're saying that they're –'

'Not married! But so what? It's not our business.'

Morag thought about that all through the evening. Next day she looked out for the young pair, hoping to see them strolling about the town, but they didn't appear. The fact was that coming across Morag had wrecked the weekend for Ellie-Rose. She insisted on going back first thing on Sunday morning.

'But why? What have I done?' Beech implored.

'Nothing. It's nothing to do with you. It's just that . . . I can't bear it, all hugger mugger like this. I want to go home.'

Outwardly Beech was all understanding and consideration. Inwardly he was seething. Who the hell did she think she was, to treat him like this? He'd given up a weekend's polo to be with her at Oyster Bay . . .

The following Tuesday, as she was sitting in the suite at the Waldorf Astoria, her telephone rang. The desk clerk announced she had a visitor. A Miss Morag McGarth was asking to see her.

Ellie-Rose gasped. For a space of five seconds her head whirled with memories.

'Miss Craigallan?'

'Yes. Send her up.'

At the gentle tap on the door she braced herself, went to open it, stood back. Morag came in, surprisingly elegant in dark brown serge trimmed with moire silk. She obeyed Ellie-Rose's gesture of invitation to take a chair in the sitting-room.

'So you did remember me?' she queried.

'Yes. I wondered if you had recognised *me*.'

'It was the name.'

'Ah yes.' They sat for a moment looking at each other. 'You've hardly changed a bit, Morag.'

'But you have.'

'Yes.' She sighed.

'Why do you sigh? Surely you're happy?'

'You mean, because I've got money and a place in society and all that?'

'You say it as if these things aren't important –'

'Oh, they're important. But they don't make you happy.'

Morag leaned forward. 'So is that why you spend a weekend in a hotel with a man you aren't married to?'

Ellie-Rose drew in a breath of surprise at the directness of the attack. 'What has it to do with you?'

[326]

'Nothing, perhaps. If you'd seemed head over heels in love, perhaps I wouldn't have come. But . . .' Morag held out a hand. 'Why were you there, Ellie-Rose?'

'Oh, what does it matter!'

'Are you going to marry him?'

'I shouldn't think so. In fact, I think it's all over. I don't know how I got into it in the first place.'

'Ellie-Rose!' Morag said, shocked. 'How can you talk like that? About something that ought to be serious?'

'Don't be silly, Morag. He wasn't the first, you know.' For some reason she wanted to hurt and overpower her visitor. She didn't want to have to justify her actions to her.

Morag had to take a grip on herself. 'My dear,' she said, 'I know the world's changing. I know I live a long way off from the bright lights of New York, but I can't believe your father would want you to behave like this –'

'Oh, Papa! So now you hold him up as a model, do you? You know very well that you were living with my father in those days. Why is it so different for me?'

'We were in love, Ellie-Rose.'

'And what good did that do? Mama soon sent you packing.' Ellie-Rose shook her head with vehemence. 'No, the more I look around me, the more I see that love is one of those day-dreams that get you nowhere. If it exists, which I doubt, it's a muddled thing that misleads you, so one may as well follow one's own inclinations.'

'You can't do things like that without harming yourself and others, Ellie-Rose. That young man, for instance –'

'Oh, don't waste any sympathy on Beech! He can take care of himself. And the same goes for me, I assure you. So, you see, you've wasted your time coming here. Unless,' she added with intentional cruelty, 'you came to see Papa?'

Morag shook her head. 'I inquired first at the desk if he was here. They told me he was at Carmansville.'

'Oh yes, at Chateau Craigallan! You should have kept in touch, Morag. He has money to throw away these days.'

Morag rose. She fastened her pelisse at her throat with hands that trembled. 'I'm sorry to have taken up your time,' she said. 'It was a mistake to come. I only thought that . . .'

'What?'

'I don't know. That you were a little lost? That you might need someone . . .?'

'Need someone!' Ellie-Rose broke out. 'You're years too late with your concern and sympathy! Where were you, when Mama and Papa were living like strangers in the same house at Brown Bridge? Where were you, when Cornelius went away and I had *no one*?'

'Ellie-Rose –'

'Now you come here, disapproving of me –'

'It's not that I disapprove, my dear. I was worried . . . I don't understand what's gone wrong. Your father was so close to you –'

'Oh, yes, close – except when there was wheat to think about! Wheat, money, investments! How can a mere human being hold his attention compared with those?'

'Have you said that to him?' Morag challenged. 'Have you told him you're lonely?'

'Lonely? I'm not lonely. I have more friends that I know how to keep up with. What do you mean, lonely? I don't need your pity, so don't come here getting tearful over me, Morag McGarth! Go back and live that cosy little life you preferred to us. I don't need you!'

Morag went to the door. There she paused and glanced back. 'If ever you want to talk to someone . . .'

'Get out!'

Down in the carpeted lobby, Morag looked about her with uncertainty. Men in top hats and fine broadcloth coats walked in and out at the gilt doors. Outside the traffic of Fifth Avenue roared by. She felt dazed, bewildered by the city, and by the interview that had just taken place.

Ellie-Rose was terribly unhappy. That was clear to see. So young and so pretty – and so strangely desperate. What had gone wrong in her life? Why wasn't she, like so many girls of her age, looking forward to a happy marriage with some suitable young man? Conventional and middle-class, perhaps – but Morag understood better than most that happiness can come in conventional wrappings.

When she asked the doorman to hail a cab for her under the pillared canopy of the great hotel, the direction she gave was not for the ferry to Long Island. 'I want to go to Carmansville,' she said.

Rob Craigallan enjoyed coming to Carmansville and roughing it on the site of his new house. He'd had a little cabin built in the grounds, and here he'd play the gypsy for a day or two, safe in the knowledge that he could go back at any time to the comfort of the Waldorf or eat a meal in the Nestor Inn up the road. He could confer with the architect, harry the builders, argue with the landscape-gardener, then go into New York for a day at the Exchange, and still be in time for an evening at his club with some business friend.

He was surprised when one of the men came to say a lady was inquiring for him. 'My wife, you mean?' he asked, for Luisa had taken to dropping by in hopes of being asked her opinion on the house.

'No, sir, it ain't Mrs Craigallan. She says you know her, though.'

'All right, show her in.' He cleared away the plans and diagrams from a chair in honour of the visitor.

When she came in he was trying to tie the tapes round a sketch map of his property. The workman closed the door behind her. She moved into the centre of the cluttered room, saying nothing. He raised his head and saw her. A giant hand seemed to seize him in a grasp of iron and then let him go. He drew in a breath, shuddering from the pain. 'Morag . . .'

'Hello, Rob.'

'Morag! Where have you been? I looked everywhere for you!'

'I'm living at Oyster Bay now,' she said. 'I got a job in New York at first because I had to get treatment for Gregor –'

'Gregor! How is he? What happened? Sit down, sit down! Oh, Morag –! You've . . . you've taken the living breath out of me.'

She sat down, loosening her pelisse and drawing off her gloves. A quick glance at her hands showed him that she wasn't toiling as a servant. They were white and smooth except, when he took them, he could feel a rough place on her left forefinger.

'I'm sorry if I've given you a shock. I wanted to talk to you, Rob. I see a lot about you and Ellie-Rose in the papers –'

'Never mind that. Tell me about Gregor. How is he?'

'Oh, you'd like him, Rob! He's very smart and bright. I think he's a handsome boy, but then I'm biased.'

'The burns? What about the burns?'

'He has a scar. It's been a long time fading. But it isn't much – it sort of half-closes one of his eyes so that he always seems to be studying things very deeply. He's bright at schoolwork.'

'Oh, Morag! Why didn't you let me know where you were? I'd have paid for doctors –'

'I thought it best, Rob. Everything had gone so wrong... And I managed all right, you know. I worked for a dressmaker while Gregor had to see a skin specialist at first, and then when I had a little money saved I moved out. The doctor said the mountains or the sea coast would be better for my chest –'

'Still got that cough?'

'Yes, but it's nothing, I'm used to it. I always intended to move down to Florida. I made friends there during that winter – remember?'

'Oh, God, yes –!'

'But somehow it never seemed the right time to go. Gregor was doing so well at school it seemed wrong to disturb him: and everything goes on well enough. I have a little business of my own, you see, Rob. The summer season, there's a lot of people at Oyster Bay, and I sell a lot. In the winter I take it easy, getting up when I like, sewing and designing, making a good stock of pretty things for the next season. Muffs, shirtwaists, nightdresses – all exclusive designs. But you don't want to hear about that –'

'But I do! I want to know everything you've been doing! Dear heaven, Morag, if you knew how I've missed you! I hired detectives, I made inquiries. Over a year, I kept looking for you ...' To his own surprise, his voice broke. 'Morag, Morag ... why didn't you write to me?'

'I thought about it often,' she said with a sigh. 'I even wrote the letter more than once. But I never posted it. I felt ... that Luisa would never forgive me.'

He shook his bowed head. 'She never thinks of all that now. She lives her life, and I live mine. In a way, I think she's happy. She has a "friend" in New York, a decent enough fellow – after all, why not, if it makes her feel better?'

'And you, Rob? Do you have a "friend"?'

'I'm no angel, Morag, but . . . no, I don't have a "friend". Maybe I just couldn't find anyone who measured up to you.'

'I'm sorry. You must have been lonely?' She was hearing the echoes of Ellie-Rose's words.

'Well, I've kept busy. And there are the children, of course. Cornelius has turned into an expert on agricultural bacteriology!'

'Good heavens!' She gave a shaky laugh. 'What on earth is that?'

'You may well ask! It's a sort of science that he and a few other fellows seem to be inventing as they go along. There's a great future in it. You always said Cornelius was clever, didn't you?' He patted her hand fondly.

'Yes, and Ellie-Rose? How is Ellie-Rose?'

'Oh, she's fine, fine. Gadding about in New York. She sees something of her mother, who's "in" with the nobs, you know. And there's a young man she looks like marrying – come from a fine family, the Troughtons. Oh, Ellie-Rose is right on the crest of the wave.'

'You're sure?' she persisted. 'Girls of that age need someone to talk to, you know. And I can't imagine that Ellie-Rose can talk to her Mama.'

'No, that's true. You can't have a conversation with Luisa.' He laughed, without bitterness. 'In the end I came to accept that. And Ellie-Rose has always known it, I think.'

'Then who does she talk to?'

'Well . . . me, I suppose.'

'But you're not always in New York. I read in the papers that you're here and there, as guest of honour at some affair, as consultant to some agricultural inquiry. And the building of this place must take up a lot of your time.'

'Yes it does, but it's going to be worth it, Morag! It'll be a very handsome house. And when it's finished, you see, I'll let Cornelius have a place to put all his books and equipment, and Ellie-Rose can have a boudoir and a bedroom and all that, and invite her fine friends –'

'But in the meantime they're not seeing much of you. You know, Rob,' she said, rather urgently, 'if you look back at your own life . . . don't you remember how everything seemed to crowd in on you as you came to that age? So many new things to learn, so many decisions to take . . . At a time like that, young people need all the help they can get.'

'I suppose so, but my two seem able to take care of themselves.'

'That's how it looks, maybe. Still, I can't help thinking that young people are never so sure of themselves as they seem.'

'You may be right.' He always found it difficult to disagree with her when she fixed him with those great dark eyes. 'And speaking of children, when can I see Gregor?'

She went white. 'I . . . I don't think that's possible.'

'Why not?'

'Who should I say you are?'

'His father, of course,' he said, hurt.

'But Rob . . . I've told him his father is dead.'

They were silent for a moment. Then he said, 'Well, you could introduce me as a friend.'

'No, Rob.'

'Damn it, I want to see him! I've a right to!' He caught back his angry tone. 'I'm sorry, I didn't mean it like that. You've brought him up this far without help from me, and I've no right to make claims. But Morag – I want to see him. I . . . I've wondered so often what happened to him, how you both got on. Let me meet him, Morag. Please. I won't let him know who I am.'

She held out against it for a long time because she could sense the danger in it. But nevertheless, some sense of pride wanted to show off the boy to Rob. Gregor was their son – the product of their love, and a credit to them both. 'All right,' she said. 'If you come to Oyster Bay you can put up at the Sagamore and drop in on us like an acquaintance. You must promise me not to distrub his view of life, Rob. He's never had a father. It wouldn't be easy for him to come to terms with it now. Besides, he thinks I'm a respectable widow lady. And . . . I'd hate him to learn otherwise.'

'I promise, Morag.'

When she got home she regretted giving her permission for them to meet. But it was too late now. She'd let her concern for Ellie-Rose prompt her to seek out Rob. She should have known that couldn't be the end of it. She could only hope Rob would look about him now, and see that his daughter was unhappy and needed him.

Rob went back to New York that evening resolved to spend more time with his children. What exactly he could do for them he wasn't sure, but Morag's earnestness had impressed him.

Ellie-Rose was dressing for a party when he came in. He called to her as he passed her bedroom door: 'What are your plans for this evening?'

'I'm expected at the Roystons. I didn't expect you back so soon, Papa?'

'Oh, there wasn't anything more I could do at Carmansville for the moment.'

She came out into the drawing-room of the suite, radiant in a gown of champagne-coloured glacé silk, her dark-blonde hair held back with roses of brown silk. He eyed her with approval. 'Say, you look marvellous. I hope the Roystons are going to appreciate you!'

She shrugged.

'I suppose you wouldn't change your mind and come out to dinner with me instead?'

'Papa!' She was taken aback.

'Just an idea. I don't want to break into your fun –'

'No, no, I'd love it. The Roystons are such a bore!'

'All right then, just let me have twenty minutes to bath and change and I'll be with you. Meanwhile you could telephone to the Roystons to make some excuse.'

He took her to a French restaurant near the Park. She was delighted to be with him, sparkling and bright, eager to accept all his suggestions about food and wine. Her spirits were perhaps a little too high. There was something almost feverish in her gaiety, although he didn't notice it.

And then, when the *asperges a la mode de Rheims* were brought, she seemed unwilling to try them. She said she was too hot, fanned herself with the feather-and-gilt fan, complained that there were too many gasoliers in the room, making the air unbreathable. He sent for some iced water for her, which she sipped thankfully.

Then he was hailed by a male friend who stopped to chat about the stock market, and invited them to join him and his wife. It seemed only polite to accept. Rob could sense that Ellie-Rose wasn't pleased. After she'd toyed with the main course, she rose. 'I have to go, Papa. I'm expected at the Roystons, remember?'

'But I thought you'd –'

'Oh, well, it's better if I show up. You will excuse me, Mrs Dubinski?'

'Such a sweet girl,' Mrs Dubinski murmured as they watched her thread her way through the tables to the exit. 'Don't you think so, dear?'

'Absolutely. Now, Craigallan, tell truth – are you really interested in those oil shares?'

When Rob got home, Ellie-Rose was in bed. He was rather pleased that she hadn't stayed out too late at the Roystons. The truth was she never went there. All she'd wanted was to get away from the Dubinskis.

Rob's first visit to Oyster Bay caused him a lot of anxiety. He rehearsed what he was going to say to his son a thousand times on the way. 'How do you do, Gregor, I'm an old friend of your mother's . . .'

To his surprise Morag and Gregor came to the jetty to meet him. 'How do you do, sir?' the boy said gravely, holding out his hand. 'Mother tells me you knew each other in the old days.'

'H.how do you do?' stammered Rob, staring at him.

He was twelve years old, tall and slender, with the pale clear skin of his mother marred only by a narrow fold on the temple and cheek bone by the left eye. As Morag had said, it gave him a shrewd, studious appearance. He was well-dressed in the knickerbockers and loden jacket of the schoolboy, a peaked cloth cap pulled down over his reddish hair.

He was composed and calm, more so than either of the adults. It was easy to see that he had undertaken the role of man of the house. Morag explained to Rob later, as they sat chatting after the boy had gone to bed that evening, that she had sometimes been unwell and Gregor had to take charge. 'He hired a salesgirl to look after the shop for two weeks last summer,' she said with a laugh. 'He made me stay in bed! Oh, he's got a mind of his own.'

'I'm glad he looks after you. From now on, Morag, if ever you need anything –'

'Oh, we manage fine, Rob. We like our life the way it is.'

He couldn't stay a pang of envy at the words. She was happy in a way he had scarcely ever known. She and the boy asked for nothing, and found satisfaction in what they had. Perhaps this was the way to live. Perhaps always being at work, always quick to make money . . . perhaps that didn't really bring happiness.

'I may come again?' he asked when he took his leave the following day.

'The hotel closes down at the end of October, Rob. You wouldn't find anywhere to stay.'

'You wouldn't ask me to stay with you?'

'No,' she said quickly. And then, seeing his hurt look, 'It would look odd, Rob. And we haven't the room.'

'Of course. Well, give my regards to Gregor and tell him I hope to see him next time I come.'

'I will.' Gregor was at school. She'd seen no reason to keep him at home. To do so would have attached too much importance to Rob's visit.

When he got back to New York he was already planning his next visit. The funny little house with its downstairs made into a shop and workroom, the quiet little town, the air of content that seemed to be everywhere – they made him look back on the past twenty-four hours as idyllic. If only he could tell Ellie-Rose about it! He was sure she'd love the place. But it was difficult to talk to Ellie-Rose about Morag, and besides, it might get to the ears of her mother.

His daughter was out when he got back. She came in as he was going down to the hotel restaurant for lunch. 'Come and eat with me?' he suggested.

'No thanks, Papa. I'm not hungry.'

'You ought to eat more,' he said, suddenly anxious. He couldn't exactly establish what it was about her, but she looked somehow unwell.

'Oh, don't fuss,' she said, and flounced past him into her bedroom. Inside, she shut the door and threw herself into a chair. So much for Beecher Troughton, she told herself bitterly.

But what had she expected? They had both know it was all over when they came back from Oyster Bay. The interview she'd just had with him only underlined how utterly apart they were.

She'd gone to see him by previous arrangement at his bachelor apartment. He was edgy and unwelcoming as he showed her in. 'I hope this is really important,' he burst out. 'I've got people waiting for me at the bank –'

'It's important,' she said. 'Are you going to ask me to sit down?'

'Of course.' He placed a chair. 'Ellie-Rose, what's on your mind?'

'I'm going to have a baby.'

'What?'

'A baby. I'm pregnant.'

'Oh.' It was a gasp of dismay. Then he said, 'Are you sure?'

'Certain.'

'And it's mine?'

She sprang up, going scarlet. 'Beech!'

'No – wait – I'm sorry. I didn't mean it quite like that. But . . . I wasn't the first, Ellie-Rose.'

'No, you were the second,' she flashed. 'Of two.'

She sat down again, looking at him. She expected him to say 'All right then, let's get married.' She had nerved herself to accept that. She didn't love Beech, and he didn't love her, but she was expecting his baby and they might make a go of it. There was as much chance of happiness that way as any other.

'Well,' he said, 'this is awkward.'

'It certainly isn't the best news I've had, but it will be all right, Beech.'

'You mean you're going to get rid of it? Is that why you wanted to see me? For money to see to all that?'

She leaned back and half-closed her eyes. He wasn't going to ask her to marry him. All at once she understood that she was quite mistaken in expecting it.

'I think Walter Meywald knows someone who does that kind of thing,' Beech was saying.

'Please,' she said through clenched teeth, 'don't discuss me with Walter Meywald!'

'No, of course I won't, but I'll get the address. I'll find out how much you need. There'll be no problem about money.'

'Don't bother,' she said. 'I'm not going to get rid of it.'

'Look here, Ellie-Rose . . .' He studied her anxiously. 'You're not going to make trouble? My Dad would raise the roof if he heard about this.'

'I'm not planning to go to your father with the news. Don't be scared, Beech, you won't have to face his wrath.'

'You can sneer about it, but you don't know what he's like. If anything happened to wreck my marriage to Kitty Highclare, he'd kill me.'

She sought in her purse for a handkerchief, with which she dabbed her lips. 'So it's Kitty Highclare you're going to marry?'

'I don't have a mind of my own on this,' he said with resentment. 'I have to do as I'm told. Look here, Ellie-Rose – you and I were never in love. You knew that.'

'I think I hoped things might change.'

'But they didn't, did they? So, that being so, we've no claims on each other.'

'You don't think a baby makes a difference?'

He drew back, easing his neck in his stiff collar. 'You're trying to make me feel guilty. You knew what you were up to, Ellie-Rose; you were no lilywhite innocent.'

'How charmingly you express yourself, Beech.'

'What do you want of me? If it's money, you can have it. More than that I can't do.'

[337]

She nodded. 'So I see. I'm sorry I bothered you with this little problem, Beech. You can rely on me not to trouble your conscience – that is, if you have one.'

'Oh, stop behaving like a tragedy queen! You're not the first girl to get into this scrape. You've always been so sure of yourself, Ellie-Rose. Now's the time to prove it. Don't come crying to *me*.'

She rose quickly and made for the door. 'Why did I ever think you were an exciting, rewarding sort of man?' she flung at him as she opened it to go out. 'I must have been out of my mind!'

And now, with the painful interview behind her, she sat in her bedroom trying to think what to do next. She was angry, hurt, disappointed, uncertain. For the first time in her life she seemed to have lost her sense of direction. She didn't know whom to turn to. Certainly not her mother – Luisa was the last person she could confide in. And not her father – it would be so painful to have to tell him that the daughter, of whom he was so proud, had made such a fool of herself.

Morag . . . She could go to Morag. Morag would listen to her and tell her what to do.

22

SHE COULDN'T STAND THE lower saloon in the ferryboat, although it was almost empty of passengers. The air was sickening with the smell of stale tobacco, steam coal and piston oil. She found a place on deck towards the stern, where she sat holding the edges of her fur-trimmed cape together to keep out the cool breeze. She watched the gulls swoop by, listened to their eerie call, and thought they sounded as lonesome as she felt.

Morag gave a cry of pleasure when she opened the door to her. 'What a surprise!' she exclaimed. 'Come in, come in.' She took her hands to urge her in. 'Why, child, your hands are like ice!'

'It was chilly on the boat . . .'

'Can I get you something hot? Some soup. I can heat it up in a moment –'

'No thanks, I couldn't.' The idea of soup was nauseating.

'Coffee, then? Or tea?'

'Tea would be nice.' She felt she could swallow some tea without retching.

Morag led her into a little room at the back of the shop. 'We don't have a proper sitting-room,' she apologised. 'Forgive the clutter.'

A checkered cloth was spread on the floor to catch snippets of thread and scraps of cloth. On a table were lengths of fine voile, and folded paper patterns. There was a workbox with scissors, reels of silk, pincushions, a needlecase. By the table, facing the stove, was a chair. Morag pushed away her work and led Ellie-Rose to sit down. She put the tea kettle on the stove.

'The crossing was rough for you,' she remarked.

'It wasn't the crossing,' said Ellie-Rose.

Morag turned to glance at her. They gazed at each other. Ellie-Rose nodded.

'Oh,' said Morag. Then, after a pause, 'The handsome hard young man you were with when I saw you?'

'Yes.'

'Does he know?'

'He doesn't want to know.'

'But if it's his baby –?'

'There's another girl he's expected to marry. He made it quite plain he doesn't want that spoiled.'

'But my dear, I repeat – if it's his baby?'

Ellie-Rose held out her hands towards the stove. She shivered. 'I don't even think we like each other very much,' she said.

Morag busied herself making the tea. The steam from the kettle made her cough for a moment. A voice called from upstairs, 'Are you all right, Mother?'

'Yes, darling, I'm fine. It's just a tickle.' She looked apologetically at Ellie-Rose. 'Gregor worries about me. He's doing home study in his room.'

Gregor? Ellie-Rose frowned. That was the baby in Morag's arms all those years ago. My half-brother, she said to herself with a start. 'He's . . . how old now?'

'Twelve. Shall I call him down to meet you?'

'No, thanks. It's you I came to talk to. I . . . I don't seem to have anyone else,' she said, unaware of how piteous she sounded.

Morag handed her her tea. 'Lemon? Milk?'

'Lemon if you have it.'

'Of course,' Morag bustled away to an alcove, to return with slices of lemon. She watched Ellie-Rose put a sliver in the tea and then said: 'You can talk to your father, surely?'

'I can't bring myself to tell him . . .'

'But you must, sooner or later, my dear.'

[340]

'Not if I get rid of the baby.'

She saw Morag stiffen.'

'You think that's wrong?'

'What I think doesn't matter. It's what *you* think. Is that what you really want?'

'That's why I came to see you. I thought you might know someone. Older women know these things.'

'No,' said Morag. 'I can't help you there. In any case, perhaps you ought to think of it more deeply. You might regret –'

'Oh, of course I shouldn't! It's the only sensible thing to do! This baby wasn't conceived in love. I don't want it – I never wanted it. I shouldn't love it once it was born. I don't think I'm capable of love.'

'My dear lass!' Morag said, putting a hand on her arm. 'What a terrible thing to say.'

'It's true! I don't love anybody.'

'You love your father –'

'But only when I'm the centre of his attention! It makes me angry and resentful when he's off with his business friends –'

'It's natural to want to be first with –'

'And Beech – I didn't love Beech. I was just . . . curious to see what it would be like to go to bed with someone like him.' She cast a shivering glance at Morag. 'I suppose you think that's despicable.'

'I can see *you* do,' Morag replied. 'Drink your tea, dear.' As Ellie-Rose obeyed, she went on: 'I think it's a mistake to warp your life by having such a low opinion of yourself. I made that mistake for years. The religion I was brought up in taught me to think that physical love was a sin, and I punished myself for a long time for my mistakes. But, Ellie-Rose, in the end nothing is gained by being unforgiving to ourselves. It's true, we must try to be better – but we ought not to hate ourselves for falling short.'

'You've come to terms with yourself, is that it?' Ellie-Rose challenged her. 'You feel you've balanced the books?'

'I don't know that I'd put it that way. I'm happy, at least.'

'How old are you, Morag?'

'I'll be thirty-nine next birthday.'

[341]

'Thirty-nine! Middle-aged nearly. And what have you got to show for it? A poky little shop in a dozey little town, and a bastard son!'

Morag winced, but then shrugged. 'Using hard words doesn't change it. I don't deny I've seen hard times. When Gregor was a baby I went through three or four years of hell. But since we came here I've found contentment. I don't earn much, but we get by. You know, Ellie-Rose, having a baby isn't such a disaster. And you're better off than I was. You have your family to support you.'

'Can you imagine my mother's face if she knew? Can you imagine the scene?'

'But that would only be at first –'

'No, she'd be ashamed. She'd send me away to have the baby. She'd put it out to nurse somewhere.'

'Your father can handle her. He'll see everything is all right, Ellie-Rose.'

'But you don't understand!' Ellie-Rose cried, bursting into tears. 'He'll be so shocked – so disappointed in me!'

Morag sprang up to catch the toppling cup and saucer. She put an arm round the girl. 'There, there,' she soothed. 'Is that what's wrong? You can't bear to see him disappointed in you?'

'He has such high hopes for me,' sobbed Ellie-Rose. 'He's building this stupid house at Carmansville so that . . . so that I can bring my fine friends there. He'll be so . . . so hurt!'

'But he'll get over it, lass,' soothed Morag. 'He loves you. He'll want to help and comfort you.'

'But I don't want . . . I don't want him to help and comfort me. I want him to admire me! I can't bear to lose his admiration!'

'Admiration isn't so important as affection. Ellie-Rose, haven't you any faith in his love?'

'I haven't any faith in anything!' cried Ellie-Rose. 'It's all hopeless and meaningless! I wish I'd never been born!' She sprang up, knocking Morag's arm aside, and ran through the shop to the outside door. Before Morag could recover she was running out into the gathering night.

The wind buffeted her as she ran along the cobbled street,

going she hardly knew where. The waves roared in along the beach. She came to the jetty where the boats came in, and ran on towards the sea, her footsteps thudding on the wooden planks. Behind her she could hear a voice: 'Ellie-Rose, Ellie-Rose!'

She didn't look back. She reached the end of the jetty, and when Morag caught up with her, she jerked away from her outstretched hand. 'Leave me alone!' she cried.

'Ellie-Rose, come back indoors –'

'Why did I come to you? You don't know any more than anybody else! Nobody knows anything!'

'You're talking nonsense, Ellie-Rose! Come back home –'

'Home? Oh, God, I haven't got a home!' sobbed Ellie-Rose, and as Morag tried to catch her in her arms, she threw herself off the jetty.

The icy waters closed over her head. The bitter shock brought her to her senses. In that moment she knew she didn't want to drown. She struggled to rise to the surface, but the velvet cloak had spread out on the water, and when she surfaced she was smothered beneath its folds.

Uttering a gurgling cry of terror, she sank again.

Morag heard her cries. 'I'm coming, I'm coming!' she shouted. She ran along the jetty trying to find a rowboat. In the gathering dimness it was difficult to see one among the fishing boats moored to the jerry. At last she saw a shallop. She threw the loop off the mooring hook, and jumped in.

It took seconds for her to push off from the stanchions and out far enough to see Ellie-Rose. She was a darker blur on the dark surface of the water. Morag rowed towards her, using one oar as a sweep so that she could face the way she was going. When she reached the girl she pulled in the oar and leaned towards her. 'Ellie-Rose, take my hand. Ellie-Rose!'

The girl was still in a tangle of velvet folds. 'Help!' she screamed. 'Morag, help me! Where are you! I can't see you!'

'Here – here! Keep still, darling. I'll get hold of the cloak.'

Ellie-Rose was too panic-stricken to heed her. She flailed in the water, feeling her heavy skirts dragging her down, unable to get the velvet hood off her head. Blind and terrified, she thrashed with her arms.

Morag, pulling at a corner of the cloak, was dragged sideways. The rowboat tilted. She pitched into the water. She gasped as the near freezing water closed over her but she quickly beat her way back to the surface. The shapeless bulk of Ellie-Rose's cloak was immediately beside her. She seized it, and with her other hand, she grabbed the drifting rowboat.

It was useless trying to drag herself aboard. She couldn't do it without letting go her hold on Ellie-Rose. She could only hold on with all her strength, and cry for help.'

The men in the bar of the Sagamore Inn were called out to the rescue by Gregor. Rushing downstairs at the noisy commotion of Ellie-Rose's departure, he had raced after the two women – impelled by anxiety for his mother's health. He knew it was madness for her to run out into the windy darkness. He heard Morag's cries. Instead of vainly trying to do anything alone, he urged the fishermen of Oyster Bay out of the snug, and they hurriedly ran a boat out from the beach.

The two women were brought ashore. Gregor ran for the doctor. At his evening meal, Dr McAllister couldn't understand what was going on at first, but when he reached the McGarth house he quickly assessed the near disaster. There wasn't room there for both women, so Ellie-Rose was taken in by a kindly neighbour. Morag was put to bed by Dr McAllister's wife and given a sleeping draught.

She woke in the early morning to find her son sitting by her bed. 'Gregor! Is she –?'

The boy dispelled her fears. 'She's safe,' he assured her. 'She's with Mrs Dinwiddie next door. How are you, Mother?'

'Oh, I'm fine. How long have you been sitting there?' she whispered.

'Never mind that. Drink some cough syrup. You've been coughing in your sleep.'

Around eight o'clock Mrs Dinwiddie slipped in to see how Gregor was faring. 'I'm just going to make some breakfast,' he said, slicing bread thinly and watching the coffee pot. 'You can go up and talk to her for a minute if you like.'

'Thank you,' Mrs Dinwiddie said, hiding a smile. He really

was an extraordinary boy; oldfashioned, her husband called him. 'How are you, dear?' she inquired as she tiptoed into Morag's bedroom.

'Fine! Just fine. How is Ellie-Rose?' croaked Morag.

'Mrs McGarth dear, I'm afraid it's very sad for her. She's lost her baby.'

Tears of pity welled up and spilled over on to Morag's cheeks. 'But she's all right?'

'Oh yes. Tired and upset, but all right.'

'Thank God for that.'

'How on earth did it happen, dear?'

'Oh she . . . she slipped on the jetty, and when I went out in a boat to bring her in, I tipped over.'

'Dear, dear, what a misfortune! A lucky thing Gregor was quick to fetch help.'

'He's a good lad,' Morag murmured. 'See he gets to school on time, Mrs Dinwiddie.'

But Gregor refused to go to school. 'I'll stay at home today,' he said in a cool voice that brooked no argument. 'She's not as well as she says she is. She'll get up and try to do something if I don't stay and look after her.'

Morag had eaten very little of the breakfast her son brought her. She tried again at noon, to please him. She swallowed a little soup and some toast, but he would have been happier if she'd taken more. 'Oughtn't she to be hungry by now?' he asked Dr McAllister.

'She has a temperature,' McAllister said, putting the thermometer in its case. 'Just see she gets plenty to drink, Gregor. I'll look in again this evening.'

In the evening Ellie-Rose came to the house leaning on the arm of Mrs Dinwiddie. 'May I see your mother?' she asked Gregor, who stood like Cerberus at the door.

'She's asleep.'

'May I wait?'

The strange, shrewd glance rested on her. 'Are you still in an emotional state?' he inquired.

'A what?'

'You were very emotional last night. It wouldn't be good for Mother.'

'I promise to be calm, Gregor.'

He stood aside. 'Very well. Dr McAllister will be here soon. If he says you may speak to her, you can go up then.'

He showed her to the little room in back of the shop and offered her a chair. He himself sat down to read a book. The clock ticked on the mantelpiece.

At seven the doctor came. He went upstairs with Gregor at his heels, but at the door of the bedroom he quietly warned the boy to wait outside. Some time later he emerged. 'I think you might try offering her some warm milk and brandy, Gregor. It might do her good.'

Gregor clattered downstairs to pour milk into a saucepan. The doctor said to Ellie-Rose, 'She's asking after you. You may go in for a few minutes.'

The room was lit only by a tiny lamp on the bedside table. Ellie-Rose came to the bedside and said: 'I'm so sorry, Morag. I didn't mean to make such a fool of myself.'

'It's all right, dear lass. I'm only glad it didn't end worse than it did.'

'You heard I lost the baby?'

'Yes, Ellie-Rose. I suppose you're glad.'

'Oh, Morag – isn't it strange – I'm sorry about it!'

Morag gave a weak little laugh. 'There, aren't mortals contrary? Never mind, my love. Remember what I said about not having a poor opinion of yourself. You've been given a second chance. Use it.'

'I'm going back to New York in the morning. Papa will be wondering where I am.'

'Well you tell him what's happened?'

'I don't know. I think... perhaps not. Why should I unload my miseries on him?'

'But he'd want to help, Ellie-Rose. Why don't you let him?'

'I'll see,' she said. 'I'll see.'

'Goodbye for the present then, dear.'

'Goodbye, Morag. I'll come back and see you in a week or two.'

'I'll look forward to that,' Morag whispered.

Ellie-Rose was wrong in thinking Rob was worried about her. He took it for granted she was with her mother at her Uncle Julius's apartment. He himself was busy, as ever. The New York futures market was very active at the moment, now that all the harvests of the world's wheat were being dealt in. When he and Ellie-Rose finally happened upon each other in the Waldorf suite, he asked absently if she was enjoying the fall season and she, taken by surprise, muttered that she was.

In the two days that followed life seemed strangely ordinary... as though the strange episode of her near-drowning had never happened. She took up the social round as if she'd never been away. When, at a card party at Mrs Garrard's, she saw Beecher Troughton, he looked at her in frowning inquiry; and she replied by shaking her head in smiling dismissal. His relief was almost comical.

That evening Rob was dining in the restaurant of the Waldorf with Sam Yarwood, in from Chicago on a business trip. A waiter approached with an envelope on a salver. 'This came for you by express messenger, Mr Craigallan,' he said, offering it.

The address was written in a round, firm hand. He opened it.

'Dear Mr Craigallan,' he read, 'my mother is very ill and would like to see you if it is convenient. Yours very truly, Gregor McGarth.'

A chill ran through Rob's veins. He got up, spilling his wine. 'I've got to go Sam,' he said. 'Something urgent. Some other time, eh?'

'Bad news, Rob?'

'I don't know,' Rob replied grimly.

He had to hire a boat to take him over. Every minute of the crossing he was on tenterhooks. When he reached the door of the little house, it was open. He ran through the shop and up the stairs.

Gregor was standing guard at his mother's bedside. 'Thank you for coming sir,' he said. 'She's been very anxious about it.'

'Would you leave us for a minute, darling?' Morag said in a voice not above a whisper.

When the door had closed on him she made a little movement

of her hand, urging Rob to come nearer. Now, standing by the bedside he saw her more clearly. He was shocked at how ill she looked. The flesh seemed to have fallen from her bones. Only her eyes looked alive.

'Morag, what's wrong?' he cried in anguish. 'I didn't know you were so ill . . .'

'I got chilled,' she said. 'My chest has always been . . . a trouble.'

'You need a long holiday in some mild climate, like you had that time in Florida –'

'Ah, my dear,' she said in a gentle voice, 'no amount of mild climate is going to help this time. Dr McAllister was very very worried. He sent for a specialist yesterday, who says I have to go to . . . go to a sanatorium.' Despite herself, the small quiet voice trembled. 'I have to go to one of those mountain places, Rob, where the air is very pure and thin. Somewhere in the Rockies.'

Rob swallowed hard. 'You shall go to the very best hospital, Morag. You know I have plenty of money –'

'I didn't send for you to ask for money, dear soul,' she interjected in gentle reproof. 'It's about Gregor.'

'Gregor? Yes, of course, he has to be looked after –'

'I'm to go at once. The specialist looked very serious and said I must travel tomorrow though I'm not perhaps quite strong enough –'

'You want me to make the arrangements? You'll go by train, of course. A special carriage –'

'Rob, Rob, please let me say what I have to say. Talking tires me so. It's about Gregor. I . . . I can't take him with me. Dr Towers said that in some way, this complaint of mine seems to be handed on to near relatives and members of the same family. It seems I'm a danger to Gregor.' She turned her head away on the pillows. 'A danger to my own son . . .'

'Morag, don't distress yourself. I'll see that he has everything he needs –'

'Will you, Rob? Including love? Will you love him for me?'

He stared at her. There was a blotch of colour on each white cheek, burning almost scarlet. Her eyes seemed enormous. She was being consumed by a fever. 'I don't understand any of this,' he burst out. 'I'd no idea you were so ill . . .'

Her thin hand made a little dismissive gesture. 'I've been lying her thinking, Rob. About the past, and the future. Gregor is going to need you, but so will Ellie-Rose. Try to think about her – more than about wheat, more than the power you get from wheat.'

'But I do love her, Morag', he protested. 'And I love you. I love you both.'

'Ah,' she said with infinite sadness, 'and little good it's done us.'

'You only speak like this because you're ill. Everything seems dark and depressing. We'll soon get you well, Morag. You'll see –'

'Perhaps. Dr Towers seems to think it will be a long business. And so, Rob . . . I want you take Gregor under your wing. He's always been used to . . . having someone to love. I can't just leave him with neighbours, though they'd be kind to him in their way. He needs someone who'll take him to their heart.'

'He'll have everything, I promise you, Morag. I'll send him to a good school. I can see he's a bright lad – he deserves the best –'

'Wait, wait! I'm not asking you to spend money on him –'

'But he's my son, after all, Morag.'

'But it's not money,' she insisted, taking his hand in a tight grip. 'Don't you see? He needs more. And you must be careful. He doesn't know who you are except that you're someone I trust. He'll be grieving, Rob, missing me.'

'Yes. I understand.'

'Do you?' she said with eagerness. 'Promise me you'll take good care, my darling. Then I can go away and try to get my life going again, without breaking my heart over Gregor too much.'

'I promise.'

'Dr Towers says it may take as much as a year. I . . . I've tried to explain to Gregor. He accepts it. He's . . . very sensible . . .' She lay back and seemed to drift off into a sleep that was like unconsciousness.

By and by the door opened and Gregor came in very quietly. 'I'd like to sit with her now, Mr Craigallan, if you please.'

'Certainly, son,' Rob said, unquestioningly accepting the implied command. As he rose to leave, Morag opened her eyes. She smiled at him in gratitude as he went out, but when he hesitated, nodded for him to leave her with the boy.

He went slowly downstairs. The place seemed very quiet. He sat down by the stove, chilled and tired, his heart beating slow and thick. She looked so terribly ill. He doubted whether the trip to the mountains was in time to save her. What a fool he'd been! Why hadn't he realised how serious her complaint was? She'd had that cough all the time he knew her.

A beared man carrying a gladstone bag came in. 'Ah,' he said, 'you're the fellow she wanted sent for. Have you seen her?'

'Yes, we had a talk. How is she, doctor?'

McAllister shook his head. 'She's been losing ground for a long time. And now this chill . . . it's amazing she's been able to battle against it thus far.'

'Is she . . . is she going to be all right?'

McAllister hesitated. 'Perhaps, perhaps. Those modern sanatoriums can do wonders these days. I only wish she'd made the trip before. But the boy, you know . . . he's doing so well at school. She doesn't want to disrupt his life.'

'She's asked me to look after him.'

'You?' The doctor was surprised. 'You're a relative, then? I always thought she was alone in the world.'

'We've been out of touch –'

'That's too bad.' He eyed Rob's fine suit, the carefully barbered hair. 'She's been hard pressed for money in her time, I think. She could have done with some help.'

'She'll have it from now on, I assure you. All expenses of the treatment . . .'

'Yes, yes, that's good. But the boy? He's an odd one, you know. Old for his years.'

'Yes, I know. It's time he and I got to be acquainted.'

The doctor looked thoughtful but said nothing. 'I'd better get up there,' he said. 'She's starting on a long trip early in the morning. I just want to make sure she has strength enough to be moved.'

'Have you hired nurses to go with her? I'll pay for –'

'My wife's going. We felt it was the least we might do. A fine woman, Mrs McGarth . . .' He moved away sharply and clattered upstairs. After an interval of ten minutes he came down again, shook hands briefly, and went out.

Half an hour went by. Rob was trying to nerve himself to go back to the bedroom, expecting to find Gregor there in tears. Very quietly the boy came in. 'She's sleeping,' he said. He was quite dry-eyed, quite composed.

'Sleep is the best thing,' Rob said, lamely.

Gregor let a moment go by. 'We said our goodbyes,' he said. 'She . . . says it would only upset her to go through it all again in the morning.'

'You'll be able to visit,' Rob said in a futile attempt at comfort.

'She said not. At least, not for a long time. The specialist said . . .' He faltered a moment and flashed: 'What does he know? She'll be unhappy!'

'I know, lad. But she feels she might hand on the sickness to you, I think. Don't make it more difficult for her.'

'No, of course not. That would only hinder her recovery.'

'That's right.'

'She said you would look after me from now on, Mr Craigallan.'

'Yes.'

Gregor went to the peg by the door and took his topcoat from it. 'I think it would be best if you and I were to go now, wherever it is you're going to take me.'

'Yes,' said Rob.

He really had no idea what to do with him. Never in his life had he felt so completely at a loss. He too got his coat and came to join Gregor at the door. They stood looking at each other.

In a hesitant gesture Gregor held out his hand. Rob took it in his own. There was something strangely touching in that handclasp. There was as yet no affection, but there was trust – because Morag had told Gregor that he could trust this stranger.

Affection would come. If it took the rest of his life, vowed Rob Craigallan, he would earn the love of his son Gregor. Because

[351]

Morag had told him to love the boy, and whatever Morag said was right . . .

They went out into the pre-dawn air. It was cold and damp. Down by the jetty lights were flickering as the mail sacks were made ready for the arrival of the first boat. They went together to the shore to wait.

This was the first stage of a journey, Rob told himself . . . the journey towards understanding Morag's son. His son too. It was the most demanding undertaking of his life but he swore he would sacrifice anything to succeed . . . to make up for all those wasted years.

If his prayers had any power, the day would come when his beloved Morag would rejoin them. And if he were granted this undeserved mercy, this time they would be together for good.